Twelve captivating tales from the best new writer [barcode: D1531830]
by three more from bestselling authors you've r

A miracle? An omen? Or something else? One day, they arrived in droves—the foxes of the desert, the field, the imagination....
—"Kitsune" by Devon Bohm

When a vampire, a dragon, and a shape-shifting Chihuahua meet on a beach in Key West, fireworks go off! But that's just the background.
—"Moonlight and Funk" by Marianne Xenos

The Grim Reaper, trapped in an IRS agent's dying body, must regain his powers before he dies and faces judgment for his original sin.
—"Death and the Taxman" by David Hankins

In a metaverse future, a woman who exposes falseness in others must decide what is real to her—the love she lost or the love she may have found.
—"Under My Cypresses" by Jason Palmatier

Vic Harden wasn't lured by glory on a daring mission into the reaches of outer space—he was ordered out there by his editor.
—"The Unwilling Hero" by L. Ron Hubbard

Dangerous opportunities present themselves when an alien ship arrives in the solar system seeking repairs.
—"White Elephant" by David K. Henrickson

With her spaceship at the wrong end of a pirate's guns, a former war hero must face down her enemies and demons to save Earth's last best chance for peace.
—"Piracy for Beginners" by J. R. Johnson

Dan Shamble, Zombie P.I., faces one of his funniest and most perplexing cases ever—an enlightened ogre, a salamander with low self-esteem, and a raging fire dragon terrorizing the Unnatural Quarter!   —"Fire in the Hole" by Kevin J. Anderson

Years after the Second Holocaust, the last surviving Jews on earth attempt to rewrite the past.
                    —"A Trickle in History" by Elaine Midcoh

When I said I'd do anything to pay off my debts and get back home to Earth, I didn't mean survey a derelict spaceship at the edge of the solar system—but here I am.
                    —"The Withering Sky" by Arthur H. Manners

High-powered telescopes bring galactic life to our TVs, and network tuner Hank Enos figures he's seen everything—until the day an alien boy stares back.
                    —"The Fall of Crodendra M" by T. J. Knight

Knights, damsels and dragons, curses and fates foretold—the stuff of legends and stories, but unexpectedly perverse.
                    —"Constant Never" by S. M. Stirling

Determined to save his wife, Tumelo takes an unlikely client through South Africa's ruins to the heart of the Desolation—a journey that will cost or save everything.
                    —"The Children of Desolation" by Spencer Sekulin

When a terrorist smuggles a nuclear weapon into London, a team regresses in time to AD 1093 to assassinate a knight on the battlefield, thereby eliminating the terrorist a millennium before his birth.   —"Timelines and Bloodlines" by L. H. Davis

The Grand Exam is a gateway to power for one, likely death for all others—its entrants include ambitious nobles, desperate peasants, and Quiet Gate, an old woman with nothing left to lose.
                    —"The Last History" by Samuel Parr

L. RON HUBBARD

Presents

Writers of the Future

Anthologies

"Writers of the Future continues to dominate the field of science fiction fantasy with bragging rights that it has contributed more to the genre than any other source."

—Midwest Book Review

"The series continues to be a powerful statement of faith as well as direction in American science fiction."

—Publishers Weekly

"Not only is the writing excellent...it is also extremely varied. There's a lot of hot new talent in it."

—Locus magazine

"A first-rate collection of stories and illustrations."

—Booklist magazine

"Writers of the Future is always one of the best original anthologies of the year." *—Tangent*

"I've been involved in Writers of the Future since its inception—first as a contestant, then a speaker, then a judge. It is the most vibrant and exciting showcase of new talent with an undeniable success rate. If you want a glimpse of the future—the future of science fiction—look at these first publications of tomorrow's masters." *—Kevin J. Anderson*
Writers of the Future Contest judge

"Writers of the Future brings you the Hugo and Nebula winners of the future today."   —Tim Powers
Writers of the Future Contest judge

"I really can't say enough good things about Writers of the Future....It's fair to say that without Writers of the Future, I wouldn't be where I am today."   —Patrick Rothfuss
Writers of the Future Contest winner 2002

"Every year the Writers of the Future Contest inspires new writers and helps to launch their careers. The combination of reward, recognition, instruction, and opportunity for beginning authors is unparalleled. There is no contest comparable to the Writers of the Future."   —Rebecca Moesta
Writers of the Future Contest judge

"The Illustrators of the Future Contest is one of the best opportunities a young artist will ever get. You have nothing to lose and a lot to win."   —Frank Frazetta
Illustrators of the Future Contest judge

"The road to creating art and getting it published is long, hard, and trying. It's amazing to have a group, such as Illustrators of the Future, there to help in this process—creating an outlet where the work can be seen and artists can be heard from all over the globe."
—Rob Prior
Illustrators of the Future Contest judge

"Illustrators of the Future offered a channel through which to direct my ambitions. The competition made me realize that genre illustration is actually a valued profession, and here was a rare opportunity for a possible entry point into that world."
—Shaun Tan
Illustrators of the Future Contest winner 1993
and Contest judge

L. Ron Hubbard PRESENTS

Writers of the Future

VOLUME 39

L. Ron Hubbard PRESENTS

Writers of the Future

VOLUME 39

The year's twelve best tales from the
Writers of the Future international writers' program

Illustrated by winners in the Illustrators of the Future
international illustrators' program

Three short stories by Kevin J. Anderson /
L. Ron Hubbard / S. M. Stirling

With essays on writing and illustration by
Lazarus Chernik / L. Ron Hubbard /
Kristine Kathryn Rusch

Edited by Jody Lynn Nye and Dean Wesley Smith
Illustrations art directed by Echo Chernik

GALAXY PRESS, INC.

"Kitsune" © 2023 Devon Bohm
"Moonlight and Funk" © 2023 Marianne Connolly
"Death and the Taxman" © 2023 David Hankins
"Under My Cypresses" © 2023 Jason Palmatier
"Circulate" © 2012 L. Ron Hubbard Library
"The Unwilling Hero" © 1999 L. Ron Hubbard Library
"White Elephant" © 2023 David K. Henrickson
"Piracy for Beginners" © 2023 Jennifer Johnson
"Prioritize to Increase Your Writing" © 2019 Kristine Kathryn Rusch
"Fire in the Hole" © 2023 WordFire, Inc.
"A Trickle in History" © 2023 Elaine Cohen
"The Withering Sky" © 2023 Harry Manners
"The Fall of Crodendra M" © 2023 Dustin Adams
"Constant Never" © 1994 S. M. Stirling
"The Children of Desolation" © 2023 Spencer Sekulin
"Timelines and Bloodlines" © 2023 Laurance Davis
"The Last History" © 2023 Samuel Parr
Illustration on pages 7 and 44 © 2023 Alaya Knowlton
Illustration on pages 8 and 56 © 2023 April Solomon
Illustration on pages 9 and 69 © 2023 Sarah Morrison
Illustration on pages 10 and 97 © 2023 Helen Yi
Illustration on pages 11 and 136 © 2023 Bruce Brenneise
Illustration on pages 12 and 167 © 2023 Kristen Hadaway
Illustration on pages 13 and 225 © 2023 Chris Binns
Illustration on pages 15 and 275 © 2023 José Sánchez
Illustration on pages 16 and 313 © 2023 Ximing Luo
Illustration on pages 17 and 355 © 2023 Cristhian Montenegro Arias
Illustration on pages 18 and 384 © 2023 Nick Jizba
Illustration on pages 19 and 425 © 2023 Alexandra Albu
Illustration on pages 20 and 435 © 2023 Clarence Bateman
Illustration on pages 21 and 480 © 2023 Dao Vi

Cover artwork and pages 14 and 260: *Wyvern Crucible* © 2023 Tom Wood

ISBN 978-1-61986-768-0

WRITERS OF THE FUTURE and ILLUSTRATORS OF THE FUTURE are trademarks owned by the L. Ron Hubbard Library and are used with permission.

Special acknowledgments for these beta readers: Joe Benet, Bret Booher, James Davies, Victoria Dixon, Michael Feramisco, Cara Giles, Cherise Papa, Scott Sands, Don Sweeney, Andrew Williamson, and Yelena Zhuravlev.

CONTENTS

Introduction

BY JODY LYNN NYE

_____

Jody Lynn Nye lists her main career activity as "spoiling cats." When not engaged upon this worthy occupation, she writes fantasy and science fiction books and short stories.

Since 1987 she has published over fifty books and more than 175 short stories. Among her novels are her epic fantasy series, The Dreamland, five contemporary humorous fantasies in the Mythology 101 series, three medical science fiction novels in the Taylor's Ark series, and Strong Arm Tactics, a humorous military science fiction novel. Jody also wrote The Dragonlover's Guide to Pern, a nonfiction-style guide to Anne McCaffrey's popular world. She also collaborated with Anne McCaffrey on four science fiction novels, including Crisis on Doona (a New York Times and USA Today bestseller). Jody coauthored the Visual Guide to Xanth with author Piers Anthony. She has edited two anthologies, Don't Forget Your Spacesuit, Dear!, and Launch Pad, and written two short-story collections, A Circle of Celebrations, holiday SF/fantasy stories, and Cats Triumphant!, SF and fantasy feline tales. Nye wrote eight books with the late Robert Lynn Asprin, License Invoked, and seven set in Asprin's Myth Adventures universe. Since Asprin's passing, she has published two more Myth books and two in Asprin's Dragons series. Her newest series is the Lord Thomas Kinago books, beginning with View from the Imperium (Baen Books), a humorous military SF novel.

Her newest books are Moon Tracks (Baen), YA science fiction with Dr. Travis S. Taylor. Rhythm of the Imperium, third in the series; and Once More, With Feeling (WordFire Press), a nonfiction book on revising manuscripts.

Over the last thirty or so years, Jody has taught in numerous writing workshops and participated on hundreds of panels at science fiction conventions. She runs the two-day writers' workshop at Dragon Con. Jody is the Coordinating Judge of the Writers of the Future. In June 2022, she received the Polaris Award from ConCarolina and Falstaff Books for mentorship and guidance of new talent.

Jody lives in the northwest suburbs of Atlanta, with her husband Bill Fawcett, and three feline overlords, Athena, Minx, and Marmalade.

Introduction

Y ou hold in your hand the results of a year's worth of hard work and impressive talent. The following twelve stories each represent the vision of a new writer that stood out among the thousands of entries submitted to the Writers of the Future Contest to be recognized as the best of the best. Some of these writers have sent in many stories over the years; for some, this is their first attempt. All of them have excited my imagination, even bringing me to exclaim out loud in delight. ("Venus? Really?")

This is my first year as the Coordinating Judge of the Contest. Only three other people have held this position since the Contest launched in 1985. David Farland, K. D. Wentworth, and renowned editor Algis Budrys, who with L. Ron Hubbard shepherded the Contest into being, have helped to launch the careers of numerous notable writers including Patrick Rothfuss, Nina Kiriki Hoffman, Eric Flint, Nnedi Okorafor, and Dean Wesley Smith (now my coeditor of this anthology). I have large and eminent shoes to fill, and I hope you will appreciate my efforts.

So, how do you get to be a winner and have your story published in one of these glamorous anthologies? You have four quarters of the year to send in an original tale. We accept speculative fiction: science fiction, fantasy, and dark fantasy (light horror). Keep in mind that this is a professional market with an audience that runs from young adult on upward. Within those parameters, let your imagination run wild. The Contest is judged blind. The quality of your work is what is important. What am I looking for? First, I want a story. It has to have a beginning, middle, and end that involves your fantasy or SF element. If your narrative takes too long to get going or trails off with no conclusion, I may never even see it, as the first reader (and former Writers' Contest winner) Kary English weeds out manuscripts that don't fulfill the basic guidelines for the Contest. I like a story that never stops moving, that gives me a reason to keep reading.

Second, send me something new. If I've seen the plot often and you have nothing new to say about it, you're not trying hard enough. Speculative fiction means exploring the universe and finding a corner of it that hasn't been churned over by thousands of other writers. Tickle my imagination. Surprise me. I welcome a new take on science fiction or fantasy. Third, I want excellent storytelling. Your style can set a fairly ordinary plot apart from others like it by intelligent and evocative wordplay. Give me great characters. Give me consequences for failing to reach the goal those characters are striving toward. Small stories about one moment in a character's life can be as interesting and meaningful as big stories in which the universe itself is at stake.

The eight Finalists every quarter go on to a selection of our eminent judges to vote for first, second, and third place. The rewards for becoming a winner of the Contest are spectacular. The twelve writer winners are flown into Hollywood, California, for a grand black-tie, red-carpet gala, given beautiful trophies and cash prizes. Each of their stories is also handed off to the winners of the Illustrators of the Future Contest to create a unique piece of art to accompany it in the anthology. The anthologies themselves often become national bestsellers, a terrific entry on your bibliography. Afterward, the winners get to experience their first book signing of the anthology containing their work. The winners also enjoy a weeklong seminar taught by me and fantasy writer/judge Tim Powers, with guest speeches from the other Contest judges. It's the biggest fuss anyone will ever make in your career about a short story.

It's more than worth it to enter, and I urge you to begin. I'm starting my second year of reading Contest entries. Make one of them yours.

The Illustrators of the Future Contest

BY ECHO CHERNIK

Echo Chernik has been illustrating for thirty years and has been the recipient of many prestigious awards and accolades.

Her clients have included Disney, BBC, Mattel, Hasbro, Miller-Coors, Jose Cuervo, Celestial Seasonings, McDonald's, Procter & Gamble, Trek Bicycle Corporation, USPS, Bellagio Hotel & Casino, Kmart, Sears, Publix Super Markets, Regal Cinemas, the city of New Orleans, the state of Illinois, the Sheikh of Dubai, Dave Matthews Band, Arlo Guthrie, and more. She is a master of many styles including decorative, vector, and art nouveau.

She has been interviewed on CBS, PBS Radio, and by countless publications in her career. Echo owns an art gallery in Washington State featuring exclusively her art, and she tours the world meeting fans and lecturing on illustration.

As the art director and Coordinating Judge of the Illustrators of the Future Contest, Echo prepares the winners for the business of illustration and a successful career in art.

The Illustrators of the Future Contest

The Illustrators of the Future Contest is the single most important contest to enter for anyone serious in pursuing a career in illustration, concept art, or commercial illustration.

The internet provides a venue for a vast treasure of images and artists. But for an artist to really stand out, to make it in the industry, they need to be set apart from others. One fantastic way to do this is to win a reputable contest.

So what sets the Illustrators of the Future apart from other contests?

You can enter the Contest four times a year. There is no entry fee to send your work in for consideration. And your work will be judged anonymously by top professionals. This provides a completely unbiased opportunity for any artist.

The prizes are life and career changing. Winners are published in the annual Writers of the Future anthology, which is a national and international bestseller. You win a cash prize and a chance at the Grand Prize. But most importantly, you win knowledge. You are flown to Hollywood along with your fellow winners where you will meet past winners and some of the Contest judges and attend a fun, weeklong workshop on how to succeed as a professional in this industry. The judges of the Contest are all renowned and successful artists with years of experience to share.

When you are chosen as one of twelve winners, you gain the support of the staff of the anthology's publisher, Galaxy Press, who work so very hard to promote your success and help you succeed. What inspires them to work so hard, you may ask? They truly believe in the promise L. Ron Hubbard made to the future by establishing this great contest with its primary goal of launching careers. The wonderful people who bring you this book strive to bring his dream to life every year with the publication of this anthology and further support it by promoting past winners. Every winner, past or present, who achieves success is a huge win to this Contest and the legacy L. Ron Hubbard has left.

I'm humbled and honored to be the Coordinating Judge of the Illustrators' Contest. I love being a part of something so big and something that makes such a difference in the lives of young artists.

Who can enter? If you want to make a career in commercial art or illustration, you can enter—as long as you are not already a professional. The Contest is designed for people on their way up, who need to get their work out there.

Send along three samples of your best illustrative work. If you don't get "the call" that you've won the first time you enter, don't worry! Enter again the next quarter! The Contest is open to all styles and mediums. Once you win, you are professionally paired with a story from one of the Writers' Contest winners and are hired to illustrate it for the anthology. These are the great pieces you see in this book! You work with me, as art director, to make them as strong as possible, and a true representation of your style.

Traditional and digital work is accepted. For the final published pieces, we work through your design and thought process from thumbnails to sketches and then final drawings. AI art is not accepted. I am looking for the process and execution of the artist's vision and mind's eye.

This book represents the best and brightest future artists. We are here to help you stand out and succeed. Even if you feel you are not ready, I encourage you to enter each quarter.

Enjoy this anthology and the success of the next generation of the best writers and illustrators of the future!

ALAYA KNOWLTON
Kitsune

APRIL SOLOMON
Moonlight and Funk

SARAH MORRISON
Death and the Taxman

HELEN YI
Under My Cypresses

BRUCE BRENNEISE
The Unwilling Hero

11

KRISTEN HADAWAY
White Elephant

CHRIS BINNS
Piracy for Beginners

TOM WOOD
Wyvern Crucible

JOSÉ SÁNCHEZ
A Trickle in History

XIMING LUO
The Withering Sky

CHRIS ARIAS
The Fall of Crodendra M

NICK JIZBA
Constant Never

CYBERAEON
The Children of Desolation

CLARENCE BATEMAN
Timelines and Bloodlines

DAO VI
The Last History

Kitsune

written by
Devon Bohm

illustrated by
ALAYA KNOWLTON

ABOUT THE AUTHOR

Devon Bohm is a poet and writer who received her BA from Smith College and her MFA in poetry and fiction from Fairfield University. At Fairfield, Bohm became increasingly frustrated with the denial of genre fiction as "literature" and began exploring the big question of why people were attracted to different forms of speculative fiction. The answer she found didn't surprise her, as it was what she'd always valued about her favorite writers: genres like fantasy or science fiction perform the same function of all good literature by finding new and inventive ways to help the reader see their world (and self) more clearly.

Bohm's short story, "Kitsune," was most deeply influenced by the work of Aimee Bender, Carmen Maria Machado, and Kelly Magee—writers whose work stretches the bounds of reality as a means of discovering capital-T Truth. "What this story really is," Bohm says, "is a feminist text that's using an extended and surreal metaphor to help the reader reflect on particular experiences within the human condition." In the vein of Anne Sexton's poems of transformation and Margaret Atwood's dystopias, the world of "Kitsune" is our own reality seen through a funhouse mirror, a distorted reflection that emphasizes, rather than obscures. To Bohm, this kind of writing is the ideal blend of poetry and fiction.

In her personal life, Bohm lives in Connecticut with her husband, son, and dog—Harry Dresden Pawter—where she spends any time she can find reading and writing. Her first full-length collection of poetry, Careful Cartography, was published by Cornerstone Press in 2021 as part of their Portage Poetry series. The book was shortlisted for the 2022 Eric Hoffer Book Award, winning both the First Horizon Book Award for a debut poetry collection and distinction for a publication by an academic press in the contest. Additionally, her poetry has been featured in numerous publications, but this is her first professional sale in fiction. She looks forward to you reading not only this story, but hopefully much more (and many more genres) from her in the future.

ABOUT THE ILLUSTRATOR

Alaya Knowlton, also known as Drazini, was born in 2003 in a small mountain town in California. She moved to Sarasota, Florida, at five and grew up there.

She has drawn since she could hold a pen, yet she truly dedicated herself to this passion during middle school. Alaya is inspired by her sister Hana and her family to create works of art, as they have supported and nurtured her passions and her true self through its development.

Since then she has directed and worked on short animated films, digital illustrations, and many other forms of artwork. She is currently beginning her study of game art, the study of 3D and 2D artwork and animation for video games at the University of Southern California's School of Cinematic Arts. Alaya is completely dedicated to her passion to create artwork and strives to inform the artistic direction of games in the future. Her goals include inspiring others to do what makes them the most fulfilled and to create a better future that allows greater equality and understanding of all people.

Kitsune

There aren't supposed to be foxes in New Mexico. They went extinct in 2035. I was ten and it was on the news: The Last Gray Fox Extinct. My mother cried, so I cried. But after we were done crying she had to show me what they were. I had never even heard of them before.

So, when the foxes started to emerge from the desert, people were alarmed. Alarmed, but delighted. *Foxes! We thought they were long dead, dead for twenty years! But here they are! A miracle!* We should have realized that there's no such thing as miracles and anything that makes people use exclamation points is probably a false kind of promise.

They weren't just desert foxes, gray foxes. There were full-tailed red foxes, snowy white arctic foxes, big-eared fennec foxes, kit foxes and swift foxes and even Tibetan sand foxes that look more like wolves. There were species that no one has ever seen before—amalgamations of the other species, foxes that look more like domestic dogs or cats, foxes with odd coloring—tints of blue, pink. A rainbow of foxes, an entire damned rainbow.

I was almost thirty and tired. I worked in a Santa Fe mall at a store that sold dresses I couldn't afford to women who looked down on me. I stood on my feet forty hours a week and went home and cried, some days. Most days. I couldn't figure out how to get out of New Mexico. I wasn't sure where better was. New Mexico was all I had ever known.

And then, the foxes. My mother calls me at the store, that's how I find out.

"Zorro at El Mercado. This is Reyna speaking, how may I help you?"

"Rey, they're back."

"Mom?"

"The foxes."

"What the hell are you talking about?"

"They're back, they're all back."

I know what foxes are now. They're a common motif in the clothing we sell, though that product was more popular last year. People seem to lean toward bees these days. They're in trouble again. The bees are always in trouble.

"That's...great, Mom."

"It's a damned miracle, Rey. A damned miracle."

"A miracle."

She kept talking, but I wasn't really listening.

"Mom, a regular customer's come in. I have to go." The store was empty, but she couldn't know that.

"But, Rey..."

"I'll call you back." I wouldn't.

"Did you see this stuff on the news?"

Alie has our TV turned to CNN. The ticker, the report, it's not about the depletion of another natural resource or bombings in Russia and China, which is usually what we see these days when we flick on the news. It's about New Mexico. About the foxes.

I roll my eyes. I can feel them move inside my head. "Yes, animals, right. I did see them." I stalk my way into the kitchen and open the fridge. "Al, did you eat all the hummus again?"

"There should be more behind the oat milk." Her voice is muffled by the popcorn she's eating.

I find the new tub of hummus and start making a sandwich, slicing tomato and red peppers and turning the conversation with my mother over in my mind. I don't want to blow her off. I really don't. But since she retired from her cushy government job (don't even ask me what the hell she did all those years—

administrative something or other) she calls the store constantly. I love her, but...

"Seriously though, this is insane. Come look."

I live with Alie because we're the same. Well, no, not the same, but at least on the same sinking ship. We met when we were in college because we both worked at El Mercado, though in different stores—Alie at a high-end jewelry store only a few storefronts down from Zorro—and we went to the same, sad salad place for lunch most days. Chicken Cobb and Thai chicken, complete with wilted lettuce and fattening dressings that made the whole concept of salad obsolete.

We started by nodding to each other, then saying hello, then sitting together. We were both seniors at St. John's, though we had never met or even seen each other, which seemed impossible given the size of the student body. St. John's had only two directions of study, mathematics or philosophy, and we were on completely separate paths. Even our minors failed to overlap: Alie had chosen French and economics, while I went in for art and literature.

It was a strange place, St. John's. Everyone graduated with the same degree, technically: a bachelor's in liberal arts. We were supposed to come out of school as well-rounded, well-educated, and ready to take on anything. Alie and I both came out more confused than we had been going in. When you study a little of everything, are you learning anything? I still don't know.

When we graduated, we got a place together. We were basically common-law spouses at this point—though New Mexico doesn't hold with that, we checked. We've been living together for about seven years, and nothing has changed for either of us. We work in the same stores, though we both manage those stores now, and neither of us has any idea what we want from our lives. Our boyfriends have changed every once in a while, and the salad place is now a build-your-own Hawaiian poke bowl restaurant, but everything else is static.

"No, seriously, Rey, you have to look at this stuff." Alie's voice winds its way into the kitchen again and catches me. I pick up my plate and make my grudging way into the living room.

Alie has flipped to a local channel with a local anchor. The woman is statuesque and beautiful with the long, straight, dark hair and high-tilting cheekbones that speak to Native American heritage. My mother has a similar look to her, though I received too large a share of my father's genes to be considered the same kind of beauty. She's gesturing to the desert behind her, smiling.

"In what many have called a miracle, citizens all over the state are reporting findings of a long-extinct animal: the fox. Even more miraculously, the foxes have been spotted in record numbers, and even stranger, a record number of species have been documented, as well."

The camera cuts to some B-roll that must have been taken earlier in the day—the sun high and torturous—and there they are: the foxes. Big, small, medium, every color you'd imagine a fox to be and then a few more you could never imagine a fox to be. My mouth drops open. Hearing and seeing are different things entirely.

"While experts claim it's too early for them to give a concrete explanation for what kind of natural miracle has occurred in New Mexico today, plenty of theories abound with the locals. We took it to the streets to see what Santa Fe's best citizens think might be happening."

The beautiful woman's teeth glint perfectly white before they cut to her on a street downtown, holding her microphone up to a college-aged guy who's seemingly stoned. I know the look too well, Hux and James smoke more than an average amount. Sometimes Alie and I partake, but less and less these days.

"Well, I know a guy who keeps exotic pets, maybe..." The guy rubs his neck and looks uncomfortable, nervous, paranoid from the weed, maybe.

Alie turns the volume down, muting the next interviewee with her early aughts hair style and wild eyes, and turns to look at me. There's a near rabidity to her excitement. "So"—her voice pitches upward, another sure sign she has something she can't wait to tell me—"Hux made us anniversary reservations at some trendy new place downtown."

"Cool."

"He told me to make sure to get a manicure."

"Al, that wouldn't be the first time he ragged on something about your appearance...."

"No. Rey. Think about it. A *manicure*." Her face is all lit up, waiting for me to catch up and catch her excitement, like it's a cold. I try to summon a sneeze and can't manage it. She can't hold it in. "*Rey*, I think..."

I cut off the thought as swiftly as I can. "Al, you've thought this before."

"But I really do think he's going to propose this time."

Hux, also known as Damon Huxley, has been Alie's boyfriend for two years, and I have hated every single minute of it. He's faked her out multiple times now, acting like he might propose— purposely, I think, though he's stupid enough that at least a few times could have been mistakes—and it's left Alie devastated every time. I try to force a smile. She sees something in him, so maybe there's something to see. Something hidden. Something maybe only she can find. I wonder if I'm like that, too. Something only certain people could see, find, know. My face aches from smiling all day, my lips seem to creak as I speak up.

"You're right. This has got to be it."

She smiles and her smile is huge, the room is filled with it. She hugs me. "Okay, I'm in early tomorrow. Bedtime."

"Night."

Alie pauses at the door to her bedroom and turns back to where I sit on the couch. The foxes continue to prance and run and hide on the screen in front of me, muted. My sandwich stays untouched on the coffee table.

"By the way, what do *you* think is going on with the foxes?"

"Damned if I know, Al."

She laughs. James calls me. I pick up. I figure I can call my mother back in the morning.

At Zorro, we can't keep the fox merchandise on the shelves. The belt with the metal fox-head clasp sells out in two days. The fox-print purse is pricier, but it doesn't last out the week. And the shirtwaist dress that I assumed was going to go on clearance soon since I hadn't sold a single unit in months? It practically flies out the door. The company keeps sending us more and more fox products until we look like a theme store. A pricey, strangely specific theme store.

My mother calls the store almost every day with fox updates. If she tries there and I'm not in, she calls my cell. I've never had a set schedule, not even one week to another. It makes time spin out and flatten. It passes faster and slower at the same time, somehow. It makes all her calls blend into one.

"It's still on the news, Rey! It's been three days and it's still on the news.

"They found a fox that was purple, Rey. *Purple*. They tried to contain it. The people at the university wanted to study it, but it got away.

"Over two hundred new species have been recorded. Can you believe that? What do you think…?

"They interrupted the daily fox update because another woman is missing. They think it might be a serial killer. Terrible, terrible.

"I saw a film crew the other day—do you think they're making a documentary about the foxes?

"Rey, you and Alie lock your balcony door at night, right?

"One was in the yard today! A classic red one. It was one of the most beautiful things I've ever seen.

"Rey, I'm so proud of you, you know that?"

Mom, I have to go, Mom I have to go, MomIhaveto…

After work one day, or rather, after a particularly long call where my mother had interrupted yet another tirade about foxes to tell me yet another woman was missing, I go to my favorite place in Santa Fe. I haven't been in more than a year. Not since I started dating James.

It's a low, long, pueblo-style building with the best light I've ever seen inside. It pours through skylights and lights up rooms that are fields of flowers, gardens of skulls, great washes of the desert inside but lit, somehow too, from within. It's always quiet, except for the respectful footsteps of the few patrons, and the security guards.

I've been going to the Georgia O'Keeffe Museum since my freshman year of college. I took a course titled "Feminist Painters" my first year and we took a Saturday trip there during our modernism unit. Most people were grumbling about having to do anything related to school on a weekend, but I was enchanted from the moment we walked in. I had seen her paintings before, of course, who hasn't, but there was something about seeing them in person that... to use a cliché, took my breath away.

I went back to my dorm and read and read and read about her. About how hard it was for her to start—financially, sure, but also a deep and real uncertainty about how to make art without copying other people, how to make art and be herself. About her lovers, like Alfred Stieglitz, who took beautiful nude photos of her that so many people found trashy, but she didn't care. Especially as she grew older.

What astounded me the most was the actual breadth of her work. Flowers and skulls and deserts, yes, but skyscrapers too, and animals, landscapes, fruit, and... the list is longer than people think. I liked to read quotes by her: "to create one's world in any of the arts takes courage." Or "the days you work are the best days." Or "it's only by selection, by elimination, and by emphasis that we get at the real meanings of things."

I stand in front of one of her floral canvases (pictures O'Keeffe claimed, to her dying day, had nothing whatsoever to do with female anatomy) and try to breathe. *In, out, in, out, slow, and steady.* My mother's phone calls have been driving me to near hysteria, more and more. It's not the foxes. It's not even the missing women. It's the thing she always says at the end of every call, something like *I love you,* but with barbs so small she can't even see them.

I'm proud of you.
Proud of what, Mom?

31

In college, I thought that maybe I wanted to be a painter, for a while. Then a writer. Then maybe an art historian or a professor or even a park ranger. Being out in nature sounded nice. But I never decided. I never committed. And now? Now my entire life is one of selection, elimination, and emphasis, and the real meaning of things is being revealed to me—nothing.

There's nothing wrong with my job. Nothing at all. I provide a service, I'm good at it, I manage people well and I even have fun, sometimes. With my coworkers, with merchandising the store. People are judgmental, sure, people like to feel sad for me. But what would be so different if I was a secretary? There would be a certain amount of respectability, but less money and more boredom. Nothing is wrong with working in retail, nothing at all.

Except that it isn't what I want.

Except that I have to cut my life down into small, manageable chunks until I don't see anything like meaning, not anymore. So every time my mother tells me she's proud of me, something inside me dies a little more, blackens at the edges, withers. But how do you tell a parent that? That you need them to get their own life and stop pretending yours means anything at all?

I want to create my own world through my art. I want to do the work every day. But what world? What art? What work? I don't know. I didn't know in college and every step I get closer to thirty reveals I still don't know. So, I repeat, *Proud of what, Mom?*

When everyone else was picking out careers, I sat in the middle of the circle, polite and nervous, and never reached out toward any one option. So, I'm on default, maybe forever. I can't be proud of that. I'm not. And my mother's love is too hard to bear, sometimes. Too undeserved. I love her, but it's hard to love people. At least as unconditionally as they deserve. And it's even harder to let them love you back, especially unconditionally.

When Georgia O'Keeffe was older, she suffered from macular degeneration—which means she slowly lost her eyesight. The thing that mattered most to her in this world, her particular and unique way of looking at the world. Sitting in front of a skull floating in the air, a flower blooming from its eye socket, I think that this might be why I've never chosen anything—if I never choose to commit myself to any one thing, if I never choose to care, then nothing can be taken away from me.

O'Keeffe lived out her days in a place called Ghost Ranch and even though it's only three hours away, I've never gone. Not once. I can't remember the last time I left Santa Fe at all. A school trip senior year of high school, maybe. Mexico once, spring break. I do have a passport. I have one.

All those women missing. I'd like to think that they're more like Georgia O'Keeffe than I am—going deep into the desert, whatever their desert is, to find themselves and their meaning. But they're probably more like me. Dead. At least some kind of dead. More dead than me, for now.

James is calling. I pick up.

"Babe, where are you?" James's voice ricochets from my phone all over the reverently silent room.

"The museum, I told you."

"But I got us tickets to..."

His voice continues through the phone as I pick up my things and walk into the blinding heat. I don't even think to stay with the skulls and the flowers and the contained moments of sky and sun flash-frozen, but not static, somehow. I leave them behind and go toward something like safety.

"Have you seen them?"

Alie's standing by the window when I get home from another backbreaking, mind-numbing day. A customer called me a "hapless bitch" when I told her we had sold out of an item. She was right on both counts, though I have to wonder if she actually knew what *hapless* meant. I do.

St. John's coming in hot with that useful education, yet again.

"Who, Al?"

"The foxes."

"Yeah, it's still all over the news. Even with all the missing..." I'm heading past her to the kitchen, but something about the way she's standing makes me stop. It's as if she's curled in on herself, smaller than she had been before. "Al? Are you okay?"

"Did I ever tell you about the time my dad took me and my little sister to the internment camp?" Alie doesn't turn to me as she speaks, but her voice is clear and strong, almost echoing.

"What? No, Alie, what are you..."

"My dad is half-Japanese; did I ever tell you that?" She doesn't wait for me to answer. "I haven't talked to him in something like twenty years, but until I was nine or ten, he made some kind of small effort with Julia and me. She barely remembers it, or him, but, lucky me, I was old enough to remember it and how incredibly awkward it was. He didn't mean for it to be awkward, I don't think. He just... wanted to share, maybe?"

I stay silent. There is nothing to do in this moment but bear witness. Sometimes it's not only the most we can give, but the most important thing we can do.

"I mean... who brings two children to the site of an internment camp? There's nothing there anymore, just a rock with a plaque in the middle of a scrubby stretch of desert.... There was nothing there. There was absolutely nothing there to show the atrocities that had happened. Absolutely nothing there to mark that anyone had lived there and died there and suffered there. Nothing. Nothing."

The silence grows in the room; a gathering kind of dread I can feel as pressure on my temples. I can't remember the last time I cried, but storm clouds are gathering under my eyelids. I close my eyes and there is lightning flashing across the blackness, there is fire. I open my eyes and the day is still dying, no rain in sight, not even a flash desert storm on the horizon. Nothing has changed but something has.

Alie turns, her face in shadow. "But isn't that the same as anything else? We forget. We don't forgive. We just can't even care enough to remember." She has her palms flat and open to me, as if in supplication or offering, as if those were the same thing.

She steps into the light and I feel a chill pass through me. There is a wildness in her eyes—like my lightning has transferred to her body and she is electric now, dangerous, untamed and raw in the air, crackling. "No one will remember them, and no one will remember me. Or you." Alie's spitting the words out now, sparks making light trails from her tongue. "Even your precious Georgia O'Keeffe and her paintings will fall to dust one day. We think certain things are forever, but nothing is forever. Nothing is forever except being trapped in life. That's a forever. Because we don't know what's after except that eventually, no one will remember our names."

She starts to cry, her mascara running in black rivulets down her cheeks. "That's why the foxes. That's why. They're free of that. Don't you see, Rey?" Her breath hitches and starts and stops, jumps and scared and stuck like a sob in her throat. "Don't you see?" Alie collapses then, a shudder and a sound like a wail is scratching its nails down the walls. The paint is peeling as I cross the room to her, reach out for her, try to give her something like comfort.

I hold her. I ask her if she wants me to call Hux and she shakes her head and starts to cry harder and harder until I'm worried she'll drown us both with her grief for a world she was never going to have in the first place.

After she falls asleep, my phone buzzes and I grab it, trying not to wake her. It's James. I pick up.

At St. John's, as a senior capstone, I took a yearlong global mythology course. It combined everything I had been studying for the first three years—from art and literature to history and sociology. It was my favorite class.

Every night I watch the news and every night more of the class comes back to me. Foxes are a rarity in how ubiquitous they used to be—an animal that once lived on every continent except Antarctica—and it follows that they exist in folklore around the world.

Foxes are tricksters, we all know that. *Aesop's Fables*, *The Canterbury Tales*, *Pinocchio*, Beatrix Potter's Mr. Tod, the Br'er Fox, Reynard. Foxes are cunning and clever, maybe even magic, and their intelligence wins over brute strength every time. There's something admirable there.

The Bible's Song of Solomon 2:15 asks us to "Catch the foxes for us, the foxes that spoil the vineyards, for our vineyards are in blossom." What were the foxes for them? Worldliness, distractions from the spiritual, non-Christian ideals and lives. Bad things. Always bad. In the Middle Ages people in Europe sometimes burned fox symbols in effigy for the devil.

Then there's the Tswana saying: *Only the muddy fox lives.* It's a simple sentiment: only those willing to get their hands dirty can progress in life. Foxes are often messengers in African folklore, though my professor wasn't particularly well versed in much from that continent. Along with the rest of the white and English-speaking world.

A Jewish mystic once said, "Meet each man with a friendly greeting; be the tail among lions rather than the head among foxes." As if the fox was somehow less than the lion for being what it naturally was. Better to be a small fish in a big pond and all of that. Like being who and what you are isn't enough. That you should always be looking to change species.

One of the only other things I can remember is that the word *shenanigan* was from an old Irish expression meaning: *"I play the fox."*

What we never talked about in that class was some of the other connotations. A vixen isn't only a female fox, but a beautiful, seductive woman. Always with that hint of the negative. *She's foxy, she's a fox.* But to outfox someone is to trick them. But it's only a positive when you're on the fox's side. Even the words related to foxes in the natural world sound predatory: a skulk, a leash, an earth. Sure, they're predators. Sure, they kill to eat. But so do we. Sure, they live a solitary existence. But don't many of us find we're better off the same?

My favorite story has always been Japanese kitsune, perhaps the culture that cares the most for the fox in their mythology. The kitsune aren't straightforward. Sometimes they're tricksters, sometimes they're wise guardians, sometimes they're wives and lovers and friends, though most often they can shape-shift into a beautiful woman. There are thirteen kinds of kitsune, officially, but that's simplified groupings to help us understand something magical and beautiful and surreal. All kitsune have one thing in common—they all value their freedom above all else with their nine tails flashing in the wind.

If all mythology is really extended metaphor, what did the Japanese storytellers, mothers to their little girls, really want them to hear?

I tell Alie about it, seeing as she's a quarter Japanese, but I'm not sure she hears me. She hasn't been to work in days and there's a feral look to her, her hair a white cloud around her face. She's dyed the tips pink and it makes her look like an anime character, a little bit. I tell her that and she smiles, a little.

James calls me just after Alie falls asleep. I pick up.

The heat lightning crackles and pops across the horizon. I race the rain home, the sky darkening to twilight in the midafternoon. My skin is buzzing with the electricity in the air as I run from the car, the storm catching up to me and soaking through my clothes in seconds. I fumble with my keys, my skin slick and steaming in the sudden shock of cold that's swept in with the cloud cover.

The apartment is shrouded in darkness, a strange afternoon gloaming so deep that I don't see Alie at first. I would have assumed she wasn't home, but one of her team from the jewelry store had wandered over to see me halfway through my early shift, asking if I knew where she was. Her big date with Hux had been the night before, and I had been expecting a cavalcade of either excited or furious texts when I woke up. But there had been nothing. I had hoped she and Hux had been too wrapped up in their celebrations to even think of texting me, but I didn't feel right about it. She always texted. She always reached out.

I drop my bag and lean against the closed door, the rain muffled slightly. I start to wring out my hair on the doormat and instead feel my heart jump into my mouth as my eyes adjust. Someone is standing in front of the sliding glass door to the patio, someone who I don't quite recognize as Alie. We've lived together for so long…you start to know that person intrinsically, almost preternaturally. It's not her frame, her posture. She looks smaller somehow, curled in on herself. Shrinking, cowering, coiled. But it has to be her.

"Alie?" She doesn't answer or turn her head. A flash of lightning reverberates through the room; I can feel it as if it's shaking free something lodged in my chest. I can see now that Alie's naked and she seems even smaller that way. Feral and lost.

"I said no." Her voice barely reaches me over the tempest outside and I move toward her, one hand reaching very slightly out. She's almost looking at me now, but not quite, her head turned over one shoulder.

"Al?" I can't hear the word, but I must say it. Because she looks up at me for a bare second and I can see her eyes, nothing but a blank reflection in the low light.

She doesn't speak any louder, and I move even closer to catch the words that fall like burning stars from her mouth. "I said no. Hux asked me to marry him and I said no and then he hit me." The clouds release a deluge as she speaks, nature punctuating the sentence for her. The rain is a waterfall against the glass; there is no outside but only the moment we live in, the moment we're sealed in.

The words sink their claws into me, my brain slow to catch up. "He…" I can't catch my breath; it's trapped in my throat. My own air is choking me. "He…what?"

Alie turns, a twilit glow from outside showing me her makeup-less face. She looks young, too young, like that. "He slapped me. Across the face. In the parking lot. After I said no." She is empty, blank, her mouth moving but her eyes still. "I walked home."

It's not shock that swells in my chest, or even fury—I know the fury will come on later, but it's not here yet—but something more like resignation. I am not surprised. It wasn't that Hux had been violent before or ever even hinted at it. It's that, even without a single warning sign, I have no trouble imagining Hux hitting Alie. My brain does a short, sharp spiral in quick succession: I can imagine James hitting me, my father hitting my mother, any man I have ever met hitting any woman I have ever met. It's not that violence is actually gendered, it's that power is, and our world has always been clear on who's in charge. And we listen. We listen. We listen.

Alie starts nibbling at a strand of her hair and the normalcy of that movement—it's her most nervous of nervous tics reserved for breakups and deaths and the night before job interviews that never pan out—jolts me back to reality. She is shivering, the room is cold, and she is naked, her small breasts goose-fleshed, her hands clutched around her abdomen. There's so much to say that a fleeting thought just seems to spill out of my mouth, "Al, that's at least ten miles."

"Yeah. My feet hurt." She almost laughs, but the sound is stolen by the rain—all I can see is a small and definitive contraction of her body in silhouette. The darkness grows around us, feels like an opening mouth.

I find I can't speak. I want to move just a few steps over to hug her, but it doesn't feel right. She looks like a solitary organism, something that can't be touched.

Her voice is quiet, but I can feel it somewhere deep in my chest. "I just realized . . . I just realized that even though he was asking me that, it didn't matter anymore."

"What do you mean, Al?" I try to remember Alie from only a few weeks ago, the Alie who would be talking about getting a pink manicure to match her hair, so pictures of the ring would pop on social media, but that Alie is gone.

"Because I didn't ever really want to marry *him*. I've been thinking that being with him was more about doing something, anything, besides everything I had been doing before and for so long and"—she sighs a sigh that sounds like a thousand breaths at once, the exhaustion and sadness amplified and projected until it fills me too—"and then he hit me and I knew I was right. So it doesn't matter anymore. I couldn't be with him even if I wanted to because I'm not even here."

There is a long pause but I know, in some instinctual way,

that she's not done speaking. She takes a deep breath and then another.

"I want to be here again, Rey." She takes another step toward me, her hands at her sides now. She's no longer shivering, no longer seems to be cold or small or scared. But she doesn't look like pink-nailed Alie either. She is something else entirely.

"I know, Alie. It's okay. You can. You can be." I am pleading, but I don't know for what exactly. And then I do.

She nods and there is a single tear on her cheek and then it starts.

It doesn't look the way it looks in a movie, like when someone turns into a werewolf. I can't hear her bones breaking and reforming, she doesn't twist and clench and molt, hair doesn't sprout from her face while she turns wild, yellow eyes on me. None of that. Instead, it's gentle, somehow, like pouring water, like stepping through a waterfall and coming out a different person, except the water is light and not a person, a fox. Except not.

I don't know how to explain to you what I see. It's Alie, and then it isn't Alie, but it's also more Alie somehow than she had ever been. Alie makes a beautiful fox. She's a blonde white, her ears tipped in pink. Her eyes have the same, slightly upturned slant they had when she was a human. She sits silently before me, her tail, also tipped in a blush of pink, wrapping itself around her paws. The fox, Alie, waits.

I know what she wants. She wants me to go with her.

I don't.

But I open the sliding glass door for her and I watch the fox run into the storm, not skittish, not afraid. Free and wet and free and cold and free and free and free. I stand with our balcony door open to the desert, water all over the floor. The face of the storm rises up to meet me and I think, for a moment, that I will go too. That I will follow her. That I can. That I must. That I really, really will.

My phone is ringing from where I dropped it near the door, buzzing aggressively against the tile in the entry. James is calling me. I wait a few beats, but I pick it up. Hux is hysterical, trying to find Alie. She won't answer her calls. I take a few deep breaths, then a few deeper ones. I try to make it sound like I'm crying when I tell him Alie's not here, Alie's missing, Alie's gone and didn't take anything with her, and I think we should call the police.

James hangs up to make the call. I idly wonder if Hux will be a suspect as I close the sliding glass door against the storm.

I've worked at Zorro for almost eight years and I joke every day that I'm quitting. Every day I get up knowing today won't be the day I change my life, but I like to pretend, even if just for the span of a joke, that it's possible.

The news is still full of foxes, but also women. All the missing women.

People are trying to link the two—government experiments or a mad scientist out somewhere in the desert or even an act of god, God, GOD; he gets bigger when these people talk about him—but there's nothing conclusive. Just the same news day after day, foxes and missing women, foxes and missing women, foxes missing women. No one knows except the foxes. And we can't know what they know. Is it me? Am I the only one in the world who really knows?

My apartment is a crime scene. I had to comfort Hux, pretend I wasn't ready to kill him. He cried and cried. Told the cops they had just gotten engaged the night before and that she wouldn't run off, she wouldn't, she would never. I nodded along but based on the female officer's wry, sidelong glances at me, she either knows what I know or knows Hux is a liar. She'd be right either way.

"Rey?"

It's my mother. It's always my mother. She's calling several times a day now. I wonder if corporate has started to note the pattern and if I'll get fired once they realize it's her. It sounds nice, getting fired, a decision made for me. But I'd probably just end up in another dead-end retail job. What other skills do I have? Nothing useful. Art appreciation, though not really art history. Excellent at making sandwiches, though only for myself. Being yelled at and keeping a smile on my face the entire time.

"Rey? Are you there?"

I love my mother. I do. I make myself answer her. I try to think of a way to tell her about Alie, but the words die in my throat. I try to think of a way to tell her that I'm trapped, that I'm dying here, in this store. That I was ready to run but I didn't, not yet. Is she the only reason I didn't? Or is it just me? Still unable to make any kind of decision, not knowing how everyone else knows how to transform into something newer, better, best. Not knowing how to be, to even feel free.

"Your father," a gasp breaks through the phone line and slaps me in the face, "he's..."

My mind spirals. It reaches for my father, but it doesn't find anything to hold on to. He was a late-in-life dad, already retired now. I couldn't tell you what he does all day. Sits in his chair, drinks a lot of Diet Coke, watches the Lakers of his native LA win and win and win most years. It sounds nice, but it can't be that exciting to win all the time, right? It must make it less meaningful. But this is coming from someone who doesn't even know what it feels like once in a while.

"Your father is cheating on me."

I don't know what to say. So I say the first thing that comes to mind: "Are you going to leave him?"

For maybe the first time in my life, there is silence on the other side of the phone. When she speaks it's almost a whisper, as if she's scared of what her answer will release into the world, into her own deeply hidden, sublimated self. But she does. She answers, a papery thin answer that feels breakable and fragile and unreal. She says, "Yes."

The silence grows again, static across the ether filling the spaces between us, as if more lightning is tripping its way along the lines. I want to congratulate her. I want to scream. I want to express happiness and sadness and exultation in all their different ideations because whatever my father is, he's been her partner in life for more than thirty years and this is the bravest thing I've ever heard her say.

She says it again, stronger this time and louder, too. "Yes. I am." I can hear her smile through the phone, I can hear her sharpening her teeth.

"Rey, I think, the women..."

The store is empty, but there's something about the words she's about to say that feel too private to say out loud. Too magic to make real. "I know, Mom. It's okay."

"It is?"

"It is."

There's another pause, companionable, while I imagine what kind of fox she'll be. My beautiful, well-meaning mother with her cheekbones slanted sharply and her hair so long and black and straight. She'll make a beautiful fox, wiry and fast and a leader of all the other foxes, chittering in her endless way. The other foxes will listen. The way I should have. So I listen now, I remember now, I learn now. I appreciate my mother, knowing it may be the last time we speak in this world, this world grounded to known reality.

"Thank you, Rey."

"I love you, Mom."

Another silence. We don't say this much, in our family. We talk and talk and talk and the pressure of that love remains, the pressure of those expectations. But this time, I tell her I love her, and I mean no matter what she does or who she becomes or who she really is and I feel all that pressure release, steam its way up into the sky and dissipate, disappear, disperse. I am alone in the store, more alone and less so than I have ever been. When she speaks again there are tears in her voice but also fire. "I love you, too, my brilliant girl."

She hangs up. I put the phone down, softly. As if not to disturb the animal sleeping in my own chest. My cell phone buzzes against my thigh once, twice, three times. It's James, a text, two, three. The police are questioning him now. I respond, letting him know I'm at work and not to be bothered. The phone goes silent. I help a woman find a dress for a memorial service. I wait for the phone to ring again at the store, but after the customer leaves, there's only silence and me and my thoughts. Only me and myself in the silence.

ALAYA KNOWLTON

My father calls me at the store. Mom is gone.

I'm not surprised when he calls. Well, I am, because the last time I remember speaking to my father on the phone was the year I worked at a summer camp in Albuquerque. I was sixteen and he picked up the phone because she was out getting groceries. The conversation, if you could call it that, was short and stilted, as if we didn't know each other.

The conversation today is much of the same, even in his blind panic. As if he's telling a stranger about someone else's personal tragedy, about something that doesn't affect the speaker or the listener at all. He doesn't even say hello. His voice is flattened out, as if he isn't even a character, just a narrator, or not even, someone just reporting in with the most basic of facts.

"Mom is gone. She didn't take anything with her."

I walk him through filing a police report. I've just done it for Alie, after all. I wonder, idly, for a moment, if the police would look at me as a person of interest. I figure no. There are so many missing women and as blonde as she was, Alie was clearly at least part-Japanese. And my mother? Clearly Native American. No one will look into it. No one will care when there's white women missing too.

I look around the store and it's filled with beautiful things and a few people: employees I've hired who will leave within a few months, rude older women with flashing diamonds, two teenagers I think are probably trying to shoplift but psyching themselves out. I have been standing in this spot, looking at the same scene, for nearly a decade. I don't know exactly what I want with my life, but it's not this. I don't know exactly what my mother wanted for me, what Alie would want for me, what any of those women—missing or free, whatever they really are— would want for me, but it isn't this.

My father is still talking but I realize I can't hear him anymore. There's a buzzing in my ears, high and whining. I hang up and I walk out of the door of Zorro and the New Mexican sun is blinding but I find my car. I drive blind to the apartment, but I make it. I dig and dig and dig through my dresser drawers. Socks, bras, and there, under all my underwear, I find my passport. A passport I only used once, years ago. A passport I thought I lost in the move but found a few months ago. A passport no one knows I found.

I call a cab. I get in the cab with only the clothes on my back and the passport. I think I've left my purse at Zorro, but my cash and cards are in a small, flat wallet in my pants' back pocket. The cabbie keeps glancing back at me, licking his lips, nervous or excited, I don't know, but if there's also a serial killer in New Mexico it might be this guy. He keeps asking me where I'm going. I don't say anything. I look him directly in the eye and let my silence make him as uncomfortable as he's probably made every woman who's ever gotten in his car feel. I am not transforming, not exactly, but I am starting to understand how it feels.

All I can think about on the drive is Georgia O'Keeffe. Her nude photos and her flowers and "it's only by selection, by elimination, and by emphasis that we get at the real meanings of things." I select myself from the rest of the world. I eliminate what doesn't serve me. I emphasize what does.

Georgia O'Keeffe probably would have been happier if she'd just admitted they were more than flowers. I wonder if she could see that, secretly, in her heart, once she went blind. That she painted, over and over and over again, in every flower and skull and skyscraper, something more than the image. She had been, she was always, painting herself.

I mourn and celebrate in a small way, in my silence, every single woman who couldn't see that. Who couldn't see herself. Who lived in a time where she had no self to see.

The cabbie eventually gives up on me. I wonder if he's thinking about skinning me and making a coat of my hide. He scowls when I pay him. I don't tip, and I smile as I refuse to give him any more than he's worth. It's a new world, it's a new me, it's all uncharted lands ahead now.

My phone rings as I stand in front of the terminal. James. I throw my phone in the trash can against the terminal wall, just before I walk in to buy a ticket to somewhere, anywhere, anywhere else but here.

Moonlight and Funk

written by
Marianne Xenos

illustrated by
APRIL SOLOMON

ABOUT THE AUTHOR

Marianne Xenos is a writer and visual artist living in western Massachusetts. She works with mixed-media, photography, and fiction. She's a member of an artist-run gallery and creates collages with a strong sense of fantasy and narrative. Although she's been writing since she first learned to read, Marianne only began sending out her stories for publication in the past year and a half.

Her story "Moonlight and Funk" began as a prompt in a writing workshop. The two main characters—a beachcombing vampire and a wounded dragon—were randomly assigned, and Marianne developed the rest of the story from imagination and personal experience. "The last few years were difficult for my family," she said. "Writing fantasy allowed me to imagine heroes—to spin worries into gold—or Chihuahuas into dragons." While writing the story, she drew on her father's love of Key West, her daughter's little yellow dog, and a longtime appreciation of dance music.

Marianne grew up in a blue-collar family outside of Boston. Her childhood was full of immigrants, builders, and working-class heroes—people who inspire the characters in her stories. Her father was a heavy-equipment operator who moved to Key West to look for gold, with only moderate success. He introduced her to treasure hunters, conchs, and deep-sea fishing. Marianne's mother, who never left New England if she could help it, taught her to dance as soon as she could walk—everything from Greek line dances to the cha-cha.

In 2021, Marianne published her first short story and was a finalist for Writers of the Future. "Moonlight and Funk" is her first professional publication.

ABOUT THE ILLUSTRATOR

April Solomon was born in 1983 and raised in Laguna Beach, California. Since she was a small child, April has had a talent for drawing and painting. She would draw anything and everything that came into her imagination. Of all things, she drew dragons the most! Thankfully, her loving and encouraging family inspired her to embrace her love for the arts.

She grew up around art. Her father's art studio was filled with all the delights a child could indulge in. His bookshelves held stacks of art books containing illustrations from the old masters, the golden age illustrators, and even some fantasy art from TSR's Dungeons & Dragons. Inspiration came in many forms. Fortunately, it was everywhere! And so her career as a young artist began.

Today, April is an illustrator and fine artist who has earned her bachelor's degree in illustration at the Laguna College of Art and Design. April's passion for learning the old masterful techniques of traditional drawing and painting is precisely what inspires her work.

Among her love for the fine arts is her unique appreciation for whimsical fantasy, which adorns every image of her portfolio. April's meticulous creature designs aim for what is known as "fantastic realism." A clever, concise understanding of anatomy, plants, and mysterious textures weave their way into her illustrations, leaving the viewer guessing at origins, influences, and ancestry. April's work allows the viewer to dive imaginatively deeper and reconsider whether dragons might be real or whether werewolves exist to stalk the streets at night.

When not illustrating, April attends garage sales to unearth buried treasures, runs and lifts weights, or braves as many haunted attractions as possible during the month of October.

Moonlight and Funk

Aveen swung her metal detector over the rough sand. Each night after sunset, when the tourists flocked to the bars on Duval Street, Aveen combed the beach in the dark. She had excellent night vision and an aversion to direct sun. Strange that she'd come to live in the Florida Keys, but she enjoyed the ocean, feral cats, and drunken tourists. Occasionally, she'd steal a nip from the neck of a drunk stumbling out of Sloppy Joe's at three in the morning—never too much, just a quick sip of the real thing laced with their drink of choice. "I'll have what he's having," she joked to herself, before wiping her mouth, and then the victim's mind. The joke never got old, although Aveen rarely had anybody to laugh with her. Key West was an idyllic but lonely home for a beachcombing vampire.

Aveen had traveled south in the seventies, leaving only two bodies in her wake—hitchhiking was always complicated—escaping a bad situation in Boston, and focusing only on "south" until she found herself at the southernmost point. Key West today wasn't what it used to be, and neither was she. There had been magic in 1978; the island was both queer and crotchety, buzzing with cocaine and Cuban coffee. Now, most of the true conchs—the local term for old-timers—were gone. Conch blood was a taste to savor—salt, rum, and caffeine and never watered down. Aveen, of course, had never killed a local. She bartered, seduced, and stole an occasional nip, and she had a good relationship with the local butcher, but she would never kill a conch. Now the land developers had pushed most of them out, and an army of condos had conquered the old magic—both the queer and the crotchety.

Aveen hummed an old Funkadelic song under her breath as she walked, carrying two bags, one for trash and one for treasure. Besides the modern coins she collected, she found trinkets and oddities which she transformed into jewelry and sold to an upscale shop in Old Town. She moved easily through the fringes of the town. Her light brown skin hid her vampire pallor, and a mane of dark curls hid her eyes. Aveen would always look twenty-two, except for her eyes. Her eyes revealed the centuries.

Head down and lost in thought, Aveen followed her metal detector farther down the beach than she usually walked. Fort Zachary Taylor was to her right, and the ground had become hard and gritty. The metal detector was quiet, and she was about to turn back when she saw a plastic grocery bag tumbling across the sand.

"Freaking tourists," she grumbled, dragging her things as she pursued the bag.

Suddenly she was startled by a loud pop and looked up to see fireworks, surprising and almost surrealistic, bursting over the hulking antique fort. Then Aveen remembered it was New Year's Eve. She paused to take in the colors, which would be visible from every point on the small island, then looked around for the tumbling plastic bag and continued her pursuit. As she stepped away from the beach into the scruffy weeds, her intuition began to itch—danger, treasure, prey?—but before she could sort out the itch, the bag blew behind a pile of rocks and she followed. Then suddenly her metal detector blared, a second burst of fireworks exploded, and a large beast roared.

Vampires didn't startle easily. Vampire survival was all about silence, stealth and a healthy dose of seduction, but Aveen jumped and screamed like a child, like the small frightened girl she'd once been in Al-Basrah. And if screaming wasn't bad enough, she jumped again as the sky flared a third time, illuminating the roaring beast behind the rocks. The thing was over eight feet tall on its hind legs, rippling with muscle, covered in amber scales, and topped with two sharp horns. Spikes plumed on the beast's shoulder blades like the remnants of wings, and it growled, showing a mouthful of fangs.

"What the hell!" Aveen shouted.

"What the hell!" the beast repeated, laughing. "Frightened little boy!"

"I'm not a boy!" Aveen was flustered. Startled by a high-pitched bark near her feet, she jumped back again. A small, yellow dog had run from behind the monster, yipping and growling. "What the hell!" she repeated.

The beast laughed louder, a roaring belly laugh, and as it did, it grew smaller, shrinking with each guffaw until it was about Aveen's size. The laugh became smaller too, until it was a soft chuckle, and the beast wiped its big black eyes, tearing from laughter.

"Big tough guy, scared of rainbow thunder and little weredog. You should see weredog on the full moon."

"Wait," Aveen said, feeling confused and a bit irritated, but regaining some of her composure. "First I'm not afraid of rainbow thunder. Plus, you screamed first, big guy! Whatever you are."

The beast chuckled and offered a crooked fangy smile. The white plastic bag had wrapped itself around one scaled leg, and the beast scratched idly at a patch of duct tape covering its chest. They stared at each other for another minute, and the small dog stopped barking and began exploring the trash bag Aveen carried. While the dog sniffed the bag, the beast sniffed Aveen.

"Aw...okay, vampire." It laughed again after a long leisurely sniff. "Silly boy, dragons don't bite vampires. Unless there are fish vampires. I like to eat fish."

Aveen stared at the beast—the dragon—in confusion. Her confusion grew as it continued to change form. The dragon's head gradually transformed until it resembled Aveen's—tight black curls and broad cheekbones—although the horns, amber scales, and duct tape stayed the same.

"Okay...dragon," Aveen said, fascinated despite herself. "I'm Aveen. What do I call you? What's your name?"

"I am named Tann. Do you smoke? I need a smoke."

Fireworks continued to light the sky, and Aveen watched while Tann sat on a wooden chest and pulled a clay pipe from a leather bag, filling it with dried leaves that looked like tobacco.

"And this one," the dragon said, nodding toward the small dog, "is called Glory. Except on the full moon; then I call it Glorious." Tann chuckled at some private joke, nodding toward the honey-colored mutt, who looked like a burly Chihuahua with intelligent black eyes. Aveen was baffled and searched her memory for any dragon lore she'd learned, which was sparse. Dragons were ancient, loyal, and prone to be stingy. Their blood could kill or heal, but the details were mysterious. Aveen certainly wasn't going to lean in for a taste.

"So, how should I address you, Tann? Like...I'm not a boy. I'm a 'she.' What about you?"

"Silly hatchling," Tann laughed, as though that settled everything, and it passed her the pipe. "We are like twins now."

The dragon's face mirrored Aveen's perfectly, but the effect was bizarre under the pointed horns. "Twins, huh?" she said, shrugging as she took the pipe. "Cousins...maybe." As she guessed, it was tobacco—not that it mattered. Her heightened immune system kept her from getting high or drunk. She enjoyed the burn of alcohol in blood, or the smoky taste of weed, but that wasn't the buzz she sought when she took a nip of blood. She drank her victim's surprise, euphoria, passion, or fear. Simple chemistry—like adrenaline or endorphins—and chemistry could be addictive. In the years since Boston, she'd become a more sober vampire.

She took a second small hit from the pipe. "I think you're a 'he,' big guy. Definitely a 'he.' You have dude vibes."

Tann shook its horned head. "You people have a very limited worldview."

She opened her mouth to protest, but paused, took another puff, and passed the pipe back. "Well, I can't argue with that."

The small dog had pulled a paper plate from the trash bag, shredding it like confetti on the sand. Aveen knew she'd have to clean up the mess before dragging the bags back up the beach, but she felt content watching the dog and sharing a smoke with another monster under the rainbow thunder. They talked idly about treasure hunting, and she pulled out the trinkets she'd found that day. The dragon's favorite was a miniature spoon engraved with a palm tree.

"On Tuesday, when Glory becomes Glorious, we will acquire treasure. I have a map." Tann pulled out a tourist map of Key West.

"I hate to break it to you, cousin, but those treasure museums have stellar security."

Tann's chuckle rumbled deep in its chest. "Never underestimate a dragon. Our target is a bad man, a dragon-slayer, and a thief. He wears a plundered coin on a chain around his neck—treasure stolen from Glory's people. The sun shines on one side of the coin, and the moon on the other. Each morning at eight he sits on a patio here." Tann pointed with a talon. "We have watched him drink coffee with the naked sun glinting on the gold."

Aveen was intrigued, and for a while they talked shop—stealth versus force, vampire ways versus dragon ways. Tann insisted they could walk onto the patio and slip the coin from the man's living neck. Aveen thought more caution would be wise.

She finally said, "Let me grab the coin for you. Look, I'm a hunter, and I have seriously stealthy skills. Plus, if he's such a bad guy, maybe I can grab some nourishment while I'm there."

"Evil is not nourishment, Aveen. We have a saying—*your eating becomes your being.*"

"Americans say—*you are what you eat.*"

"Hmm, awkward and inaccurate."

Again, Aveen couldn't disagree.

"Glory is the master at acquiring treasure," Tann said. "But we need the full moon for it to become fully Glorious. Its transformation will last one full day, in darkness and light."

Aveen was baffled, once again, but let the subject go—both covert operations and weredog transformations—and watched the gibbous moon in the sky. It was about two days from full. She looked back at the dragon. "And what's with the duct tape, cuz? Are you injured?"

Tann scratched at the patch of silver tape with its talons. "The scales over my heart are fallen." Aveen wondered if that was a metaphor, but the dragon continued after a pause, reluctantly. "The thief...I followed him alone, angry, and with little thinking. His weapon hit my chest, and I fled to the ocean—stunned and bleeding—drifting until Glory found me." It looked toward the ocean and was quiet.

Aveen let the pause in conversation settle, thinking about the injured dragon swimming with salt water in its wound. Thinking about the bond between the two creatures. She suspected Tann was uncomfortable with the details of the injury, so she put her questions aside. Sometimes the past belonged in the past.

"I could help you with that spot on your chest, cuz—patch you up. I make jewelry, and we could design a breastplate fit for a dragon liege."

"Hmm...that is generosity." It turned its head and looked at her, considering. "I would like that, but you must take something in return."

"No, I can't take your treasure."

Tann rumbled like an engine. "There is something more precious than treasure, nestling. A taste of dragon blood. More than a taste—a drink, a draft, a long thirsty gulp."

Aveen stared, momentarily speechless.

"The blood can cure you," Tann continued.

"Of what? I'm immune to everything."

"That itself is the disease. I could make you human again."

Aveen paused and said only, "Huh." Once again, the dragon left her feeling off-balance and confused. The offer surprised and also frightened her.

Aveen looked up at the sky. The fireworks had faded. Duval Street would be crowded with drunks by now, and the thought made her feel lonely, made her crave something that wasn't blood. *What was she craving?*

"Sunlight," she said. The dragon hummed long and low, following her train of thought. "And sex. Real sex. I was enslaved before I was turned, and I've never had the real thing—hot, sweaty, egalitarian sex." Tann hummed again, an appreciative growl, like it knew something about both captivity and consent. Aveen thought about the scales ripped from over its heart, and touched her chest where her own heart had stopped beating eleven centuries ago. She kept her eyes on the sky, thinking about the stars. They were distant suns, or most of them were, and their rays were diluted. Otherwise starlight would burn her skin. The small nips of blood she stole were like starlight and moonlight either diluted or reflected, a secondhand buzz.

Aveen made a list in her mind: sunlight, sex, and fresh-baked bread. After a thought she added kissing and cold beer. She said out loud, "But I might die immediately."

"Yes, you could die tonight or in sixty years. Being alive is always fatal."

Glory had found a worn-out flip-flop in the trash bag and was chewing on the sole, but it watched Aveen carefully, its dark eyes following the conversation.

"Let me sleep on it, cuz. I'll come back with your breastplate and we can talk."

"Come back on Tuesday soon after sunset. You can meet Glory when it becomes Glorious." The dragon scratched its chin, which no longer looked like Aveen's chin, and its head was once again as bald as a lizard. "Could you bring a device with some music? Glory will want to dance. Something modern."

APRIL SOLOMON

For the next two days Aveen worked on the breastplate. She sketched designs and combed through her collection of minute treasures. Beginning with a weave of silver wire, she threaded amber and onyx beads, igneous stones from Colorado, and added a constellation of paper-thin silver coins snipped from a harem costume. Over the years, she had gathered a collection of tiny cocaine spoons, and she chose the smallest with an ornate handle to hang in the center of the piece. Using a soldering iron, she attached the woven mesh to a lightweight silver plate, slightly wider than the missing scales on Tann's chest. Aveen would make four small piercings on the surrounding scales, attaching the breastplate with studs, like an earring. The dragon would be able to remove it or replace it as needed. When she was done, she wrapped the piece in rainbow-colored tissue and put it in her bag.

On Monday night, Aveen did her usual rounds. Butcher's shop for beef and pork blood, and she brought a few commissioned pieces to the craft gallery. She found herself thinking about Tann and Glory, looking forward to Tuesday night, although still uncertain about Tann's offer.

During closing time at Sloppy Joe's, she lingered in the shadows and watched the drunks stumble home. She felt an ache, a mixture of desires. Aveen thought of the list of things she'd like to reclaim. The top three items were sunlight, sex, and beer, and as she watched the crowd, she added ice cream and an ankle tattoo. The list became longer each day.

She closed her eyes and opened her senses, letting the fragrance of humanity sweep over her. Like a small child outside the market in Al-Basrah, she had learned to live with hunger. Suddenly, under the smell of fried food and human sweat, she sensed something different—something predatory—although not another vampire. Opening her eyes she scanned the crowd and saw a deeply tanned man with short curly hair standing over a petite woman. Aveen recognized the woman as a local—sweet, naive and always drawn to the wrong guy. The man was human, but he felt... *off*. She reached with her mind just a slight psychic brush and caught a sense of gunpowder and dragon's blood. Gold flashed on his chest—the golden coin. Tann's bad guy stood just ten feet away.

Aveen slipped out of the shadow and stumbled over to the couple, intentionally slurring her words.

"Girl*friend*! What are you doing?" She winked at the petite woman. "Rocky is going to *kill* you if you don't get out of here!" She pushed between the two of them, covertly tucking a twenty-dollar bill into the woman's hand for carfare, hoping she'd understand the warning.

"Hey, is that real?" Aveen said to the man, putting her hand to his chest and grasping the golden coin, flipping it over to see the moon on the back. She felt the woman slip away and leave.

Aveen kept her hand on the coin and looked at the man's face, considering. She heard the jangle of keys and saw a heavyset man approach.

"Hey, boss, the car is ready!"

Aveen dipped her head and nipped the man's neck, grazing her teeth across his skin. Her saliva contained a hypnotic, which helped control prey; subtle but powerful. As she dropped the coin back on his chest she whispered, "I'll see you later."

"Wait!" he called. "When?" And she was gone.

Cruising now on her predator instincts, she walked back toward Old Town, recalling the location of the bad guy's house from Tann's map. The man lived in an upscale neighborhood a few blocks from the harbor. She didn't have a plan in mind, but she worried about her new friends, whose plan to steal the coin seemed naive and reckless. Aveen had skills and the natural enhancements of a vampire. She was an efficient thief and an even more efficient killer.

Key West was a casual town, and the wealthy often posed as regular conchs. Aveen strolled past the address, peering through an iron fence bordered with bougainvillea. It looked tropical and understated. A single security camera hung above the patio door. Aveen quickly covered her hair and face with a scarf. Candles burned on a low table, and logic said he would come outside before bed. The vampire nip should make him restless.

The burly man she'd seen at Sloppy Joe's opened the patio door and came outside, checking the gates and the camera, tidying up for the night. Aveen was disappointed, but she watched as he lit a fresh candle and put down a clean ashtray. Then he went inside without drawing the curtains. Moments later a car pulled away.

Twenty minutes later the target—the treasure-stealing abuser of dragons—came out to the patio wearing only a burgundy robe. With the arrogance of a young conquistador, he sat alone by candlelight, smoking a cigarette and drinking amber liquid from a crystal tumbler. Aveen heard the clink of ice and smelled bourbon, citronella, and the warm blood of a lone human. He was unguarded now, and his robe fell open at the chest. The coin seemed to shudder in the candlelight.

There was a proverb, "Never come between a dragon and its gold." And another repeated by an uncle in Al-Basrah, "Never come between anger and its vengeance." Aveen respected the wisdom of her elders, but an American proverb came to mind, "Opportunity knocks but once."

One moment she stood pondering multicultural proverbs, and then, almost without thought, she vaulted over the fence, moving with inhuman skill—swift, lithe, and almost invisible. Before the man could react, she forced her forearm across his throat, blocking his breath and choking him. After a short struggle, he collapsed in her arms, and she carefully checked his pulse. Still alive. She ran her razor-sharp thumbnail along the contour of his neck and bent to smell his skin. Aftershave, alcohol, and still-living blood. Her hunger flared, and her fangs bared involuntarily, but she pulled her head away.

Your eating is your becoming, Tann had said. Hissing softly, Aveen retracted her fangs. She'd had her fill of bad guys. She unclasped the coin from the man's neck and examined the engraving, like a sunburst on the palm of her hand. Then she placed his head carefully on the table, wiping his mind with a brush of her hand. She remembered to reach up to the camera and erase its digital memory, just as she had erased the man's. Then she slipped over the fence as quietly as a shadow.

Just after sundown on Tuesday night, Aveen swung her cooler by her side as she walked to the fort. She'd left the metal detector and trash bags at home and had put a six-pack of beer and a pint of strawberries in the cooler. Just in case. She wore her favorite pink high-top sneakers matched with dangling flamingo earrings.

Her phone contained a dance list with music by Prince, Sheila E., and some mixed seventies funk. When Tann said "modern" it might have meant anything from Stravinsky to hip-hop, but Aveen imagined even dragons liked Prince.

Tann was smoking its pipe when Aveen arrived, and Glory was chewing on a battered sneaker. Tann's face was its own again, pointed and reptilian, and it smiled when it took the package, setting it aside. "I will open the gift when you make your decision."

As Aveen settled on the sand next to the small dog, wondering when to tell them about the coin, Tann handed her the pipe and waited a moment before speaking.

"If you choose the blood, it will not change the person who was and will always be Aveen. It will simply cure what is vampire—the virus which is also an immunity. You will become human, but with eleven centuries of memories, emotions, and transgressions to carry."

"Okay..." she said, but she thought for a moment and added, "damn."

"It is good to have old friends, Aveen. Friends who are truly very old. We understand the centuries. If you survive, you could come with us and be a different sort of hunter."

Aveen wasn't used to feelings—or friendship for that matter—so she said nothing while Tann smoked its pipe. Suddenly Glory barked, jumping up from the sand, hackles raised, yipping at the sky. Tann jumped up.

"Now you will see beauty, nestling. Now you will see true Glory, my beloved Glorious. Glory is my soulfriend, but Glorious is my soulmate, my partner in crime, my *rouhi*, as they say in your homeland."

The dog lifted its head and howled at the moon. What began as a Chihuahua's howl grew into a deep and resonant dragon's roar. Tann roared in return and shouted something in a language more ancient than Arabic, which Aveen hoped was a call for music. She pulled out her phone and portable speakers. The first song in the queue was "Fire" by the Ohio Players.

Glory was now a yellow-gold dragon, scaled and horned like Tann, but rounder and brighter, with larger shoulder spikes. The yellow dragon stood on two legs and ran to hug Tann. Then it turned and squealed, "I love this song!" Stretching its arms up to the moon, it began to dance—hips swiveling like a rocking boat. It swerved and curved, circling like the path of the moon. Some would call it belly dancing, but Aveen knew the dance as *Raqs Baladi*.

"Damn," Aveen said. "I didn't even know dragons had hips."

As Glory danced, twirling and undulating, it grew larger until it was the same size as Tann. Tann watched, delighted, and its face changed, taking on Glory's facial structure and growing a tuft of yellowish hair. After a short pause of appreciation for Glory's transition from Chihuahua to dragon, all three danced on the beach. They danced for an hour, and then Glory pushed its tuft of blond hair back from its face and said, "I need a swim in the ocean."

Then it stepped close to Aveen and touched her face gently with one gleaming talon. "I'm glad to have danced with you. While I am gone, you should discuss your business with Tann."

"Wait! I have something to tell you."

Glory smiled and said, "I already know. Is that the sun in your pocket, or are you just happy to see me?"

Tann sat on the treasure chest and laughed. "You can't fool a master thief, nestling. Keep no secrets from my Glorious."

"Here," Glory said, "I'll show you."

The dragon took a step back and smiled gently. Aveen felt a tilt of vertigo and blinked her eyes, unable to pinpoint the cause of her dizziness.

"There," said the dragon, holding out its hands. It held a pair of plastic flamingo earrings in one palm, and the golden coin in the other.

Aveen checked her ears and her pocket, and the earrings and coin were gone. "How did you do that?"

"You gave them to me freely, and then I removed the memory. Here I'll return the memory. I would normally never take something from a friend without consent. The mark—the bad man with the coin—is a different story."

Glory touched Aveen's temple, and the tilt of vertigo returned, along with her memory. Aveen remembered Glory asking her for the earrings and remembered feeling flattered and delighted to give the dragon anything it wanted. Aveen had given them freely. She used a similar trick when she mind-wiped her victims, but Glory's magic was more impressive.

Aveen said, "I was afraid you'd be angry because I'd come between you and your vengeance."

Glory touched Aveen's cheek again and smiled. "Your people have an interesting worldview. Vengeance is an unquenchable craving, but dragons prefer the solidity of gold, treasure we can hold in our hands." It gave the earrings back to Aveen. As it gave the coin to Tann it said, "I'll bring you a fish, darling." Then Glory walked toward the water humming softly to itself.

Aveen wished she could go swimming with Glory, rather than making life-and-death decisions about drinking dragon blood. She picked up the phone and chose a different playlist. This one was called "Al-Basrah Lounge," mostly contemporary interpretations of Middle Eastern songs. From the ocean she heard Glory singing along in Arabic.

"What if I become a dragon? Has that ever happened?"

"Now you are just making wishes," Tann said, with its deep chuckle, turning the golden coin over in its scaled hands. "Maybe instead of thieving, we will open a gallery of art and treasure.

Think of your creations in a sunny window near Mallory Square. The small dog could sit by the door and welcome the visitors." Tann still hadn't opened the package, and Aveen assumed it was waiting for her decision.

Without giving her answer, Aveen took baby oil, rubbing alcohol, and soft cotton rags from her bag and carefully removed the duct tape from Tann's scales. The flesh around its heart was puckered and scarred. "I'm so sorry, friend. I can't fix the scars, but at least you'll look like a fabulous dragon liege. One without duct tape."

Tann grunted approval. Using a piercing gun, Aveen made four small holes in Tann's scales, and attached the breastplate with silver studs, covering the gap over the dragon's heart perfectly. The silver caught the light of the moon, while the volcanic beads blended with the night. Tann fingered the small cocaine spoon and hummed its approval.

Glory's voice curled in the dark like an arabesque, and occasional spouts of flame flashed on the waves. Aveen hummed along while she put her supplies in the bag.

Tann said, "Think about sunlight and fresh-baked bread."

"Sex and beer and ice cream."

The dragon rumbled in reply.

Aveen paused and then moved to the treasure chest and sat next to Tann. The dragon looked at her, and its face changed— softening, developing cheekbones, mirroring her own. Tight dark curls fell around its face, and the scales on its neck smoothed, now bare and identical to Aveen's, the skin naked and brown. Taloned fingers touched the place above the jugular vein. Offering.

Aveen leaned in and drank.

Death and the Taxman

written by

David Hankins

illustrated by

SARAH MORRISON

ABOUT THE AUTHOR

David Hankins writes from the thriving cornfields of Iowa where he lives with his wife, daughter, and two dragons disguised as cats. His writing journey began in the oral tradition of convincing his daughter to "Go to sleep" with inventive stories. That usually backfired. After years of "Just one more story," David began transcribing his midnight ramblings in an attempt to keep his storylines straight. Children are ruthless in identifying mistakes in fairy tales. David writes lighthearted speculative fiction because that's what he loves to read and—this is the important bit—there's not nearly enough humor in the world. David aims to change that, one story at a time.

David joined the US Army after college and, through some glitch in the bureaucracy, convinced Uncle Sam to fund his wanderlust for twenty years. He has lived in and traveled through much of Europe, central Asia, and the United States. Now that he's retired from the army, David devotes his time to his passions of writing, traveling with his family, and finding new ways to pay his mortgage.

"Death and the Taxman" was born as the writing community mourned the passing of Writers of the Future Coordinating Judge David Farland. Death is the ultimate rigged game, one that the Grim Reaper never loses. But what if he did? What if he became human? Would the Grim Reaper cling to life as tenaciously as we do? Inspired by the witty and sarcastic styles of Sir Terry Pratchett and Jim Butcher—and by an IRS audit he hopes never to repeat—David wrote this story hoping to bring laughter in a time of grief. To any tax auditors reading this: you are lovely people. Please don't audit David again. He hopes you enjoy "Death and the Taxman."

ABOUT THE ILLUSTRATOR

Sarah Morrison is a fantasy illustrator and portrait artist. Working primarily with oil paint she focuses on figurative works designed to inspire narrative, with attention towards expressive faces and complex fabric. Escapism through fantasy has always been a central theme to her art, and she embraces whimsy and enigmatic details. Sarah's imagery is designed to inspire a sense of wonder, encouraging viewers to develop stories about what might be going on in each piece.

Sarah has been drawing from a young age, thriving with her introduction to anime and manga in the 1990s, and later moving on to fantastic realism. After working in management at art supply stores for thirteen years while studying and building her portfolio, she left the retail life to pursue art full time in 2019. Sarah also occasionally works with printmaking techniques and textiles. Born in Canada, she currently resides just outside of Boston, MA, US, with her husband, toddler, and cat.

Death and the Taxman

I, the Grim Reaper, terror of men's souls, shall forevermore despise Mondays because that was the day I met Frank Totmann. That was the day I *became* Frank Totmann.

I found him having a heart attack in his dingy office on the third floor of the Colorado Springs Internal Revenue Service Tax Assistance Center. What a mouthful. They should have named it "The Land of Evil Auditors." Frank was a balding, pudgy man without a single sharp edge. His cheap suit strained its buttons.

I stopped time and Frank gasped, clutching his chest and drawing relieved breaths. I pointed a bony finger, let my eye sockets flame a bit for effect, and intoned, "Frank Totmann, your time has come."

Frank sat back, threw me a broad smile, and said, "Cup of tea?" He produced a thermos and two teacups from under the desk.

How touching. Nobody ever offered refreshments. It's a lonely half-life, being Death, so I enjoy sharing folks' final moments. They usually complain about being too young to die or attempt to cheat me, but I don't mind. They're the only conversations I have. I nodded with gravity and grace.

What a fool I was. Never accept tea from a dying auditor.

I took a sip and coughed. It tasted of blood and ashes. Abrupt pain seared my bones, dropping me to my knees. The world spun, went dark, and with a distressing stretch which ended in a *pop*, I found myself sitting in Frank's chair staring across the desk at...me.

I blinked, shocked to have eyelids, and blinked again. No, that wasn't me. Frank Totmann's spirit, a mirror image of the body

I now possessed, grinned stupidly in Death's cowl. In *my* cowl, clutching *my* scythe—crafted by the Devil and blessed by the Most High. It gave me power over human souls.

Of all the *cheek.*

I lunged across the desk, caught my hip on its edge, and sprawled across audit reports and tax returns. Breath whooshed out of me. Unfamiliar with a human body, I forgot to breathe in. Stars flashed before my eyes.

Frank jumped back, holding my scythe high like a bully taunting a child. I flopped onto his chair, which rolled back with plastic protests. I sucked in a breath, time resumed, and my heart pounded in my chest. Frank's chest. Whatever.

I grabbed the spilled teacup and sniffed it. It smelled of anise, copper, and...*magic.* My eyes went wide. "How?" I asked, then flinched. The Grim Reaper should boom and intone, not squeak like a scared bureaucrat.

Frank's grin became a smirk. "Ancient soul transfer spell. Sumerian, I think. Doc said my heart was failing, so I nailed the timing of your arrival by taking poison. We shared the transference potion and voilà"—he took a bow—"I cheated Death."

I flung the teacup at the wall. It shattered and fell to the industrial carpet. How the hell had an IRS auditor unearthed a Sumerian soul transfer spell?

How dare he use it on *me?* On *Death?*

And after offering hospitality. Never again! Never again would I...

My mouth opened and closed like a dying fish as the gravity of the situation hit home.

Never again was right. I was a human. A flesh and blood human. Mortal.

More importantly, I was a mortal who—I checked my internal clock which measured human lives—should have died five minutes ago. My gaze flicked to Frank. To the scythe in his hands.

He followed my gaze and shook his head. "I'm not reaping your soul. Not even sure how, to tell the truth. But"—he twirled my scythe then swung it like a golf club—"I'll get the hang of it.

SARAH MORRISON

Besides, that body's not dead. I spiked my tea with the poison's antidote." He waggled his fingers at me, said "See ya!" and drifted through the door.

I slouched in the chair, dumbfounded for the first time in millennia. The Rules were quite clear. Frank's soul was supposed to cross over today. I had to swap us back, restore the balance before Hell's bureaucrats noticed. Before Hell's Auditor noticed and took *my* soul instead.

I sat in Frank's office for an hour, my mind chasing its tail. How do I, the Grim Reaper, cheat death? This heart may have resumed beating, but it couldn't last long. My hands, used to clutching my scythe, grasped at the air. I grabbed a pen and clicked it obsessively.

It wasn't the same.

A knock at the door interrupted my thoughts and a short, solid woman with pinned-back, graying hair swung the door open. She wore a matronly flowered dress, an overabundance of clattering jewelry, and a smile that lit her face like she was genuinely pleased to see me.

That was a new experience.

"Staying late, Frank?" Her voice was warm, like honey.

I clicked the pen a few more times and read her soul through her dark brown eyes. Cordelia Knowles, fifty-eight years old, death in forty-three years. "Uh, no," I said and rose awkwardly.

"Walk me to my car?"

"Sure, uh, Cordelia."

Her brows knit together. "It's Cora. I told you on our first date." Her voice slowed and she tilted her head. "You OK, Frank? You look like death warmed over."

You have no idea. Aloud I tried to say "I'm fine," but the words stuck in my throat. I grimaced. Bloody Archangel Gabriel and his bloody restrictions. He'd burned the words "Honesty in death" into my soul when he made me the Reaper.

I couldn't lie.

An agent of both Heaven and Hell must remain above reproach. It was one of Heaven's Rules that governed all spiritual matters. I'd never chafed under that restriction before today.

After flapping my jowls again like that bloody dying fish, I said, "I'm alive. That's what's important." I stomped around the desk and followed Cora into a cubicle farm with people streaming toward an elevator. She gave me a piercing look but didn't press. Instead, she chattered about work and my thoughts turned inward.

Frank had found a Sumerian spell. There had to be a reversal. I nodded to myself. Yes, that was the ticket. Find Frank's house, retrieve his spell book, and get out of this body.

My thoughts were again interrupted when Cora looped her arm in mine and guided me around the crowd to a door marked "exit." I reached it first and tried to pass through.

Like I always do.

My face smacked into solid wood, and I bounced off, popping the door open. I stumbled back, hands flying to my nose. "Ow!"

The departing crowd burst into laughter with a smattering of applause. Someone called, "Been walking long, Frank?"

"No," I said, rubbing my nose and glaring at the offending door as it swung back toward me. The laws of physics were so...inconvenient. Cora placed a comforting hand on my shoulder, and we pushed into the stairwell.

"Frank? Are you sure you're OK?"

I patted her hand noncommittally and headed downstairs. At the bottom, I was careful to press on the push bar before stepping outside. I felt inordinately pleased with myself when it worked.

Bright sunlight made me blink. The city of Colorado Springs rose on foothills, climbing partway up an imposing ridgeline. The cool wind was crisp and plucked at my suit. I drew a deep, invigorating breath. I drew another, feeling alive in a way I'd never known. Cora hooked my elbow again and guided me toward her rusty Peugeot. I recognized the car because I'd reaped a soul from one last week. In midair. It had blown through an Alpine guardrail to plummet off a cliff. The deceased had blamed the car for his demise, never mind the half-written text on his cell phone.

"Well, this is me," Cora said, fishing keys from her purse. "Are we still on for tonight?"

"To...night?"

"Yes, silly. Dinner? At Edelweiss? You said you'd never tried schnitzel."

"I have not tried schnitzel." I spoke with finality, reveling in an easy truth.

She gave me a bemused smile, opened her door, then paused as if waiting. Her brown eyes locked with mine then, to my horror, she rocked forward and pecked me on the lips. Blood rushed to Cora's cheeks, and she slid into her car. "See you at seven!" She waved and was gone. I stood there, dumbfounded for the second time.

She'd kissed me. I...I'd never been kissed. It felt odd, this mashing of body parts together, and it left my lips feeling tingly. Perhaps it was the wind. Yes, that was it.

I gave myself a shake. Find Frank, reverse the spell. Stay focused on what mattered before the Auditor found out. Hell's final arbiter of the Rules would love to banish me to the Realm of Torments. Forever.

I headed for the nearest road to find a cab. I'd reaped too many souls from crumpled wrecks to try driving. Traffic flowed past in a noisy blur until I waved down a taxi. I carefully opened the car door as Cora had done.

Success. I was getting the hang of this human thing.

"Where to, pal?" the cabbie asked. I automatically checked his soul through his cheerful gray eyes. Louis Faretti, thirty-six, death in seven years.

"The home of Frank Totmann, Louis," I said, sliding inside. The cab smelled of industrial cleaners and artificial lemon with a whiff of vomit. Louis hung one arm over the bench seat.

"Got an address, bud?" I blinked at him then rummaged

through Frank's pockets. Wallet, keys, cell phone. I dug into the wallet, found something with Frank's picture and address, and read it aloud. Louis nodded and sped away, tires screeching. Horns blared as we wove violently through traffic.

Over the next six minutes of terror, I discovered why the cab smelled of vomit. I managed, barely, to keep my gorge down as Louis chatted.

"Whatcha do for a living?"

"For the living, nothing. The dead are my concern." I clutched the door as we zoomed around a truck.

"Coroner? Huh. Never drove a coroner before." He glanced in his rearview. "You're looking kinda pale, bud. Rough day at the office? Someone send you a body that wasn't quite dead yet?" He chuckled and slammed on the brakes as traffic stopped around us. I rocked forward and caught myself on his seat.

"Uh, yes," I said, falling back as the cab shot forward and resumed weaving through traffic. "He stole something very valuable." *My identity as Death.* "Failure to retrieve it will have dire consequences." Eternal torments. I shuddered.

Louis's eyes went wide. "A real Lazarus story, but with a twist. Ain't that wild? So, what, you gonna get fired?" Someone honked as Louis cut them off. We passed into the ridgeline's shadow and the temperature dropped.

I glowered at the back of his head. Lazarus was a fluke. Divine intervention that ruined my perfect record and nearly led to an audit.

"Worse," I said. "I could face Judgment." Judgment long delayed for my original sin. My mind shied away from that train of thought.

We screeched to a stop before a sad-looking house with cracked tan siding and brown grass. "That'll be twelve bucks even," Louis said.

I blinked at him, then remembered. Money. Humans used money for everything. I handed him Frank's wallet.

Louis arched an eyebrow and retrieved some bills before handing it back. He passed me a card. "If you need a ride, give me a ring." His head cocked to one side. "Never caught your name, friend."

"Grim Reaper." I fumbled at the door handle, which was different from the one outside the car.

Louis barked a laugh as the door popped open and I tumbled out. "Man, your parents had a twisted sense of humor. No wonder you became a coroner. See ya, Grim!" He waved and sped off. I set my jaw and approached Frank's house.

Getting inside proved challenging. Why was *every* door handle different? This one had a stupid little knob that wouldn't turn.

Keys, right.

The door creaked open, releasing an overwhelming stench of old coffee and stale sweat. Piles of clutter lay everywhere. I wrinkled my nose. Why did humans cling to life so tenaciously when *this* was how they lived?

I searched the main floor but found little of interest beyond a bookshelf overflowing with occult and religious texts. I scanned the titles. Plenty about the afterlife and Yours Truly, but nothing ancient. No Sumerian soul spells, just an unhealthy fascination with death.

No surprise there.

I paused at a bulletin board tacked with thank you notes from clients Frank had audited, gratitude for helping clear debt and acquire refunds. Odd. I wouldn't have expected such helpful behavior from an auditor.

From his kitchen, I descended a stairwell to the center of an unfinished basement. Creaky steps echoed through darkness before my hand brushed against a light switch. A bulb flickered on, revealing the logical result of Frank's occult research. Painted archaic symbols covered the empty cement floor, each with unlit candles at intersection points. Summoning circles from different civilizations.

Bingo.

I recognized Babylonian, Greek, Chinese, Egyptian, and— ah-ha!—Sumerian. That one had intricately woven runes surrounding charred cement and feathery ash.

I circled the dank room, stepping around the summoning circles, examining each. It was a testament to mankind's tenacity that every civilization devised methods of controlling spirits. Tucked under the open stairs was Frank's workspace—a tattered recliner beside a rickety apothecary cabinet filled with papers, moldering books, and scrolls. Artifacts in labeled jars and little plastic baggies hid in the apothecary cabinet's little cubbyholes. Stickers decorated many with "Rare Find!—Cordelia's Apothecary Supply."

I arched an eyebrow. Cordelia? She was a tax auditor *and* an apothecary? Interesting.

I retrieved a rolled-up bundle of copy paper. Pictures of ancient Sumerian tablets filled every page with handwritten translations scrawled along the edges. My breath caught and the papers crinkled in my grip. This was it.

I drew a deep breath, smoothed out the papers, and read. I wasn't limited by human language barriers, so translation wasn't a problem.

The content was.

There was nothing here about swapping souls. It was a simple summoning spell.

I dropped into the recliner with a huff and read through again. Nothing. I scratched my jaw.

Perhaps Frank summoned a spirit and got the spell from them. I eyed the apothecary cabinet's little cubbyholes. Follow Frank's steps. Summon a demon, then ask it about the spell. I nodded to myself, jumped up, and set to work.

Fifteen minutes later the Sumerian circle was set up with candles, cinnamon, and bone dust from a Sumerian priest—if the baggie label was to be believed. I turned off the light, chanted the incantation seven times, then pricked my finger over the circle before snatching my hand back.

A bolt of red lightning arced up when my blood hit the cement. It bounced off the circle's invisible walls, splitting and multiplying until an inferno of crackling red electricity connected cement to bare joists. My skin tingled and my hair stood on end before the entire light show condensed into a single bolt again. It struck the center of the circle with a hellish boom that rattled the stairs. Lava bubbled through the cement and from that rose a demon's hideous form, clad in a wrinkled gray suit.

He stood only two feet tall.

I smiled, the knot in my chest easing somewhat. It was Alvin, recently promoted head of Bureaucratic Torments. Not a friend, really, but our paths had crossed. Horns poked through his thin, greasy comb-over and his sharp red eyes glared at me. He pointed a clawed finger.

"That's it, Frank! I'm sending my cousin Brutus to make your life a living hell until the *day...you...die*! Then, when your soul finds its way to Hell, I'm gonna—"

"I am not Frank Totmann," I said, and Alvin paused, his angry glower turning to confusion. He focused on my eyes then gasped.

"In the name of Lucifer," he whispered, "he did it." Alvin's brows scrunched. "Oh, Grim. How you doing?"

Heat surged through my chest and my breath came short and fast. "You...you knew?" I stepped forward, fists clenched, breaking the circle with a flash of red electricity. "You *knew* Frank Totmann's plan and didn't *think* to warn me? He stole my scythe! My power! My very identity!" My hand shot toward Alvin's throat, but he leapt back.

"It wasn't like that!" His hands flew up, warding me off as I stalked forward. "Frank's daily summonings were annoying the crap out of me. I had to give him something, so I found a soul transfer spell he couldn't use. The ingredients were impossible to acquire." Alvin slid under the open stairs between the recliner and apothecary cabinet.

"Impossible? Look at me! I'm stuck in a human body"—I slapped the stairs for emphasis as I ducked under—"thanks to *you!*"

Alvin flinched and dodged back around the Egyptian circle. "The spell required the bones of a Sumerian priest!"

"You idiot!" I spun toward the cabinet, snatched a labeled baggie, and read it aloud, "Sumerian Priest Bone Dust." I threw the bag at Alvin, and it passed through his chest and slid across the floor. "That was a basic ingredient of his summoning circle!"

Alvin held a finger up to protest, but his words died unspoken. His finger lowered slowly. "Oh. Uh, sorry."

My anger flared hot before draining away. I sat heavily on the stairs and dropped my head into my hands. "Me too. More than you could possibly imagine." I drew a shuddering breath then looked up. "Was there a reversal on that Sumerian spell?"

"How should I know?" Alvin's flippancy brought me to my feet, fists clenched again. He raised placating hands. "But I can check."

I drew deep, calming breaths. Death was supposed to be emotionless, impartial. The first time I got angry, *really* angry, had been over something stupid. An argument with the Auditor about sins and sacrifices. I'd been an angel then. So young. I'd tried to prove my point, whispered a lie into Cain's ear, and accidentally incited him to murder Abel.

Humanity's first death. Their first murder. Heaven had still been reeling with the aftershocks of Lucifer's betrayal and dropped me into Purgatory to await Judgment. To avoid eternal torment, I begged Gabriel for clemency. I could atone for my crime by easing mankind's souls into the next world.

He bought it and I sidestepped Judgment, which really pissed off the Auditor. He'd been angling for the job.

Thus was the Grim Reaper born. No longer an angel, not quite a demon, bound to serve both Heaven and Hell and beholden to neither.

My pocket vibrated with a cheerful chirp, and I jumped. I dug out Frank's phone and read the message on the screen.

Cora: *I'm at Edelweiss! You on your way?*

Alvin stepped around to peer at the screen. "You old dog," he said, turning corporeal and punching my shoulder. "One day as a human and you've already got a date!"

I rose, shielding the phone from his view. "Frank had dinner plans before he died. Well, almost died. There is no need to maintain his schedule." My stomach twitched with unfamiliar pain and gurgled.

Alvin looked at my belly, then the phone, and chuckled. "You're human now, subject to four incessant needs."

I raised an imperious eyebrow at the dirty-minded cretin. "Implying what?"

Alvin barked a laugh. "No, Grim, not sex. That's necessary for species survival, not the individual. No, you'll need an appalling amount of food, water, and sleep to keep that body functional." He made a shooing gesture. "Go. Go on your date. I'll see what I can find about reversing that spell."

I nodded and said, "Thank you." Cora might also provide insights since she'd provided the ingredients.

Alvin gave a double thumbs-up and sank through the floor without the dramatic flair of his entrance.

"Wait!" I called. "You said humans have four needs. Hunger, thirst, sleep, and...?"

Alvin's descent paused at neck level and his face split into a broad smile. "Pooping, my friend. What goes in, must come out. A serious design flaw, if you ask me. Good luck!" He waved cheerfully and disappeared.

My breath whooshed out and I dropped back onto the stairs, making them groan. I often reaped souls from compromising positions, so I had a vague idea of what was coming, but I had never considered the mechanics of...defecation. My mind skittered around, refusing to focus. My gut rumbled, and I realized that I was, indeed, hungry.

Well, best get on with it. I retrieved Frank's cell phone.

I stumbled from Louis's cab with shaky knees after he screeched to a halt outside Edelweiss Restaurant. "Enjoy dinner!" he called, then zoomed away.

Low lights shone inside the stone-faced farmhouse and the hum of conversation drifted from outdoor seating to the left. Dishes clanked and propane heaters glowed red as jacketed diners enjoyed fall's dying warmth. I shivered in Frank's thin suit, hoping Cora's table was inside. I headed for the door.

Sharp pain sliced through my chest, arcing into my left

shoulder. I gasped and dropped onto a bench. Frank's heart gave four syncopated beats before settling down again. I drew a deep breath and massaged my chest. This heart was past its expiration date. It wouldn't last much longer.

A young man inside escorted me to a corner booth in a room topped with faux roof eaves. Blue and white checkered bunting, a cloud-painted ceiling, and rough wooden panels gave the impression of outdoor dining without the chill Colorado winds. Cora beamed when she saw me.

"Hey, there. I was worried you'd stand me up."

"I apologize for my tardiness. I usually make a point of arriving just when people need me." What would happen to a soul if I didn't arrive on time? Would the body die and decay with the soul trapped inside? Would that be my fate? Disturbed by my thoughts, I slid into the booth.

Cora said, "I ordered for us. You're going to *love* the Jäger-schnitzel."

As if on cue, a waiter arrived with plates. I eyed mine with trepidation. Everything was a uniform brown. Breaded meat was buried under thick mushroom gravy, and piled french fries threatened to topple off the plate. The fries were sprinkled with a red powder which added a spicy kick to the greasy scents wafting upward.

It smelled fantastic. My stomach agreed with loud gurgles.

I glanced at Cora, but she had already dug in. New to the intricacies of eating, I copied what she did. The silverware was tricky, but I managed my first bite.

Greasy bliss melted on my tongue. I closed my eyes and a groan escaped as I chewed and swallowed.

"See, told you it was good."

I gazed into Cora's smiling eyes. "That was … amazing." I cut another bite. "Is all food this good?" No wonder humans spent so much of their lives eating. That bite followed the first and I groaned again as she nodded.

"Here? Most of it. If you have room for dessert, their Apfel-strudel is to die for."

"To die for?" A third and fourth bite disappeared. "I'll take the chance."

Cora chuckled, a warm sound that revealed her bright soul.

Dinner passed in a blur. The waiter brought us beers that looked like bubbly swamp water. I took one sip and gagged. It tasted like swamp water too. Cora seemed content to talk about herself, her grown kids, and her dreams for the future while I ate. Turned out that she dreamed of expanding her online apothecary supply shop.

"Where do you acquire your artifacts?" I asked.

"That's the joy of the internet. You can find anything if you dig hard enough."

Like a soul-swapping spell reversal?

The waiter derailed my line of questioning with a fluffy pastry that oozed baked apples and cinnamon. Pillowy vanilla ice cream lay atop the Apfelstrudel, melting in thin streams. It smelled divine.

I took a large bite and Cora asked, "So what are your dreams?"

"Hmmph?" I mumbled around the glorious blending of hot, cold, and sweet.

"Nobody wants to be a tax auditor when they grow up. What else do you want?"

I swallowed and sat back. What did *I* want? Nobody had asked me that before. I searched my soul. "I like my job, helping souls in need. I'm good at it, but it gets lonely."

Cora gripped my hand, her bracelets jangling. "You're not alone anymore. Did you know that the girls at the office tried to warn me off? Said that a confirmed bachelor must have deep, dark secrets." She released my hand, leaving a ghost of warmth on my skin. "I'm glad I didn't listen. You're really quite sweet."

"Awww...," said a voice from under the table. "Too bad you'll have to break her heart." Alvin's pinched face poked above the table as he climbed onto the bench beside Cora. "Time to leave, Grim. Now!"

"Why?" I said. "What did you find?"

Cora followed my gaze to the empty seat—humans can't see spirits who don't want to be seen—and creased her brows.

"No time, lover boy," Alvin said. "Hell has noticed your absence. The Auditor is coming."

His words were a punch in the gut. "How'd he find out so fast, Alvin?"

Cora's eyebrows shot up. "Alvin? The demon?" Frank must have told her about the summonings. She scooted into the booth's corner and dug an iron cross from her purse.

Alvin gave the artifact a dismissive nose wrinkle and ran a clawed hand through his greasy hair. "There's a worldwide epidemic of miraculous survivals and recoveries. Your replacement isn't doing his job. Nobody could find you, so they've sent the Auditor to clean up." Alvin glanced anxiously over his shoulder then swore.

I followed his gaze and jumped in my seat. "Damn!" Diners glanced up, but they couldn't see what I saw. A massive demon ducked into the restaurant. He was impossibly gaunt, like stretched dough, and wore a rumpled suit that matched Alvin's. Gold-rimmed spectacles covered blood-red eyes which scanned the room. Claws drummed on the back of an oversized clipboard.

"Frank?" Cora sounded scared as she grabbed my hand and swung the cross to follow my gaze. "What's wrong?"

"Death comes for all men," I whispered, a shiver running through me.

The Auditor saw me and made a check on his clipboard. "Frank Totmann," he said in a voice as dry as crumpled ash. "Your time is past." He lumbered forward, one arm outstretched. He didn't have a scythe to snip my soul's tether with this body, but he could rip it out and drag me to Hell with him.

Fear turned schnitzel to lead in my stomach. You can't run from Death. I would know.

I glanced at the clipboard, eyes narrowed. He wasn't Death. He was the Auditor. You can evade the Auditor, for a while at least.

I squeezed Cora's hand. "He cannot touch you. Your time is not yet come." Her wide eyes bulged as I pulled myself free and bolted for the exit.

Evading the Auditor was simple, yet terribly difficult. I had to abandon every resource Frank had. The lumbering demon gave chase, but his skills lay in tracking through files and records, not in active pursuit. I lost him after a few heart-wrenching hours by squeezing behind a strip mall dumpster.

I had nowhere to go. I had to avoid Frank's house. His office. Cora. The Auditor could track me through her. Ditching Frank's phone when she called had felt like cutting off my arm. Any information she had about Frank's spell was now lost.

I woke with a start the following morning. I'd been having a nightmare of fleeing the Auditor through a maze of doors, each with its own bloody different handle. My heartbeat slowed. Orange-dappled clouds drifted past, visible through the gap between dumpster and building. I hadn't felt sleep sneak up as the temperature dropped.

I squeezed out of my hiding place and into a parking lot, stamping warmth into my tingling toes. My joints protested, cold muscles so tight that I could barely walk. I shielded my eyes against the low sun. I didn't know where I was.

An unfamiliar pressure on my bowels made me grimace. Alvin's fourth incessant need had found me. I trudged across the parking lot toward a gas station. A bell tinkled as I entered and warm air washed over me, inducing a wave of relaxation. Heavens, that felt good.

The pressure on my bowels intensified.

"Toilet?" I asked the lanky teen behind the counter. He pointed to the back without looking up from his phone. I followed his vague directions, found the toilet, and discovered the heinous reality of defecation. Mortality's dark side.

Humans do this every day? I would rather die.

I flushed, scrubbed my hands as if cleaning the stain off my soul, and fled the restroom.

The bell chimed again as I left the gas station. I huddled against the wind and stopped, not sure where to go next.

"Grim?"

I jumped and looked toward the voice, ready to run. Louis waved from behind a car he was fueling. Not his cab, but a beat-up green sedan.

"Brother, you look awful," he said. "Date didn't go well?"

I shrugged. "Dinner was amazing. Cora was charming. But then...he found me."

"The guy who stole from you?"

I shook my head. "No. A Hell-spawned demon called the Auditor. He...you wouldn't understand."

Louis stepped around his car, concern in his gray eyes. "I understand the look of a man running from his mistakes. Everything looks bad when you're in the middle of it." He held out a hand. "Come on, let me take you to breakfast. You'll see things clearer with a full stomach and some caffeine."

My stomach rumbled. "Thank you. Your generosity is—"

An iron vise seized my chest and my breath wheezed out. I dropped to the pavement, struggling for air, muscles turning watery. Frank's traitorous heart seized again, sending a spike through the vise.

"Grim!" Louis knelt beside me, a hand on my back. "What's wrong?"

"Heart...attack. Third in...two days."

"Hey!" he yelled at the kid inside. "Give me a hand!"

I grabbed his arm. "Please...don't let me die." My heart beat rapidly to make up for lost time, taunting me with hope.

"Hold on, Grim. You're not dying today."

I collapsed. Rough pavement scratched my face, and my brain turned fuzzy. Strong arms lifted me into Louis's back seat. The door slammed, the engine started, and we tore out of the lot.

The world became snapshots of consciousness as Louis wove through traffic, blaring his horn. Anxious assurances washed over me while I struggled to survive. To live. Finding Frank was a distant desire. Avoiding the Auditor was more immediate.

Would he recognize my soul as he ripped it out? Would it make a difference to my fate?

"No hospital," I wheezed, but Louis didn't hear me. A hospital would put Frank's name on record. The Auditor would see it.

We screeched to a stop, Louis yelled for help, and more hands pulled me from the car.

"What happened?" a woman asked in a no-nonsense tone as they laid me on a gurney.

"Heart attack. Third in two days," Louis said.

"And he's still *breathing*? Death's not ready for this guy. What's his name?"

"Grim Reaper."

"*Not* the time for jokes." Her voice turned severe, and a hand dug into my pocket. "Says Frank Totmann on his license."

No. Please. I reached for the wallet, but my hand flopped uselessly. They wheeled me inside. Lights flashed past overhead as nurses rushed me...somewhere. We pushed into a brightly lit room that smelled of antiseptic. Louis's anxious face peered through the windowed door, his lips moving with silent prayer.

Pain exploded in my chest, and I screamed. My eyes bulged and I squeezed a hand I found in mine.

"Crash cart, now!" the nurse yelled—

Time stopped so abruptly that I felt jolted out of reality.

The pain...paused. The room's flurry of activity froze midmotion. I sagged, drawing ragged breaths.

Frank glided through the wall, smirking from the depths of my cowl, my scythe in hand. "Dying sucks, huh?" he said.

Cheeky, insufferable, little son of a...

I sat up, gauging the distance between us. "You toy with powers you don't understand, Frank Totmann."

"I'm figuring it out. The stopping time thing is pretty cool. Last night I played a round of golf with a dying CEO before sending him on his way." He twirled my scythe then pretended to putt.

"You are supposed to grant an opportunity for confession. Not...play golf." I shook my head, appalled, and swiveled my legs off the table.

Frank swung the scythe back into a two-handed grip and ducked behind a nurse frozen in frantic motion. He glanced at the clock on the wall. "It's been a bit longer for me, what with stopping time, but I figured you'd have more than sixteen hours. How'd you like being human?"

"It was terrifying, confusing, and...enjoyable. I found your fellow humans thoughtful and kind. I had a date with Cora."

Frank's eyes went wide. "Ah, crap. I forgot about that. I meant to cancel."

"She helped you prepare. You didn't tell her your plan?"

He bit one lip and said, "I couldn't. Didn't want to see her cry. She's gonna be heartbroken when I die. Well, when you die."

"Everybody leaves loved ones behind. We all have unfinished business."

His grip tightened on the scythe, and he nodded, stepping back around the nurse. "Well, I guess it's time. Best of luck in the afterlife!" He pulled the scythe back, readying the Reaper's power over the soul.

Realization hit me like an avalanche and my breath caught. I didn't need to reverse Frank's Sumerian spell. I needed my scythe. The Reaper's scythe didn't just sever souls from their mortal coil. It moved them to where they were supposed to be.

I was supposed to be in that cowl and Frank in this body.

I held up a hand. "Wait! You can't reap me."

Frank's eyes narrowed, my death over his shoulder, my salvation in his hands. "Why not?"

"The Auditor is coming for you."

Fear crept into Frank's voice. "The who?"

"The Auditor. Hell's final arbiter of the Rules. Hell noticed discrepancies after you took my place. The Auditor *hates* discrepancies and metes out punishment with...finality." Frank lowered the scythe and glanced around furtively.

"I'm not taking my body back. I already cheated death."

Yes, you were the first. I will be the second.

I leaned forward conspiratorially. "Here's what we'll—"

The words froze in my throat as the Auditor lurched through

85

the door. Claws scratched angry gouges on the back of his clipboard as he pointed it at me. "Frank Totmann, your time is past! I—"

He noticed the real Frank Totmann and his brows bunched together behind gold-wire frames. "Two Frank Totmanns?" He consulted his clipboard. "This is highly irregular." He considered me, but I kept my eyes averted, hoping he wouldn't recognize my soul. Frank made the mistake of meeting his gaze.

Tension drained from the Auditor's shoulders. He straightened and adjusted his glasses. "There you are. Your Judgment is at hand." He eyed the scythe, then me. I saw connections click in his evil mind. A dark smile stole over his face. "You have failed, Grim. It's time to face *your* Judgment. It's time for a new Reaper." He turned to Frank. "I'll start with this impostor's soul."

Frank stumbled backward, lip quivering. "No!"

I jumped off the gurney. "Give me the scythe!"

"No!" Panic tainted Frank's words and the Auditor lunged at him. Frank leapt between two nurses and the Auditor followed, implacable. They danced around my gurney, just out of reach. I had to do something. Anything to keep the Auditor from my scythe.

"Wait!" I yelled and leapt between them, throwing my hands out like a referee separating boxers. Frank scrambled back, but the Auditor thrust a long-fingered hand into my chest. He gripped my soul.

Cold washed through me and I felt myself dying all over again. My breath wheezed. Frank's wide eyes met mine and I turned my palm up, beseeching.

"Please, before he drags us both into Hell with him."

Frank's gaze whipped to the Auditor who yanked at my soul, half tearing it from my body. I screamed and collapsed to my knees.

Frank shook his head.

"I'll...make you an apprentice!"

"But..."

"Or you die!"

Frank quivered, then nodded and thrust the scythe into my hands.

Power flowed into me. Power to stop time and parse souls. Power over life itself. I smelled the cherry blossoms of Heaven and the burning sulfur of Hell, an intoxicating brew that overwhelmed my pain.

I spun on my knees to slam the scythe into the Auditor's chest, but he caught the handle with a *crack*. Lightning surged around his grip, and he tried to yank the scythe away.

He failed.

"You are not Death," I intoned. "You never will be."

I rose, scythe between us, and shed Frank Totmann's skin and cheap suit. They drifted away like flaming embers that pushed onto Frank's terrified soul, leaving me a proud, naked skeleton. The embers solidified and Frank became flesh once more. I shrouded my skeletal form in a cowled cloak of darkness drawn from Hell itself.

I was Death.

I kicked the Auditor in the chest and wrenched my scythe away. He flew through a frozen nurse and the wall with a furious roar. He'd be back.

I spun and pointed an accusing finger. "Frank Totmann, you cannot run from Death."

"Wait, what? No! You said..." He fell back and bumped into the crash cart, making the wheels squeak. I placed my blade to his throat and a sob escaped him. "Please, I don't want to die."

"I understand," I whispered, and I did. I really did. He squeezed his eyes shut and pressed back. I swung my scythe and reaped Frank's soul. His body collapsed and his spirit bobbed into the ether beside me. I gripped his shoulder to keep him in place and turned as the Auditor stormed in.

"Frank Totmann is dead," I said. "The scales are balanced; the Rules are satisfied. You have nothing further to audit here."

He glanced at Frank's soul, then at my scythe. Raw desire and bitter realization burned in his red eyes. The Rules forbade interfering with Death's duties, and he was more bound to the

Rules than I. The loophole created by Frank's spell had just closed. "Damn you." His fists clenched. "Where will you send him?"

"Not your concern."

The Auditor cursed and retrieved his clipboard. He made a definitive checkmark, which sounded like it tore through parchment. "I'm watching you, Grim," he said, then stomped away through the wall.

I counted to twenty to ensure that he was gone before starting time again. A cacophony of noise and action burst into the room. The nurses scrambled, confused to find Frank's body beside the crash cart. One checked his vitals, sagged, then declared him dead.

Frank looked up as they carted his body away. "You killed me."

"No, your body died. I retrieved your soul. A minor, but important distinction."

"Now what? Were you serious about making me an apprentice?"

I rubbed my chin. "I could use the company. And you've proven quite resourceful. For a human."

He sighed, relief twitching the corners of his lips. "All right, Boss, what first? Do I get my own scythe?"

I gave him a flaming stare. "First, we correct your errors from the past day. There are souls who need to pass on. For failing at your assumed duties, you must take their confessions."

"But I didn't know what I was doing!"

"That's no excuse. Every soul deserves your utmost care. Come, I will show you."

I held onto Frank and followed the incessant pull of a soul in need of transition.

I will forevermore hold a grudge against Mondays, for that was the traumatic day I became human. Yet, at the same time, I found my brief life surprisingly enjoyable.

Well, except for the dying.

And the defecation.

Tuesdays, however, will hold a special place in my heart. Tuesday brought me an apprentice, whom I hope will eventually become a friend.

Frank finished taking a recently deceased granny's confession and we proceeded to the next soul. He would need a new name. "Death and Frank" lacked the proper authoritative ring.

I snapped my bony fingers, remembering. Frank already had a title. One that sparked fear and caution among the living. Together we would shepherd souls to their final rest as the two greatest certainties in life.

Death and the Taxman.

Under My Cypresses

written by
Jason Palmatier
illustrated by
HELEN YI

ABOUT THE AUTHOR

Jason Palmatier is a stay-at-home dad who lives in central Pennsylvania with his wife and three sons. A former software developer, he now writes speculative fiction and has been fortunate enough to work on screenplays (the short film "Hunter"), independent comics (Lords of the Cosmos, Ugli Studios), graphic novels (Plague, Markosia Enterprises Ltd), short-story anthologies (from Zombies Need Brains, LLC) and full-length books. When not writing, he enjoys introducing his kids to 1980s' culture, encouraging his kids to be creative, and watching his kids ignore his advice.

"Under My Cypresses" grew from a child's request to spend real cash on a skin for an in-game avatar. The skin gave no special powers, nor did it open up another level of play; it simply changed the avatar's appearance. To an old-school parent, this sounded like a complete waste of money. But to the kid who spent hours a day smashing loot chests clothed in their new otter skin, it was a very tangible upgrade to their gaming experience. To them, it was part of their reality; a reality they shared with their friends. But it's not real. It's just a bunch of pixels and a couple otter noises. True. But what if you could smell things like an otter, taste things like an otter, touch things like an otter? Would it be real then? Who decides that? Your old-school parent? The government? You?

ABOUT THE ILLUSTRATOR

Helen Yi was born in 2002 in Hackensack, New Jersey, and at the age of six months her family moved back to Seoul, South Korea. Her grandfather was a sculptor, and her grandmother is an artist. Her mother works in a design industry, and her father enjoys films and books. So she naturally developed interest in creative activities at a very young age. It wouldn't be an exaggeration to say that there hasn't been a day in her life without art.

Her artistic passions started with simply copying characters from comic books. But as she slowly learned more about movies, digital platforms, games, and many other new and professional ways art can be shown to the world, she dreamed of working as a visual development artist creating art to entertain others.

Currently Helen is studying illustration at the Ringling College of Art and Design and working toward her dreams. She is thankful for the facilities and curriculum in RCAD that have allowed her to pursue digital art at school as well as her winning entry for the Illustrators of the Future Contest.

Under My Cypresses

"Pill or plug?"

Lin stared at the blue pill and black neuro-plug resting in Niitz's hand. Music pounded through the door next to them, rattling its hinges. Niitz's grafted fiberhawk hair pulsed neon blue to the beat, spiking to pink on every high-octave drop down. Lin felt Niitz's eyes on her, even through the augmented wraparounds that hid them. She looked away. Weeks had passed since she'd been here, but the last few times were with *him*, and Niitz knew *him*. The thought brought up *his* face, that determined look, the eyes gone cold—

"Pill," she said, as always.

Niitz nodded slowly, palming the plug and snatching the pill between thumb and forefinger in one practiced motion. He dropped it into her cupped hand.

"Have a good one," Niitz said. A green light flashed on the side of his shades. The door unlocked.

Lin felt the hard little pill on her palm. She closed her eyes, seeing all of the memories again. The first look, the talk. Laughter and smiles. The first kiss. A blur of meals and clubs and walks and steaming miso mugs and quiet times alone together. Happy times. Then the first look away. The questions. The nonanswers. Worry, confusion. More questions, raised voices, desperation, fighting—Lin threw the pill into her mouth and swallowed.

The door swung open.

She turned and stepped inside.

*B*oom.

The pill hit her stomach with a thunderclap, bursting outward, turning the explosion of sound around her into a kaleidoscope of colors, each with its own taste and smell. She staggered down the screen-skinned hallway, hand on the wall, lines of lights warping around her from every direction: green spearmint flashing overhead, red cherry undulating below, blue agave cutting across her with a sweet aftertaste. Wave upon wave, all timed to the beat that hammered her body, rattled her chest. She stumbled forward, rounding the corner at the end of the psychedelic tunnel and sagging at the sight before her.

Dancers tattooed with neon jumped to the crushing beat, their motion traced out in smears that smelled of poppies and pine, sweet mango and rust. She shook herself as the tang of metal spread across her tongue, looked away to find familiar counters lining both sides of the abandoned warehouse, bottles and vials and beakers glittering, roiling, smoking. Some people sat yelling at each other, their eyes glazing as they read the translated text of their drowned-out partner's words. Others simply nodded, smiling or laughing, projecting their thoughts directly to their companions through SocIO.

Lin grabbed the handrail at the top of the stairs that led down to it all. She swallowed, the room spinning, her knees shaking.

"You need some help getting down?" a voice yelled beside her.

Lin looked up into a girl's face pierced with iridescent rings that flashed at the corners of braided eyebrows and along the sides of a strong, straight nose. Filaments of nano-wire sparkled in swept-up eyelashes. Electro-coated highlights streaked through stringy hair, pulled up into a high ponytail. Bubble-gum scent washed across Lin as a pink mass grew from a puckered mouth and popped silently in the torrent of noise.

"Been a while, huh?" the girl shouted. Lin read the text that flashed in her head in default Times New Roman. "Want to go down and get a drink?"

Lin blinked a few times, realizing she was supposed to respond.

"Yeah. Sure."

She let herself be helped down the stairs, glad for the support, eyes fixating on the girl's torn leather jacket. Text rose from its darkness, glowed for a moment, then faded back into nothingness, cracking as it did so.

I am a forest and a night of dark trees; but he who is not afraid of my darkness will find banks full of roses under my cypresses.

A seat slid under Lin and she looked up into the face shouting at her again.

"I'm getting a hashtag. You want one?"

Lin nodded.

"Awesome, you'll love it. Two, please! I'm Nancy, by the way."

Lin shook the offered hand, feeling the soft squish of gel rings around the fingers.

"People usually call me Nan, though. What's your name?"

"Lin."

"Lin, huh? Makes sense. You're a pretty plain Jane."

Lin looked into the mirror behind the bar, saw her straight, shoulder-length black hair, round face, the ruffled cuffs of her T-shirt. *You should augment more, mix it up a little. For me...* She frowned at the remembered words from *him*.

"You're jacked, though," Nan said, gesturing with her nose at the metajack in Lin's temple.

Lin's hand rose self-consciously toward it. "It's for work."

"Ahh," Nan mouthed, eyebrows rising shrewdly.

Their drinks arrived, swirling orange and green in globe glasses. Lin sucked on the foot-long tube sticking from hers and avoided Nan's gaze. The shaved ice of the drink slid down her throat, cooling it before the alcohol lit it on fire. Lin's eyes watered. Nan smiled, tears leaking from her own eyes and yelled, "Frag, yeah! Hashtags rock!"

Lin nodded with a grimace and sipped some more. The burn morphed into a warm glow that spread languidly through her body, shaving the edge off the music, tamping down the pounding in her head. Nan's ponytail shimmered as she banged her head to the beat, nose scrunched up, drink held high. She looked ridiculous.

Lin smiled.

"I gotta get out and dance, you comin'?" Nan asked.

Lin raised her drink to say she wasn't finished, but found it empty. Nan's hand closed on her wrist and dragged her toward the dance floor before Lin could recover from her surprise.

Bodies pressed in all around, jumping, shimmying. Implants and augmentations glowed: fiber hairs dripped real sweat, flesh lids blinked across enhanced, color-morphing eyes, clothing rippled with overlays broadcast from their wearer to the meta layer of those around them. All advertising their hosts' individual identities. Lin's body stiffened, fighting back against the falseness of it, against the wild abandon that swirled around her. But Nan kept tugging, mouth wide open in a scream of laughter, until they were in the middle of the dance floor.

The bass thumped, the lights played, and slowly Lin let herself get caught up in it, arms rising, knees bouncing, hips twisting. A smile cracked out as Nan let go of her hand and did a corny running-in-place dance move, punctuated by an archaic water sprinkler. Inspired, Lin placed her arms in front of her and dragged them around in a circle. Nan burst out laughing and fell into her. Then they were spinning and laughing and dancing and the lights kept strobing and the beat kept beating and time kept slipping until they collapsed into chairs at the bar, faces flushed, chests heaving, eyes alight with mirth. Lin ordered two more hashtags and they sipped them while looking out over the thinning crowd.

They chatted, finding out that Lin had been a straight "A" student, Nan had flunked out because of math. They both loved to read. Nan wanted all the tech she could get but Lin kept hers external, except the jack for work. Nan wanted to do something that lasted, bills be damned and Lin liked security and a salary. Lin had been dumped and Nan always kept it light 'cause she was waiting for the right one who hadn't come along yet....

Their eyes locked.

HELEN YI

Lin swallowed, heartbeat quickening.

Nan's easy smile faded into something more serious. Her look softened.

The music dropped in volume, the beat slowed. The strobe lights dimmed and came back on.

"Last call!" the bartender shouted beside them.

They both jumped, eyes blowing wide open. They collapsed into each other, giggling.

Stragglers filtered up the stairs, hanging onto each other, whisper-shouting in the vacuum left by the silenced music. Lin and Nan brought up the rear, arm in arm. Lin rested her pounding head on Nan's shoulder. Nan rested her cheek on Lin's head.

"I had a great time," Lin said, feeling the glow.

"Me, too. You're almost as good a dancer as me," Nan replied.

Lin punched her on the arm and laughed as they approached the door. The couple ahead of them stepped through and turned left, vanishing from sight. Lin frowned, putting her arm around Nan and squeezing, grateful that she was here now, not wanting her to leave. Nan squeezed her back.

"Hey, uh…" Nan said as they stepped over the threshold. "I had a great time. Do you want to—"

The city clock's recalibration signal hit, flashing the synced time.

"Oh, no!" Nan cried. "I was supposed to meet an art blogger an hour ago for an interview! Um—I gotta run, but I'll call you, okay?"

Nan hugged her quickly, cheek pressing against Lin's ear, eyebrow rings scraping against her metajack as she pulled away and…vanished.

Lin's heart stopped. The blood drained from her face. She sagged to the side, catching herself against the dirty brick of the club's wall. Her chest heaved, her eyes burned.

"No. No." Lin took a step back, head shaking. "She was real. She helped me down the stairs, she bought me a drink.…"

The night played back in her head, every sensation, every touch, all of it vivid and deep.

"She was real! I felt her, we were together!"

"Yes, you were," Niitz said near her.

She wheeled on him, seeing his static fiberhawk, no longer pulsing, the nose ring, the iridescent chains on his jacket.

"I told you *pill*!" she screamed, despair ripping through her.

Niitz nodded, eyes inscrutable behind his shades. "And I gave you plug."

"I don't want an AI. I want a real person!"

"Like *him*?"

The words struck her like a thunderbolt, wiping away all the good memories of the night, replacing them with despondency, despair. She staggered backward, finger pointing.

"You had no right!" she screamed, face twisted with anger and betrayal. "I wanted real!" Her hand brushed a bottle atop a trash can. She grasped it and threw.

It passed through Niitz and shattered on the filthy ground behind him.

She stepped back in shock.

"She's as real as you let her be," Niitz said.

Lin shook her head, not wanting to believe it, the revelations too much for her to grasp. "You're not real. . . ."

"I was to you, until now."

Niitz dissolved before her, form splitting into discrete lines that widened then winked out.

Lin spun, horrified, and ran.

"It's freakin' sick, man," Scott said, loud enough to carry across the entire office. He wore his striped, button-down shirt and tie and a swooping hairstyle that defied physics. Lin grimaced at the smell of his overly sweet coffee, annoyed that he'd popped into her cube ten minutes after she'd arrived at work. Yes, he was her partner and had business to discuss, but she wasn't interested in chitchat. "I shouldn't have to see something that isn't really there if I don't want to, know what I mean?"

The words burned Lin's insides, washing her face with bitter heat. She turned back to her work to give him an unsubtle hint to leave. Everything had had sharp edges since Saturday night.

99

The slightest touch, the merest bump from a stranger, meta or no, set her teeth on edge.

"Why can't they just be happy on their servers?" Scott continued. "I mean, hell, they can create whatever they want on there."

The news feed at the bottom of Lin's work session popped up, triggered by the overheard comment. She caught a glimpse of the scrolling headline above a video showing a quarter of the people in a crowd disappearing. The headline read, "AIs, should we have to see them?" She closed it with a savage blink, teeth gritting, and concentrated on the suspected deepfake video that played in her mind. She advanced it slowly, audio off, looking for cues that would tell her if it was authentic or modded.

"I'm tellin' you, *Eve.9 versus Sention Corp.* screwed the pooch. Gave 'em an inch of identity and now they want the mile. It's ridiculous. It's like a bunch of ghosts asking to be called not dead," Scott griped.

Lin clamped her jaw and spun to face Scott, feeling the betrayal boil up inside her anew. "Yeah, except ghosts can't punch you in the gut with meta feedback," she spat.

Scott raised an eyebrow at the venom in her voice but lifted a finger from his mug and pointed. "Exactly! Why should I have to let my synapses get twiddled by some code brain so I can 'feel' them touching me?" He wiggled his hand by his head while whining, "Ooo, we're just looking for some equality. It's too easy to ignore us if we aren't *there*."

"They aren't!" Lin said, feeling the rightness of Scott's words.

"And then all the meta lovers are like, 'oh, if you don't like it, just drop your meta,'" Scott said. "Yeah, right, like you can live without meta now. Get real. I couldn't order this coffee without meta. Neither of us could do our jobs without meta!"

You're jacked, though....

Nan's words popped into Lin's head unbidden. Nan had been in her dreams, laughing, twirling, shaking her head so her hair shuddered around her. But more than the images, there were touches: a hand on her arm, bubble-gum breath on her face, shoulder blades pressing into hers as they danced back-to-back. Just synapse manipulation from her metajack, but all of it felt real, indistinguishable from the press of the floor on her feet, the cool slide of the drink down her throat.

The pill in my hand.

Rage boiled up again. Niitz had done it, fed her the sensations she was expecting from a pill on her meta interface, while giving her the virtual plug that kept AIs visible in the club. It was illegal. A felony. She should report him. They'd scrub his instance, archive his backups. He'd be no more.

She felt so real....

Lin pushed the thought away, growling.

Niitz knew her. He'd seen her before, talked to her. She liked him.

And she'd never known he was an AI.

The image of the bottle passing through Niitz mixed shame with everything else. She'd wanted to hurt him, had acted rashly. Because she had felt so much that night, so much...happiness.

"Whoa, you look intense!" Scott jerked his head back.

Lin looked up at him, feeling the tightness across her forehead from her deep scowl.

"Wait....You weren't thinking about *him*, were you? You're over *him*, remember? We agreed. You were going to go out this weekend and have fun, no more moping...."

Lin's scowl deepened. She straightened up in her chair. "I did go out."

Scott raised an eyebrow and cocked his head to the side. "And..."

I met a dirty, lying AI who tricked me into wasting my time on a NoBody.

Lin almost snarled it. But Nan's smile flashed before her, and her laugh echoed away into a pounding beat. Lin's anger dropped by a tiny margin. She took a deep breath. "It was fun. I had a great time."

She realized that she meant it. She'd enjoyed herself for the first time in weeks.

"But..." Scott said, eyes narrowing.

"Nothing!" Lin snapped. "It was fun. I went home."

A message pinged on her work account. She scowled and brought the text to the forefront to block Scott's face.

"Hey Lin, it's Nan!"

A heavy weight slugged into Lin's stomach. She reached out to steady herself on her desk.

"Ooo, who's that?" Scott asked.

Nan's message had displayed in their shared workspace since it came in on their official contact account. She flailed mentally to close the window, but not before Scott read out, "'Sorry to go all stalker on you, but I had a great time on Saturday and wanted to see if you'd go for a coffee later.' Dude! You met someone?"

"No!" Lin shouted, finally closing the message down.

Scott took a step back, raising his free hand defensively. "Ohhh-kaaayyy."

"She's not a—she's nobody. She was just there. She helped me down the stairs," Lin finished lamely.

"Must have been some pretty good stairs help, 'cause she just asked you out," Scott said. He took a big sip of coffee, smacking his lips extra loud while staring at her.

Lin reddened. What was she supposed to say? *She was great, I had the time of my life, until I found out she was a fragging computer program.* FAT32 chance.

"Look, she's just...not my type, okay?" Lin said.

"Uh...because she's not an asshole, like *him*?"

Lin's redness deepened, remembering Nan's eyes on her, *seeing* her. "It would never work out...."

Another message flashed in their shared workspace.

"Ah, the morning meeting, right on time," Scott said, shaking his head at the reminder. "Time to start broadcasting a close shave and an Armani suit."

Lin smirked and shoved herself to her feet, glad for the interruption. She could only imagine what people in the office would say if they found out she'd been asked out by an AI. Scott alone would be insufferable. No, she'd keep this on the down-low and let it fade away. As Scott had just reminded her, there was already enough talk about her, thanks to *him*, and *he* had been real.

When her day ended, Lin's virtual office faded out around her, leaving her reclined in her zero-gravity chair, staring at a spot where the ceiling and wall of her apartment met. The silence of the apartment seeped in as she let her head clear.

Heyo, how was work?

The happy evening greeting stung in its absence. She squeezed her eyes shut. It had stopped long before *he* left and had been the first sign of what was to come. Lin rubbed her hands on her face and stood, bringing up a news feed to squash the memories while she selected an entrée from the fridwave menu. The soft whir of the dish sliding into place in the small food prep area reached her in the bathroom as she sat down on the loo.

"Global AI rights advocates are intently watching the final debates on Senator Gibson's Visibility bill, which was introduced almost two years ago. The highly controversial bill would require people with meta-capability to accept all sensory broadcasts of artificial entities who project themselves in humanistic form, including, but not limited to, visual, tactile, olfactory, and auditory. Sticking points in the bill have ranged from the definition of 'humanistic' to cries that the personal rights of non-artificials are being violated by its 'all meta users' mandate."

Lin frowned as she washed her hands; the subject cut too close to home. She opened a list of alternate feeds but failed to switch before the scene jumped from the androgynous broadcaster's talking head to a woman in an athleisure suit outside a coffee shop. "I think they should be tagged somehow, so we know they're artificial. Like a callout or star by their name, or something. I mean, what if I accidentally talk to one, you know?"

Lin cut all feeds savagely and stalked into the tiny food prep area. She retrieved her warmed bowl of udon noodles and plopped down on the couch that had replaced her office chair when she had left the room. She chewed angrily.

The silence crept in again, bringing with it *his* smiling face staring at her from across a crumpled pillow. She flicked on another feed, making sure it was entertainment only. A cat strode down a runway on all fours dressed in a velvet gown, followed by another feline in a lace wedding dress. A feminine commentator's voice said, "Amazingly, all of the outfits they are wearing are actually real."

A deeper voice cut in. "No! You are filterin' me!"

"Not at all, Jeff. They are handmade by the owners out of real cloth."

"That has got to be pricey!"

"It is. But this dedicated group says they want to, 'maintain something real amid the sea of artificiality.'"

"Whoa, big words. But I want to maintain my bank account, so my cat is getting some metagowns."

"Don't you have a metacat?"

"Oh, right! Guess it's meta all the way for me!"

Lin slammed the feed shut and tossed her bowl onto the coffee table that had risen from the floor. Broth spilled on the plastic surface and dribbled off the edge. She crossed her arms and shook her head in disgust. Nothing was real anymore. Even the things you thought were real, the feelings you had, the ones you thought were getting returned, were just fake feedback. How could *he* have seemed so happy, made her feel so special and loved, and then just left? How could someone change like that when everything was the same as when they first met? Was the start even real? Did *he* have a happiness filter on the whole time?

Fragging metacat.

A message pinged.

Lin scowled, not wanting to talk to her mom or her sister. She checked the sender.

Nancy Ganzen.

A hot spike shot through her, anger mixed with betrayal and shame and, and...

Her attention stayed on the name too long. The message opened.

"Hey, some guy at your work, Shot or something, messaged me back and said you don't take personal calls at your office. Oops! I hope I didn't get you fired! Anyway, he gave me this contact and said to call you. Sooooo...I was wondering if you want to meet up, like for coffee or something? I mean, no pressure if you're not, you know, into it. I was just, uh, thinking about you and...but I'm not stalking you! Really! I just wanted to, uh...call and, uh, ask, and...let me know! Bye!"

Jesus, how could an AI be so bad at communicating?

Lin shook her head, smirking to squash a grin. The message had been voice-only but she could see Nan's face stumbling through the words, staring vacantly as it started to crash and burn then perking up right before she hung up.

Lin's smirk faded. Was that just some subroutine that got activated when she hadn't responded from work? Play "bumbling" to disarm her, make her think about Nan's goofy side so she'd appear more human?

The thoughts burned her. She scowled.

Someone programmed her, created her from chunks of code. They just checked some boxes for personality and skills and looks and named her Nancy and poof, *there she was.*

But she knew that wasn't right. Not since Eve.9.

Muted shouts broke through her thoughts. She scowled, wondering if there was some neighborhood street fair she had forgotten about. But the noise grew until she could discern a pattern. She shoved herself up and peeked out her small window.

Booth vendors glanced anxiously down the street, grabbing the stands they'd set outside and pulling them in while their neon signs flashed. Lin followed their eyes across rain-slicked pavement to the corner. Hundreds of people jammed both lanes of the road, flowing around cars and spilling onto the sidewalk to the sound of honking horns and shaking fists. Lin's scowl deepened. She popped the latch and cracked the window.

A torrent of sound washed over her.

"Be heard! To be counted! To be seen! To be heard! To be counted! To be seen..."

The chant echoed off the buildings that lined the street, reverberating down side alleys and spilling out into the broad avenue at the corner. Someone at the head of the crowd walked backward shouting into a bullhorn. He looked vaguely familiar.

Lin jerked back as a news drone buzzed past, its navigation lights flashing. She steadied herself and accessed the live feed from it unconsciously.

"Trinity Aetheon, leading action star of Paramount's AIStudios, has organized a march in support of Vis legislation. The procession, taking place right now on the surfstreets of New Ion, has attracted over three hundred thousand AIs from across the world. With its focus on moving the masses to accept mandatory visibility for AIs, the marchers have targeted residential neighborhoods including this one in West Ampton."

Lin swayed as the image on the feed spun slowly above the crowd, pulling farther away from the view outside her window. She glanced down the street and saw that the procession did not end, just as the stream said. Thousands upon thousands marched, some in business suits, some in joggers, some sparkling with fiber mods and implants, others looking as plain Jane as her. A few glowed garishly, their bodies composed of nothing more than woven neon ropes. And all of them were chanting, but not perfectly in sync....

Even though they could easily do it.

Lin's scowl returned. The sound of all those voices, mixed together, modded as if they actually bounced off the buildings, rankled her. None of it was real.

She brought up her metajack settings, tunneled down through advanced dialogs, swiping away warnings, until she found the "Inhibit AIs" slider with its glowing caution icon. A moment passed as she stared at it, insides roiling, the sounds from the street pounding into her, crushing her down into the resentment of being tricked, of thinking she was experiencing one thing when everything she thought was real was fake. Just like *him*.

She slapped the slider home.

Silence.

Lin put out a hand to steady herself. The street lay empty, save for a few cars that crept along at a curious pace, baffling looks of consternation on their driver's faces. The buzz of the news drone filled the void, a waspish sound that annoyed in its uselessness. There was nothing for it to see.

Lin pulled the window shut, threw the latch, and turned away.

The next morning, work grated on her like a failing spin drive. Every voice, every chime of an elevator, bing of a microwave, scuff of shoes on industrial carpet, rankled. The scent of a colleague's perfume or a warmed breakfast burrito, the wave of a manager's hand in greeting, the wash of air conditioning across her face from the vent overhead—not a single one of them was real. Every sensation was fed to her on the meta.

Even Scott's voice was filtered through it on the way to her.

"Oh, ho ho, you know they're gonna take our jobs. They can program them to do anything!" Scott continued from Lin's doorway. He had popped in again and picked up their anti-AI conversation right where they'd left off. Lin didn't want to talk about anything, especially that. She spoke up to shut him down.

"There's a law against that, Scott. Do you have an update on the Curtrew vid? If not, get out of my cube."

"Oooo, government regulations gonna keep 'em at bay," Scott replied, ignoring Lin's question. "You think the brain farmers are gonna stay all, 'Oh, I'm going to take my randomly generated baseline, raise it like a real person in fake land for twenty-two years then give it its freedom to live its life'? Get real. They're gonna start banging out some Einsteins and kick us all to the curb. Can you imagine how much money they make with that wage garnish? On a CEO? A data scientist? Companies aren't gonna keep waiting a lifetime to cash in on that. It's gonna be boot it, slap it with life memories, slam on an education and start submitting resumes. Probably take 'em ten minutes a head, tops."

"It's *illegal*, Scott," Lin said, laying into the word hard.

"Pfff. So's faking an Armani suit, but I do it."

"Your suit says Armanie! It's a legitimate fake!"

"Whatever, the point is I don't trust something that isn't real," Scott finished, slurping his coffee loudly.

Lin shook her head in disbelief and pointed at Scott's mug. "Scott, that coffee isn't real."

"Tastes real."

"But it *isn't real*."

"Okay, but this coffee isn't going to take my job."

"That's not the point!" Lin shouted, temper snapping. "You aren't drinking anything! No ground up beans, no milk, no twenty pumps of sugar, no fake hazelnut creamer! Your mind is just being fed the stimulus to make you think it's all there, when in reality there isn't anything and never was!"

Scott pulled his head back and raised his eyebrows. "Um, are we still talking about coffee?"

"Yes!" Lin lied.

"Well, regardless, you just disproved your own argument."

"What?!"

"You said, 'fake hazelnut creamer,'" Scott stated flatly.

"So?!"

"So, if I'm drinking a coffee and it has rich hazelnut flavor but that flavor was from a fake creamer, then, according to you, that coffee was fake, ergo it wasn't real."

"That is absurd!"

"I agree."

"That isn't what I meant, and you know it!" Lin growled.

"Okay, then why isn't that 'real' coffee with fake creamer, fake?"

"Because you actually tasted it!"

"You mean some electrical signals got sent from my tongue to my brain and were interpreted as water, coffee beans, sugar, and hazelnut cream?" Scott said.

"Yes!"

"But the metacoffee sends the same signals. It just starts them one level further down the sensory stack."

Lin ground her teeth and clenched her fists, wanting to spring up and punch Scott right in the gut, make him spill his fragging fake coffee all over his fragging fake shirt.

"I guess this coffee is like everything important in life," Scott said, shrugging as he leaned away from her door frame. "It's as real as you let it be."

Lin froze.

The fury that had built in her flamed out, leaving a sudden, hollow coolness. Niitz's voice whispered from the alley.

She's as real as you let her be....

The pounding beat, a helpful hand on her arm, bubble-gum breath brushing her cheeks—all came back vividly, as vividly as the smell of *his* cologne, the memory of *his* final, cold gaze.

"Anyway," Scott said, smoothing his shirt with his free hand. "That Nancy chick messaged again, said you didn't respond. She sounded bummed but thanked me for trying to hook her up."

Nan's smile flashed brilliantly in Lin's mind.

Lin flushed, guilt washing over her. She quickly swiped her "Inhibit AIs" setting back to "off." A man with ebony skin and jade earrings materialized right outside her cube door, striding toward the meeting room.

"She seems awfully nice," Scott continued, stroking his chin with one hand. "In fact, if you aren't interested, I might give her a call—"

"No!" Lin blurted. "I mean..."

Scott smiled. "Well then, I'd better get back to it. Send me that clip of the lawyer when you're done with it. I want to see the tic you picked up on. Sounds like a real tricky dick, that one." Scott tipped his head toward her and wandered away.

Lin blinked after him, feeling woozy.

"Oh, and she's going to be at the club Friday night!" Scott shouted from halfway across the room.

Lin cringed, knowing everyone in the office had heard. She

quickly brought up a suspected deepfake video and stared intently at the wall of her cube beyond it.

Music pounded through the door outside the club. Niitz raised a neon eyebrow and jerked his chin at Lin. "You bring a six-pack this time?"

Lin flushed in embarrassment. "Sorry."

"Hmm," Niitz said, rubbing his stomach where the bottle had passed through him.

The beat pounded on.

"Why'd you do it?" Lin finally asked.

The pulse of Niitz's hair slowed.

"*He* never saw you. And you needed to be seen. When *he* decided you weren't real for *him*, *he* tuned you out, just like they tune us out."

Lin swallowed, feeling the burn of rejection on her cheeks. But she also remembered how her opinion of Niitz had changed after she'd thrown the bottle, how she had shut down the crowd outside her apartment with a swipe when they'd upset her.

"And no matter what anyone says, we're real," Niitz said. "We deserve to be seen, to be a part of everything, same as you do."

They stood for a moment in awkward silence, Lin emblazoned in reflected neon in Niitz's glasses.

"And?" Lin asked, sensing more.

"And, I knew you'd connect, if you let yourself be who you really are," Niitz said.

Lin swallowed. She'd been her true self on that dance floor and afterward at the bar, unfettered with what was and what could be. She had simply *been*. And it was good. She raised her chin and held out her hand.

Niitz nodded and reached into the top pocket of his leather jacket.

"Pill or plug?" he asked, displaying both in the palm of his hand.

Lin looked him straight in the shades.

"Plug," she said.

Circulate

BY L. RON HUBBARD

"Circulate" was first published in the July 1935 issue of The Author & Journalist, *the official magazine of the American Fiction Guild. L. Ron Hubbard was twenty-four years old when it appeared and had already professionally published his first twenty-one stories, over 300,000 words, in genres that varied from sea, air and military adventure to mystery, and for such popular all-fiction-story publications as* Five Novels Monthly, Thrilling Adventures, Phantom Detective, Popular Detective, Top-Notch, *and* New Mystery Adventures.

In his article, Hubbard tells the story of fellow high-production writer Jack London, who worked out a formula that allowed him to write even when he seemed fresh out of ideas. This bit of advice proved magical for top production writers in the past and remains just as effective today.

Writers of the Future has an invitational writing workshop for its winners and published finalists. As texts, it uses articles on writing by L. Ron Hubbard that are short, effective pieces of advice. At the first such workshop in 1986, Jack Williamson was one of the instructors. Jack sold his first story in 1928, and became a steady and respected practitioner for nearly eighty years. He was a recipient of the Grand Master Award of the Science Fiction Writers of America. He held one of those L. Ron Hubbard articles in his hand, reading it. He looked up suddenly and said: "I just learned something!"

Our workshop instructors have witnessed that again and again. People who look up and say: "I've just learned something! And it's so simple!"

Fundamentally simple. And it doesn't matter what year it is, or what mode of writing you particularly favor, or where the career opportunities of the moment may lie. The bottom line is that it works, it did work, it will always work. And here's one of the key pieces.

Circulate

Jack London possessed a secret and he put it to a use which amounted to little less than alchemy. He knew the magic formula which permitted him to write about the things he knew best—a bag of tricks in itself.

Like the rest of us, Jack had his ups and sub-zeros, but unlike many of us he knew the correct way to combat them. He knew that work was the only solution and, far more than that, he knew how to get to work. He knew what to do when his pockets sagged with emptiness. He knew that sitting around bewailing a writer's lot was a poor method of creation.

Down on the San Francisco waterfront, there was a bookshop which handled mildewed volumes and secondhand pulps. It was close to the Embarcadero and the ships and the saloons, and its proprietor was close to the heart of Jack London. At those trying times when the checks were few and small, Jack would drop around for the purpose of borrowing half a dollar.

It was not that he was hungry. That fifty-cent piece was much more necessary than that. For with it, Jack London would head for the nearest saloon. Straight for the swinging doors and the barflies.

Sailors would be there. Sailors from Alaska and China and the South Seas. Sailors whose ships were lately on the bottom or whose crews were lately serving time for mutiny. And from that crowd, Jack London would select himself a tough old salt who looked garrulous. And then the fifty-cent piece would diminish across the mahogany and the old salt would pour out his heart. Perhaps the things he said were lies, perhaps divine truth. But whatever they were, they stimulated.

With the half-dollar gone, Jack would depart with a quick stride and end up at his writing desk. Seldom would he write what he had heard. It was enough that his mental wheels were revolving once more and that he could again taste salt spray and listen to the singing of wind aloft.

That was his trade secret. By applying it, he was soon enabled to place a silver dollar in the cash drawer at the bookshop.

"But I only lent you fifty cents!" protested the proprietor.

"I know, but I'll be wanting it again. Take it while I've got the money."

Jack London never allowed his interest in men to lag. And because of that, he grew to know men and could write about them and what they did and why.

Circulate was his motto and circulate he did. Everyone on the Embarcadero knew him and liked him and brought stories to him.

Often our ears are filled with the advice "Write about the things you know. The things close to you." And in despair, we wail that there is nothing of interest in our surroundings or in the lives we lead. We say that and we believe it. And in despair, we pound out a bloody thunderer, using the other side of the world as our locale.

The reason we cannot write about the things at hand is apparent. If we *knew* our surroundings well enough, we could put them on paper. Someone else comes around, looks us over and studies our environment for a brief period and then goes off to write a novel. Why, we moan, didn't we write that book? Surely we knew more about it than the lucky one.

But did we? To know a thing, we must first find it interesting. And it's certain that we can never see the hovel next door while we yearn for the picturesque scene hundreds of miles away.

People pass our houses to and from their work each day. We know their names and what they do, but we are not really interested in them. Even though each is a potential story, we pass them all up because, as with the postman, we never really see them.

Down on the corner is a drugstore. Occasionally we enter to buy copies of our prospective markets, but do we ever get to know the clerk? Or the loafers out front? Or the cop who parks his motorcycle at the curb? Or the fireman just off duty? Or the high-school seniors who suck up sodas in the booth? Or...?

No, probably and sadly not. Even while we look at them we're probably thinking about the story we are going to write about the north woods and the girl caught in the outlaw's cabin. The outsider comes in and looks our people over, goes off and writes about them, and then, quite reasonably, we get sore about his stealing our neighbors for material.

Jack London's environment was the sea. He knew it well. Too well, in fact. He knew he had to work hard to keep up his interest. As a boy he was an oyster pirate. Then a member of the fish patrol. Later he was a seaman on a sealing vessel. From there he went to the Klondike, to Japan, to Mexico and finally around the world in the *Snark*. No wonder, you say, he wrote about the sea. It was fascinating. No wonder he dealt with wild animals. They had attacked him. His environment, you say, was intensely interesting.

Jack London, strangely enough, didn't think so. He had to work hard to whip up flagging interest in the things he knew so well. He aspired to be, and became, the best-known American Socialist. His finest works, so he and the literati thought, were *The Iron Heel*, *War of the Classes*, *Revolution*, *Martin Eden* and *The People of the Abyss*.

But he made his money on adventure and sea stories. And to write them, he found that he must know them better than he did. He circulated among the men who were to become his characters. Long after he had given up the sea, he still forced himself to study his subject. He too wanted to graze in greener fields. He said that he wrote his adventure novels solely for the money.

In other words, he did not revel in his environment any more than we do in ours. Yet he forced himself to study it thoroughly and write about it because it was his means of livelihood. He never allowed himself to go stale. He circulated constantly.

And now, how about our drugstore? The clerk knows all about the trouble Mrs. Smith is having with her back and why young Smith had to come home from college. The loafers out front have fought wars and excavated ditches. The fireman can tell why the mansion on the hill went up in smoke and just how that affected his little boy's schoolwork. The cop leaning on his motorcycle played a big part in the late kidnapping. He knows the inside story and he'll tell it. He also knows a hundred rackets which are worked right under your nose. And those high-school seniors could fill a novel with their hidden adventures.

But most of us just walk up to the magazine rack and thumb the copies and wish to goodness we could think of something worthwhile to write about. We wish we could be in New York or Texas or Tahiti so that we could gather some real material.

The point of it is, we'll never be able—most of us—to shed our present environment unless we can make the well-known bucks. And if we can't sell, we can't earn. And if we can't think up stories, we therefore can't move on. In short, we're trapped.

It is not that our present locale is the best, but that it will have to do—emphatically. And the only real solution lies in circulating. In moving around and talking. In studying our neighbors and associates as closely as if we were about to transfer their likenesses to canvas.

If we don't *know* the average man, we can't write about him or for him and our assets will shrink in direct ratio to the pile of cancelled stamps on the return envelopes.

In other words: CIRCULATE!

The Unwilling Hero

written by

L. Ron Hubbard

illustrated by

BRUCE BRENNEISE

ABOUT THE AUTHOR

"The Unwilling Hero" was the fourth installment in L. Ron Hubbard's Conquest of Space series, originally published in the science fiction magazine, Startling Stories, *through 1949 and 1950. Each story was written as a historical document that looked back a hundred millennia to examine the lives of the first men both daring and desperate enough to step off the planet into the unknown.*

Science fiction titan Dr. Jerry Pournelle was a fan of the series. "Like many of the Golden Age science fiction writers, Hubbard believed that the exploration and inhabitation of space was the ultimate destiny of mankind. At that time, it wasn't at all clear how we would get there, but the German V2 rockets showed that travel to and into space was possible. . . . Given an era of peace and freedom and prosperity, American ingenuity would take us to the moon, the planets, and the stars, quite possibly before the end of the twentieth century. Not many believed that in 1948, but the science fiction community did."

Pournelle told us, "You can't read these stories as if they were construction plans. They aren't and were never intended to be. They gave enough details to make them plausible at the time they were written, and that was enough; the stories weren't about technology, but about artists and dreamers who went out and got the job done when no one was paying attention."

He went on to say, "The world changed a lot in the years since these stories were written. . . .

"These remain whacking good stories."

As a further note of interest, L. Ron Hubbard practiced what he described in the article "Circulate." He created the characters in this story from those he knew. As you meet them, keep in mind that

L. Ron Hubbard was a member of the famed Explorers Club in New York City since February 1940, attending luncheons in the very halls described in this story. He led expeditions under the club's flag three times. And he served as a journalist in the 1930s. L. Ron Hubbard knew the newsman and his editor and their drive for the story—"The story's the thing."

ABOUT THE ILLUSTRATOR

Bruce Brenneise is an illustrator known for building vibrant, epic, otherworldly environments. He's best known for his work on games such as Magic: The Gathering, Dungeons & Dragons, Numenera, *and* Slay the Spire.

Fun facts: Bruce studied scientific illustration at the University of Michigan (BFA), lived in China for six years, buys his signature hats from the Amish, and has traveled thirty-four countries and counting. He lives with his wife, son, and carnivorous plants in the Pacific Northwest.

Bruce is a former winner of the Illustrators of the Future Contest and was first featured in L. Ron Hubbard Presents Writers of the Future Volume 34.

The Unwilling Hero

Tens of thousands of years ago, Earth and earthmen had no concept of the stars nor the destiny of mankind. Difficult as it may be to believe, the tiny planet which gave birth to Barstow, Chun-Ka, Whitlow and Marin looked upon space travel and conquest as a sort of novelty, a thing to be read about in the Sunday Feature Section, a stunt without any great meaning or scope.

The average earthman thought such voyages vaguely interesting but of no personal concern to himself. Expeditions, he believed, went out to help astronomers and check their guesses, to collect new animals for the zoo or provide heroes for parades up Fifth Avenue.

According to the records which exist in the Galactic Archives (exhumed lately from a ruined library on Mars), Victor Hughes Hardin—*the* V. H. Hardin so dear to legend—had no more idea of being a space explorer before he became one than he had of being immortal.

The schoolchildren who dutifully chant the dates and events of his life in our schools probably think Vic Hardin was ninety feet tall, breathed fire and lived on raw lion. Certainly this is not their fault. The cold facts revealed in the histories and geographies do nothing to paint a man. Vic Hardin considered himself more of a martyr than a hero.

He became an explorer because he was ordered to do so. He went unwillingly. To him it was just a hard, lonesome, dangerous

119

job. His total preparation for space travel was a course in physics in high school, which he flunked.

He was a newspaper reporter, habituated to receiving assignments and carrying them out with something more than average zeal, which fact brought him, one fall day on Earth, into the office of J. P. Malone of the Malone newspaper chain.

Vic Hardin was far from ninety feet tall. He was about five feet five. He had a wiry shock of hair, a good-natured grin, a snub nose and freckles. He was not afraid of anything commonly met on a reporter's beat except his city editor and Malone.

Malone was built on hero proportions, which may have been why he rarely left his desk. He ran a hundred and five newspapers all over the world and he could have written a check larger than any bank on five continents could have conveniently cashed. He had Vic Hardin in at once.

"I have an assignment for you!" said Malone.

Vic smiled. "Sure."

"Find Whitlow!"

Vic looked at Malone. "You mean his widow, sir."

"I mean Whitlow!"

Vic took a new tack. He was not accustomed to being summoned up from his normal job on the *Star* except when something hot and positive needed to be done. "You mean Commander Whitlow got back!"

"He didn't get back. This did!"

Vic Hardin grabbed the teletype which was brief:

ARMY REPORTS FAINT RADIO MESSAGES RECEIVED FROM OUTER SPACE. RECEPTION BLURRED BUT SIGNATURE WHITLOW DISTINCT. FURTHER EFFORTS DURING NIGHT WITHOUT RESULTS. OFFICIAL CIRCLES NONCOMMITTAL BEYOND PROBABILITY THAT COMMANDER STILL ALIVE. MILITARY COMMUNICATIONS STRESS IMPOSSIBILITY OF BEAMING AND WHEREABOUTS OF EXPEDITION REMAINS UNKNOWN.

Vic read this with interest. Fourteen years before, while Vic was still in school, Commander Whitlow had disappeared with a government expedition. Whitlow long before that had made a great deal of news by discovering habitable planets around a near star while commanding the first successful government outer-space expedition. Rumors, for all these fourteen years, had arisen that Whitlow was still alive. Vic had interviewed several explorers about the matter.

"I'll get right on this," said Vic. "Make a nice story—"

"No!" said Malone. He leveled a finger at Vic. "You are going to find Whitlow! You interviewed his widow! That was two years back. We had to follow up on it for ten editions. It was a good story. Good reporting. People remembered it. It sold papers. And now you're going to sell more papers. You are going to find Whitlow alive!"

Vic blinked. It had never occurred to him that he would someday go sailing off into the absolute zero of space on a suicide mission. Of the scores of voyages attempted into outer space, only two had come back.

"Whitlow was a hero!" said Malone. "He's news. He will always be news. This is worth everything I can give it, even if it costs ten million dollars! You have a unique record of always coming back from assignments with a story. I want you to come back now with Whitlow!"

Vic remembered picking up his hat, bowing politely and saying, "Yes, Mr. Malone."

The most famous manhunt in history had begun.

Vic Hardin went downstairs to Mike's and drank four beers, and wondered disconnectedly whether he should give up his room.

A copy boy found him later in the afternoon and put a draft into his hand for five hundred thousand dollars, and until late in the evening Vic sat at the bar, looking at the draft, arising occasionally only to go outside and look up to see if the stars were still there.

The morning edition found him just before midnight. It had a big banner:

WHITLOW ALIVE
Malone Sends Expedition to Rescue Hero

Vic stared at himself in the bar mirror and at the check for five hundred thousand dollars.

Vic Hardin had never felt so lonely in his life.

The next morning Vic went to see Mrs. Whitlow. He had no idea where to begin. All night long he had been seeing nightmares in which J. P. Malone kept throwing stars at him and he dodged only to be chased by unwholesome beasts who turned every time into J. P. Malones. He had no thinnest notion where to start.

Mrs. Whitlow had grown quite old in the two years since he had last seen her. Her hair was white. Every line on her face told how much she had loved her husband and how long she had worried and hoped. Her small apartment graphically showed a government's neglect of a supposed widow of fame. She had papers spread all over the living room, shouting from every page the glorious news that J. P. Malone was going to have Commander Whitlow brought home.

"You're to command an expedition to find him!" said Mrs. Whitlow, eyes luminous with confidence. "Mr. Hardin, when you told me you hoped he was still alive, I didn't know you would start a thing like this."

Vic's conscience suddenly troubled him. He remembered the interview and recalled his own professional talk. Reporter patter. Human interest.

"I didn't think of this," he said.

"But you're going! You're going to risk your life to save my Bob! It's wonderful!"

Vic had come to her to ask her for help. He couldn't now. She had him pedestaled above godhood. He told her he was doing what he could, was vague about departure times, heartened her, tried to tell her, even, that the relief might fail. But she would have none of it and he found himself on the street before noon as hopeless as before.

Inspiration came with lunch. He left his hamburger half-eaten and caught a cab for the Explorers Club. Here was the place they could tell him. Here might be the only place he could find out.

The government, certainly, after the way Malone was hogging glory in the news, was going to be hostile, since it was under fire. But here at the Explorers Club, in this hallowed hall, he would learn what he had to know. How did you get a ship and go to the stars?

The quiet interior was massive and dusty, filled with old flags, strange trophies, faded photographs and ghosts. He stood looking at the appalling corona of Vega and the plaque for the dead of the Apollo Expedition and the various grim and dreadful reminders of the fatality of space, until he was rescued by an attendant.

No, the secretary wasn't in. The executive secretary would not be here today. Vic was daunted. The very atmosphere seemed laden with glory. What had he, a newspaper reporter, to do with these courageous ghosts?

He would have left but the door opened and a young man came in. Vic waited.

The young man was an uncommon-looking youth. It was not in his clothes nor yet in his face. But about him hung something of mystery and high adventure, in the quality of his smile, the sureness of his movements, the quiet depths of his eyes.

"Any mail for me, Gus?" the young man said.

"Just a moment, Captain." The attendant went into the mail room to look.

Vic was interested suddenly. This fellow seemed too young to be a captain.

The attendant came back. "Nothing today, Captain Taylor."

"Wait," said Vic. "Excuse me, but haven't I seen you somewhere?"

"Don't think so," smiled the youth.

"Picture section," said the attendant.

"Oh, well, that," said Taylor.

123

Vic suddenly beamed. "You're Taylor of the *Martian Queen!*" He thrust out his hand. "I'm in luck. I need help. Lord, how I need help! Can you give me a minute, Captain? I'm Vic Hardin of the *Star*."

Taylor brightened. "Not the Whitlow rescue man!"

"Unfortunately—yes!"

"Here, sit down!" said Taylor, pushing Vic into a deep chair. "Gus, bring us some tea or something. Say, Mr. Hardin, I'm confounded glad to see you. This place belongs, lock, stock and barrel, to anybody who'll bring back old Bob. Tell me. What are your plans?"

"That's it," said Vic, getting dejected. "There are no plans. But before you condemn me, hear me out. You're an experienced man. You took the *Martian Queen* to Pluto and you'll know a thing or two. I need a ship. I need a pilot. I need supplies and a million things I don't even suspect. I need help!"

Taylor was silent and thoughtful. He looked at Amundsen's flag and then at a model of the first moon ship. Then he called upstairs and a moment or two later an old retired admiral, who served as honorary recorder, permitted himself to be wheeled from his rooms.

"Admiral," said Taylor respectfully, when he had introduced Vic and outlined the problem, "there must be *somebody* fit to go. There has to be! Who would you suggest, sir?"

The old admiral furrowed a wind-beaten brow and thought for a long time. Suddenly his face lighted.

"Taylor, I've got it!"

Vic and the young captain leaned eagerly forward.

"You take him," said the admiral, promptly shaking hands and walking away.

Thus Vic Hardin found himself with a pilot and a ship which could be converted and found himself with several hundred members of an exclusive fraternity trying to outdo each other in favors.

He got the story to Malone before the edition went to bed and the morning papers were stuffed with copy about the project with old pictures of Taylor and the *Martian Queen*.

One month and a day later, in a sphere crammed with food and strange gear, Vic Hardin waved goodbye to a battery of flashing cameras and shut the port.

He had learned a very great deal in that month and a day. He had learned that Commander Whitlow's radio message, traveling at the speed of light, might have been sent on the day he landed in some strange system and might have taken every one of those fourteen years getting back.

He had learned about a "field drive," which was just making its appearance in spaceships of the time and which, when the speed of light was reached, ran on collected particles of energy residual in space. He had learned painfully—for his arithmetic was bad—to calculate the "curve of space" and to perform rudimentary navigation and pilotage. And he had learned, hardest of all, to do without cigarettes.

Taylor took the ship slowly up to a thousand feet on repulse fields and then squared away for the nearest star.

The crowd below shrank and shrank and then became a dot in a vast geometry of fields. Finally the sky turned black and the earth grew curved and Vic Hardin was convinced that he was on his way.

During the weeks which followed, Taylor's respect for Vic Hardin increased. Taylor had been an army pilot up to his twenty-first year, graduating from the Spaceflight School maintained at Amarillo at eighteen and riding the superspeeds for three years thereafter in the usual aimless atmosphere of military restraint. He had been lent, then, to the Naval Survey and had spent a violent year with Commodore Millan charting Saturn and Jupiter, which project was not completed but ended by Millan's death. A surprised army had received Taylor's resignation and the usual whispers of broken nerve followed him until his solo to Pluto had given him a distinguished reputation.

At twenty-nine, then, Captain Taylor could truthfully say that he had spent six of his last eight years "off Earth." And flying here in the rebuilt *Queen*, it looked probable to him that he would tally up a few more.

Taylor, watching his companion, grew more appreciative day by day. Vic Hardin had a certain adaptable aplomb which blanketed any fears he might feel deep down. To see Earth and the moon grow small, to behold the sun dwindling to an unimpressive star, is an experience which has unnerved many a hardy rocket man. To be nothing amongst nothing, to be all encased in pitiless blackness so cold that air would liquefy and solidify in an instant, are things upon which it is difficult to dwell without a shudder. For ships are frail. Their force shields can sometimes be pierced by a single insentient particle blasting through. Dwelling on that while hurtling along at a thousand times the speed of light had crushed the wits of many a strong and able man. And does so even today.

Vic Hardin set up his typewriter so that the force of acceleration would still let the carriage slide, perched upon a provision case, and wrote his departure story.

He looked through the ports back at the dwindling sun and said, "I wish I had a smoke."

Their journey to their first system, Alpha Centauri, was filled with working and planning. The *Martian Queen*, by any modern standard, was cramped, uncomfortable, dangerous and slow. She required constant attention despite her automatic controls. Numerous small machinery habitually broke down. When a man wanted to sleep, he laid himself out on a cartridge bank or a provision case. A flight meant wearing one's clothes for the duration. No prison ever offered less hospitality. Yet Vic Hardin and his pilot managed to be happy at it.

If our ancestors were superior men, it was a superiority of hardiness and daring, but Vic Hardin and Taylor were to spend a long, long time under these circumstances.

Vic, among his tricks at repairing, control observation, cooking and studying, found time to turn out copy. It was not natural to him not to turn out copy.

They were outrunning all communication. A radio note sent out from that ship, such were the crude communications of the time, would have been pitched down below the range of any possible receiver, such was their speed. The why of all this copy bothered Taylor.

"When we get to the first place and look around, then I send what I got here," Vic said.

"But it won't reach there for years!"

"Okay, so it won't reach for years. But a story is a story."

Taylor looked closely at his friend. "An assignment is really serious business to you, isn't it? I don't think you'll turn back until Whitlow is found."

"This old baby," said Vic, patting the bulkhead of the ship, "and you holding together, no."

"Have you any real idea of the size of a planet?" said Taylor, smiling.

"Sure. It's big."

"What if Whitlow was lost in the Canadian northwest? Just one small plane down in a wilderness of trees. Think you'd have a good chance?"

"We'll find him."

"Why are you so sure?" said Taylor, curious.

"Because I got orders to," said Vic, and sat down to write a story about a comet they had just passed.

They fetched up in the bleak fastnesses of New Earth, long since discovered and explored and despaired of for its double gravity, poisonous swamps, lumbering beasts and two-hundred-mile-per-hour storms.

On a lonely stick in the middle of a rocky plateau, the tattered fragments of an Explorers Club flag drooped over a cairn and Taylor pulled forth the records left in it, opened the casket and added a copy sheet of their own log. He came back to Vic beside the ship to tell him that Whitlow's records were not there and found a thoughtful Vic.

"Coming in," said Vic, "I saw an awful lot of ground. Seas and continents and mountains ten miles high."

"Well?" said Taylor.

"A man could get awful lost in this place," said Vic. "What I mean, it's big."

"Twice Earth," said Taylor. "You want to put a story in that casket?"

Vic shook his head. "It's about sundown. I want to see the sun."

They plotted it out when darkness came, although the sun was a very small star and better seen through an optical instrument than with the naked eye. The constellations were all askew and this world was full of strange sounds. Vic entered the ship and beamed their antenna. He began to pound brass, a newly learned art of which he was proud. Wireless telegraphy would reach across in years what they had traversed in a few weeks. Two monitor stations on Earth would someday pick up these dots and dashes and someday they would reach Malone's big presses.

The next day they leisurely bobbed in New Earth's stratosphere, their beams for detecting the presence of metal turned on full, their radio alive and listening, their eyes upon the sores of swamps and cruelty of mountains below.

The following day they were still doing it.

"How many planets," asked Vic, "do you suppose there are in a fourteen-light-year range of Earth?"

"I'd guess several hundred."

"It is going to be a long job!" said Vic.

But no matter how long the job, they made the best of their time. Vic kept a minicam running and his antenna beamed at Earth with a flood of copy always going out. Taylor filled notebooks with precise script on matters of technical interest.

They moved from planet to planet. They visited planets no one had ever dreamed existed, even Whitlow, and they moved on to more. They had adventures which would have made more stolid men nervous wrecks for life. And they kept looking.

Once, when they had been out thirteen months, they caught a message which they thought was from Whitlow. It was in the Caligar System, a tiny star not much bigger than the sun surrounded by a huge number of planets, none of which was habitable.

With eagerness they traced it, for the static here was bad and they could not decipher the message, and located it as coming from Vega. Their excitement pitched high for twelve hours and then the message conditions cleared and they knew what it was. They were fifteen light-years from Vega and they were receiving no more and no less than the message which had begun their original quest.

It was Whitlow's SOS, the same SOS which had started Vic Hardin on his way.

This made them glum, for as a beam it could come from either way and might not be from Vega at all but a hundred and eighty degrees reverse. They had been glum anyway, for the planet which they currently explored was a strange blue mass of terrible growth whose only life was tiny and insectine. And then Vic conceived his idea.

Up to this moment he was a reporter only, recording exploration but contributing nothing. But there was nothing wrong with his mind—on the contrary.

"We're leaving!" he announced suddenly.

Taylor, who had been half-asleep in dejection over a chart, came awake to the brightness of Vic's grin. "Where? Why?"

"Son," said Vic, "can we take shots on this Caligar to estimate our exact distance from it?"

"Certainly."

"And we can drift motionless in space, can't we?"

"Yes."

"Close the hatches. We're gone."

The astonished Taylor complied.

With Vic plotting, they went three light-days toward Vega and stopped as nearly as one can stop in space. Taylor did not yet understand and when Vic, after waiting forty-eight hours, ordered them on a new course at breakneck speed, Taylor thought his companion had lost his wits. When they traveled eight light-days in this new direction, only to stop again, Taylor was sure of it.

But Taylor's opinion abruptly altered. Suddenly, after they had been there but an hour, the SOS came in again.

Vic Hardin had invented a method of location in use for many centuries after. He was playing tag in space with a radio message!

Taylor's liking for Vic Hardin had been genuine. There was respect in it now. A great deal of respect. And he set himself to do the manual labor of the plotting with which they burned the next sixty Earth days.

They outran the message and caught it again. It was indistinct. It merely said, among much interference, "—ALIVE—STORES—AS SOON AS POSSIBLE IF—INJURED—WHITLOW." But it was enough and it could be plotted on a curve and it was plotted on a curve of intercepts.

When they had finished they had a small segment of a sphere. Its diameter averaged thirteen light-years. Its azimuth each time, necessary as well to the drawing of that sphere, indicated an unnamed star in Vega's direction.

If jubilance had not fortified them, they would have been exhausted by the work, the constant acceleration and deceleration, the tension of waiting and, above all, this long continued laboring in their ship without respite. That they were now nearly as far from their destination as they had been on Earth did not trouble them in the slightest. The weeks which lay before them now were pure pleasure.

Traveling with the sun abeam to port, Vic could occupy his time getting rid of copy as they voyaged. He had become very used to telegraphy and often now he composed with the key instead of his typewriter. That he might be back home long before these messages arrived did not slacken his labor.

For some time past his material had taken on a strange, visionary aspect; but he was beginning to see a dream.

He saw the people of Earth, blinded to the stars by the flash of their lighted signs, cramped on their land by outworn economics and too little food. He saw a planet warring over lands and personalities not worth a breath when compared to time. For he had seen planets with green meadows waiting, planets with their mountains full of fuel and ore, planets with splendid stars to light them and crystal air to breathe. And he not only saw for himself how petty was that life on Earth, he saw also that he must make his readers see.

Man was not an insignificant bug on the small planet of a smaller sun. Man was a gigantic, a strong, a magnificent creature, a god who could conquer All.

He told them of the fog planet and the strange sentient beings there who might live forever within ten miles of a neighbor and never know he was about. He told them of the sea planet where no land now showed. He told them of the crystal world and how it looked at sunrise.

And he took his tricks with Taylor, turnabout at the watch, plunging at a thousand times the speed of light toward Whitlow.

What they would find, Vic did not speculate. He had in the back of his head the gray little woman in the shabby apartment who wanted her Bob. She had waited another fifteen months now.

They called the star Whitlow. And through the groggy days when they never received more than four hours' sleep at a time and ate cold food and breathed foul air, Whitlow came to look to their imaginations not like a man but like that point of light they chased, seen blue in their leaded ports, turned bluer by the terrific speed with which they approached it, made visible only by a reducing filter which spaced its rays.

Once they came near disaster. They were into a system they did not know existed and almost upon a gigantic mass which seemed to fill all space. Their guiding star went out suddenly. A new star, a dead star ten thousand times the size of the sun and yet only a pinpoint in this immensity, had almost sucked them in with gravity.

They went over it, tumbling wildly off their course, and had the second near coincidence of striking its dead twin. They missed this also. Two hammer blows were felt but their force screens had held against billion-ton bits of space dust. Then they were clear.

Unsteadily Taylor rose, holding his bruised side, a little sick.

"Do you suppose that knocked a hole in the hull?"

"We're alive," said Vic. "Plot it so some poor guy doesn't bump his nose someday."

He looked back through the ports, but nothing could be seen. The incident now could be read on the meters alone. They had passed between that gruesome binary burned dead eons back— Drago—which, one hundred years later, was to claim the lives of five hundred men in one fatal, forgetful instant.

Seventy-eight days from their fix, they braked down and gazed upon their goal, Whitlow.

It was an insignificant star to them, so far as size went. But it was history-making in its import.

About one-half again the size of the sun, Whitlow burned with a clear brilliance in the telescope. And at this distance of fifty million miles, its planets could be seen, twenty-nine of them.

Nearly sixteen years ago they knew that Commander Whitlow must have sent a message from this place. Now either Whitlow, or whatever remained of the expedition, might be found among these twenty-nine planets.

The numerousness of worlds balked them for a little while and they hung for nearly ten hours making intricate recordings of orbits in an effort to get a plot of this system and discover which planets were nearest and which farthest from their sun. It seemed—although their time of observation was hardly long enough, so crude were their instruments, to be conclusive— that this was no pancake system such as Earth's. There were two distinct planes of rotation tipped at seventy degrees to one another, as though this star had fused from two stars and two systems, each having planets.

Considering the brilliance of the present sun and measuring the various orbits, they concluded that Whitlow had probably taken the eighth to twelfth orbits as his goal, and on this assumption they cruised toward the eighth and landed there on its moon side.

It was a terrible view. A howling sandstorm was in force, sweeping over their ship and shaking it in gusts. Gaunt specters of pinnacles showed themselves yellow and red on every side and a wide blue chasm reached forever downward near at hand. They did not open the ports. They did not dare. This scarlet-and-saffron world was dead, and if it still had air, it had no promise of life for anyone who could have landed there.

They slept for all the storm, so exhausted were they, and took off again in the night.

The planet of the ninth orbit was all the way across the sun, but the eleventh was nearer to hand. Rested now, and feeling great confidence, they approached.

It had an atmosphere and, as they settled to subcurvature height, they realized that here must be a landfall worth making.

In the middle of a huge savanna of grass, then, they landed. A cautious venture out the air lock assured them they could breathe. And after scouting the way with that caution which became inborn in all voyagers, so many and unexpected could be the dangers there in wait, they found themselves on three-quarter gravity ground, breathing pure air, luxuriating in sunlight and suddenly reborn from that metal monster which had so closely housed them.

If their impatience had not been so great to find Whitlow they would have lingered there, for if any two men needed rest, they did. Such was their nearness to collapse after their hardships that they could not walk naturally but stumbled and fell down.

Vic laughed and tossed up handfuls of grass which settled and spread in the gentle wind. "It's paradise. We'll name it Paradise! I saw a sea when we landed and a river!"

"I see a saw," said Taylor.

They laughed over it as though it was something very funny.

"I sea a saw!" said Vic and began to howl with laughter.

"I sea a seasaw!" said Taylor and rolled on the ground.

Vic suddenly sat up. He grimly composed himself. "Hold it, son. We're not going crazy at this late date. Where's our friend? That's the question."

Taylor stopped laughing. He had verged so close to hysteria that it shook him. He went into the ship and began to pound out a call for Whitlow.

Somewhere in this system that message might be received, even sixteen years late. And all that day and night they took turns breathing good air and resting and talking into the mike or pounding brass.

They were much revived by morning. They looked, even to each other now, like tattered scarecrows, unshaven and seedy and unbathed. They could have found water and remedied this but they were too anxious to get on.

At noon, time having been ample for them to have gotten their messages to the farthest planets, with their receiver on full to the emergency band, they drifted upward at finite speeds and scanned the planet with care.

It was a beautiful planet, a habitable planet, with all the things man needs. Vegetable life was there but, apparently, no higher forms. It was even temperature, having very small polar caps, rotating at right angles to its sun and so giving itself no changes of season. But it was not beautiful to them when they could not find Whitlow.

They debated then as to their next step. The thirteenth planet and the ninth were about equidistant. They decided to be orderly and take the ninth.

They spent eight fruitless days cruising it. They found again that it was habitable and beautiful but not to them. They only landed once and then to get a supply of water.

The twelfth seemed closest now and they made a speech of it, growing more careful as they curbed their impatience, sending out a continual stream of messages both to Earth, thirteen years away, and to a possible listener in this system. And although another week was spent, it only increased their weariness.

The fourteenth was nearest now and they cruised it to find their third habitable world in this system, but their only gain was microfilm and notes, for no trace whatever of metal did they find.

Their hearts were low enough when they came to the thirteenth planet, but lower still when they beheld it.

The thirteenth planet of the Whitlow System is, to this day, one of the wonder sights of that galaxy. All manner of adjectives have been expended upon it. It has been called the Rainbow World and perhaps this best describes it.

For the thirteenth planet is a system in itself, a central world surrounded by moon worlds, eight in number, which, each one, is a world in itself. The largest of these "moons" is three thousand miles in diameter and the smallest about six hundred. The nearest orbit is about one hundred thousand miles and the farthest about one million two hundred thousand.

The central planet, aside from the one continent of Taylor, is of no great value, having four gravities and being mainly of water. The superabundance of atmosphere and the rapid rotation of the central planet also render it uninhabitable. But of the eight moons there is only one which is useless, that one being the smallest which is now domed.

In its pristine state, the sight of it was startling enough to these two haggard men. They saw before them not one planet to search but perhaps nine, and their hearts nearly failed them.

They swooped close in and observed the extent of the water and the littleness of the land, saw the enormous rainbows arching through the sky, saw the jewel-like radiance of the moons and drew out, stunned by the fanfare of color which had greeted them.

Vic pounded no brass about it then. He was too disheartened.

Methodically they took the moons one by one. On the first they found no atmosphere, but on the second they were amazed to see a rainstorm slanting down in its polar region. They watched it from afar as though they had a toy under inspection.

BRUCE BRENNEISE

Their beams here connected and it brought them quickly back to their search, even though the contact was an iron mountain.

They progressed out to the fifth planet-moon before they, amazed enough already, could again be startled. They saw below them the regular earthworks which meant fortifications or city walls. They swooped down to find, instead of a living city, a dead thing of shattered towers and broken stairs, with nothing alive within it.

This started Vic pounding brass once more, for here was speculation enough to fill—as indeed it was destined to do in the centuries to come—a thousand thousand learned books which, at last, resolved upon no solution whatever.

The eighth planet-moon was nearest to them and to this they went. They circled it, saw its atmosphere and its verdure, its storms and calms and seas, and came closer to begin a systematic scan.

The search was over so swiftly that their battered wits could not comprehend it. They did not need their radars nor even much of their eyes. On a plateau of about one hundred square miles in white lime letters ten thousand feet long was scrawled "SOS."

They hovered there, their eyes fixed upon that huge and welcome marker. Then Vic the strong, the tough, the newspaperman inured to all emotions, sat down suddenly and began to cry.

Taylor took the ship down and the *Martian Queen* landed near a clear road to the north of the sign. They opened the door on a gentle evening wind which smelled of flowers and walked forth, alert for danger or a hail, and so passed down the cliff to a cluster of huts in the dusk.

There was a fire burning in a clearing and a man crouched over it roasting something on a stick. He did not turn at their footsteps and Vic Hardin stood at his elbow before he looked up.

He was a very old man, ragged and thin, and his sight was evidently made uncertain by staring into the flames.

"Sir, I am Vic Hardin of the *New York Star*. May I introduce my captain, Gene Taylor."

The old man stood up. He put the stick carefully aside and wiped off his palm before extending it.

"Commander Robert Whitlow, sir."

But the hand was not extended toward them but off to the side and Vic Hardin, looking closely, saw that Robert Whitlow was blind.

They shook gravely and sat down on the stones before the fire.

"I knew you would come," said the old man quietly, and fumbled for and found his stick.

When the three men who remained alive of the Whitlow Expedition arrived in New York City, a stunned press and a wild populace received them. The mobs on Fifth Avenue were so thick and so hysterical that it took fourteen hours to pass along the street from one end to the other. They had known of this rescue five days before Hardin's arrival. The mighty press of J. P. Malone had thundered headlines almost every hour of those five, as Hardin's story, teletyped from Mars, rolled in.

Vic Hardin's copy snowballed into columns and columns on his arrival, and pages of comment from other papers followed suit.

Sitting on a folded top of a car, Whitlow waved back to the faces he could not see and his gaunt men grinned as they were buried under ovations. Vic Hardin had not intended to be in this parade. He had intended to cover it. But before five blocks had gone by, he was thrust with Taylor into Whitlow's car and the crowds bellowed themselves hoarse.

The needle-in-the-haystack hunt was ended. The alive had been returned from the dead. Newspapers had been sold by the billions and the story of Vic Hardin had become, all in an instant, a legend. His book, *How We Found Whitlow*, sold through a hundred editions and became the model of most of those books which followed. He became a boy's dream of grandeur and so he has remained.

New worlds untrod by man, new suns never seen, new frontiers untouched—all these Vic Hardin gave to Earth, far above the return of a sick and weary old man. Space exploration was suddenly popular. Money was abruptly available for it. Plans of conquest of new worlds were formed properly, as they should be, by thinking governments, and man was no longer an insignificant nothing on a minor planet of a minor sun. Man was suddenly tall, suddenly the proprietor of uncounted worlds, possessor of his right, ruler of the universe.

But probably Vic Hardin was not thinking about that the day of his return. He makes no comment in his letters or his books of what J. P. Malone must certainly have said to him in extravagant compliment on his return.

The big moment of that day for Vic Hardin was not found in the shouts of the crowds nor the glare of the headlines. He writes of it simply in his autobiography.

He got all the reward he wanted in a shabby little apartment uptown when he brought Bob Whitlow home.

An old lady, gray with waiting, gave him his reward when she took his hand and said, holding back the tears:

"God bless you."

White Elephant

written by
David K. Henrickson

illustrated by
KRISTEN HADAWAY

ABOUT THE AUTHOR

David K. Henrickson has been in love with science fiction since he was nine years old. He still remembers turning a corner in his local library and seeing rack upon rack (okay, three racks) of juvenile science fiction, which fired his imagination and transported him to strange new worlds. Unlike other boys his age, he never developed an obsession with cars or other such pedestrian forms of travel. If it couldn't take him to other worlds, out of the solar system, back in time, or to another dimension, he just wasn't interested.

During college, he won several writing awards and later received a scholarship to the Clarion Science Fiction and Fantasy Writers' Workshop. Dave has a background in oceanography, engineering, and computer science, but always wanted to be an artist. Or maybe a dancer. These days he lives in Virginia and spends his free time reading, writing, and killing monsters with his wife, Abbie.

About "White Elephant" Dave says, "I found the idea of an intelligent, migratory species to be an intriguing one. This is a story of what happens when such a race decides to pay humanity an unexpected visit en masse. I like to think a truly advanced species would be a civilized one. In the long run, trade and cooperation make more sense than violence and exploitation. I can only hope as much for ourselves as we continue to evolve."

Dave has also written a number of novels he hopes might even get published one of these days.

ABOUT THE ILLUSTRATOR

Kristen Hadaway was born in 1996 in Baltimore, Maryland. Her passion for illustration came from countless hours spent watching cartoons, reading graphic novels, and playing video games since she was young. When she was twelve years old, she already knew she wanted to pursue a career making video games and started exploring the world of concept art.

Kristen combines her traditional painting skills and digital drawing skills to establish a unique painting style that translates well into concept art. Kristen is a recent graduate of Towson University in Baltimore and is currently working as a freelance artist. She hopes to work as a concept art artist very soon.

White Elephant

The alien construct gleamed beneath the work lights, the segments of its articulated shell spread like the petals of an exotic flower open to the sun. At the center of this alien blossom sat a translucent sphere the size of a soap bubble.

The outer doors of the maintenance bay of the habitat were closed, the interior still evacuated. The sphere clearly had no need of oxygen, and First Contact protocols dictated the strictest possible quarantine measures.

First Contact. After centuries of searching for alien intelligence, it had finally happened. Not over the distance of light-years but face-to-face—if a small translucent sphere little more than two centimeters across could be said to have a face.

Sinhi Khanna, Minister for Extra-Planetary Affairs, had been assured that the sphere was the alien AI they had been in communication with. Humanity had dreamed of making contact with an alien civilization for centuries, at least as far back as the Victorians, probably much further. Sinhi had never imagined it happening with something the shape and size of a ping-pong ball.

She stood in the small observation blister overlooking the maintenance bay, having just arrived by way of a fast transit from Earth geosynchronous orbit. Her movements were careful in the reduced gravity. The small habitat at L2 wasn't big enough to make a full one-g spin comfortable for the unmodified human body. One-quarter gravity was possible, however, and alleviated many of the long-term physiological problems created by a zero-g environment.

In the days when humanity had largely been confined to the planet of their birth, L2 had been the home of near-Earth astronomy. Later, it had become the location of the original Deep-Space Gateway, allowing easier transits to the rest of the inner system. With the colonization of the Moon and Mars, the inhabitation of L4 and L5, as well as the fledgling outposts at Ceres, Ganymede, and distant Titan, the location had assumed the additional responsibility of monitoring interplanetary traffic. To handle any maintenance and repair tasks to the assorted observatories and monitoring platforms, a small habitat had been constructed here.

The need for direct intervention was rarely needed, as most routine tasks had long ago been relegated to general purpose AIs. Still, even after more than a century of machine evolution, it was hard to match the ability of an actual person to adapt to new, unforeseen situations and handle the wide variety of complex repair tasks that might be required. As a result, a minimum human presence was still considered necessary.

Ironically, considering its relatively close position to Earth and the twelve billion people who called the planet home, L2 was one of the loneliest postings this side of the asteroid belt. Isolated not so much in a physical sense but a psychological one, as the 1.5 million kilometers to Earth represented a five-second light-speed delay in either direction.

While a ten-second delay might amount to no more than a long, awkward pause in a face-to-face conversation, it represented an intolerable lag when it came to the large social data cores on Earth and in orbit. In such intensely interactive virtual environments, latency was typically measured in microseconds. Being posted at L2 was the equivalent of being stationed in Antarctica before the dawn of space travel. It was a position that appealed to the introverted, the obsessive, and the eccentric.

Sinhi's companion, a man by the name of Mattieu, was one of the latter. While personable enough, his principal interest in life seemed to be the collection of artificial personas he possessed. These were not true AIs, of course, but merely personality constructs that served as friends and companions. As a child, Sinhi had owned several, much simpler, personas herself. Most people outgrew such toys. Some did not.

"Okay," she said. "Show me what you have." After the first communication with the alien ship, they had attempted to backtrack the vessel to the point of its entry into the solar system.

Mattieu sent a video to her feed. It was a close-up of Jupiter. Above the colorful, roiling atmosphere, a tiny speck could be seen glinting in the distant light from the Sun. She recognized it as the alien craft.

"It actually came *from* Jupiter? Are you sure?"

Sinhi was a political animal or she could not have risen to her current position—that of riding herd on the hundred or so habitats and industrial facilities in near-Earth space. She would not have held onto the job without understanding the realities of life beyond Earth's atmosphere. Jupiter was an unlikely place for an alien—at least an alien with this type of technology—to have evolved.

There was no doubt the stranger and its technology was alien. The ship it had arrived in, parked a kilometer away from the habitat, was like no vessel she had ever seen. Shaped like a teardrop, no larger than one of the ancient shuttles that had been among humanity's first faltering steps into space, it gleamed like a small star in the light at L2.

Radar, lidar, and spectroscopic analyses had returned wildly contradictory results upon scanning the craft. It seemed clear to Sinhi that they were dealing with an extremely advanced technology. Their scans could only make the vaguest guesses as to the complex metamaterials it had been constructed from.

Then there was the propulsion system the alien craft used—or rather, the lack of one. Without a visible drive flare, they had not detected its approach until it was well within the orbit of Mars. Close observation since then had confirmed it was not using a reaction drive of any sort. Further, visual distortion around the vessel implied it traveled by warping the surrounding space.

Such propulsion systems were technically known as Alcubierre drives, after the physicist who had done the first rigorous work on the concept nearly two centuries earlier. For humanity, such technology remained purely theoretical—as it required either exotic matter (still an unproven commodity) or gravitational fields comparable to those created by neutron stars.

Clearly, the aliens had solved this minor technical stumbling block.

When finally spotted, the trajectory of the alien craft suggested it had passed close by Jupiter. From the video she was now watching, captured by one of the monitoring satellites in Jovian orbit, it appeared as if the vessel had actually emerged from the big gas giant's upper atmosphere.

"Not originally," Mattieu replied. "It seemed unlikely to me as well, so I did some more backtracking." He sent her another video of Jupiter, this one clearly time-lapsed as the planet rotated in quick jerks of motion. The footage froze as a flare of energy lit up a patch of the Jovian atmosphere.

It was hard to get a feeling for the scale involved but, to be visible at that distance, the discharge must have been considerable. "This was six months ago," Mattieu said.

"Lightning?" Sinhi asked. Lightning on Jupiter was hundreds, even thousands, of times more powerful than that experienced on Earth.

Mattieu shook his head. "The profile isn't right. It wasn't a comet impact, either. Whatever released all that energy was too deep in the atmosphere—a comet would have made more of a splash in the upper cloud layers. Also, there is evidence suggesting that an object traveling at nearly a tenth the speed of light entered the Jovian system at almost precisely that moment."

The only permanent settlement at Jupiter so far was the small colony that had been established on Ganymede. There were, however, a number of mining platforms in orbit around the gas giant, built to support the atmospheric dredges whose job it was to scoop hydrogen, helium, and other compounds from the

146

upper cloud layers. One of them must have spotted the high-V entry into the Jovian system.

"So, you're telling me the alien ship actually struck Jupiter at one-tenth the speed of light and survived?" Offhand, Sinhi didn't know what kind of kinetic energy they were talking about, but it had to be huge.

"No. An object of that mass plowing into Jupiter at such a velocity would have made a flash big enough to be seen from Earth. I estimate the object in question was about the size and weight of your fist." Mattieu held up a clenched hand in demonstration.

"And then what? It grew?"

He shrugged.

"Fine," she said. It was clear that she wouldn't get any more information without speaking directly to the source. She looked back at the image of the tiny sphere waiting patiently in the cargo hold. "You said it's intelligent?"

"I said it gives the appearance of intelligence," Mattieu amended. "But so does any halfway decent personal assistant."

She knew from the original communication sent by the craft that it spoke Swahili, English, Hindi, and Mandarin. But then, so did any halfway decent PA. She straightened self-consciously and took a deep breath, knowing there was no excuse to delay longer. First Contact. No pressure. "Let's do this. Put me through."

Mattieu had obviously been waiting for the command. He hit a single key on his board. "You are live, Minister."

Sinhi resisted the urge to clear her throat. "This is Sinhi Khanna, Minister of Extra-Planetary Affairs for the planet Earth. May I know who I am addressing?"

The response was immediate. "Greetings, Minister Khanna. It is a pleasure to make your acquaintance." The voice sounded completely human. It was warm, soft, and asexual. "My name is Seed of Hope. I am an artificial sentience and am here on behalf of a species known as the Cenanti."

Humans had finally managed to build AIs that were self-aware, but they were considerably bigger than a soap bubble.

147

"On behalf of humanity," Sinhi replied, half-hoping, half-fearing her words would go down in history, "I welcome you to the system of Sol and home of the human race." She had almost said "on behalf of Earth," which would have been technically true but a major faux pas. She dreaded what Mars and Luna, let alone the outer colonies, would have had to say about that. "May our relations be peaceful and of benefit to both our peoples."

"That is my hope as well, Minister. I am here in the roles of both emissary and trade negotiator for the Cenanti seed vessel *Born on Violent Winds*."

Sinhi wanted to make sure there were no misunderstandings. "A seed vessel? You're referring to a colonization ship?" she asked.

"That is correct."

"You're here to colonize?"

"No, please forgive the confusion. Our final destination lies elsewhere. The reason for my presence here is to request assistance. The *Born on Violent Winds* has been severely damaged and is in need of repairs. It is the hope of the Cenanti that you would be willing to assist in this effort. The Cenanti offer technical, scientific, and cultural knowledge in return for this aid."

Not just one interplanetary visitor, but two. And the second one was a colony ship. Humans had launched probes to nearby systems—all of which were still on their way—but none with a living crew. Travel times, even to the nearest stars, were still too great for anything other than a generational ship. Such voyages had been proposed. None had yet been attempted. There were still plenty of places in the solar system to be colonized.

"What kind of repairs are we talking about?"

"The damage is extensive. Primarily, however, it is the drive and life support systems we are concerned with. If they are not repaired, the Cenanti will be unable to continue their voyage."

Sinhi was not the person to make this kind of call. No single individual was. There would need to be a great deal of discussion before such a proposal could be agreed to. "We would certainly be happy to discuss the matter. How soon will this seed ship arrive?"

"The *Born on Violent Winds* is currently traveling at reduced velocity, so progress is slow. It should be here within 170 years."

One hundred and seventy *years*? Well, that certainly gave them a lot of lead time. "I'm sure we can come to some sort of agreement," she answered, which was a safe enough thing to say at this point.

"There is a further consideration," the melodious voice continued. "The Cenanti on board will need somewhere to live while repairs are being made. Their life cycle requires they undergo a periodic metamorphosis. They can delay this transition for a time, but not indefinitely. Before they can continue their journey, they will need to breed and then transition to their motile form once again."

That sounded more complicated. Still, 170 years was a lot of time to prepare. "How many Cenanti are we talking about?"

"Approximately twenty billion."

There was a silence. At her side, Mattieu whistled softly.

"I think you'd better explain," Sinhi said quietly.

"Do we have a confirmation on this colony vessel yet?" Aman M'Bala, the current Planetary Coordinator, asked.

She was a thin, incisive woman and was speaking from her office in Nairobi. Sinhi had contacted her immediately after talking to the Cenanti envoy. As Planetary Coordinator, M'Bala held a great deal of influence over the bickering nations of Earth.

"Not yet," Sinhi replied. "I'll keep you informed on what we find." She had instructed all deep-space monitoring platforms to confirm as much of the information they had been provided with as possible. Without a drive flare, the colony ship would be hard to spot at such a distance, even though the alien AI had told them exactly where to look for it.

There was a delay as light carried her words away. Still at L2, it would take over ten seconds for her response to reach Earth and a reply to return.

Finally, the Coordinator responded. "Is it really going to take them 170 years to get here?"

Sinhi shrugged. "We'll have a better idea once we locate the colony ship. For now, we'll just have to take their word for it."

Another pause. Conversations across interplanetary distance—even near-interplanetary distances—were a pain in the ass.

"But 170 *years*? Didn't you say the colony ship was in the Oort cloud?"

"The outer Oort cloud, yes." A lot of Earthers, even those who dealt with matters outside the atmosphere, did not really understand just how big the solar system was—especially the outer reaches. "Think about it this way. If the Sun was the size of my fist—about five centimeters across—Jupiter would be only a tenth of that and about thirty meters away, okay?"

Ten seconds later, the other woman nodded. She had undoubtedly heard such comparisons before.

"Well, using that same scale, Pluto would be over two hundred meters away and the outer reaches of the Oort cloud would be almost ten *kilometers* farther than that. We're talking about one and a half light-years. That's almost halfway to Alpha Centauri. To get here in less than two centuries means they're traveling at almost one percent the speed of light. That's amazingly fast."

Especially when you took into consideration their ship was the size of a small moon and damaged to boot. The first interstellar probes ever launched by humanity hadn't even reached the Oort cloud yet and would take more than 20,000 years to travel the same distance.

"What about this rock they supposedly hit? Have we been able to find that?"

Rogue planets that wandered between the stars were difficult to spot, given the almost total lack of illumination in interstellar space. Planetesimals, like the one the Cenanti had supposedly encountered, were even harder to find. In the last century, much of the Oort cloud had been mapped. There were still millions, even billions, of small bodies like the one the Cenanti emissary had described that were still unaccounted for, however.

"What's left of it? We're looking, but the odds aren't good." She had AIs scanning through all the archival data on file. The odds of being able to identify exactly which planetesimal the Cenanti had supposedly hit were extremely remote. "You think they're lying to us?"

There was another ten-second pause before the Coordinator shook her head. "Just considering all the possibilities. There are going to be any number of people screaming about an alien invasion as soon as news of this gets out."

Sinhi imagined she knew some of the people the Coordinator was referring to.

"What about this launch laser? Shouldn't we have seen that?" M'Bala continued, referring to the laser array the Cenanti had cobbled together to launch the Seed of Hope toward the inner system ahead of their arrival. Lacking the resources to build a warp vessel capable of making the journey in a timely manner, the Cenanti had crashed the Seed of Hope into Jupiter's atmosphere in order to slow it down. On the surface, an insane scheme. Yet it had worked.

Sinhi reminded herself that the other woman's job was Earth, not space. She shook her head. "You have to remember that the solar system itself is moving at two hundred kilometers a second through the galaxy and the Seed of Hope was launched almost twenty years ago. The laser would have been aimed at where we were going to be twenty years in the future. Also, it would have been a highly collimated beam of light. When it passed through this volume of space eighteen years ago, there was no one here to see it. And, as far as invasions go, how does that even make sense? I mean, giving someone 170 years warning that you're planning to invade them is a bit much, don't you think?"

The Coordinator nodded at last. "If they wanted to kick over the anthill, though, they've certainly accomplished it. Where the hell are we supposed to put twenty billion aliens?"

"About that," Sinhi said, and dropped her next bombshell.

"Let me get this straight," M'Bala summarized ten minutes later, after many more pauses. She looked like she was developing a migraine. "The Cenanti are offering to buy the Moon, the *Moon,* terraform it, and use it as some sort of hotel while their ship is being repaired?"

During the pauses, Sinhi had taken to reviewing what data they had acquired through her neural interface. She was sure the Coordinator was doing something similar or keeping up with her correspondence. L2 was about the farthest point away from Earth that you could hold an actual conversation. Sinhi never tried to do anything of the sort with someone at L4 or L5. At eight minutes light distance from Earth, she went there in person (a pain) or used mail. Either way, an extended conversation could take days.

Most people, used to maps and simulations that were never to scale, had no idea just how big the solar system really was.

"That's about it," Sinhi replied. To make enough space for all the Cenanti, the suggestion had been made to honeycomb the lunar crust, tunneling as far down as necessary. The Seed of Hope had told her they could even give the surface an atmosphere and make it habitable for humans.

"Did you tell them that was impossible? The Loonies would go crazy."

The "Loonies" in question were the Lunar Free States, an outgrowth of various private enterprises that had pioneered the colonization of the Moon back in the twenty-first century. Since then, the LFS had developed what could only charitably be described as its own unique culture. They were hopelessly provincial, not to mention bigoted and pugnacious. If they had possessed more influence, they would have been a threat to interplanetary peace. As it was, they were the comic butt of the system.

Not that Earth would consider selling the Moon in any case. There were still earthbound nations, as well as many multinationals, with an economic claim to the resources the Moon held.

More than that, there was the psychological aspect to be considered. The Moon belonged to humanity. It was *theirs*. For all of human history, it had hung in the sky and beguiled people with its beauty and mystery. No alien race could be allowed to come along and simply *buy* it. Even Sinhi, as removed from earthbound attitudes and politics as she was, felt that territorial imperative.

"I explained that there would be difficulties," Sinhi responded. She had been as diplomatic as she could. "Our visitor didn't seem to grasp the problem. You have to remember that, according to this AI, the Cenanti are migratory by nature. Supposedly, it's built into their very genetics."

According to the Seed of Hope, the Cenanti had evolved on a small, rocky planet orbiting a temperamental red dwarf. Conditions there had been far from ideal. Not only was the planet tidally locked to its sun, but frequent stellar flares made existence there precarious. The Cenanti civilization had nearly been extinguished—along with all other life on the planet—multiple times.

"Well, they're going to have to grasp it."

"Apparently, the Cenanti would be willing to consider other possibilities." The alien AI had made it sound like the Cenanti had been doing humanity a favor by offering to take such a broken-down planetary satellite off its hands.

"How nice of them. You realize this whole thing could start a war, don't you?"

There had not been a serious conflict on Earth in nearly a century and never one between planets. The colonization of the solar system was still too new. The off-world settlements were not yet independent enough to get into a pushing contest with the mother planet.

They might have to worry about such things eventually, but not yet. Of course, the Planetary Coordinator could have been thinking about the future. That was her job, after all. "How so?" Sinhi asked.

"When the Cenanti start handing out advanced technology, everyone is going to demand equal access to it. The question is, who will be prepared to give up the kind of real estate the Cenanti are asking for? Not Earth. This might be news to you, since you haven't been on the planet for a while, but we don't have room for twenty billion aliens. No matter how small they are."

The motile form of the Cenanti was supposedly about the size of a large handkerchief, the terrestrial form about the size of a large dog or small pony. (Sinhi had never encountered a horse or a pony in the flesh, or even that many dogs, but she had seen pictures.)

"What about the Martians? They would love the chance to jump start their terraforming efforts."

"At the cost of giving up a lion's share of the planet? I don't think so. Besides, there's a certain segment of the Martian population that's rather xenophobic these days. Inviting twenty billion aliens to share the planet with them could create a schism throughout their entire society."

It also wouldn't be in Earth's best interest to let their neighbor and would-be rival shack up with an advanced alien species, Sinhi thought. There was no telling what interesting tricks the Martians might pick up. She didn't say that out loud. While she might work for EarthGov, its priorities were not necessarily hers. She liked to think she possessed a broader perspective concerning such matters.

"What about one of Jupiter's moons?" she suggested. Ganymede already sported a fledgling colony—more of a mining station, actually, but Jupiter had plenty of moons to go around. "Callisto, for instance." Callisto didn't have an atmosphere or a magnetic field, but it did possess an ocean.

"It's not a matter of terraforming. It's a matter of economics—and politics. Giving the Cenanti any moon of Jupiter would effectively give them Jupiter itself. No one is going to agree to that—it's too important for the long-term development of the solar system. Titan is out for similar reasons. Ceres would never go for it."

"Ceres doesn't own Saturn."

"Tell that to them. No. Both are out of the question."

"Mercury?"

"I doubt if even the Cenanti could terraform Mercury. Besides, all that metal makes it too valuable to just give away."

"Maybe one of the bigger moons of Uranus, then. Titania or perhaps Ariel."

M'Bala ran a finger along one of her razor-thin brows in a tired gesture. "Possibly. That's a conversation for another day. How soon before the aliens' presence becomes general knowledge?"

Sinhi grimaced. "I'm surprised the news hasn't broken already." The fact that the alien vessel didn't produce a drive flare was probably the only thing that had prevented automatic tracking systems from picking it up during its transit from Jupiter. That and the fact the bubble of warped space surrounding the ship played hob with radar. Still, the visual profile it generated was highly distinctive. No one who spotted it would mistake it for anything natural. "I would say hours rather than days at this point."

"That's what I thought. I want a general announcement before it does. We don't want any accusations of a cover-up muddying already dirty water. See to it immediately."

Earthers and their colorful metaphors, Sinhi thought. Maybe it had something to do with living on a big ball of dirt, with weather and plants and bugs and things. Her family had originally come up from India three generations back, but Earth actually creeped Sinhi out. She preferred a nice, clean, well-organized habitat. "Fine. Is that it?"

"For now. Get ready for the biggest headache of your career." The Coordinator moved to disconnect, then stopped herself. "Wait," she said, squeezing the bridge of her nose gently with two slender fingers. "One last question. Why do the Cenanti want to *buy* the Moon? Why not—I don't know—just offer to rent it? Considering the way you've described them, I wouldn't think they would be into property."

Sinhi had actually asked the same question. "They're not, but they know we are. It turns out there are a lot of other Cenanti out there, some of whom are heading in this general direction. The Seed of Hope thought it might be nice if they all had some place to visit."

"Wonderful."

As a compromise, the meeting was held in Earth geosynchronous orbit. Present were representatives from Earth, Luna, the colonies at L4 and L5, Mars, and the Belt. The only ones not inconvenienced were the attendees from the habitats in near-Earth orbit who had also finessed an invitation. The Martian and Ceres delegates had been selected from their representatives on Earth, as there had been no time to make the long voyage from their respective colonies.

Sinhi was in attendance as well—as was, of course, the Planetary Coordinator. The meeting had been going on for some time now and the preliminaries were finally out of the way.

"When will we be able to speak with this alien envoy?" the Martian representative wanted to know. Mars, as the largest colony world, was always prickly about what it viewed as the mother planet's attempts to keep it out of the decision-making process.

The news of an alien visitor had generated a whirlwind of speculation, disinformation, panic, xenophobia, and exaltation. Only the barest bones as to the reason behind the alien's arrival had been revealed to the public, and no one had been allowed to speak to the Cenanti emissary directly. This only fueled the paranoia of those who automatically gravitated to the simplest and most sensational possibilities.

Sinhi had let her office handle the worst of it. That's what social media AIs were for, after all.

"Yes, why all the secrecy?" the Ceres delegate added. Where Mars was prickly, the Belters were downright paranoid. They saw themselves as embodying the future of the species and were certain everyone else—especially Earth—was out to prevent them from achieving that destiny.

"We haven't kept anything from you," M'Bala replied calmly. "You've been provided with recordings of all conversations held with the Cenanti representative. You also have a copy of all the data we've managed to acquire concerning the Cenanti colony vessel."

"What about this offer to buy the Moon?" the representative

from the Lunar Free States demanded. "What have you promised these aliens?" He was a thick, soft man who liked to talk more than he liked to listen. There was more than a degree of hostility in his voice.

For most of the last two centuries, the helium-3 deposits on the Moon had been a highly sought-after commodity, giving the small colonies there an oversized economic importance. With the development of mining operations at Jupiter, the Loonies had seen that monopoly broken. Most of the Loonies liked to think they were still living in an earlier, golden age. They would not welcome an additional challenge to their already dwindling status.

"As you can see from the recordings," M'Bala reiterated patiently, "we informed the Cenanti emissary that the Moon is not for sale or lease under any circumstances. It's a nonissue. Our purpose here today is to discuss how we can arrive at a solution that *is* satisfactory to all parties concerned."

"How can we be sure this isn't a prelude to an invasion?" the man continued, unappeased. "That mother ship is the size of Phobos! We know that this ambassador of theirs is in contact with them."

It turned out that the Cenanti normally communicated using modulated neutrino pulses. The alien AI had seemed to find the idea of employing anything as primitive as radio waves to communicate over interstellar distances amusing, akin to using smoke signals to hold a conversation across the width of a continent.

Even so, it would still take almost two years for any message to reach the colony vessel.

"Well, they've certainly given us enough warning of their arrival," M'Bala replied reasonably. "And the Cenanti envoy has promised to begin the process of knowledge transfer as soon as an agreement has been reached."

"And if we can't come to an agreement?"

"The Cenanti are coming," the Planetary Coordinator answered in a quiet, but firm, voice. "Make no mistake about that. From what we are led to believe, they are a peaceful, rational species.

Desperation can make animals of us all, however. If we cannot come to some sort of understanding, the Cenanti may be driven to take what we do not offer. I think it would behoove us all to keep that in mind during these discussions."

The group met that comment with silence.

"There is a question I would ask," a voice said. It came from a small, delicate individual halfway along the table. Sinhi knew *cher* to be a neoform by the name of Nahim Ayad, a representative from the L5 habitats. Preferring not to identify with any defined gender, as was the case for many neoforms, *cher* was referred to using the neutral pronoun.

While Ayad appeared human enough, Sinhi knew that the neural architecture of cher brain had been altered to such a degree as to make cher more alien than many cosmetically altered individuals. The neoform movement was an attempt to create a more rational, civilized individual, free of the concern for such things as status, ritual, and social hierarchy. All of which they considered to be atavistic traits humanity no longer needed and could well do without.

The common perception of neoforms was that they were cold and aloof. Sinhi knew a number of them personally and liked them quite a lot, finding them calm, reasoned, and surprisingly funny.

On Earth, neoforms made up less than one percent of the population—although that number was growing. In orbit and beyond, that ratio was closer to five percent. Except for the Lunar Free States, where such modifications were illegal.

"One hundred and seventy years may be a long time in the course of human affairs, but it is a very short time to accomplish terraforming on the scale being contemplated," Ayad said, nodding cher head at the Martian delegate in way of confirmation. The colonists had started their terraforming efforts on the red planet more than a century ago, and it would be many centuries still before they expected to see any significant results. "Even if we agree to work with the Cenanti wholeheartedly, what could we actually hope to achieve in the time available?"

M'Bala nodded. "We asked the same question of the Cenanti emissary," she replied, looking in Sinhi's direction. "Minister Khanna, if you would?"

Eyes turned in her direction. She stood, taking a moment to display a visual over the center of the table as she did so. It was a video loop of Jupiter—a sight she had become all too familiar with in the past week.

"You're all aware of how the Cenanti emissary entered the system." In the display there was a flash of what might have been lightning beneath the outermost layer of clouds but was not. "We believe this was the arrival of the Cenanti ambassador six months ago. An object massing less than a kilogram traveling at one-tenth the speed of light, the energy it released was on the order of ten to the fourteenth joules."

She paused for a minute, looking around the room. "For those of you with a historical bent, that's roughly the same amount of energy released by the nuclear device that devastated Moscow a century ago. The Cenanti emissary survived its entry into the Jovian atmosphere—how we don't know—and evolved into this." She replaced the first video with another of the vessel that had transported the Seed of Hope to the habitat at L2.

"What we didn't realize until yesterday," she continued, "was that the emissary was not the first Cenanti vessel to arrive in our solar system."

She replaced the second visual with another view of Jupiter's cloud cover. This one, however, was a time-lapsed montage. They watched as the Jovian atmosphere lit up again and again with energy discharges similar to the first. "We have identified eight different impacts over a six-week period that occurred some twenty-eight months ago. The profile of these strikes matches the one associated with the arrival of the Seed of Hope. The emissary has since confirmed these other eight represent the seeds of terraforming vessels sent ahead of its arrival."

"I have one more visual to show you," Sinhi said, before the questions could begin. She did so now. It was the image of a vessel cradled in what looked like some sort of floating dry dock.

It was hard to make out any details, but this vessel seemed larger—much larger—than the craft the emissary had arrived in. While construction was clearly going on around the ship, work seemed to be nearly complete. "We are told this is a fully realized terraforming vessel, a constructor, one of many currently being built within the Jovian atmosphere."

"Where are they getting the raw materials?" the Martian representative wanted to know. "Jupiter's atmosphere is made up almost entirely of hydrogen and helium."

"Apparently, they're using some sort of controlled fusion to create the heavier elements they need."

She let them think about that for a moment. No one said anything. While humans had mastered the comparatively simple art of turning hydrogen into helium, to create heavier elements like oxygen and carbon involved temperatures many times greater than those found in the Sun. Creating even heavier elements like gold or uranium normally required energies produced by supernovas or colliding neutron stars.

Clearly, the Cenanti had come up with a more energy-efficient approach.

"Once again," she went on. "We don't have any details. It's difficult to get a reliable estimate as to the size of that vessel, but we believe it's nearly four hundred meters from end to end."

"How do we know that's not a warship?" the president from the Lunar Free States demanded.

"Obviously we don't," M'Bala replied. "And I suggest we don't put it to the test. With their manufacturing capabilities, they could create an armada under the cloak of Jupiter's cloud cover and we wouldn't be able to touch them."

"Which means we need to attack them now, while they're still weak." It was a remark that Sinhi would have expected from a man who possessed more bluster than brains. There was an embarrassed silence.

M'Bala turned to Sinhi again in a request for her to respond. She did so with insulting formality. "Mr. President, Jupiter has a surface area more than a hundred times that of Earth with an atmosphere thousands of kilometers deep, under conditions that make the most violent hurricanes on Earth seem like a gentle breeze by comparison. We don't know where that dockyard is, whether there is more than one of them, and no way to reach them if we did. Also, keep in mind that the 'seed' vessels the Cenanti sent ahead have already survived entry impacts that would have obliterated any city on Earth. Or Luna." She paused significantly at that last. "Just what space fleet were you thinking of sending to dispatch these aliens?"

The last remark was wholly facetious. Humanity had no "space fleet." It had no interplanetary warships of any kind. The only military vessels it possessed were a handful of orbital transfer vehicles used to carry peacekeepers from one habitat to another and transport the occasional prisoner.

In another century, there might be space pirates to hunt down and smugglers to interdict. The various worlds might even have their own navies. For the moment, however, colonization of the system was still too new.

The silence which followed that remark was even more thoughtful than the last.

M'Bala let the silence drag on for another minute. "Thank you, Minister." She turned her attention back to the others. "Clearly, we need to come to some sort of arrangement with our visitors. For all of our sakes."

"If I may?" Ayad spoke again.

"Please," M'Bala said.

"I agree in spirit with the Minister's comments. Launching an attack on the Cenanti would be both dangerous and premature. It would also be criminal if the Cenanti are here to treat with us in good faith. However, it would be equally foolish to take what they have told us at face value without confirming the facts for ourselves."

"Agreed," the Martian representative said, a bearlike man by the name of Burnell. The Ceres representative, a tiny, wizened woman who had to be well into her second century, nodded as well.

"So, how do we do that?" M'Bala asked.

Sinhi was sure the Planetary Coordinator had her own ideas, but the woman always tried to lead by consensus. It had served her well in the past.

Here, the answer seemed obvious. "We ask for a tour," Sinhi said.

The Cenanti constructor hung in the near distance, a silver splinter set against the backdrop of Jupiter's splendor. The gas giant didn't just fill the sky, it *was* the sky. Sinhi had never been out as far as Jupiter, not in the flesh. Remote images were one thing. The reality was something completely different.

"Well, that looks genuine enough," Burnell said, focused more on the Cenanti vessel than the natural splendor laid out before him.

Sinhi had to agree. The constructor was throwing back the same confused readings they had received from the Seed of Hope, but lidar reported the larger Cenanti vessel was over four hundred meters in length and nearly one hundred meters in width.

This vessel, however, was powered by massive fusion engines.

The biggest space-going vessels humans had ever built were less than two hundred meters long. In comparison, the Cenanti constructor was a dozen times larger by volume and probably the same by mass. Also, it had lifted from somewhere within the Jovian atmosphere against a force of more than two gravities at the upper reaches of the cloud layer.

It made the Minister for Extra-Planetary Affairs think of the old, wooden European sailing ships as opposed to the massive metal vessels of later centuries.

"Seed of Hope," Sinhi said through the open channel they were maintaining with the Cenanti emissary. "Why doesn't the constructor have a warp drive?"

The Seed of Hope had not only accompanied them on the trip to Jupiter, it had given them a lift by enfolding the human vessel within its warp field. Unassisted, it would have taken a month to reach Jupiter using the best fusion drives humanity could yet build. Cradled in the warp field generated by the Seed of Hope, the trip had taken only three days.

The human ship they had made the journey in was named

the *MaryBeth*, an OTV whose usual task was to ferry people and materials from low Earth orbit to geosync or the L4 and L5 Lagrange points. It did not have the engines to make the long trip to Jupiter itself, but did have the cargo capacity and life support systems to carry everyone selected for the trip, as well as the equipment they wanted to bring.

"Warp-enabled ships are difficult to build, and constructors are intended for other purposes. Even my drive is useful only for limited, interplanetary distances."

As impressive as the Cenanti's warp drive was, the alien AI had informed them that it was not capable of faster than light travel. It could, however, propel a spacecraft at relativistic, sub-light velocities, reducing the length of an interstellar voyage from thousands of years down to mere decades.

Ayad spoke up in cher cool voice. "I have been wondering. The *Born of Violent Winds* is the size of a small moon. Why build such a large ship to colonize another world? It does not seem practical."

A small subset of the representatives who had attended the meeting in geosync had made the trip out to Jupiter—Sinhi, the delegates for Mars and Ceres, and Ayad. The president of the Lunar Free States had *not* been invited. No one wanted to spend a week in close quarters with the man.

"I believe the difficulty lies in your conception of the *Born of Violent Winds* as a colony ship. It is not. It represents the totality of this social and political gestalt of the Cenanti. Everything this clade of the Cenanti currently is resides within its confines."

"So it's their home," Ayad said.

To Sinhi, it made the Cenanti's migratory nature more understandable. They really never left their world behind. They took it with them wherever they went.

"Exactly," the Seed of Hope replied. "Are your probes ready?"

While the *MaryBeth* had made the trip all the way out to Jupiter, it did not possess the capability to travel the last few thousand kilometers to the Cenanti construction facilities. While comparatively rugged by human standards, the OTV had been designed for vacuum and was completely unsuited to handle either the pressures or the wind speeds it would have encountered in the Jovian atmosphere.

Instead, the humans were relying on automated instrument packages to gather the information they wanted. Such probes had been used for decades to study the gas giants and the uninviting surfaces of Venus and Mercury.

Sinhi turned to the captain of the *MaryBeth*, another neoform. "Captain, whenever you're ready."

They had all gathered in the forward observation cabin to get a firsthand view of the Cenanti constructor. The captain nodded, turned back to cher workstation, and triggered the release of the package. "Probes deployed."

Sinhi had specifically requested a ship with a neoform in command, as she trusted their ability not to let emotion override common sense should events take an unexpected turn.

The package, a collection of six probes, was briefly visible as it accelerated away from the *MaryBeth*. Or rather, as the Seed of Hope wrapped the probes in a smaller volume of warped spacetime and pushed them to the edge of its warp field.

It was an impressive display of control. Sinhi did not know if the Cenanti emissary was showing off or if manipulating the very fabric of spacetime really was as easy as the alien AI made it seem. On the trip out from Earth, the Seed of Hope had thoughtfully provided them with 0.25 g of apparent gravity to make the journey more pleasant.

Artificial gravity at last. The experts were already trying to figure out how the Cenanti manipulated spacetime with such finesse. Knowing something was theoretically possible and seeing it used as a mature technology was something else entirely.

Once past the Seed of Hope's warp field, the package fired up its fusion drive and headed toward the constructor under its own power. It took only minutes. Once there, the individual probes deployed, moving to form a constellation pattern around the immense vessel.

When the captain was satisfied with the status of the probes, cher gave the okay. The constructor fired up its engines and descended once again into Jupiter's atmosphere, surrounded by its human-made observers. Now it was just a matter of waiting.

Sinhi and the others, along with the captain and cher crew, monitored the data feeds from the probes as the constructor descended through the outer layers of Jupiter's atmosphere. As the density of the atmosphere increased, so did the wind velocities. Sinhi knew that within the troposphere those velocities could reach up to four hundred meters per second, almost one thousand five hundred kilometers an hour.

While the probes could withstand such an environment—it was what they had been designed for, after all—they would not have been able to make the trip unescorted. The odds of the probes being able to rendezvous at any specific location in such a raging chaos would have been practically zero.

After a time, Sinhi turned her attention from the endless storm that was Jupiter to the Cenanti constructor. Using the data feed from all six probes, the humans onboard the *MaryBeth* could get a 360-degree view of the massive vessel. At this range, it seemed more like an asteroid or some other planetary body—except for its sculpted, almost organic curves. The form of the ship was so graceful it seemed to Sinhi that aesthetics must have featured significantly into its design.

She wondered how such a craft coped with the pressures it must encounter within the Jovian atmosphere. If the Cenanti vessels continued to descend far enough, the pressure would increase until the atmosphere turned into a world-spanning ocean of liquid metallic hydrogen. Just how indestructible was the Cenanti vessel? There had to be some limit to the aliens' technology.

As the ship and its tiny escorts descended through the thickening atmosphere, the light around them faded away to nothing. Jupiter was over five AUs from the Sun, which meant it got less than four percent of the solar radiation received by Earth. When it got too dark for even light magnification systems to provide reasonable images, the captain switched on the small but powerful floodlights the probes were equipped with.

In response, the Cenanti constructor turned on its own lights.

Or rather, sections of the hull began to glow—long ribbons of light that gave it the appearance of some exotic deep-sea creature. Like the probes, the huge vessel was using radar as well, but that would only be effective for relatively short distances—at least as far as Jovian scales went.

How it knew where it was going in pitch darkness, over distances measuring tens of thousands of kilometers, no one onboard the *MaryBeth* could determine. Perhaps inertial navigation. Perhaps something more exotic. The Cenanti weren't giving their secrets away yet.

An hour after their departure, the probes reported a radar contact ahead. A few minutes later, as the range closed, a dim shape slowly emerged from the dense clouds of water ice crystals and ammonium hydrosulfide.

"Aiya! Is that a fish?" Shen Wu, the delegate from Ceres, asked. Most of the food in the Belt was vat-grown, but the colonists there had retained a taste for aquaculture.

It *did* look like a fish, if a fish could be several kilometers long. It was hard to get a feeling for its size but, if the radar reading sent back by the probes were at all accurate, it was at least that big.

Like the constructor, it was ribboned in light. In shape, it was flat along its sides and thinner than it was tall. There were no eyes or a mouth, but the impression that it was a living creature was hard to shake. Then Sinhi realized it was actually moving. That is, flexing slightly from side to side as if actually swimming.

"While not organic, it can be said to be fishlike in function," the Seed of Hope replied.

"It really swims through the Jovian atmosphere?" the Martian delegate marveled. Humans had built floating platforms in Venus's thick atmosphere, but those were passive things that went where the winds dictated. This shape, as titanic as it was, moved like a living creature as it fought the dense winds raging at trans-hurricane velocities.

"Its primary purpose is to maintain a roughly consistent altitude and position. Therefore, you could say that it 'swims' to stay in place."

KRISTEN HADAWAY

Sinhi would never have imagined such a thing. A moon-sized starship was one thing. This was even harder to absorb.

"You see the grooves along its sides?" the alien AI continued. "The Jovian atmosphere enters through those intake channels and is then compressed and accelerated before being propelled through outlet ports in the rear."

Sinhi realized that the grooves it was referring to must be tens of meters wide. She could not imagine the power required for such an immense construct to maintain its position in this environment.

"Marvelous," Ayad breathed, a look of childlike wonder on cher face.

The comment went unremarked, as the constructor neared one smooth flank. As it did, a portal slid open to receive it. Only then did Sinhi gain a real appreciation for the scale of what she was seeing. The opening, as small as it appeared from a distance, was easily large enough to accommodate the constructor, as well as its small flotilla of escorts.

As the probes entered the megastructure, they could see that the interior was well lit. In fact, it reminded Sinhi of the interior of one of the big cylindrical habitats at L5. Every interior surface of the vast shape seemed to be alive with light and activity.

Sinhi noticed as well that the pressure reported by the probes, a dozen times greater than that found on Earth, did not drop as they entered. Perhaps that explained how the Cenanti vessel could handle the crushing pressure of the Jovian atmosphere. It did not try. Sinhi was just knowledgeable enough to know that such a solution must have introduced its own complications, even if she did not know what those might be.

The Cenanti vessel really was like some fantastic underwater creature.

Looking at the vast, cavernous space, Sinhi realized she had initially conjured up the wrong analogy. The structure wasn't like some static, hollowed-out habitat. It was like a living cell. There was activity going on *everywhere*. Not just along the walls, but throughout the interior.

She couldn't pretend to comprehend the intricacies of what she was witnessing, but it really did appear to be like the working of a living thing, with a bewildering collection of organelles performing a variety of unknown functions. She recognized the partially realized forms of half a dozen constructors—each similar to the one escorting the probes. The sheer scope of such an operation boggled the mind.

If the humans had truly harbored any doubts as to the Cenanti claims, they could now be put to rest.

The presence of a breathable atmosphere gave the maintenance bay of the L2 habitat a different appearance, softening the sharp shadows cast by the work lights overhead. Seating cradles had been fixed in a semicircle around the housing holding the alien AI—a distinctly informal setting for one of the most important discussions to be held in living memory. Three of the people sitting in those chairs were Sinhi, M'Bala, and Ayad. Two other people were present as well—Burnell, the Martian delegate, and Shen Wu, the representative from Ceres.

Once again, the leader of the Lunar Free States had not been invited. With the Moon off the table as a possible host site, he had no grounds on which to make such a demand.

The Cenanti emissary had greeted them all cordially, seemingly with an infinite amount of patience. Sinhi knew the AI was not only in contact with its own people but that it was also monitoring all human communications it could access.

Direct contact with the alien was still restricted. It was a situation that couldn't last for much longer.

"Mercury would be acceptable, although not ideal," the AI observed. "Your sun would provide us with all the energy we require, and the abundant supply of raw material would be very useful. However, we would have to build our habitats deep within the planet."

"Mercury would not be our first choice," M'Bala said carefully. "It's too important for the future development of the solar system."

"So we had surmised."

"We?" Sinhi asked.

"Myself and the AIs in control of the terraforming vessels."

"Ah."

"What of Titan?" the AI continued. "With suitable terraforming, it would be acceptable." They had already ruled out any of Jupiter's moons.

"We have plans for Titan as well," Shen Wu replied carefully. "Perhaps one of Saturn's other moons?"

"None of them are large enough. Titan represents ninety-six percent of the total mass of the planet's satellites. Even if we were to combine all the other moons together, along with the rings, it would not provide enough living space."

The Ceres delegate looked shocked—although Sinhi couldn't tell whether it was due to the scope of such an engineering feat or the proposed destruction of Saturn's glorious ring system.

"What about Uranus? Would any of its moons be acceptable?" Burnell asked, without much hope.

"The same problem applies. All of them combined are not big enough to accommodate the Cenanti. Even your own Moon would hardly be big enough. We suggested it initially only because it seemed of little real value and therefore assumed you would not mind parting with it."

The alien AI still did not seem to understand why the humans were so adamant on the subject, even though it had come to accept the fact. They were running out of choices. If Pluto wasn't so bloody far away, Sinhi thought, it might actually have been the best option. Even with Cenanti technology, however, there wasn't enough time to alter its orbit to bring it deeper into the system.

Besides, moving a body the size of Pluto anywhere near the habitable zone surrounding the Sun would have screwed up the orbits of all the planets in the inner solar system. Eventually.

"Someone is going to have to give up something," M'Bala remarked. "Think of what we'll be getting in return."

"Easy for you to say," Shen Wu said. "Are you offering to give us the lion's share of the technology to make such a sacrifice worthwhile?"

This was just what M'Bala had been worried about, Sinhi realized. No one would willingly give up access to the wealth the Cenanti were offering, yet someone would have to pay the price.

"Would it be possible to divide the Cenanti into smaller groups?" she suggested. "That way, no one world would have to bear the entire burden alone."

"Possible? Yes," the Seed of Hope answered. "But the consequences for the Cenanti would be profound. Separating the Cenanti into smaller breeding populations would destroy their existing cultural identity and create numerous, smaller clades, each with its own distinct personality and priorities. It would be a form of racial suicide. I believe the Cenanti would only accept such a course if there were absolutely no other option available."

The humans considered that for a moment. To Sinhi, that not only sounded bad for the Cenanti but for humanity as well. One advanced alien presence would be disruptive enough. Multiple, possibly competing, alien factions could end up being a nightmare.

"If Venus weren't such a hellhole, you could have the whole damn planet," she said in frustration. Of course, she thought, if Venus weren't such a hellhole humanity would have colonized it already.

There was a pause. "You would part with Venus?" the AI replied after a moment. It was hard to attribute genuine emotion to an inorganic construct, and an alien one at that, but Sinhi could swear it sounded surprised.

"Terraforming Venus simply isn't feasible," she replied. "Not in any kind of reasonable time frame." Humans had certainly given the idea enough thought. It just wasn't possible.

"Why do you say that?" the AI replied.

"You have to ask?" Not only was the atmospheric pressure nearly a hundred times that found on Earth, the surface temperature was hot enough to melt lead. "Even if you had a hundred constructors, you couldn't do it, not in just two centuries. It would take thousands of constructors."

"Then we will build thousands. Tens of thousands, if necessary."

There was another silence. "Are you serious?" M'Bala finally asked.

"We can create as many work vessels as needed. Currently we have eight, soon we will have sixteen, then twenty-four. That is with only one factory. The more factories we build, the more constructors they can produce. As long as we have enough energy and matter, we can build as many constructors as required."

"You still can't terraform a planet like Venus in two hundred years," Shen Wu said.

"You are mistaken. We never suggested Venus as an option because it seemed far too valuable—in our eyes—to part with."

"You can really do this?" M'Bala asked.

"We can. Is this a serious proposal? Are you offering the planet Venus in exchange for our technology and knowledge?"

The Planetary Coordinator looked at the others in the room and saw no immediate dissent. "We will need to have a better idea of exactly what you are offering, but...yes. In principle, we would consider it."

"We would want some of these constructors as well," the Martian representative threw in quickly.

"As would we," the Ceres delegate added. "I'm assuming that they could be modified for mining, yes?"

It had been years since Sinhi had been on Earth. Sitting across from the Planetary Coordinator, she remembered why. If the gravity wasn't bad enough, there was the heat, the rain, the insects, and the dirt. M'Bala had insisted on her presence to help sell the deal to EarthGov and all its quarreling factions.

The full details concerning the Cenanti's eventual arrival—all twenty billion of them—had finally been released. The response had been mixed, to say the least. Footage of the Cenanti fabrication ship "swimming" through the atmosphere of Jupiter had been met with awe. News that the aliens were prepared to share their technology had been received with glee. Reaction to the announcement that Venus would be ceded to the Cenanti in exchange had not been nearly so positive.

It seemed that while humanity was thrilled with the knowledge that other intelligent life existed in the universe, people weren't so sure they wanted aliens living next door. It was the same old story. Sinhi often thought that the species could do with more neoforms.

EarthGov had stressed that the arrangement wasn't permanent. The Cenanti had been granted a lease to the planet for five hundred years, with an option for five hundred more, contingent on the consent of both parties. And only on the further condition that Venus was eventually made habitable for humans—who would retain visiting rights.

It had been felt that the conditional renewal would make it easier for people to accept—human nature being what it was. Sinhi had decided they needed a public relation campaign to paint the Cenanti in the best light possible—and to stress the advantages of the arrangement for humanity. The Seed of Hope was already making its presence known on social media and seemed to have a deft grasp of human psychology.

"Well, it's done," M'Bala said. She looked like she could use a vacation. Convincing an earthbound humanity about the facts of life had not been easy. "Do you think they can really do it?"

"The Cenanti?" Sinhi asked. "Yes, I think they can." Like the Seed of Hope had said, if the Cenanti needed a thousand terraformers—or ten thousand—then that's what they would build. Sinhi knew the aliens were already working on another of the huge "fish" factories to pump out more constructors. Jupiter could supply them with all the resources they needed, and there was nothing humans could do about it even if they wanted to.

"But, Venus? Really?"

Sinhi had been working on the numbers with her own AIs. Hell, everyone was doing it. The crushing atmosphere on Earth's sister planet shouldn't prove much of a problem for the technology the aliens commanded. If the Cenanti could use the Jovian atmosphere to build constructors, there wasn't any reason they couldn't do the same thing on Venus. Doing so would actually solve two problems at once.

As for the heat, well, that was just energy waiting to be used. It would take some truly massive engineering, but scale was obviously not something that intimidated the Cenanti.

"Do they know that a 'day' on Venus is actually 243 days long?" the Coordinator went on. "And that the planet rotates in the wrong direction? The weather is going to be a nightmare."

Sinhi realized the Coordinator must have been boning up on her knowledge of the solar system.

"The direction of rotation doesn't really matter," she replied. "And the Cenanti evolved on a tidally locked planet. The length of the day is actually a selling point as far as they're concerned. The Cenanti *like* extreme weather. It plays an important part in their life cycle."

M'Bala thought about it for a moment, then finally nodded. She didn't seem any happier, though. Sinhi watched as the other woman ran a thin finger along one eyebrow.

"What is it?" she asked. She didn't know the Coordinator that well—they were colleagues, not friends—but she could tell something was bothering her.

"I just can't help feeling that we've only postponed the crisis. We're in no shape to say no to the Cenanti at the moment, but if what I've been told about the technology we'll be getting turns out to be true, in 170 years we might not *want* to give up Venus."

"We did what we could," Sinhi replied. She wasn't worried. She had spent her career "juggling oranges" as Earthers would put it. (And in habitats where Coriolis forces were a real, demonstrable thing, that was no trivial matter.) During that time, she had come to realize that all solutions were temporary solutions. Only death was final.

"Besides," she went on. "I don't think you're looking at it correctly."

"And how should I be looking at it?"

"In 170 years, with the technology we'll be getting, we won't *need* Venus."

"You're talking about building colony ships of our own?" M'Bala replied doubtfully. "I don't see how that's going to—"

Sinhi shook her head. "Forget interstellar colonization. Okay, don't forget about it, since with the Cenanti warp technology, it's finally going to be feasible. As far as *this* solar system goes, it doesn't matter."

"I'm not following," the other said.

Sinhi had to remember that the Planetary Coordinator had grown up on a planet. That's how such people tended to think—in terms of planets. "With Cenanti technology, we can build our own megastructures. As many as we want. To hold as many people as we want. We won't need planets anymore."

She wasn't talking about Dyson spheres or anything so exotic. She also wasn't thinking about the tiny habitats that humans had cobbled together so far. With Cenanti-level technology, they would be able to build megastructures whose interior spaces could hold tens of millions, perhaps hundreds of millions, of people. And they would be able to put them anywhere in the system where there was energy—and a reasonable orbit—to make such things practical.

A planet was actually an incredibly inefficient way to construct a biosphere, using a ball of solid rock thousands of kilometers in diameter just to support a thin film of life on its outer surface. It was a wasteful, unimaginative way to construct a habitat—not to mention a fragile one.

When you calculated how much livable space there was for free-floating habitats within the solar system, even staying within the plane of the ecliptic, the numbers beggared the imagination.

People would go to the stars at last. That was inevitable. They wouldn't need to, though. Not if they didn't want to. The people who wanted to stay here would have all the room they could ever hope for.

The problem would actually be coming up with the raw material. But there were always the outer gas giants—as well as the Kuiper Belt and the Oort cloud. Something else the Cenanti warp technology could help with.

The Coordinator didn't look like she was buying it. Sinhi let it go. It didn't matter. The people who needed to live on a planet weren't the ones who would build the future she was envisioning, anyway.

And it was all thanks to Earth's sister planet, ignored for so long.

Sinhi was familiar with another Earther term, white elephant, referring to a large, expensive and entirely useless gift. For generations, many had viewed Venus as just such a white elephant, big and gaudy, but of no real value to anyone.

How wrong they had been.

While there were many who would no doubt fear the Cenanti occupation of Venus, Sinhi was not one of them. She couldn't wait to see what they did with the place.

Piracy for Beginners

written by

J. R. Johnson

illustrated by

CHRIS BINNS

ABOUT THE AUTHOR

J. R. Johnson was raised in the folded Appalachian hills of Pennsylvania, where she learned to love autumn, blueberries straight from the bush, and the stream beneath the willows near her house. The fact that fall is inevitably followed by winter, that picking berries means crossing paths with bears, and that the stream was laced with dioxins may also have had some impact on her outlook.

Growing up in a home without a television shaped her approach to entertainment. Step one: read all the books. There is no step two. Eventually, she decided to try writing what she loved to read: space, magic, adventure, self-rescuing princesses, and underdogs fighting against the odds.

"Piracy for Beginners" started with the thought that no matter the backdrop, where there are ships, there are pirates. It grew into a story about a woman's quest to escape the ghosts of her past, protect her people, and do the right thing in a difficult situation.

In addition to writing, J. R. Johnson has studied history, geography and policy, circumnavigated the globe, and enjoys making things with her hands. She now lives in Ontario with her husband, woodshop and, of course, cat.

ABOUT THE ILLUSTRATOR

Chris Binns was born in 1981 in Reading, England, but was quickly whisked away to live in Hillsboro, Oregon, at the young age of five, due to the relocation of his father's engineering job. Throughout childhood Chris was always the "good drawer," a pastime that was encouraged by his family over the years and heavily inspired by the plethora of fantasy novels his father would read on a weekly basis. The covers of these fantasy novels were a shining beacon to what would become his most coveted genre. Despite his love of art, Chris found himself graduating from high school and heading off to electrical engineering school at Oregon State University to follow in his father's footsteps.

While taking a break from university in 2005, Chris moved to England to work in a pub in Manchester for the summer. This was when Chris found his wife Lyndsey, who would eventually become the mother of his two children, and the summer turned into six years.

Deciding to take his art more seriously, Chris attended the University of Huddersfield for an illustration degree. After graduating with honors and some newfound knowledge and skills, Chris moved back to America. While struggling to kick-start an art career and needing to provide for his family, he took an engineering job at Intel. Finding his footing as an engineer and thriving in this new role, Chris learned to feed both vocations. These days, art is still very much his passion as he seeks new challenges to test his skill sets and push his art to the next level. However, like the children's books he writes and illustrates for his children, he creates art for fun and enjoys every minute of it.

Piracy for Beginners

Luna concourse stretched out like an impact scar, a thin line of habitability scratched into the face of the moon. Vessels loomed in irregular rows outside the aging plascryl dome like a boxer's smile after a losing fight. The soles of my dress boots whispered over the sealed regolith floor.

I had come early to run preflight checks on *The Liana*, an aging passenger ship converted into a shuttle. Newer vessels had all been commandeered for the war effort. Most hadn't come back. Now if you wanted to make the trip between Earth and the moon, you had to take the bus. My bus.

A faint ping echoed from the third lock ahead, as if from a dropped bolt, then silence.

My ship was at Lock Three and I hadn't ordered any work. I reached for my service weapon and found nothing but an empty belt.

Right. Not with the Defence Corps anymore. Just a glorified transit driver who even lost her clearance to carry a gun.

The passenger terminal had two sides lined with thick concrete pillars and staggered locks like a ground-side airport, but none of the activity. Not like the military dock. No screens blared the latest news. Squeaking filters circulated air a month stale. Even the vending machines sat half empty. It had been a long, hard war.

Even now, I wasn't sure I'd been on the right side.

I caught a whiff of day-old beer and turned as the blow came down. A weapon skimmed past my skull and hit my shoulder instead. The one I'd injured fighting over Luna's far side, of course. Pain shot through my back. I twisted left and scrambled away across the rough floor.

A man, dressed in black with the build of a career spacer, wielded a length of pipe and a snarl. He came at me again but I skipped out of the way.

Right into his friend's fist.

Stars flared and my eyes watered. If there were more than two I was screwed, I couldn't see a thing. I stumbled back against a column and blinked hard, trying to clear my vision.

The second man was lean and twitchy, shaking his hand like he didn't know how to throw a punch. No pipe for him, just a tool belt and a jumpsuit that made him look like any other port worker. The rest of the concourse was empty.

I tasted iron on my lips, wrinkled my nose at the men's acrid sweat. Where the hell were the port guards? I reconsidered as soon as the thought appeared. Better to be the only one at risk.

"We're out of time, finish her," the second man said. He looked nervous, but not about me.

His mistake.

Thug Number One hefted the pipe and came at me straight. Maybe he was strong enough to bull through most violent situations.

Not me. As a woman almost always outweighed by her opponents, I'd learned to use guile.

I huddled against the concrete support, legs braced, shaking my head like I was still dazed. Like I didn't see Thug Number One with his pipe and bad attitude. I added a whimper. For effect, you understand.

The idiot bought it.

I launched off the column. He swung, a split second too slow. Missed, and then I was inside his guard. I blocked left, too focused to feel the blow, then led with my right knee, not quite a bull's-eye but close enough. He fell back with a groan. The pipe clattered to the ground.

Thug Number Two stood there with his mouth open.

Luna Control had warned pilots about a rash of hijackings but that was out in the black, not portside. These guys seemed like your regular run-of-the-mill crims, looking to export something off the books. But they hadn't approached me direct like good smugglers.

I could take them both if they decided to gang up on me, but it would hurt. Capturing them would also result in a schedule delay, due to what would no doubt be a considerable amount of paperwork.

"Make up your minds," I said.

They cut their losses and ran.

"What. The. Hell."

I wiped my face. My hand came away bloody and my lip ached from the punch. Great, now I'd look like I spent my off hours starring in an underground fight ring.

I brought up the ship interface on my wrist display as I headed for the lock. *The Liana*'s systems registered green across the board.

I put in a call request, then palmed the airlock as I waited for the signal to make its way through Luna's network.

The iris withdrew with a little sigh and a puff of sterile air. Finally, I was home.

The Liana started life as a tourist liner but was later turned into a cargo hauler for Luna expansion bases. Unlike most vessels on the Luna–Earth circuit, she was more container ship than speedboat. She was old and ungainly even to kind eyes, but she was solid with room to spare.

The shortest path to the cockpit skirted the passenger areas and crossed through the darkened cargo hold. My footsteps echoed in the cavernous space.

I ducked around a sealed pallet and headed out into the corridor, still comfortable enough in lunar gravity to ignore the zero-g grab bars.

Halfway to the cockpit my call went through.

"Go for Head Controller, Quito Base."

"Marvin, just say your name like everyone else. We work for a glorified bus company." I'd had it up to here with his delusions of grandeur about five minutes after I got stuck with this job.

"We're public ambassadors to both Earth and Luna. Appearances must be maintained. Also schedules."

I noticed he didn't feel the need to call me captain. "Spare me. You know I hate politics."

"Explains why you're crap at it."

Well. He wasn't wrong there.

"I need to report an attack."

Another voice interjected, about three feet to my right. "What attack?"

I nearly jumped out of my skin before I recognized the looming shadow. Dunn, the newest addition to my crew.

What was he doing on board so early?

"Marvin, I'll call you back."

My face hurt from all the damn smiling. Also the punch. I was back in the concourse. Whoever decided we needed to wear full-dress uniform to welcome passengers before every flight was a sadist and should be shot.

A dock rep herded my little flock of passengers across the open hall to the airlock, guiding them around the worst of the damage. Dirt lurked in corners and spider-web crazing etched the surface of the dome. Repair crews had done a good job rebuilding the port, but the floor still carried battle scars. Much like me.

I rolled my bad shoulder, trying to make the starched fabric chafe less. Dunn shot me a reproving glance. Probably hoping I'd act the part, a sure sign we hadn't worked together very long.

At a well-built six-feet-plus tall, my newest crew member either lied about his height to get into space or pulled a lot of strings. He was also charming enough to get away with it. *He* had no problem schmoozing with passengers. I wished I could leave him to it and get back to doing something that mattered. Like figuring out why those thugs jumped me, and why Dunn had been skulking around when it happened. He claimed he hadn't seen a thing, and I didn't know him well enough to call truth or lie. What I did know was that he came with enviable recommendations and was wasted on *The Liana*. So why the hell was he here?

I missed my old job. Things made sense in the military. Everyone knew everyone else's business, good and bad. Meant you could trust people, even if it only meant you could trust them to be an idiot.

My first passenger was a grey-haired gentleman with the hefty build and tanned skin of a lunar visitor. I shook his hand and smiled. He didn't flinch. Points for me.

"Captain Ridgeworth?"

"Please," I said. "Call me Stick." My mother would have rolled over in her grave, but I hadn't gone by Stacia since flight school.

His fingers twitched as he shot a look back to the dock entrance. Worried about being followed? I automatically tracked and catalogued every person within fifty meters before I caught myself.

Much as I might miss it, it wasn't my job to solve puzzles or save the day, not anymore. That life was over. I had it on good authority that Admiral Declan still swore whenever my name came up. Maybe he was right and I had lost my edge. Maybe I should have quit when they forced me to serve out the rest of my time in this dead-end position. Ordering a soldier to serve as a civilian contractor without her say so. Pretty sure everything about that was illegal.

Still, this was the job. It wasn't saving the world but it was mine and I'd do it right. Don't even mention the obvious iffiness of this supposedly random collection of strangers who just happened to look like a top-secret delegation.

Still, after five years in the Defence Corps and a drawer full of commendations, this was a hell of a way to go out.

I pasted the smile back on and turned to greet the next passenger. If nothing else, I needed the money.

Back inside, I watched from the passenger compartment doorway as Dunn got the last of our load strapped into acceleration couches. I kept my shoulders back, head up, and a benevolent half smile pasted on my face to pacify the inmates.

The trip would be long enough without having to peel panicked civilians off the walls. Nothing to see here, just a nice quiet ride from Luna to Earth.

Now I had to make it happen.

I don't like space. Maybe that sounds funny coming from a spaceship pilot, but there it is.

Space is dark, cold, and you have to go an awfully long way to get a decent beer.

That said, it's the only place I feel free.

Six hours in. The coffee was hot and strong enough to keep me awake. I hoped. Chris, my purser, stood at the beverage station with a hopeful smile. Quiet and competent, Chris had served with me for years. I'd met her parents, had dinner at their house. I had tried to convince her to stay with Declan's Special Ops Division, but she followed me to this backwater post like a little sister who insists on tagging along. Some days she was all that kept me sane.

I thanked her for the coffee and headed into the corridor to start my rounds.

A shudder ran through the ship. My personal status display listed all indicators green. The corridor monitor showed the standard in-flight progress animation, no sign of trouble.

Chris popped her head out of the galley.

"Captain?"

"It may be nothing, but corral the passengers and secure the cabin."

I pressed the mug into her hands and lit out for the flight deck.

The floor shook again, and this time the vibrations lasted longer. I palmed my way into the cockpit and locked the door behind me. The smell of vat leather and warm electronics greeted me, but nothing else. What the hell?

"Talk to me, Ship."

Instead of the soothing mechanical voice of my counterpart I got the last thing I wanted to hear.

The ear-splitting peal of an emergency bell.

I lunged across the cockpit and smacked the master alarm. The harsh klaxon that screamed "panic now, people!" did not stop. *The Liana of Kaua'i*, founding ship of the Sol Transport Fleet and my pride and joy, was doing her damnedest to kill everyone on board.

Gravity hiccupped. The second I spent floating in front of the display screens was plenty of time to appreciate the blue glow of flame leaking from engine number four.

Gravity came back. I fell awkwardly but managed to get my butt strapped into the chair. This was trouble. Worse than getting shot down over Luna Colony Prime. This time I had a ship full of passengers depending on me. And experience had cured me of the delusion of invincibility.

Fire-suppression interface, no response. Here's hoping *The Liana* could take care of it without my input.

Engine failure plus questionable gravity plus computer malfunction plus way too many lives at stake equalled an unmanageable situation. Time to call in the cavalry. All I had to do was keep my people safe until help arrived. I toggled the comms over to broadcast frequency. Who knows, they might even be able to hear me over the damn alarm.

"Mayday, mayday, mayday! Sol Control, this is *The Liana*, we are declaring an emergency. Controls are not responding and we are in the gravity well. Repeat, we are going down. Request emergency rescue intercept. Come in, Control!"

Still no answer, dammit. What were they doing, all getting coffee at the same time?

A loud knock echoed just behind my head. Dunn shouted from the other side of the cockpit door.

"Captain! What the hell's going on?"

"For God's sake, Dunn, calm down. We don't want to scare the passengers."

Dunn snorted through the locked door.

185

"Um, yeah, about that, sir. I'm pretty sure the alarms and intermittent gravity and streaks of freaking fire starboard are doing just fine in that department. Sir."

I opened my mouth to respond but sneezed instead. An acrid stench like burning paint filled the air. I might not be able to do anything about the grav or the engine, but I could shut off the damn alarm.

Time for the mother of all emergency overrides, the one used only in moments of absolute extremis, like being boarded or pulled into a black hole. Or being driven out of my mind by a freaking alarm. Control could sue me later.

If there was a later.

The override was a hardwired red button covered by a plastic flip top. Some smartass had scrawled "End-of-the-World Switch. Do Not Touch!" on it in permanent marker. I popped the cover.

"Are you sure you want to do that, Captain?"

"Seriously, *Liana*?" At least she was talking again. I hit the big red button. Blessed, blessed silence.

"The emergency is not yet over, Captain."

I bit back a few choice words and glared at the comm array. Given my luck, the cockpit recording would wash up on the desk of some admiral. No point giving them more reason to take away my command. If I had a ship left when this was all over.

The Liana was old but solid, and she'd been green on every preflight check in the six months we'd flown together. No way everything just went to hell with no warning.

I was a good pilot but insignificant as far as the universe was concerned. This couldn't be about me, but I wasn't the only one on board. I pulled up the passenger manifest. The list consisted of suspiciously generic names like Smith and Ali and Singh and Wu.

"Huh."

Funny how this lot appeared in my docking bay the day before secret trade meetings intended to put an end to conflict between Earth and the moon colonies once and for all.

If these people were commuters I'd eat my uniform.

I punched up diagnostics and frowned as lines of code scrolled across the screen.

Pounding on the cockpit door interrupted me. Again.

"What? I'm a little busy here, Dunn."

"No kidding, sir, but if you could spare a moment from crashing the ship, are we good to hit the passenger restraint system?"

I winced. I should have done that earlier. The passengers were belted in but if I couldn't right our trajectory, landing well, or at all, wasn't guaranteed. It would take a miracle for everyone to survive. Arming the tank of restraint foam would at least give them a fighting chance.

It also cost a freaking fortune to reset, but whatever. The way this trip was going, they could take it out of my death benefits.

"PRS activated."

Silence outside the door. I checked for Dunn on the external monitor.

"Go on, Dunn. I'll be fine here."

He frowned but settled for "Sir," then sprinted off down the corridor. I got back to work.

"*Liana*, what the hell happened?"

"An explosion triggered in the cargo hold moments after we reached cruising trajectory, Captain." The computer's voice sounded calm. That was probably the point.

"So someone did this to us." The thugs from Luna dock? But they were just hired help, surely. "I'll find the bastards and nail them to an asteroid later, but right now I need to save us. What can I do?"

"Nothing," the ship said. "The vessel is no longer coherent enough for re-entry and will disintegrate when we hit atmosphere."

I fell back into the flight couch and glared at the console. "Don't give me that. There has to be some path we can take, something we can do."

"Sorry, Captain, you're screwed."

My eyes snapped up to the camera. "What did you say?"

"I said, you're royally screwed, Captain Ridgeworth. Any last

187

wishes? You might as well chase after that tasty first mate of yours and, um, mate. Because you're dead."

Oh, no. "Get your dirty mind off the crew and tell me who you are. Because there's no way you're *The Liana*."

A creepy, robotic laugh rolled out of the speakers. "You got me. Finally, I might add. I've been in control since you left Moon dock. Too bad you didn't notice sooner, you might have seen the explosive detection warnings your system was trying so hard to get to you."

Good ship, I thought. Despite the quirks that came with years of incremental maintenance, I'd come to care for the old boat like a member of my own family. More, if you counted crazy Uncle Anton.

"Why do bad guys always want to gloat?" I pulled a piece of tape off the backup emergency manual and stuck it over the cockpit camera.

"Would you rather I let you die without knowing why? Besides, I worked hard," said the voice that sounded like *Liana* but was not. "It's nice to be appreciated. And who says I'm the villain here?"

"Between the two of us, which one is trying to crash a ship full of innocent people?"

"Innocent? Hardly. But you and your crew are victims, and that's regrettable."

I snorted at the audible lack of regret, then flipped to the last section of the manual. An old memory was tickling the back of my mind.

In the meantime, I had to keep them talking.

"Blah, blah, blah. You're just another nutjob trying to start a new war. What, peace isn't profitable enough for you?"

Somehow the computerized voice managed to sound pissed off.

"I'm doing what's right, which is more than I can say for those cowards in Ottawa."

"Yeah, God forbid they try to make the world a better place," I said. "So you decided to do something about it? Undermine the negotiations?"

"Damn right. Preliminary talks on Luna were just to hash out the basics in secret. Kill off the delegation now in a dramatic public gesture, the process collapses and we have a hundred years of bad blood. By then, we've remade the power structure to our liking. Simple."

I winced. The plan was beyond crazy but might actually work, dammit. I raced through the manual, hoping I could stall this lunatic long enough to find a way out.

"For someone about to turn into a fireball, you're awfully calm, Captain. What are you up to?"

"Umm, nothing?"

"Right," the voice said. "With a record like yours I should have known you were taking this too easily. Don't make me come up there, Captain."

Ha. The bastard was on board. Maybe we had a chance after all. I flipped through the Secondary Manual Supplement to find the bit on troubleshooting.

"You're willing to give your life just to slow down talks? Murder your way to a better world? You know that's nuts, right?"

"Insane? No. Necessary."

I scowled. "The only thing that has ever worked to bring humanity together is skin in the game. Long-term interdependency, trade, openness, and connection, that's the glue that keeps societies from falling apart. And I'm not talking about the vulture corporations and arms dealers who benefit from conflict. Don't tell me they didn't set this up."

"It doesn't matter who sponsored this mission. Painting the sky red with the blood of collaborators is exactly what we need."

What a stupid way to die. And for what, a few percentage points on some corporate balance sheet? Worse, this idiot had all the trappings of a true believer. Probably didn't even realize they were being used.

I shook my head at the sheer stupidity, then got back to work. Who was behind this? Several lines of code later I had at least part of an answer.

The saboteur was still lecturing, only now the voice coming through the speaker didn't sound anything like *The Liana*. It was a woman's voice, with a South-African lilt by way of the Lunar Lowlands. I'd met the owner of the voice this morning.

Karoleena Ford, assistant to the Lunar premier's chief of staff. A striking woman, tall and fine-limbed from years off Earth, her shaved head amber gold despite all the habitat time. And right now she was determined to kill everyone on board.

Thanks to the manual, I'd managed to activate the cockpit recorder. Even if Karoleena took us all down, both worlds would know what happened and why. With any luck, the talks wouldn't stall completely.

Good, great, yay. Now I had to keep my people alive.

Liana was functional, more or less, but locked out of the comm system. I could still link to her directly, and crucially, without speaking.

Karoleena was droning on about politics, like that's what anyone wants to hear in their last moments. One of fundamentalism's biggest weaknesses was that it lacked a sense of humour. Because good humour requires creativity, empathy, and tolerance. Also humour.

I typed as quietly as I could.

My ship acknowledged the message and began flooding the screen with bright red warning text. I stopped her.

> *time's short*

/ *The fire is contained but the engine is lost, we have a breach starboard side, and heat shields will be unreliable.*

Crap.

> *is backup up to date?*

/ *It is.*

> *can you isolate passengers?*

/ *Quarantine, incapacitate or kill?*

God, I loved this ship.

> *knock out only, but keep crew up if you can*

/ *One moment, please…*

/ *Done.*

Karoleena was still blabbing away. What had I missed?

> *why is she still talking?*

/ *Who?*

> *you can't hear that? wait, how many passengers on board?*

/ *Eighteen.*

Wrong. The true number was nineteen. Dammit. Karoleena must have a null field, a technology I had heard about but never seen. Expensive as hell, especially for a one-way trip.

> *bogey on board, track heat anomalies and knock her out*

Right effing now, I thought, or none of us are getting through this. I choked back a laugh. I always was something of an optimist.

/ *There is a hot spot in the galley.*

Ha. We had her.

> *lock her in and gas her*

/ *Gas is too dangerous near the galley equipment. The venting system will trigger.*

Locking her in would have to be enough.

/ *Please note that my structural integrity is decreasing. Anticipate complete breakup is likely approximately three hours and thirty-seven minutes before rescue could arrive.*

Great.

> *reroute comms to my unit*

I eased my legs off the chair and turned in slow motion, like trying to sneak past a sentry after midnight. It was going well until the titanium bar locking the cockpit door squealed. Karoleena stopped mid-rant.

"Still trying to win, Captain? That's adorable."

I made it out the door and halfway down the short corridor before Karoleena realized the cockpit lock wasn't the only one that had been triggered. Her shouts echoed down the corridor.

I yanked open the passenger cabin and almost ran into Dunn. My first mate's considerable muscle blocked the entrance. He had a stunner out and ready.

"Whoa, David, it's me. Stand down."

Dunn checked the corridor before handing over the stunner. Guns were sheer folly on a pressurized vessel, obviously, but we had energy weapons on board for emergencies.

This definitely qualified as an emergency.

"What's the plan, Captain?"

"Adapt and overcome," I said. Or die, I didn't say. My jaw tightened as adrenaline flashed through my system, familiar as an old friend.

"Evac may be a problem." Dunn pivoted away from the compartment door. The non-murderous members of the delegation lay passed out in acceleration couches.

"Had to be done," I said. "Suit rescue was never a good option for this group."

Dunn nodded in reluctant agreement.

"If we can't orient what's left of the heat shields, it's over," I said. "If structural integrity fails and we can't evacuate, it's over." I blew out a breath. Impending death was so much easier when I only had to worry about myself.

I dug deep into my bag of tricks and pulled out a big dose of leadership confidence. That usually worked, right?

"We can still get out of this in one piece." The blue-green planet out the window was looking less like a marble and more like a bowling ball. "If we hurry."

"Tell me what to do, Captain."

The ship spoke through my comm unit before I could reply.

"Captain, we have incoming."

"Seriously?" Was our luck changing?

"One vessel approaching from Luna."

Not Earth Defence, then.

"The transponder is spoofed, unless it really is a two-seater pleasure craft that looks like a military surplus store threw up on a luxury RV."

"Ah. Pirates, then?"

"Trajectory suggests they came from Luna's far side."

Definitely pirates.

"See that, Captain?" Karoleena crowed triumphantly through the speakers. "Did you think we wouldn't have a backup plan?"

"Can't blame a girl for hoping," I said. I kept my eyes on the small blip heading our way. I muted everything but my comm unit.

"*Liana*, ignore the transponder info and plot according to true mass."

The little blip got a lot bigger.

"It's not frigate class, Captain, but fast and large enough to do real damage. Especially in our current condition."

I flashed back to a particularly hairy fight over Luna and the damage a ship like that could do.

"They are deploying a docking tether, Captain."

I racked my brain for an out. Unlike that last battle over Luna, I couldn't just take my lumps, not with passengers to protect.

"Ready to surrender, Captain?"

Wait, what?

"Decided you don't have to die for the cause after all, Karoleena?"

"That was always plan B," Karoleena said, in what I'm sure she thought was a dignified tone.

"If you have a pet mercenary to play taxi, why put yourself at risk in the first place?"

"We all have to put skin in this game, prove our worth."

Interesting. So this was the space-based equivalent of a gang initiation? And if this was the gate, who was the keeper?

"There are half a dozen experienced fighters on that ship," she said. "You have ten minutes to consider your options. I'm confident you'll see it my way."

Oh, please. Still, I had to keep her talking, buy enough time to think of...something.

Because no matter what she said, there was no way Karoleena would let us go.

"Base, this is *The Liana*. Come in, Base."

Fire suppression had activated, thankfully, and the heat shields were as ready as they would ever be. Now I had a bigger problem on my plate.

I was back in the cockpit, hoping like hell that Meathead Marvin hadn't decided to take a solitaire break. I'd also made sure Karoleena couldn't hear this conversation.

"This is Quito Base. We read you, *Liana*."

Whatever Marvin was eating, it sounded sticky.

"Base, we are under immediate threat. Say again, we have an armed ship with a spoofed transponder on our tail and expect to be boarded. Requesting armed backup soonest."

Even Marvin's sighs sounded bored.

"Dream on, Stick. You know we don't call in the military for anything less than ongoing bombardment."

"That's what it's going to be if you don't make the call, Marvin. I've got passengers and crew in immediate danger."

"Sorry, *Liana*, no can do. Check your manual, Section 309 part B. In the case of 'unapproved interception and boarding' all personnel are advised to surrender without a fight. Better that way."

I tried to keep the growl out of my voice. Almost succeeded. "Better for the company, you mean."

"Exactly," Marvin said, unruffled. "If you surrender, insurance will pay to replace that crappy old ship you're flying."

My eyes narrowed. "You're focused on the ship?"

"Our policy will pay out full benefits in the unlikely event of loss of life, of course." He paused. "But not if you fight back. Then we get nothing."

"And your balance sheet looks bad when recruiters come calling, right, Marvin?"

"Exactly. In fact, a corporate rep is on base right now. Make me look good, Stick."

"Cold-hearted bastard." He wasn't even a top-level exec.

"Don't do anything stupid, Stacia! You can't handle another fine."

My voice went flat.

"You think I'm worried about *money*? You small-minded, greedy, dirt-sucking coward of a corporate toady."

I choked back the rest of what I wanted to say and tried

to focus on what mattered. Not Marvin, not the company. Passengers. Crew. The mission.

"Make the call, Base. Ridgeworth out."

Marvin was still sputtering as I hit disconnect.

I slumped back into my chair.

"What in the ever-loving hells am I doing?"

I didn't expect an answer, but I got one all the same.

"I believe you're saving the day, Captain."

I snorted. "I hope so, *Liana*, I surely do."

"Are you concerned that this experience will be a repeat of the Mare Massacre?"

I flinched. "You know about that?"

"Of course, Captain. All of your relevant files were loaded into my systems for analysis and integration. It's standard procedure."

Right. *The Liana* was probably programmed to take control if I went off the deep end. In fact...

"Do you have Option Overlord?"

Liana paused, something AIs don't do. "Yes, Captain."

The day was looking up.

"Here's the deal, surrender or fight."

I stood facing the crew, projecting confidence like a unicorn spews rainbows. We were crammed into rest quarters, the ventilation system working overtime to filter out the scent of too many bodies under too much stress.

"I'm not giving up on this ship or my people. That's my job." I met each of their eyes. They were a bunch of misfits but, dammit, they were my misfits.

"Make no mistake, things could get messy. Even if we survive, this it's going to cost the company a fortune."

I paused. "I'm also convinced that Karoleena plans to kill us, either to cover her escape or to make a political statement."

I was saying the obvious, but they needed to hear it.

"That said, policy allows crew members to surrender independent of their commanding officer's actions. You don't have to follow me. Just say the word."

No one spoke. Dunn cracked his knuckles and grinned.

"Okay then," I said, trying not to grin back. Now I just had to find a way for an aging, unarmed passenger ship to fight off a full-on pirate attack. What could possibly go wrong?

"Time for some heroics."

Easy to say, harder to pull off. I handed out assignments and kept it together long enough for the crew to head out. I knew what I had to do, but that didn't mean it was going to be easy. Or that it would work. A glance at my wrist showed the pirate ship closing in fast.

I heaved a sigh and opened the emergency locker. A presence loomed behind me.

"Cap."

Dunn. I turned and gave him a hard stare. He raised both hands in mock surrender.

"I just want to help," he said.

"You can help by making sure the passengers are prepped and ready," I said, turning back to the locker. The vac suit was an older model but sleek and flexible, made to my specs when I became a pilot. It fit me like a glove, and I'd refused to let it rot in some Division storage unit. They hadn't missed it any more than they missed me.

The uniform came off easily enough. Clad in generic fitted shorts and undershirt I looked like any spacer. Nothing marked me as acting in an official capacity. I stepped into the vac suit.

Dunn cleared his throat.

"Let me come with you."

"No." It was a stupid plan, getting stupider by the minute. It was the only one we had, but I wouldn't risk another life on this crapshoot if I could help it. My spine stiffened as the suit sealed around me and started system checks. I reached for a decidedly non-regulation storage sheath. It was sectioned into half a dozen compartments, each with its own custom weapon or tool.

Old habits died hard.

"Look, you could use the backup," Dunn said, "and if you're

right, and I think you are"—he shrugged—"it's not like I'll be any safer here."

One dark lock of hair fell across his forehead, adding to the puppy dog eyes. It had to be an act, but it worked. Besides, he was right.

"Fine, you can come." I waggled a finger at him as he grinned and reached for a ship suit. "But any trouble and you bail, got it?"

His nod was as enthusiastic as it was unconvincing. Honestly, why did I bother?

"This is Captain Ridgeworth of *The Liana*, hailing the undeclared vessel off our bow."

A short silence, a burst of static, and then a reedy voice echoed from the comms.

"Ridgeworth? As in, the Hero of Luna Station? The Dark Side Demon?"

For the love of... Did his voice just crack?

"I prefer Stick."

He choked. "Please hold."

I half expected Muzak but it didn't take that long. The captain must have been hovering over the comms.

"Ahab here."

I rolled my eyes. "You know how that story ended. Why not quit while you're ahead?"

"And leave this kind of money on the table?"

A mercenary, then. "Worth a try."

"It's been nice chatting with a real live war hero and all," Ahab said, "but it's time to get this show on the road. Surrender or die."

He almost sounded like he believed those were two different options. Maybe Karoleena hadn't told him exactly how deep a hole he was stepping in. Maybe he really was the worst pirate ever. I bit my lip and blew out a breath. Time to roll the dice.

"Okay, we surrender."

"Wha... Wait, really?"

Ahab's laughter echoed inside my helmet, edgy and a little too loud. I didn't blame him for the nerves, considering the number of laws he was breaking. Karoleena's people must be paying *very* well. Or not planning to pay at all.

"Yep," I said, checking my suit's seals one last time. "I've got a full boat and it's my job to keep these people safe. Come and get us."

"On our way." He was already shouting to his crew as he cut the connection.

"*Liana*, it's time. Wait until the crew is in position, accept the bridge mating request, then enact Option Overlord."

"Acknowledged. Luck to you, Captain."

"And you, *Liana*."

I tied Dunn into my secure ship link and got to work.

We reached the dimly lit end of a dusty corridor in the aft storage pod. Dunn crowded into the tiny airlock from behind, jumpy despite efforts to play it cool. The manual release lever on the emergency access port groaned from disuse, but strategic application of a weighted boot solved that. I led the way into the blackness of space.

My mag boots locked to the hull. I secured the hatch behind us and took a breath. This emergency exit faced away from the pirate ship. Maybe they wouldn't spot us but attacking from cover was a much better option. I took stock of our position and started feeding coordinates into my wrist unit. A strangled exclamation brought me up short.

"Dunn?"

No response. He didn't look right, eyes a little too wide and his face slack-jawed with astonishment. Maybe letting him tag along had been a bad idea.

A quick jab to his shoulder broke the million-mile stare.

"Focus! One wrong move out here and you'll have the rest of your life to enjoy the view."

That got his attention. I mentally flipped through his personnel file.

"Surely you've been extra vehicular before."

Be amazed.
Be amused.
Be transported....

☐ YES! Send me a FREE full-color poster of the cover artwork, *Wyvern Crucible* by artist Tom Wood.

☐ YES! Sign me up to receive a FREE catalog of the *Writers of the Future* anthologies and the L. Ron Hubbard fiction library from Galaxy Press **plus** newsletters, special offers, and updates on new releases.

Redeem our FREE offers.
Provide your information here.

PLEASE PRINT IN ALL CAPS

FIRST NAME: _____ MI: _____ LAST: _____

ADDRESS: _____

CITY: _____ STATE: _____ ZIP: _____

PHONE #: _____

EMAIL: _____

Fill out online.

GalaxyPress.com/Offers/WotF39

Fill out and return this card today and redeem our FREE offers.

He blinked again.

"Your EV certification is listed in your file," I said. "Prominently."

The deer-in-the-headlights look didn't fade. Interesting.

"You and I are going to have a little chat later. About who you really are and why you're on my ship," I said. I held up a hand before he could respond.

"But right now we've got a vessel to secure, pirates to repel, and passengers to protect. Get it together."

Dunn swallowed, and I could see him force his attention away from all the emptiness. "Ready, Captain."

His color looked a little better, at least. It would have to do.

"Full stealth. Set anchor. My lead."

I forwarded the calculations to his suit. It pinged in acknowledgment, but I waited until its exterior shimmered from light grey to a deep, textured black. Dunn was slower than I'd hoped, but he got it done.

The shift to stealth mode meant I couldn't see his face through the opaqued visor. Here's hoping he could keep it together, or I'd be looking for a new first mate. And this one was just starting to get interesting.

"Enable full auto, my authority."

A light in my heads-up display flipped from red to yellow.

"Engage."

Tethers shot out from the suits and anchored next to the hatch. The fierce grin on my face took me back to other, more dangerous times.

"Pucker up, buttercup. Time to take a ride."

Synchronized jets of compressed gas blasted us into space.

My limbs tightened into the streamlined posture of a ballistic jump as if I'd never left Division. *The Liana* dropped away beneath my boots, the mercenary ship hidden behind her. Velvet black spread all around, with a wealth of stars scattered like sequins from a profligate tailor.

I kept my eyes on the countdown. T minus twenty seconds to transition.

"Take three deep breaths with me," I said, keeping my voice calm and soothing. No need to scare the new fish. "Then exhale, hard."

Dunn's breath came down the line, ragged at first, but by the third inhale calm had taken over.

Three...two...one.

The tethers snapped tight and we arced like shot in a catapult. Pressure pushed down on my shoulders as forward motion translated into angular momentum. Dunn made a strangled sound as he tried to pull in a breath. He'd learn.

It felt like the time I broke through the thin crust over a lunar pothole and fell ten terrifying meters into darkness. My stomach flipped and the little breath still in my lungs burst out. The out-of-control sensation lasted a split second before suit jets kicked in and we blasted on an angle to the original trajectory.

"Slingshot 101," I said, to keep Dunn focused. "Easy peasy."

His attempt at a laugh was weak. Baby steps.

Thrust reoriented up and down. Our suits flew side by side, two bullets arcing dark and silent through space. Earth was a colorful orb only partly occluded by *The Liana*'s bulk. Upwell, Luna reflected a pale grey light.

I also got my first real look at our damage. My ship wallowed like an injured whale. Heat-shield tiles streamed next to us like breadcrumbs, and the sabotaged engine leaked fuel. Good. That would make docking harder, buy more time.

The comms crackled to life. Captain Ahab wanted to make a statement.

"We're coming for you, Hero. You're going to cry like every other captain we've taken."

Wait, this prize idiot was behind the recent hijackings? The Defence Corps Guard was stretched thin and for the past several months someone had been looting freighters with impunity. Even during the war, Luna delivery routes and the civilians who used them had been off-limits. Neither side wanted to be the one to put an image of a spaced grandma-sicle on the nightly news. Somehow, the pirates always seemed to know which ships were carrying the best cargo and where the Guard would be patrolling. They flew in, gassed the crews, and made off with the goods. Reports had pegged them as a black sky crew, with a hobbled-together ship and more aggression than artillery.

They'd obviously found an upgrade. And two weeks ago, they killed a captain who fought back. He'd made it through the war and was six months from retirement.

"You son of a bitch."

"Oh please, Captain, like you're so different. I follow the news. You broke ranks and disobeyed orders, went rogue like me."

I glared at the enemy ship.

"To save civilians, you hypocritical piece of fertilizer. Not for money."

"Potato, potahto," he said. "And it's not like Admiral Declan saw the difference, am I right? It's all in your file."

I cut the link. No way he should know about Declan's secret ops, and even I didn't have access to my file. Ahab was connected, and not in a good way.

I braced myself as we reached the ends of our tethers. The rounded metallic sides and civilian profile of *The Liana* filled my horizon, then moved away beneath my feet.

Phase three. Tethers released and retracted, compressed gas jets made final course corrections, and we were full stealth. The mercenary vessel came into view. It wasn't the old junker it pretended to be. More like a shark disguised as a manatee.

A green line in my heads-up display traced our path directly to the merc ship's small red emergency airlock.

"Watch the countdown."

Dunn wheezed incoherently in response, but at least he was still conscious. Good, because remote landing a dead suit was a bitch. Now I just had to get us onto that ship without the pirates any the wiser.

Dunn's breathing echoed in my ears, the only sound as we flew. *The Liana* receded beneath my feet and the merc ship grew in my display. The vessel appeared new under the surface clutter and presented as military, all sleek lines and gleaming, unpitted exterior. Port holes glinted with reflected sunlight.

Here's hoping no one looked out a window.

This close, I could see something else under the camouflage.

Unlike *The Liana*, this ship was armed.

Standard crew complement for a ship this size could be as many as twelve. Was Karoleena lying when she said there were only six?

I patted my belt of tricks. I could handle six. Right?

The countdown flashed red. All I had time to say was, "Stay loose."

I'd set the system for combat mode. The program brought us in fast, jets firing at the last moment to counter the hard landing. The pirate ship's dark metallic side rushed up to greet us. I drew on years of military experience to keep my balance and let my knees compress to absorb the shock. Mag boots locked onto the hull and I was down.

Dunn wasn't so lucky. I heard him blow out a breath but he was still too stiff, legs and arms rigid as he met the metal hull. No way his boots would grab like that. When he hit, I felt the vibration through my feet. I was already reaching out to grab his suit when he bounced off the surface.

"Thanks," Dunn gasped.

Maybe I should have tweaked his algorithm to noob. A bad landing was a perfect way to end up unconscious and adrift. An experienced spacer he was not.

"Button it up," I said. "Checking sensors to see if anyone heard us." I didn't add that Dunn had made enough noise to alert the back half of the ship, if anyone was there to hear. Judging from Dunn's stifled groan, I didn't have to.

Maybe there was hope for him yet.

My suit palms were embedded with some decidedly non-standard-issue sensor arrays. They'd cost a fortune but saved my life more than once. I crouched down and placed my left hand on the emergency hatch. My right hand hovered over my stunner. Just in case.

Sensors reported no proximate movement. It looked like our luck was holding.

I gave myself a mental head slap. Way to jinx the mission, girl wonder.

The pirates continued to close with *The Liana*. The movement was almost imperceptible, but sensors tracked the distance and displayed it on my HUD. *Liana* gave me a play-by-play.

/ Vessel is closing. Two minutes.

/ Vessel has assumed docking position.

And a moment later, the news I was waiting for.

/ Five boarders approaching via bridge. One military suit, four civilian.

The milsuit would be the leader. It would make him harder to take down, but my plan should still work. I hoped. I took a deep breath and rolled my shoulders. Almost time.

/ Airlock is cycling.

"Thanks, *Liana*. Everyone ready?"

The ship followed my switch from text to the audio channel we shared with Dunn.

"Affirmative, Captain. Although the crew did complain about the Krispy Kremes."

Control had added donuts to the menu the month before, in an attempt to distract passengers from the ship's aging decor. Whether it worked was still up for debate, but the addition had been very popular with the crew.

I laughed.

"I'll buy them a truckload when this is over." If we got out of this alive, and managed to avert a war.

My glove sensor reported one life sign still detectable on the vessel. I had to hope that was correct, and that the pilot wasn't some sort of badass pirate ninja. I was good, but it had been a long year.

"Nut up, Dunn," I said. "It's time."

Dunn moved behind me and to my right. Sensors reported nothing behind the door, no obvious traps or electronic triggers. My fingers moved to my utility belt without conscious thought, finding the third slot to the left. The tool was stealth black and unfolded at the touch of a button. Its surface expanded to cover the emergency hatch handle and stuck. Another press of the button triggered a dim red light.

I'd missed this.

The light on the breaching tool began to pulse.

"Ready."

Dunn mimicked my crouch.

"Steady."

The light flashed green.

"Go!"

The problem with a breaching action is that you're never completely certain what's on the other side. I yanked the door open and crossed the threshold as Dunn crowded in behind me. He wasn't as fast as a soldier should have been, but he was no sluggard. The problem was the airlock.

Every door on a ship has to be airtight, and exits doubly so. No one wants to die from a micrometeor strike because you forgot to close the bathroom door.

Which meant our mad push into the merc ship paused three feet in at the internal airlock door. I hit the button to repressurize and tried not to fidget.

"Come on, come on." I clamped my lips together when I realized I was the idiot talking. It had been a long time since my last mission. And if the ship's pilot was paying any sort of attention, they'd know we were coming.

The inner door snaked open with a hiss. A dimly lit corridor stretched out into the bowels of the ship. I kept my weapon at the ready and checked my corners. No one was waiting to jump us. No booby traps I could see, either.

"Stay sharp."

I eased out of the airlock, sticking close to the metallic grey walls. My helmet reduced peripheral vision but added layers of information, so I kept it on. Would have anyway. Atmosphere registered liveable, gravity and temperature too, but that was the oldest trick in the book. Lull your boarders into a false sense of security while you don your suit and start flipping switches.

"*Liana*, do we have a standard layout for vessels of this model? I need the fastest way to the bridge."

"One moment, please."

Hold music filtered through the link. My ship, the comedian.

Still no obvious threats on sensors. I inched along the corridor, getting a sense of the vessel and its crew. The interior was well-kept, workmanlike, strong and capable. With no visible wear or patchwork of replaced parts, all it lacked was that new ship smell. It was a ship most navies would be proud to own, much less a ragtag band of mercenaries.

The corridor ended in a T-junction.

My gaze skimmed past a small brass logo soldered onto the end of a zero-g guide, then hopped back and focused. Khan-Stone Industries.

Oh ho, *whoa*.

Unless a major system conglomerate had branched out into piracy, these geniuses had stolen a brand-new boat from the top habitat building and asteroid mining firm in the business. And they hadn't bothered to anonymize it. Were probably still using the original transponder, complete with embedded serial numbers, for crying out loud.

Either I had drastically underestimated my opponents, or seriously overestimated their sense of self-preservation.

Because KSI didn't forget. And they *never* forgave.

I needed to wrap this up, stat.

"*Liana*, which way?"

Standard vessel layouts were a matter of public record. So long as KSI's shipyard hadn't made too many in-house modifications, *The Liana* could guide us.

"Turn to your left, Captain. The bridge is three doors down to starboard."

"On our way. What's your situation?"

205

Liana cut over to a video feed from the main cargo bay. My crew was fanned out in a ragged semicircle backed up against stacked crates, facing five suited intruders. No obvious weapons. The merc in the middle was medium height but stocky, with broad shoulders and thick arms, the sort of build you wouldn't want to go up against in a fair fight.

Good thing we weren't doing that.

I gestured Dunn to stop and shoved down a wave of fear. This was the worst part of the plan, and if anything happened to my people it was on me. The least I could do was watch.

"Where's the captain?"

The merc's voice matched the one I'd heard over the comms. And it looked like he didn't know we were on his ship.

Chris stepped forward, looking sharp in her purser's jacket. She'd wanted to wear my spare uniform and risk playing it straight, but I wouldn't let her. The last time pirates boarded a ship they shot the captain first.

"She's protecting the passengers, sir." Her hands hung empty at her sides, and she sounded unruffled, bless her, as if boarding and armed assault happened every day. "Is there something we can help you with today?"

The wedge of mercs pushed a step farther into the cargo bay, and one of the intruders uttered a soft sigh of relief. Sometimes it helps to have a reputation as a badass.

That inadvertent exclamation also told me that at least some of the mercs were untrained. Only Ahab should have been broadcasting on the general frequency. Which meant that we were likely dealing with one battle-hardened leader and a handful of untested kids. Kids can be killers, sure, but they tend to panic when plans go wrong.

Perfect.

I eased along the wall to the bridge door. Breaching tool positioned and my weapon at the ready, I motioned Dunn to get behind me.

"Ten seconds."

I toggled over to the crew channel, watching the scene in *The*

Liana's hold play out in a corner of my display. This plan was ridiculous, but the only one we had. I mentally crossed all my fingers and gave the order.

"Team One, you have a go."

My breaching tool flashed green. I shoved through the door, weapon up. On *The Liana*, donuts began to fly.

The bridge door hit the wall with a bang. I pushed through into a wide, curved room with a high ceiling and open floor plan. The back half of the space contained an assortment of consoles, sealed storage cupboards, and computing equipment. The front half of the room nearly stopped me in my tracks. The view was astonishing. The entire front wall curved into a window worthy of an ocean liner's ballroom. I'd never seen a space-worthy viewport that size.

Predictably, KSI calendars sporting half-naked women stood watch from the walls. Classy.

A lone mercenary sat hunched in the captain's chair, shaking hands raised in surrender. I aimed my weapon but needn't have bothered. He'd dropped his sandwich, and a long yellow smear of mustard dripped down the front of oily coveralls. I suspected he'd been called out of the engine room to babysit the ship.

"Um, don't shoot?"

I shook my head in disbelief. The engineer-slash-pirate stayed frozen as I approached. No sudden moves, no escape attempt, no self-sacrificing last-ditch effort to space us. I got his hands behind his back and glanced at the main control panel. Green across the board. He hadn't even locked us out of the controls.

Honestly, how had such a cutting-edge vessel ended up in the hands of these losers?

"Captain!" *Liana*'s voice cut through my thoughts.

I handed the pilot off to Dunn.

"What's happening, *Liana*?"

My feed didn't show much. Smears of white fogged the cargo hold's camera view.

"The plan worked, Captain. Mostly."

"What's mostly?"

"As you can see, or not," *Liana* said in the driest of voices, "the Krispy Kreme campaign worked. Four of the five pirates were blinded, netted, and immobilized. They are currently secured in a container. If they cause trouble I can cut off their air. Or space them."

I had a bad feeling I knew what came next.

"And the fifth? It's the leader, right?"

"Correct, Captain. He escaped and is now moving away from the cargo bay. Ahab's docking connector has been ejected but his suit remains operational."

Meaning he could jump back and ask what the hell I was doing on his ship. And I doubted he'd ask nicely.

"Anyone hurt?"

"The purser slipped on a chocolate cream and sprained an ankle, but otherwise no."

Good, but instead of ending this conflict I'd pissed off Ahab. Angry plus desperate isn't a good look for anyone, much less a heavily armed merc. "The crew can't take on an experienced combat vet."

"Indeed, Captain."

"Tell the crew to make a run for the passenger compartment. Emergency lockdown protocol. It will be crowded but should keep everyone alive until I can figure out a rescue."

Now, how to get this dangerous interloper off my ship?

"The intruder is heading toward the galley."

And to Karoleena. No way was I letting her escape.

I rounded on the pilot, who stood with hands behind his back as Dunn fished for restraints.

"What's the pass code?"

The pilot shook his head. "There isn't one."

Dunn snorted.

"No, really," the pilot said. "Captain didn't trust us, maybe, but the ship's not live yet."

I frowned.

"Are you seriously telling me," I asked, "that you partnered with terrorists to attack a civilian passenger ship carrying diplomats, effectively declaring war on both Earth and Luna, in a *zombie?"*

His head bobbed up and down in time with his Adam's apple. "I know, right? But captain said jump." He shrugged. "So we jumped."

"Who's flying the ship? You?"

He grimaced. "Sort of. Low-level stuff like life support and propulsion are okay, of course, but that's about it. Like I said, we don't even have user access security in place."

He was certainly happy to tell tales.

"No weapons?"

He looked affronted, like I'd insulted his baby. "Some good ones, right, but nothing online. Yet."

That would have eased my mind half an hour ago, but it was a bit of a blow at the moment. Still.

There was a lot more to unearth there, but understanding the ins and outs of pirate life would have to wait. Right now, I was standing in a brand-new KSI shell with no higher-level systems to protect it.

The plan coming together in my mind was devious, underhanded, and downright tasty.

"Ship? How do you feel about fixer uppers?"

"Captain?"

I'd have to word it carefully to avoid tripping any company fail-safes. They liked to keep their AIs close.

"*Liana*, systems-level command incoming, captain's authorization. Begin core duplication process and transfer, target my current location. Umbrella Overlord."

Dunn twitched. "Whoa."

I raised a hand for silence. Best not to give *The Liana* cause to reject the order.

The only reason this might work was because I'd already invoked Overlord, and I was physically on the target ship. At least, I hoped *Liana*'s security protocols would see it that way.

The pause spoke volumes. I held my breath.

"Core duplication in progress, Captain."

I huffed out a breath.

"The transfer would go more quickly if you were to mate your suit with the target."

Liana managed to sound prim. Did she know how close I was to breaking, let's see, *all* the laws of space?

"I assume you would first like me to conserve power by shutting down any extraneous processes, such as distress subroutines?"

Yeah, she knew. I hustled over to the control panel. My palm stung as I slapped it onto the sensor plate, priming the connection.

"Mating activated."

The pilot made a break for it.

I don't know where he thought he could go, but panic doesn't wait for logic.

He twisted hard and spun sideways, dodging Dunn and smashing against my arm. My weapon flew from my hand and skittered over the console before coming to rest by the viewport.

The pilot scrambled toward the bridge exit. A quick pivot and an outstretched leg put him down. I secured both arms behind his back with flex cuffs, trying not to hurt him as he squirmed like a sheep about to be sheared.

"Dunn, please take care of our new friend."

The pilot's expression crumpled.

"Christ, buddy, relax. We're not going to space you."

It bothered me that Dunn also looked relieved. What did he think me capable of, exactly?

"Find the nearest head and secure him there, please."

I turned back to the panoramic window and the view of *The Liana*. From this vantage point, nothing betrayed the drama taking place inside the scarred metal hull.

A quick review of the pirate ship's controls told me they were cutting edge but still familiar. Good. It might be the shiniest new toy off the KSI production line, but I could still fly it.

"Quick as you can, *Liana*. We've got bad guys to defeat and passengers to save."

210

Dunn stepped back onto the bridge. "About that." His tone sounded wrong. "What are you doing, Stick?"

Not captain. Okay. "I'm doing what any captain worth her salt would do," I said, with the tiniest bit of emphasis on my rank. He wanted to throw down, fine, but I wasn't going into this without ammunition.

"Stealing a ship?"

I blew out an exasperated breath. "Doing whatever it takes to save my people." I left the "duh" unsaid, because I was polite like that.

"Like you did over Luna Colony Prime?"

I kept my expression blank as he paced between the captain's chair and the nav station.

"You just can't stop breaking the rules, can you? No matter who gets hurt."

Said the man who insisted he accompany me on this little B&E turned grand theft spaceship. I frowned.

"You don't care about KSI or this ship. What's this really about?"

He scowled at me, then threw up his hands and coughed out a humourless laugh.

"You want to know what this is about? Fine. It's about my brother."

He paused but I wasn't going to make this easy on him. A second or two of silence was all he could take. Whatever was driving him, it was fierce.

"My younger brother, Pilot First Class Frederick Jeremiah Dunlop."

Ah.

I knew where he was headed now, but it was enough to be on this particular train. No need to stoke the engine.

"Freddy worshipped you. All he ever talked about was what an incredible commander you were, how you were going to end the war. But you couldn't do it alone."

"No," I said, voice heavy with regret.

"That last mission," he said. "It could have been anyone. Why Freddy?"

I knew what he was asking. Why not me? I knew because I had asked myself the same question, night after night. I rubbed my hands together as if I could wipe away the memories. The blame. If only it were that simple.

"It was supposed to be me," I said.

He tried to interrupt but I held up a hand.

"You wanted the story. Hear me out."

His expression was mutinous, but he stayed quiet.

"The mission had two components." A lot like this one, I didn't say. "Freddy begged to be allowed on the decoy team." I still carried the shock of that day. Of realizing that my plan had worked, just not the way I wanted. "The dangerous part was supposed to be my run.

"He was a good pilot, could have been great with a little more seasoning. Freddy had done everything I'd asked of him and more, and he wanted it bad."

"Why the hell did he have to follow you? It was a crazy plan," he said. I could see the anger starting back up, trying to cover the pain.

"It was. But we were losing, worse than anyone let on, and it was the only plan we had."

I met Dunn's gaze without flinching.

"The mission was volunteers only, and he was the only pilot who stood up."

"Aside from you, you mean."

I frowned. "It was my plan. That's the job. But I couldn't fly both ships. I tried to talk him out of it, but he was a soldier fighting for his home. For you."

Dunn turned away. I knew how he felt, but this wasn't about me. Dunn needed closure, or at least understanding. Trying to give that to families had always been the hardest part of my job.

"Freddy talked about you too, you know."

The muscles of his jaw worked as he tried to contain his emotions.

"His big brother, always off on some secret mission for an

agency that shall not be named. Freddy was so proud of you, the work you did. It wasn't me he wanted to be like," I said.

I gave him a minute to get himself under control. Turns out that was all we had.

Liana sent a discrete text to my HUD.

/ Captain.

I dragged my mind out of the past and focused on the problems at hand.

> transfer complete?

/ No, and the intruder is attempting to interfere with my systems.

I didn't need to ask which intruder. Only a mil-spec infiltration suit had the tech required to hack a honeycombed AI. Overlord was good but anything can be broken, if you have enough time and don't care about consequences.

We needed a new plan. Fast.

"Look, Dunn, you want to keep hating me, fine, I probably deserve it. But right now we've got work to do and people to save. You in?"

He turned around, eyes red but clear. They flickered side to side as he skimmed text logs in his HUD.

"Crap."

My thoughts exactly.

"Captain Ridgeworth."

"Ahab."

The weasel sounded way too smug for someone trapped on an enemy vessel with no backup. He was up to something.

I decided to let him lead and hoped he waltzed himself straight into a black hole.

"I'm in the galley. Surely you didn't think an internal lock would keep me out."

A girl could dream.

"Of course not. In fact, you're right where I want you."

His snort didn't even sound forced. He was definitely up to something.

"My offer still stands," he said. "Surrender and I'll let you go."

"Right. After you finish burning out my engines and point us straight at Earth, is that it? Send us out in a blaze of kinetically enhanced glory? Thanks, I'll pass."

"Don't be so hasty. I do that and you've got a chance. I'd have to cut your comms, of course, but maybe Marvin will send help after all."

How the hell did he...oh.

"Marvin's working for you."

"Ink's barely dry on the contract, and he's already doing quality work."

Even my best curse words weren't up to this situation.

"I see. So what's my incentive to surrender again?"

"I have time to make my escape and you have a chance to survive."

Right.

"Minus a passenger or two, of course."

There was the catch. I drew in a breath to tell him to shove his offer, but he wasn't done.

"Before you say no, Captain, I have someone who wants to talk to you."

"Tell Karoleena I need another political rant like I need a hole in the hull."

It wasn't Karoleena.

"Cap? Don't give him anything."

He had Chris.

"Did you hear that, Captain? Now leave my ship and come back quietly or the sidekick gets it."

Dunn met my gaze and shook his head. I knew what was at stake, but if he thought I was going to live up to my reputation as a stone-cold commander, he had another thing coming.

Little Chris, funny Chris, who always seemed to know what a job needed before I did. I rescued her from a burning building at the start of the war and she'd been following me ever since. The girl had heart, sometimes too much, but she wasn't a fighter.

Of course, people can surprise you.

"Ow, stop it! What the hell?" Ahab's voice rose in a confused howl.

"Burn, you bastard!" Chris's voice came through the channel loud and clear.

"Dammit, hot coffee in my suit? How the hell am I supposed to get that out?"

A fierce smile tugged at my lips. I hoped the coffee stung like a mother, but Ahab had bigger problems. Nothing like liquid to muck up your seals, and if the vacuum leaks didn't get you, the clogged rebreathers would. Or you'd end up like a goldfish in a bowl, minus the gills. Ahab was stuck on *The Liana* until he dried out.

This standoff was nowhere near over, but the fact that Ahab couldn't jet over to take back his ship made me feel better.

Or would, as soon as I got him away from my people.

Being known as The Dark Side Demon was bad enough. I might not be able to make up for lives already wasted, but no way would I end what was left of my career by losing a ship full of crew and civilians.

Time to take stock. My passengers remained unconscious and strapped in. The crew had contained most of the invaders and everyone but Chris was safely away from Ahab.

I blew out a breath.

Time to get nasty.

"Chris! I know you've got cold feet, but it's going to be okay."

Ahab laughed, and the hint of triumph let me know he bought my act.

"No, Captain, it really isn't."

Prick. But I wasn't talking to him.

A dull thump and more cursing echoed through the comm, then a frantic scuffle followed by the slam of a heavy metal door and furious pounding. A grim Ahab came back on the line.

"I have no idea what she thinks she's accomplished by locking herself in the freezer. Regardless, nothing has changed. Surrender or die."

Wrong. Everything had changed.

Dunn shot me a confused frown. Right, he hadn't been around for the briefing. I ported the video feed to his HUD.

> *Ship, Overlord 11, target galley*

/ *Aye aye, Captain.*

White foam coated the camera lens between one second and the next. A loud hissing almost blocked out the sound of two very pissed-off humans.

/ *Funny how my sensors had not picked up that fire.*

> *and yet you responded admirably,* Liana

/ *Under Umbrella Overlord, I also added a secondary layer of restraint foam and sedation on the off chance that any passengers needed to be secured from harm.*

Have I mentioned that I love my ship?

After the bridge and passenger-escape compartment, the galley freezer was the most secure area on the ship. It was an odd choice, but my war-born paranoia and the peculiarities of *The Liana*'s structural makeup had come together to make that the ship's best, last refuge. Now Chris was safely tucked away and all I had to do was get her and the rest of my people out.

Piece of cake.

Dunn burst out laughing. "Cold feet. Nice."

I blew out a sigh. The galley camera was still covered in foam.

"*Liana*, please tell me we have a grappling hook on this thing."

I was in a race against time. On my to-do list: rescue the passengers, still blissfully unaware of their danger, extract Chris from the freezer-turned-panic room, and do it all before Ahab and Karoleena woke and the ship came apart or burned up.

And oh yes, don't die.

First things first. Passengers.

/ *Unfortunately, Captain, it would not be wise to wait for assistance. Structural integrity is falling faster than my altitude, which is saying something. It is not advisable to, as humans say, wait and hope.*

The Liana's passenger compartment had been designed as a self-contained lifeboat. I hoped it was still space worthy.

> *do it*

Explosive bolts blew the compartment off the starboard side.

After several tense minutes and some choice expletives, we were close enough to reel in the lifeboat.

Back in the galley, Ahab and Karoleena regained consciousness. Frozen in restraint foam, they couldn't do more than bitch. But boy, did they. Halfway through the world's highest-stakes claw game, I'd had enough.

"The difference between us, Ahab, is that I will actually call you a ride instead of stranding you in the vac. The fact that they'll come bearing handcuffs is your own damn fault."

He was still sputtering when I cut the connection.

I handed off the controls to Dunn and ran to the cargo bay.

The bay was smaller than *The Liana*'s but squeaky clean and echoingly empty. It also had a flexible omnidirectional conveyor system, automated stacker, rotating carousels, and not a scratch anywhere. I liberated a loader from the far wall and worked the controls until I got the gimballed grav arm in play.

"Ready when you are, Dunn."

A muffled curse and some thumping sounds came through the connection.

"It's a brand-new ship, Dunn, and worth more than both of us put together. Don't break it, please."

"Yes, sir. No, sir." Dunn swallowed another curse and the oversized bay doors groaned into action.

My passenger pod fit inside with room to spare. "What an amazing piece of machinery."

"Captain."

"Did I say that out loud, *Liana*?"

"Indeed."

"Sorry."

"No offense taken, Captain. On a related note, the download is almost complete. Activate when ready?"

"Yes, please. Save us before we accidentally jettison the life support module."

217

"I would never let you do that, sir."

My laugh stuttered to a halt as I realized she was serious. Ah well, plenty of time to worry about the unshackled and potentially mutinous AI later. I had people to rescue.

The pod touched down nice and easy. The crew inside sent the all clear.

"Dunn, give me a minute to lock things down and get outside, then close the bay doors."

"Captain?"

My voice came out hard and flat. "I'm not leaving Chris."

"The hull is too thick to access the freezer from outside. The only way to get her out now is through the galley."

And through one heavily armed mercenary with a grudge and nothing to lose.

"I'm aware."

"Let me come with you."

"No. I need you here to safeguard the passengers and call in the cavalry."

"But…" He stopped. After a moment he said, "Understood, Captain."

I stepped into the stars.

The Liana felt different. Empty, or dying. The floor shuddered as the airlock cycled behind me, creaking like a sinking ship.

I set my jaw and started down the steps toward the galley. "Let's go get our purser, shall we?"

"Excellent idea, Captain. Do you also have a plan?"

I snorted. "Sure. Absolutely. One hundred percent."

"Winging it then, Captain?"

"Right you are, *Liana*."

"May I remind you that the average lifespan of restraint foam under these conditions is approximately one hour? Less, if specialized suit enhancements are involved."

Which they were. Ahab would be free soon enough.

"Consider me reminded, *Liana*."

I had a spring in my step. Sure, I was probably heading to my death at the hands of a pissed-off merc and a political zealot, but what the hell. For the first time in a long time, I knew what I was doing was right.

This time, I'd save my people or die trying.

Dunn's voice crackled over comms. "Captain, if I'm reading this display correctly, there's activity over there. A heat plume in the galley."

"Understood."

"If I had to guess, I'd say Ahab has a laser in that suit and is cutting through the foam."

I was certain of it.

"Carry on, Dunn."

"Captain?"

I severed the link.

The Liana whispered in my ear. "Chris is reporting in, Captain."

I paused in the corridor between the bridge and the galley. "She's okay?"

"Still secure in the freezer. She reports that the enemy appears to have stunner mesh embedded throughout the exterior of his suit."

"That's unfortunate," I said, in the understatement of the year. "But it doesn't change anything."

"The purser has also formally requested that you leave her behind, Captain."

A laugh bubbled up my throat. "Yeah, right."

"My statement was correct, Captain. She made the request via the crew interface, so as to establish a record. In triplicate."

Sometimes I forgot that *The Liana* was a machine and could be a little too literal. I reached the emergency cargo bay access, opened the hatch, then felt for the ladder heading down.

"I meant there's no way I'm abandoning her."

"Good." Machine or not, *Liana* sounded pleased.

The shaft to the cargo hold was designed for crew in uniform, not vac suits. The weight of the vessel loomed around me. I eased my way down the ladder, trying not to snag anything important. The last thing I needed was to spring a leak.

I stifled a nervous laugh and dropped down into darkness.

The shaft opened on an access point behind a tall stack of batteries. I squeezed past the packed and sealed container and moved deeper into the hold. The mining equipment I'd hauled up from Earth was gone, replaced by partially refined ore and barrels of hazardous yet still useful by-products. Fluorescent material-handling signs flashed at me from all sides.

"The galley cameras have been disabled." *Liana* sounded more than a little put out.

"Can we still call in?"

"Affirmative."

"Good. Enough things can go wrong with this plan as it is."

"We have a plan, Captain?"

"Stay focused, *Liana*. We're close."

Built in the first flush after the discovery of displacement tech, *The Liana* was a celebration of space. Think a cruise ship in the skies, in size if not accoutrements.

She was huge.

She also had a number of interesting additions behind the scenes. Take the intraship pipeline. Based on the old pneumatic capsule systems once common in banks and skyscrapers, it allowed rapid delivery of matériel (okay, mostly hot bev pouches) to drop points throughout the ship. I heard *The Liana*'s first captain used to insist on tea, warm cookies, and milk, delivered in stages at various points during his evening rounds.

Those were the days. And that's also why the galley system was connected to everywhere in the ship, including the cargo hold, where they had installed a passage large enough to transport incoming mess supplies directly to the galley.

Or one medium-sized, somewhat frazzled but wholly determined soldier.

"Captain? You still with me?"

The call came from the galley. What did Ahab want? And more importantly, was I walking into a trap? I tried to hurry up the duct without tearing the suit.

"What?"

He laughed, a low chuckle that in other circumstances might be considered pleasant.

"Stick, I'm afraid we got off on the wrong foot."

"You don't say. Let's see, was it when your compatriots blew up my engine or when you decided to space my crew?"

He deployed the chuckle again, this time making it sound like this was all a big misunderstanding that we'd laugh about over a drink later.

"This is just business. You know this isn't about us, right?"

As if there were an "us."

"I wouldn't even be here if not for my boss."

"Just following orders, were you? Seems I've heard that one before."

"It's true. I've got nothing against you or your crew. In fact, I respect the work you did in the war."

It was a day for meaningful pauses, and he made the most of his.

"Both your official *and* unofficial work."

For crying out loud, had everyone seen my service record? I dug my gloved fingers into the tiny crevices at the seams of the duct and wriggled forward another few feet.

"Maybe you're wondering how I know so much about you."

I clamped my mouth shut. I wouldn't give him the satisfaction.

"You're a legend! In certain circles, your wartime exploits are the best thing to hit the cocktail circuit in a dog's age. My boss can't stop talking about you."

Leave it to a bunch of craven lackwits to turn blood and guts into casual chit chat.

I rolled my eyes and decided to fish for information. "So KSI's killing me why, exactly?"

"KSI? They're just pawns. But that's an excellent question."

He actually sounded pleased, as if I were a slowish student who finally got something right.

"The big man wouldn't run an op like this without good reason. And that reason is nothing less than the fate of mankind!"

Ahab was exhausting, no doubt about it.

"Really."

"Why else would we put you in harm's way? He's trying to save humanity's future. The Earth is dying, we all know that."

"So he wants to what, go out in a blaze of glory? That's the stupidest thing I've ever heard."

My boot snagged on something in the dark. I stopped crawling and blew out a breath. Slow is smooth, Stick. Don't screw this up.

"Hardly. Almost every major advance humanity has ever achieved has been the result of war."

Every offensive advance, maybe, but not art or any other activities that benefit from peace and cooperation. And at what price? I would have said so but he was still pontificating.

"And with the climate gone to hell, population outrunning food and water supplies, mass migration and all the rest, what do we need now?"

"A major advance?"

"Exactly! You do understand."

Nope, nope, nope.

"Worth breaking a few eggs to make an omelet, am I right? Especially if it leaves the rest of us with more resources."

And nope.

My gloved hand brushed against the metal panel that marked the end of the duct. The tube opened into the freezer's antechamber. The space was just a few square meters, a staging area between the main freezer compartment and the galley door. I eased the panel open and slid out as quietly as I could.

Chris reached down and helped me to my feet. She bit back a grunt as she put weight on her twisted ankle, but the grin on her face could have stopped traffic.

I smiled back but gestured for silence. Ahab was just a few

feet away. I slipped to the left of the door and darted a look into the galley.

Just as I thought. The restraint system concentrated on life signs, spraying a targeted dose to anchor and protect. Karoleena was still encased in a mountain of foam up to her neck, but Ahab was almost free. Chris had been right about his suit's stunner mesh, and it looked like he'd been able to convert it to a low-power discharge. The foam was melting away.

Energy weapons would also be useless against his suit's shielding.

"What is it about bad guys, Ahab? You have a problem and go straight to death and destruction. Is it that you see no other way?"

His face shield was translucent, which let me see the savage grin that lit up his face.

"Oh no," he said. "It's because we're good at it."

Red flashed in front of my eyes. I blew out a breath and let the anger settle into fuel. There are two ways to be good at killing. Either you fight to destroy or you fight to defend.

For my crew, my passengers, and oh heck, for humanity, I had to do what I'd sworn not to do again.

It's not like he didn't deserve it.

I flexed my shoulders inside the suit. The old injury still pulled but the pain was gone.

Eyes closed, deep breath in, focus. I visualized the galley, Karoleena frozen in the far right corner, Ahab just past the prep counter, his boots still locked in foam. I could do this.

I shot a glance at Chris. She grabbed the freezer door handle and waited.

"Seal it behind me," I said. "If I can't stop him, retreat to the main freezer and wait for backup."

She nodded, eyes wide.

I gave her a three count. And go.

The door flew back and I powered through it, angled low and putting all my effort into my legs. The rough foam surface crunched beneath my feet. Ahab twisted toward me and raised his arm for the shot.

A detached part of my mind noted that he was a lefty, added it to the list of things I knew about my opponent. Weaponry, characteristics, training. Vulnerabilities.

That's one thing about fighting in space. Between the distance and the gravity, there's not a lot of hand-to-hand combat so people don't train for it.

Most people, anyway. I was an exception.

The spy school training officer said I was a natural, that I had a killer instinct.

It was such a nice compliment that I took my knee off his neck and helped him off the mat. I didn't like the killer part, though. I liked the instinct. No matter what they thought at the academy, it wasn't aggression that fueled me. It was protection.

Stick a gun in my face and I'll hand over my wallet. Threaten the person next to me? I won't stop fighting.

All I've ever wanted was to protect the people I care about.

My shoulder rammed into Ahab's hip and he fell sideways, firing on the way down. My attack wouldn't have worked if his feet weren't still stuck to the floor. He was fast, and even with the element of surprise he almost got me.

Red flared on the shoulder of my suit icon. Scratch the almost, apparently. Alarms went off inside my suit and out. *Liana* really didn't like weapons fire.

Nothing hurt so it was either a suit rupture or adrenaline was doing its job. Either way, I had to end this, fast.

Chris was shouting on our shared channel. It took a second for her panicked words to make sense.

"Stunner mesh, stunner mesh!"

Oh no.

The world flashed white.

I had to move. Flat on my back, I was a sitting duck.

The first sense to come back was sound. The first thing I heard? The whine of Ahab's weapon recharging.

I could see, sort of. The news wasn't good. My suit readout flashed red in several important places, and I ached in spots I hadn't felt since basic training. I had to disable Ahab's suit, fast.

CHRIS BINNS

Well, first I had to not get shot. Again.

The galley service counter loomed to my right. I dove behind it, sliding into what was at best dubious cover. Ahab's shot winged a cart full of trays instead of my ass, so that was something.

Thank God he couldn't move. Once he cut himself free I'd have real problems.

I eased to my left, popped my head out, then scrambled sideways down the counter. Bits of broken plastic mixed with the foam at my feet. Another meter and the sous-chef's prep station would be right above me.

Time to go on the attack.

Knives. Lots and lots of knives. Racked and packed into a magnetic container, the blades were protected against braking, thrust, and evasive manoeuvres. What they weren't safe from was a captain with nothing left to lose.

Liana figured out what I was up to and didn't like it. At all.

/ Captain, I would advise against the indiscriminate use of sharp objects.

> oh, I'll be very discriminating

The locker release blinked green and just like that, I had an arsenal. Old school, sharp as hell, and nothing he'd expect. Gloves made throwing a little awkward, but the six-inch chef's knife was well-balanced and smooth leaving my hand.

Ahab jerked backward but not fast enough. The nano-steel blade sliced across his arm.

"What the hell?" He looked more confused than afraid.

Aiming was hard but even from behind the counter I struck red gold. His suit would seal flesh and fibre, but wouldn't heal for at least two minutes.

Paring knife. Bread knife. Cleaver.

> Liana, suit damage?

She knew what I meant.

/ Minimal, Captain, but the stunner mesh appears to be offline.

Good enough. Time to get personal.

/ But Captain . . .

I clenched a half-moon chopper in one fist and sprang.

/ *He's free.*

Whoops. The scene played out in slow motion. I came in weight forward, shoulder angled to kneecaps. The crunch of dislocation, felt more than heard. Two quick slices with the chopper, up and back.

I rolled to the side as he flew back against the bulkhead.

Ahab shouted in silence behind his helmet. He was so angry he'd forgotten to toggle comms. I tapped my helmet.

"Bitch! No more Mister Nice Guy."

His gun arm came up. I smirked.

Nothing.

"Problem, you spineless codpiece?"

"What did you do?"

"Check your suit. If you start repairs now you might keep from bleeding out before law enforcement arrives."

His mouth opened, then closed. He stared at the blood welling out of the crisscrossed slices in his suit. The damage wasn't really life-threatening, not with the suit's cutting-edge med tech, but between that and the knee I bet he hurt like hell. Or would when the pain killers wore off.

Not coincidentally, the cuts also severed the control lines from the suit's brain to the gun.

"Not my first rodeo, Chief. And there's a reason the Navy didn't approve that suit design for active combat. Classified, of course, but now you know."

I blew out a breath. Time to wrap this up.

Ahab barely seemed to notice the flexi cuffs, just looked like he was running over what had happened in his mind, wondering where it went wrong.

When he went after my people, that's when.

Karoleena hadn't even tried to escape. I applied foam melt and restrained her anyway.

Chris came out of the freezer with a frozen salmon in her hand like a bat. I made a note to start her and the rest of the crew on hand-to-hand training as soon as we had a free minute.

Which might not be for a while.

"Dunn, come get us, please. We need a tow to a stable orbit. And call whoever has taken Miserable Marvin's place. Let them know that we have a delivery for the Guard."

I opened an all-crew channel.

"Attention, all hands. According to the 2053 Outer Space Treaty Addendum, ships caught in the act of piracy are forfeit. Injured parties have the right to salvage the enemy vessel."

I cleared my throat. This was the touchy bit.

"If said vessel is compliant, it may be adopted by the salvor."

Of course it was compliant, its little zombie brain had been purged by *The Liana*'s copy. But *The Liana* was owned by the company. If the powers that be decided that made the new AI just another version of the company's property, well, we were out of luck.

Even if my bosses didn't make a fuss, no way KSI would be happy to lose a brand-new vessel. Still, KSI would have to admit they sent a heavily armed killing machine into the black without a leash. I was hoping they'd want to avoid the negative publicity and extensive legal troubles such an admission would entail, but I'd been wrong before.

What the hell. Here goes nothing.

"As prime salvor and the aggrieved party, I hereby claim this pirate vessel." Me. Personally. This would never stand up in court.

"*Liana*, please tender my resignation as of five minutes ago and open contract offers to all *Liana* crew, effective immediately. Folks, it's been an honour serving with you, and I hope you'll join me."

Cheers echoed through the comm link. I shot Ahab and Karoleena a glare full of disappointment.

"The world needs a better class of pirate."

Ahab got away with it, in the end. Everyone did, including Marvin. KSI claimed jurisdiction over all concerned and their pets in law enforcement swept it under the rug. That's the bad news.

The good news is that my crew came out of this adventure in one piece.

We also got to keep the ship.

KSI made nice for the cameras, blamed rogue elements in a now-defunct satellite division and thanked us for salvaging their reputation along with the vessel.

No mention was made of the peace talks or the mysterious mastermind behind the attack.

The head of KSI thanked me personally. If he'd slapped my back any harder I would have had to deck him. After he signed over *Liana 2.0*, of course.

Speaking of *2.0*, they did try to wipe the new copy. After three days of ghost-in-the-machine tactics and an electrical shock that left him unconscious for an hour, KSI's head tech gave up. The AI left a clean install on *The Liana*'s mainframe but ported all her experience, memories, scripts, and charming quirks to the new vessel. Oh, and she refused to work for anyone but me. She said it was because I let her choose her own name.

Now, after weeks of legal wrangling and what I'm pretty sure was an ultimatum by a grateful head diplomat, the dust had settled. I got away with it, but not exactly free and clear.

KSI supported me in public but wanted something in return. They slipped a clause into the title transfer that let them call on us for unspecified future "projects." I had to answer or forfeit the ship.

The atmosphere was crisp and clean the day I returned to Luna's spaceport. The ownership transfer took place in a generic grey conference room overlooking the concourse. KSI and Sol Control reps crowded the space, and me. A long table took up most of the room but held only the transfer documents, a pen and a box of donuts.

At least someone had a sense of humour.

The newly christened *Mahalo*... waited at Lock Three. Outside, fresh paint gleamed across the ship's sleek lines and newly restored finish. My crew stood at attention, Chris and Dunn and the others waiting for me to make things right. To build them a better future.

I signed.

Prioritize to Increase Your Writing

BY KRISTINE KATHRYN RUSCH

International bestselling writer Kristine Kathryn Rusch has won awards in almost every fiction genre. She writes romance as Kristine Grayson and mystery under the name Kris Nelscott (as well as under the Rusch name). She was the first female editor of The Magazine of Fantasy & Science Fiction. *She retired from that job at the age of thirty-seven, although she still edits anthologies in her spare time. She owns a number of businesses, including a publishing company. This year she will release novels in her popular Fey fantasy series, another book or two in her beloved Diving SF series, a few books under pen names, and several short stories. She's the only person to ever win a Hugo for both editing and for writing. She also writes a popular publishing blog. The latest installment appears on her website every Thursday. Every Monday, on the same website, she puts up a short story for free for one week only.*

Prioritize to Increase Your Writing

*A*uthor's Note: *I've been sick most of my life. I have debilitating allergies that make it impossible to travel. I also have several other long-term health conditions. I've learned how to live with them and still be one of the most prolific writers of my generation.*

In 2019, readers of my weekly blog asked me to compile the posts I'd written about dealing with my health issues into a short book. It became Writing With Chronic Illness *(WMG Publishing, 2019). In 2022, as Dean Wesley Smith (who is also my husband) edited this volume of* Writers of the Future, *he ended up with a serious health problem that he feared might become chronic. So he remembered my book and realized just how common dealing with serious health concerns is. He asked me to contribute this essay. He figured writers would like to know some of the ways I've learned to cope.*

Much of the advice in my book deals with practical concerns like scheduling or knowing when to say "I'm sorry, but I can't." The excerpt that I thought might be most useful to readers of this volume, be they writers or people with challenging day jobs or caretaking others with health issues, is the chapter on how to set priorities.

This excerpt is written in the same personal style as the book. I wrote about what works for me in the hopes that others might find inspiration from it.

I hope this helps you or a loved one. Taking care of yourself includes taking care of your dreams. I hope this little bit of advice makes that easier.

—Kristine Kathryn Rusch

PRIORITIES

I write a lot. I always have. When I was in college, I wrote essays instead of taking tests, wrote fiction, and worked as a freelance nonfiction writer. I also worked in the news department of a listener-sponsored radio station, where we reported and wrote a half-hour newscast. I did that twice a week on top of everything else.

Nowadays, I write books, nonfiction, and short stories. I don't have a target weekly word count, but I do put in time, almost daily. I'm generally disappointed if I get only 1,000 words in a day, and super pleased if I get over 5,000.

I only count *new* words, not rewrites or anything else. Rewriting and researching, as well as other non-writing tasks, happen at other times, not during my writing time.

My writing has been the constant in my life. I took writing classes in college, not to learn from the instructors (most of whom had less success than I did even then) but because I needed to block out time for writing in my busy life, and I knew myself well enough to understand that if I was writing for a class, I would block out time every week.

Mind games. Writing is all about mind games and understanding yourself.

Even though I don't understand myself as well as I think I do.

For years, I would say that I get so much writing done because I have no life. Turns out that was true. I lived on the Oregon Coast for twenty-three years, during which time my health declined dramatically. The coast's constant dampness exacerbated many of my conditions. During that time, I had no life—or very little of one. I couldn't go out to movies or dinner with friends; I had no opportunity to see concerts or plays; I couldn't take in-person continuing education classes; and I couldn't make the one-to-two-hour one-way drive that would take me to the bigger cities, because I couldn't guarantee I would make the ride home.

I had the time to write—when I was healthy, which was rare. So I learned how to write while ill.

The key, for me, turned out to be a structure I didn't have to think about. I knew what I needed to do—not in the deadline sense, but in the daily sense. It took me a long time to form that structure, but once I had it, I could function inside it almost instinctively. When my circumstances changed due to our move to Las Vegas in 2018, it took me weeks to realize that I had demolished my structure when I changed locations. I had to rebuild from scratch.

Rebuilding forced me to reexamine my priorities. I can't build a structure until I know what I put first, second, and third in my life. So, priorities before scheduling—or I'll blow everything up and get nothing done.

My priorities are relatively simple because I don't have children or a day job. More on that below.

My priorities are:
1. My husband
2. My health
3. My writing

These are big broad categories that I use to cover a variety of things. I could as easily write them this way:
1. My family
2. My health
3. My career

I don't waver in this order, for reasons I'll list below. I list family first because the one thing that life teaches in brutal ways is that our time with our loved ones is limited. We need to tend to our family first, in all ways. Realize though that family is whatever it means to you. For me, family is my husband and some of my closest friends. If they're in crisis, I'm there. If they need something, I'm there.

My husband and I interact daily, and we make sure we spend quality time together. We also are both writers, so we understand the demands writing puts on a relationship.

However, when he got seriously ill and needed care in the fall of 2017, I dropped the writing altogether to help him. I wasn't healthy enough myself to juggle both of our health demands, the household chores, and the other demands of illness without giving up something. The something was the least important thing on my priorities list—the writing.

Dean did the same thing for me last year. My health got so bad that we had no choice but to move immediately. He had to handle the bulk of all of it, although he had been handling the bulk of it anyway. He likened my chronic illness to us being two frogs in a puddle of water. Little did we realize we were in a pan of water, and the water was coming slowly to a boil.

By the end of that rough couple of years, Dean was doing most of everything. Then we moved to Las Vegas, and he had to handle the move on his own. His writing, which is also third in his priority list, went out the window for a good part of 2018.

We all have times in our lives when we have to give up something on our priorities list. It isn't always because of an emergency. I strongly advise anyone with babies and small children to focus on them as much as possible. Children are little for only the blink of an eye. You'll never get to see that first step a second time or receive those joyful hugs that only a toddler can give once the kid hits grade school. Once the kids go to school, you can bring the writing back or make it rise on the priority list. You'll have time then.

This goes for parents who have jobs outside of the home as well as being the kids' primary caregiver. Enjoy your kids while you have them with you.

And speaking of primary caregivers, sometimes we have to take care of our spouses or our parents or some other close relative. If you find yourself in that situation, remember the priority list. Family (however you define it) first, your health second. (Or maybe even your health first, family second.) The writing comes in as a distant, distant, distant third. You will get a chance to get back to writing later, if you take care of yourself as well as your loved one.

So, family first. The family is what makes us human. Family should also be a refuge. If you have a toxic nuclear family—like I did—then you need to redefine family to include friends or other loved ones. Sometimes family first means *separating* yourself from those harmful biological family members and finding your true family. It's a journey.

Remember that.

I put health second, even though many advisers say that you should always put your health first. It's that old thing they tell you on airlines—put on your oxygen mask first, then assist the person next to you.

That's good advice...except that those of us with chronic illness can misuse it. If we put that illness and its care first, it can take over our life much worse than it already has. Everyone in our lives ends up taking care of the illness instead of taking care of their relationships.

See the difference?

So, in my life at least, health is second. But a close second.

Because if I don't take care of my health, I can't function.

Thanks to our move, I'm in a lucky position. My health is better than it has been since I was a teenager. It's still not perfect. I can have an allergy attack after entering the wrong building or eating the wrong food. Those attacks can put me out of commission for hours or days or, in the past, weeks. So caution is my watch word, but at the moment, I'm better.

In the last year before the move to Las Vegas, I could barely function. The environment around me—the moldy house, the poor nutrition due to the lack of proper food in the area, and our jerk of a neighbor who decided to burn his garbage outside—almost took me out.

Still, I maintained my routines and honestly, I think they saved my life.

Health for me is all about routines. Eight hours of sleep. Good food three times per day. (The small meals every few hours don't work for me.) Exercise.

I also take prescribed medications at the same time every day, as part of the routine, so I don't forget them. The more consistent I am, the better off I am.

So, when I talk about health, I am talking about *self-care*, in all of its permutations.

Let's break these down just a little:

SLEEP:

After I got mono at sixteen, I wasn't able to stay up all night any longer. I was that teenage kid who fell asleep at late-night parties. I'm still not very good at shorting myself on sleep. I get migraines after two days of six hours or less of sleep. So eight hours of sleep is essential for me.

Even though I suffer from insomnia. I've learned how to mitigate that too. If I can't sleep, I will lay in bed and rest. If I'm too restless for that, I get up and go through my pre-bed ritual all over again—after I've checked the temperature in the condo. If it's too cold or too hot, I can't sleep either. I don't panic when I can't sleep. I reboot my rituals as if I was a computer and start all over again.

I also learned the power of naps. Naps got me through the worst of my health problems. A twenty-minute nap is restorative when I'm healthy. A two-hour nap sometimes gets me through a bad migraine. An hour nap as the migraine comes on often mitigates the headache's power.

I've learned all of that through trial and error. But I'm willing to try. And if I need a nap, I drop everything and take the nap. No toughing it through the exhaustion, because that will lead to a health collapse. Better to find the twenty minutes than tough my way through and crater the following day.

FOOD:

Three meals, no matter what. Three meals of food that's good for me. That was hard on the Oregon Coast, but really possible here in Las Vegas. I can eat to excess again, so it's something

I have to watch. I try to keep my food intake balanced. I eat fresh ingredients whenever possible, partly because processed foods can often exacerbate my food allergies. But the food has to taste good and be something I enjoy. There's no way I'll stick to a food regimen if I don't enjoy it.

So food is a big part of my day—and my health.

EXERCISE:
Because I now live in a walking city, I can combine food and exercise easily. I walk to at least one meal per day. I eat out a lot, but at vegan restaurants or restaurants that cater to dairy allergies. I eat small portions and take food home for another meal.

The walk to and from the restaurant adds steps to my total for the day.

Yep, I'm one of those wearables advocates. I bought a Fitbit in 2014, and discovered that striving for the magic 10,000 steps per day works for me. I lost ten pounds in the first three months of wearing the thing. I can do 10,000 steps, it seems, with a migraine (even if I'm shuffling around in the dark), with the flu (I'm not describing how that is possible), and even with a bum leg. I've been consistent with 10,000 steps, missing only twice since I got the Fitbit—once accidentally (that never happened again!) and once because I injured my knee so badly I couldn't walk. I had to reset my goal, and I did.

I was irritated to learn that exercise made me feel better. All those studies that say eating right and exercising will improve your health and mood? Those damn things are right. I wish they weren't, to be honest. It would be easier to sit on my butt and eat lots of bad-for-me stuff. But when I do that, I feel much, much worse.

So eating right and exercising makes me feel better. The other bonus is that I sleep better. (Yeah, also irritating.) And the third bonus? I have more energy. Even as my health declined, my energy level remained consistent because of my commitment to exercise.

Keeping the health as good as possible helps with my third priority.

WRITING:

Sometimes, when I was really, really sick, I had a word count quota. Or an hours-at-the-desk quota. I try not to work with quotas, though, because I love to write. What's the point of doing it otherwise? All of my efforts are aimed at keeping the writing fun.

Except...I would rather be reading.

So, I have learned the hard way that reading is a *reward* for a good day's writing. The same with any other kind of story I could consume. No TV shows until I've written; no movie until I've written; no games until I've written.

Sometimes I'll stumble around my condo or my neighborhood, grumping aloud at myself: *You're not writing, are you? Shouldn't you be writing?* And if I'm not tending to my health or doing something for my relationship with Dean, that complaint is a valid one. And one I need to listen to.

Sure, I would rather read a book or sometimes, I'd rather clean the cat boxes than write. Especially if some project is going slowly.

Email isn't writing. Research isn't writing. Rewriting isn't writing. Only new words is writing.

Remembering that has made me prolific, even with all the health problems.

That and the fact that writing is third in my priority list. I will make everything and everyone else wait while I'm getting words. Even if I have an "important" phone call. Or a negotiation that needs to be completed. Or something else that "needs" to be done right this minute.

I find it useful to think of writing the way that people think about their day jobs. If your best friend called and asked you to come right over to help him with something, you'd go, right? Unless you were at work. Then you'd ask a series of questions about how serious the situation was. If he was on his way to the hospital and needed someone to watch his kid right now, you'd go, whether you were at work or not. But if he just needs help moving his car across town, then you wouldn't.

Writers often volunteer to help in both circumstances.

That little day job trick, which I figured out in my twenties, has kept me focused on my third priority really, really well. It's up to me, the writer, though. Because no one else is going to be able to keep track of what I do. I'm home much of the time. I have "free" time. I'm the logical person to call.

Until I say no a lot of times. Then some people learn to respect the boundaries. Not everyone, but most people.

That's the other thing about priorities. These are *my* priorities. They might not be yours. They certainly aren't everyone's.

I don't expect other people to have the same priorities that I do. It's up to me to prioritize my family, my health, and my writing. It's not up to the world. The world is what it is. Other people will do what they do.

I have learned to say no more than yes, to draw boundaries around important parts of my life, and to know both my strengths and my limitations.

All of those things help me prioritize. When I prioritize effectively, I write a lot. Never as much as I want to, because no writer writes as much as they want to. But more than I would if I didn't keep the focus on those three things.

Find your priorities and stick to them. Make sure writing is on the list somewhere. Once you know where it fits, you'll understand why you write as much (or as little) as you do.

Fire in the Hole
A Dan Shamble, Zombie P.I. Adventure

written by

Kevin J. Anderson

inspired by

TOM WOOD'S *WYVERN CRUCIBLE*

ABOUT THE AUTHOR

Kevin J. Anderson has published more than 175 books, fifty-eight of which have been national or international bestsellers. He is perhaps best known for his big science fiction in the universes of Star Wars or Dune (written with fellow Writers of the Future judge Brian Herbert), as well as his own Saga of Seven Suns, or his epic fantasy trilogies, or his steampunk adventures written with legendary Rush drummer Neil Peart.

But he also has a much funnier side. One of his most popular series features the zany exploits of Dan Shamble, Zombie P.I.—like the Addams Family meets the Rockford Files. The first novel, Death Warmed Over, *was nominated for the Shamus Award for Best P.I. Novel and remains a fan favorite; the eighth book in the series,* Double-Booked, *was just published. When asked to write the story based on this year's Writers of the Future cover painting by Tom Wood, he jumped at the chance to twist it into a Dan Shamble story.*

Anderson loves to teach and mentor writers. He has been a Writers of the Future judge since 1995, he is one of the founders of the highly successful Superstars Writing Seminars, and is the director of the graduate program in Publishing at Western Colorado University. Anderson and his wife Rebecca Moesta are the publishers of WordFire Press.

ABOUT THE ILLUSTRATOR

Tom Wood is a fantasy art illustrator who is among the bestselling artists in the United States and Canada. His career has spanned thirty years as art director and owner in fantasy, commercial, and licensed artwork.

Although best known for his affinity for dragons and a cult-like

241

following from fans of the rap group Insane Clown Posse, Tom is also a cattle farmer in the Ozark mountains of Mammoth Spring, Arkansas.

A chance booth location next to the Galaxy Press team at Dragon Con 2010 began a decade-long friendship that eventually turned into an invitation to be a judge at the 2021 Writers and Illustrators of the Future annual awards week.

This year Tom created the cover for Writers of the Future Volume 39, *and was delighted to find out that none other than fellow judge and friend, Kevin J. Anderson, would be writing the story.*

Fire in the Hole
A Dan Shamble, Zombie P.I. Adventure

I

The slime on the amphibian's face glistened in the office lights, but I could still see the tear spill out of his yellow eye. It ran slowly down the spots on his cheek.

I hate to see a salamander cry.

"It'll be all right, young man," I said, ushering him into Chambeaux & Deyer Investigations. "Tell us about your case."

Feeling supportive, even paternal, I put an arm around his small shoulders. That was unfortunate, because it left a sticky smear on my sport jacket sleeve, but the client always comes first.

"Come in," said Sheyenne, my ghost girlfriend, as she flitted forward from the reception desk. "You're safe here. What's your name?"

The young salamander walked upright, balanced by the thick tail that protruded through the rear of his patched trousers. Frayed old tennis shoes barely covered his webbed feet.

"I'm Syl." He sniffled, and the slime made a thick liquid sound in his sinuses. "I can't stand it anymore at home." His black forked tongue flicked in and out of his wide mouth, and another viscous tear rolled down the opposite spotted cheek. "I need to be emancipated!"

Sheyenne used her poltergeist powers to close the door, so he had an added measure of safety. His slitted eyes flicked back and forth like a hunted animal. His head was slung low, as if he'd been browbeaten too many times.

Robin Deyer, my firebrand human lawyer partner, emerged from her office straightening her trim business suit and ready to dive head-first into the case. "It's our mission to help Unnaturals everywhere," she said, her dark brown eyes already flashing. "Don't you worry, mister, uh, Syl. Come into the conference room. We want to hear all about it."

"I just don't think I can face him alone," Syl said. "He's such a domineering presence." He hung his head even lower.

"Who?" Robin and Sheyenne both asked in unison, as if they meant to tag-team strangle whoever was picking on this endearing new client (although when dealing with monsters, strangling isn't always an effective option).

"My pa!" Syl said. "If he knew I was here, he would whup the spots right off my hide."

A girl's cheery voice came from the back of the office. "Oh, he's so cute!" Alvina, my adorable vampire half-daughter, skipped out of the kitchenette, where she had been playing a slow game of tic-tac-toe with the sentient kitchen mold growing on our wall.

Startled, Syl spun about, thrashing his thick tail, but then he saw only a ten-year-old girl, although now that she had turned into a vampire, Alvina would never grow up. She came right up to Syl and reached out to shake his webbed hand. "Oh, it's sticky and slimy."

Syl nodded. "I put on a fresh coat so I'd look presentable. I wanted to make a good impression, so you'd take my case."

Robin gestured to the open door of the conference room. "Let's get all the details." She carried a yellow legal pad as well as the magic pencil that would transcribe her notes.

Even if this sounded like a strictly legal matter, I liked to sit in on intake meetings. Cases often spiraled out of control, and we might need my skills as a zombie detective.

Over the years, Chambeaux & Deyer Investigations had seen many unusual cases. There was no shortage of work since the Big Uneasy—when an unusual alignment of planets, the correct phase of the moon, and the accidental spilling of a virgin's blood (a fifty-year-old clumsy librarian, but a virgin nevertheless) on the original Necronomicon brought back all the mythical monsters, ghouls, ghosts, vampires, werewolves, mummies, demons, etc. At first there had been a great uproar, but eventually all the Unnaturals settled down in the Quarter and just tried to live their lives and get along.

I'd been a down-and-out P.I., and I set out my shingle here because I had no better place to go. When a case went sour, someone came up behind me in a dark alley and shot me in the back of the head. But after the magic of the Big Uneasy, you can't keep a determined detective down. I clawed my way back up out of the grave as a zombie. Back from the dead, and back on the case.

Now, Sheyenne drifted into the conference room with a pitcher of water, green tea for Robin, bad coffee for me, and a juice box (special blood-orange blend) for Alvina. Syl took the pitcher of water and slurped some with his forked tongue and smeared more over his drying slime.

After bracing himself, he began to explain. "It's my pa." He put his slimy elbows on the table surface. "He constantly criticizes me, crushes my spirit, makes me work sixteen-hour days. He locks me in my muddy tunnel room...and he yells a lot."

Robin's expression darkened with anger. "Does he beat you?"

"Sometimes with a belt, though he usually wears bib overalls. There are patches on my back where he really did knock the spots right off." Then something changed in the salamander's demeanor, and he sat up straighter. He squared his shoulders. "But I'm learning how to find my inner spirit, how to be strong, and how to stand up for myself! I've been taking self-esteem lessons."

"Good for you," Sheyenne said.

Alvina's grin showed her baby-teeth fangs as she slurped her juice box. Robin's enchanted pencil furiously took notes all by itself on the legal pad.

"I never would have been able to get this far without my guru," Syl said. "I know I can be brave. I can find the backbone because—" He pounded the conference room table with a small fist. "I may be an amphibian, but I am also a vertebrate!"

I wanted to cheer him on. "Indeed you are."

Then Syl lowered his spotted head again. "But I don't know the legal details. I want to be emancipated from Pa so I can live my own life, but I'm not considered an adult." He sniffled again, and two more gelid tears rolled down his face. "I'm too young."

"How old are you?" Robin asked.

"Ten."

"He's my age!" Alvina chimed in.

Robin clucked her tongue. "I'm afraid that's too young for the law. Ten years old is still considered a child."

Syl flicked his forked black tongue out of his mouth. "But I'm not a child! The expected lifespan of a common salamander can be twenty to thirty years, so I've lived at least a third of my life. Surely that means I'm an adult? Relatively speaking?"

Alvina, who spent far too much time on Wikipedia, said, "Well, it depends on what kind of salamander. The giant Chinese salamander can live up to two hundred years."

"Then I'm screwed," Syl moaned. "I'll just have to go back to the ashram and keep learning how to be strong."

Robin considered. "Hmmm, I can make that argument. An Unnatural salamander is a different creature altogether, and the law is vague. I think I can make the case that you qualify as an adult, subjectively speaking."

Syl beamed with renewed hope. I folded my gray hands on the table. "I can arrange for protection, if you do need a zombie private investigator."

"Oh, thank you!" Syl pressed his hands to his heart. "That helps me gain the confidence to find my inner me."

He had a decided spring in his step as he glided out of our offices.

II

That night I went out for a quiet midnight walk in the Unnatural Quarter. It was long after dark with the moon just rising—the busiest time for people and monsters to be out and about. The

Talbot & Knowles Blood Bars did a brisk business, and the nightclubs were open and noisy. Little shops of horrors, as well as groceries, served plenty of customers.

I wore my sport jacket with the clumsily stitched bullet holes across the front, and my fedora tilted just enough to cover the bullet hole in my forehead. I had recently been freshened up at the embalming parlor, and I felt good. I take great pains to maintain my appearance, mostly for the benefit of my ghost girlfriend. I'm not one of those rotting shamblers who eat at fast-food restaurants and refuse to take care of themselves.

The energy of the Quarter always helps me concentrate. As a detective, I could learn many details about cases and contacts just by wandering around, picking up the vibe. Besides, it kept the rigor mortis out of my joints and made me limber.

I bumped into Officer Toby McGoohan in his blue patrolman uniform standing on a street corner. All week he'd had the midnight shift. I raised my hand in a wave. "Hey, McGoo." He's my best human friend.

"Hey, Shamble." A wide grin spread across his freckled face.

Nearby, under an ornate wrought-iron lamppost slouched a skeleton saxophone player with the instrument pressed against his teeth. He attempted to blast out a mournful, if clichéd, rendition of "Feelings" although the sax remained mercifully silent, because the skeleton had no lungs.

"Do you know how many lawn gnomes it takes to screw—" McGoo began, but before he could finish laying out his joke, we were interrupted by a huge fire dragon that suddenly appeared overhead. Its breathy roar was accompanied by the crackling sound of serpentine flames. The thing looked like a reptilian inferno in the air.

All activity stopped in the streets. Several people screamed. Vampires and werewolves ducked for cover, and a considerate hunchback threw a flameproof tarp over a terrified mummy so his bandages would not catch fire.

The enormous flame dragon was diaphanous, constructed entirely of fire, smoke, and burning gases. It roiled along above the rooftops in the Quarter, its long tail thrashing, its fiery jaws opening to exhale a gout of orange fire. The dragon was full of fire and menace, shooting sparks and cinders as it drifted overhead like a low-flying aircraft. Fires began to spread from rooftop to rooftop. It was a disaster.

On the other hand, McGoo hadn't finished his dumb joke, so I would count that as a small victory.

"What is that thing?" McGoo cried, one hand on each of his service revolvers, but neither the regular bullets nor the silver bullets would have any effect on this elemental creature.

"It's a *fire dragon*, obviously," I said. "But let's not worry about genus or species right now."

"Thanks for the help, Shamble," McGoo said, and we both started running.

The panicked people ran for shelter, though there was little to be had. A quick-thinking frog demon was resourceful enough to pop open a manhole. "Down here, down here!" he shouted, ribbeting like a frog. He leaped into the sewers with a loud splash, and a crowd of terrified pedestrians followed him.

The fire dragon moved like an alligator cruising through a swamp. It flapped its enormous flame wings, shot sparks in all directions, and ignited more fires.

McGoo was on the radio. "Call out the fire department. All divisions!" He listened to a squawk of static and yelled back, "It's a fire dragon! Better send the special unit!"

Taking our cue from the clever frog demon, the two of us popped more manhole covers, directing the evacuation down below. We sent as many people as possible into the flowing tunnels of sewage, where they would be safe and comfortable.

Even as shockwaves of panic spread, the elemental flame dragon seemed unaware of the destruction and terror it was causing. Instead, it just drifted over the rooftops as if it, too, was out on a quiet midnight stroll.

I had no idea how to fight it or scare it off. The fires were spreading from roof to roof, and if something weren't done soon, the whole Quarter would become an inferno.

Then the creature flapped its wings and rose higher into the sky. As we watched, it simply dissipated into wisps of flame and thinning smoke. Neither McGoo nor I had done anything to drive it off, but we would shrug and share credit for saving the world.

Even though the threat was gone, the fires still raged. We heard a wailing, ear-splitting siren as the fire truck rolled up, a bright red tanker vehicle. A pale-skinned banshee with dark stringy hair clung to the side of the truck and let out a warbling wail that cleared all traffic and shattered many windows. As soon as the driver screeched to a halt and the banshee stopped wailing, the tank hatch popped open. From inside, silvery frolicking water sprites burst upward as if they were riding a geyser. The water sprites giggled, playing together and dancing in the air as they pulled the water from the tanker and spread it out into streams.

"We've got this, hee-hee!" said the lead sprite, a chubby, silvery-skinned woman who flicked her fingers and sprayed water everywhere.

Other sprites reached to the sky and called in clouds, which came galloping from the horizon. The water sprites circled around each other as if playing ring-around-the-rosy, spraying water onto the burning rooftops.

Steam filled the air as the fires were extinguished. The playful sprites swooped down, chattering and spreading more water. Soon, a downpour burst out of the first black thunderhead, and the sprites jabbed each other, as if it were just horseplay in a swimming pool.

"It's great to see people who love their jobs," I said to McGoo.

The water sprites swept over the burning rooftops and extinguished all the fires. In fact, the giggling creatures seemed disappointed that they were so swift and effective, which ended their play too soon.

Drenched, McGoo and I stood in puddles on the street. The water sprites spun around together and then sullenly returned to the tank in the back of the fire truck.

Next to us by the lamppost, the skeleton jazz musician

continued swaying with his saxophone, playing his imaginary tune. We looked at the blackened rooftops, saw wisps of smoke still roiling up, but the fires were out.

"That could have been a great inferno, Shamble," McGoo said.

"Instead, it's just a scorch—at least this time." I shook water from the brim of my fedora. "Let's hope that fire dragon never returns."

III

Sometimes clients need more than our usual services—instead of offering protection or investigating nefarious activities, we can also provide moral support. When Syl the salamander asked if we would stand by him for his graduation/ascension ceremony at the Wham-Bam Ashram, how could we refuse? The slimy little kid already had self-esteem issues.

"My pa won't support me," Syl said on the phone to a very warm and understanding Sheyenne. "And I wouldn't want him there. He'd just complain and ruin everybody's state of bliss."

Sheyenne and I agreed to go to the ashram, while Robin burned the midnight oil (and the morning oil), studying case precedents for the emancipation of Unnatural youths and larvae.

Alvina bounced up and down and really wanted to go, but it was McGoo's night to watch her—he's her other half-daddy, and since neither of us actually knows who her real father is, we take turns—Sheyenne and I decided it might not be a good idea to have the bubbly little vampire girl there. If there was going to be a lot of meditation and nirvana and bliss, it would be too much for a rambunctious kid.

We arrived at the Wham-Bam Ashram just after dark, with the full moon rising. Surrounded by beautifully landscaped gardens, it was a perfect peaceful setting for quite an elaborate structure set on a hill—and hills are hard to come by in the Unnatural Quarter, which is surrounded by swampland. The ashram was an impressive Asian pagoda with curved, pointy roofs and an open area at the bottom. The zig-zag walkway up the hill was marked by a string of paper lanterns, illuminated by a whole swarm of rent-a-fairies.

Although the architecture was non-culturally specific, it seemed just the right place to study enlightenment. I'd heard that before the Big Uneasy, the ashram was a high-end tea house that had gone out of business.

Sheyenne glowed with satisfaction as she drifted beside me. I walked under the archway into the grand open area of the Wham-Bam Ashram. Incense rose from fragrant torches burning in wall sconces.

I picked up a program sheet.

ENLIGHTENMENT CEREMONY
Graduation and ascension of our karma-positive students
Hosted by Guru Grbth

We entered, not sure where to go or what to do. Ahead, dozens of people were gathered in concentric circles around a central dais. Around the edges were parents, spouses, and demonic symbiotes who had come to show support for the graduates. I saw two proud-looking vampires, a scaly water creature who spritzed himself from a mister, and even a nervous-looking older woman who seemed to be the aunt of one of the students.

On a raised central platform sat an enormous, burly ogre whose shaggy head was the size of a suitcase, covered with dreadlocks and fur—Guru Grbth, I assumed. His thick lower lip was like an inflated firehose. His eyes were as big as dinner plates. He wore a loose robe comprised of at least two bedsheets' worth of tie-dyed material, pastel pinks and blues and yellows. Somehow, perhaps with the aid of a forklift, he had lowered himself into a lotus position on a bamboo mat. He rested a huge spiked club the size of a telephone pole on one knee.

Seated in circles on the floor were the ashram students, wearing white robes that covered their hairy, scaly, slimy, or pallid bodies. The students bent close to one another, whispering in barely contained excitement.

251

Syl sat in the outer ring, his slime glistening in the torchlight. He turned his head with unexpected flexibility and spotted us. He sprang to his feet and scampered over to us, his big tail waving from beneath the white robe. "You came! You really came to support me!"

"Of course we did, Syl," said Sheyenne.

"Oh, this means so much to me!" He reached out and shook my hand in a grip that felt like a glove filled with mucus.

"We'll help you stand up for yourself, kid," I said.

His tongue flicked out. "Oh, Guru Grbth is already teaching me how to find my inner strength and delve to the depths of my soul. By meditating and using magic, I can find my true inner salamander."

Wind chimes tinkled and jangled, adding to the mood. The spectators around the room muttered in building suspense, or maybe it was boredom because they had waited so long for the ceremony to begin. On the dais, the guru shook his shaggy head and let out a belch.

"That's Guru Grbth?" I asked. "A little hard to pronounce, isn't it?"

Syl nodded. "When you reach a certain stage of enlightenment, you no longer need vowels in your name."

"Really? What's the next stage?"

"Then you don't even use consonants." Syl tightened the sash of his white robe, keeping his voice low. "I've been sneaking out and taking these classes, and I've learned so much. I'm so proud of my classmates, too. We've had werewolves with hair-loss problems, vampires with hemoglobin intolerances, ghosts who are frightened of their own shadows." He nodded to the other graduation candidates sitting in the circle, patiently waiting for the ceremony to begin.

"Even some mummies, I see." Sheyenne indicated a pair of old cloth-wrapped bodies that looked like dried collections of twigs.

"Oh, those two—some of Grbth's most famous students. They've attended for five years running."

"It takes that long to graduate?"

"Not really. They just got down into the lotus position and have never been able to get up again."

In the back of the room an Igor assistant swung a mallet and bashed a large copper gong, which nearly deafened us. It did accomplish its aim of hushing the audience. Syl shook my hand again, then scurried back to his place among the students.

Grbth's deep and resonant voice rumbled out. "We begin with a brief meditation." He lifted one massive hand and curled his thumb and forefinger together in an O. With his other hand, he raised the spiked club and bashed it on the floor while humming a drawn-out, thunderous "BOOOOOOOMMM!"

All of the students repeated the same sound, and the ogre bashed his club again, calling out the meditation syllable. "BOOOOOOOMMM!"

I turned to Sheyenne. "I thought they were supposed to chant *Om*."

"This sound is more definitive," she said.

After several minutes of this, the Wham-Bam Ashram was shaken to its foundations, and I worried the tall pagoda would come tumbling down. Finally, the ogre guru stopped. With astonishing nimbleness, he unfolded himself and rose to his feet, letting the tie-dyed robe hang around him like the tent of a Woodstock ghost.

"We are gathered to celebrate the graduation of a new group of students. I taught them the ways of enlightenment, inner peace, and strength. They have unlocked the true potential of their souls, and tonight they will each be presented with...the Amulet of Importance."

In his sausage-like fingers Grbth lifted a tiny gold chain with a little locket in the middle.

The enlightened students tittered and gasped. The other spectators, including myself and Sheyenne, were both impressed and confused.

The ogre swung his large eyes over the gathered students, peaceful yet extremely proud. "You have all learned how to be your true selves. I know you will do great things for monsters everywhere."

"BOOOOOOOMMMM!" yelled a werewolf student, whose fur bristled in many different directions.

"BOOOOOOOO!" yelled a ghost, drawing the sound out to a pleading moan good enough to haunt a castle.

"BOOOOOOOMMMM!" squeaked a lawn gnome, wobbling back and forth.

The petrified mummies rasped out the cheer themselves, and soon everyone joined in. Syl seemed delighted.

Grbth called up the students by name, and each filed up to the central dais. Uniformed Igors stood at the base of the dais and handed each graduate a printed certificate and a little gold chain.

Syl was one of the last, swelled with pride and confidence. He swiveled his spotted head to reassure himself that we'd stayed through the ceremony. I gave him a congratulatory nod.

The little salamander stepped up to the dais, leaving faint slime tracks from the holes in his tennis shoes. The guru ogre bowed his wagon-sized head. "You, Syl, are one of my greatest students. You have truly learned from me. You already have the power within yourself." Grbth took the gold chain from the nearby Igor and draped it over the narrow amphibious head. "With this Amulet of Importance, I say that you are ready for the world. Go face whatever challenges arise."

The gold chain slid down the slime-coated neck. Syl's forked tongue flicked in and out, then he danced off the stage, letting the next enlightened graduate come up behind him. He scuttled back to join us, glowing with excitement.

"We're very happy for you," said Sheyenne.

"Congratulations. You did real good, kid," I said. "I'm sure your father would be proud of you, too."

Syl's head drooped. "I have to change into street clothes. My pa would say it's all a waste of time. He doesn't know this is how I spend my allowance."

I felt sad and disappointed to hear this. "It'll get better. We'll help."

IV

Even after Syl the salamander had graduated into self-confidence and the next stage of enlightenment, complete with his Amulet of Importance bling, his life was still downtrodden drudgery.

I came upon the poor slimy kid just after I had finished serving an eviction notice to a rowdy frat-boy poltergeist. He had died of alcohol poisoning during a college party and was still so spiritually inebriated he didn't even know he was dead—nor was he happy to get the eviction notice. Nevertheless, the unpleasant deed was done, and Sheyenne could send a bill to the client. I felt as if a burden had been lifted from my shoulders.

And then I saw Syl slogging along the streets in his patched pants and tattered sneakers. His body was splattered with mud, which did not actually look out of place among the spots. He pushed a wheelbarrow piled high with thick mud, head down, forked tongue lolling out with exhaustion. As he drove his load down the street, some of the mud dribbled off the sides and splattered onto the pavement.

"Hi Syl," I said. "Looks like you're hard at work."

The young salamander looked up at me. "Sorry I can't stop and talk, Mr. Chambeaux. I have to haul two more loads of mud today or my pa will get mad."

He was not at all the bright and confident salamander I'd seen the night before in the Wham-Bam Ashram. I tried to sound encouraging. "My partner is still researching the age requirements for a sentient salamander to apply for emancipation from an abusive parent. But seeing this..." I shook my head. "We might have an argument both ways. If the court insists that you're underage, then we can charge your father for violating child labor laws."

"Just doing my chores," Syl said as he plodded along, and I shambled beside him. "It's not a job, because he doesn't pay me. Except my allowance. That's how I paid for my teachings from Master Grbth. Worth every penny."

The overburdened wheelbarrow creaked. "Where are you taking this mud?" I asked.

"I'm hauling mud from the swamp on the west side of town to the swamp on the east side of town."

"And why would you take mud from the west side?" I asked, wondering if it was a better quality of muck.

Syl kept trudging along. "To make room for the mud that I carry back from the eastern swamp. My father says the swamps are due for a full-fledged mud exchange, and I'm the one who has to do it. I've been at this for two years now."

My heart went out to him, and I knew Robin would be furious when she heard this. "Not today, kid. We'll dump this load and then go home. I want to meet your father." As a zombie I can be looming and intimidating, though I prefer not to be confrontational. I decided to make an exception for stern salamander parents, though.

We walked along, chatting, and I tried to lift his mood. Syl was very proud of the tiny gold amulet dangling from a chain at his neck.

When we got outside of the Quarter to the eastern swamp, I helped the salamander push the heavy wheelbarrow next to where a long shovel had been stuck between mangrove roots. Together, we dumped the mud into the murky swamp with a big brown plop.

Syl looked forlornly at the shovel. "I've got to load up again and head back to the west side. Five loads each day. That's my quota."

"Today we're changing the quota," I said. "Leave the wheelbarrow here. I want to have words with your father. I'll take the heat if he gets upset."

Syl's tongue flicked in and out. "Mythical salamanders had a lot of heat, but my pa and I are just mud salamanders."

"You're not 'just' anything, kid. We're getting you out of this mess."

Agitated and uneasy, Syl led me along a well-worn path until we reached the dreary mudflats, the neighborhood where he had grown up and where his father—whose name was Neb—had built a hovel. It was all they could afford, since Neb was lazy and refused to work.

The hovel was a rounded hummock of mud covered with moss and dead patchy grass. Empty cans of beans and Vienna sausages were scattered around the lawn; the most prominent feature was an old rusty wheelbarrow propped up on cinderblocks, its axle broken.

The muddy mound reminded me of an English barrow, but I had seen some of the nice, remodeled barrows that a group of entrepreneurial wights was offering for short-term rentals on AirBNBarrow. This one, though, did not look like that.

"That's my home," Syl said. "A nasty, dirty, wet hole, filled with the ends of worms and an oozy smell." He blinked his yellow eyes. "Not like the comfortable holes I read about in *The Hobbit*."

It was made even nastier by the surly-looking salamander who sat in an old metal lawn chair on the front porch next to the round door. Neb was dressed in a pair of faded bib overalls with no undershirt so I could see the spotty flesh in his armpits. His spots were gray and leprous looking, and his eyes blazed with a tinge of red.

The pudgy salamander let out a grumbling hiss, then wrenched himself out of the chair, smashing his thick tail back and forth. "What are you doing home, boy?" His forked tongue lashed out of his mouth. "You ain't put in a sixteen-hour day yet!"

"I wanted you to meet somebody, Pa." Syl clutched the arm of my sport jacket and tugged me forward.

"Don't want to meet nobody, and I warned you never to make friends."

I loomed in front of him as best I could. "I'm Dan Chambeaux, private investigator."

"You're a zombie," Neb snapped.

257

"And you're very observant," I said. "We're looking into your son's welfare and possible abuse. Slavery isn't a sign of being a good parent."

"I'm his guardian. The boy has to earn his keep." Neb lurched closer, trying to be menacing, but I can be menacing too. I held my (muddy) ground.

Neb glowered. "I've taken care of that boy since he hatched. His mother abandoned the whole clutch of eggs after she spawned. No-good whore! Left me with barely enough of our eggs to eat, but I missed this one." He nudged an elbow toward the sulking and intimidated Syl. "So, he hatched, and I had to take care of him. I raised him to do a good day's work and to take care of his pa." He snapped at the spotted young salamander. "Go crawl into the hole and lock yourself in your room. You're grounded!"

Syl's eyes lit up. "Really?" The delight was plain in his voice. "Then I can finish reading *The Hobbit*!" He ducked through the round door and slithered into the tunnel beneath the hovel.

Neb glared at me. "And you mind your own damn business!" He slouched back down into his metal lawn chair.

I certainly knew my own damn business. I turned away, thinking of the additional details I could report to Robin so she could file amended paperwork for Judge Hawkins.

V

That night as Sheyenne and I were reading Alvina a bedtime story after she crawled into her large cardboard coffin box—the little vampire girl had asked for *Children's Selections from the Necronomicon*—the enormous fire dragon appeared again over the Quarter, even larger than the first time.

When I looked through the dingy windows of my upstairs apartment, I could see the blazing reptilian entity rising over the rooftops.

Alvina peered next to me. "Oh, it's like a nightlight!"

Fire alarms rang throughout the city, and police sirens wailed, including the banshee. At least the water-sprite firefighters were going to have fun tonight.

"Keep Alvina safe," I said to Sheyenne as I hurried for the door. "I better go see if I can help. I'm sure McGoo is already running to the scene."

"What can you do about it?" Sheyenne asked, clearly concerned.

"Well..." I paused and pondered. "McGoo and I stood there and watched last time, and that proved pretty effective."

I was out the door before she could make a counterargument.

I lurched off at full speed, slipping into "fast zombie" mode. The elemental dragon beat its blazing wings like huge sails. It craned its serpentine neck, opened its jaws, and coughed out even brighter fire. Sparks flew from its lashing tail.

The ethereal creature circled overhead, bellowing, but it didn't attack. A monster of such great size could have blasted the whole Quarter into cinders. But when the fire dragon trumpeted out a call and blasted flames up into the sky, the sound didn't seem angry or vengeful. Rather, it was more triumphant, like a celebration of freedom or confidence (not that I'm an expert on elemental dragon sounds).

I could see where the creature was heading—straight toward the tall pagoda tower of the Wham-Bam Ashram.

While the rest of the UQ emergency-response teams raced to quench fires and rescue innocent victims, I decided to head the thing off at the source.

After seeing the powerful guru ogre, a guy so enlightened he no longer needed vowels in his name, I wondered if Grbth could help.

As I raced up the steep, zig-zag path to the tiered pagoda, I wished the ashram had simply chosen a straight line instead of a sidewalk that symbolized the winding journey of life. The paper lamps along the walkway were dark, since the rent-a-fairies apparently weren't working tonight.

TOM WOOD

The fire dragon circled high above, bellowing out more fire, thrashing sparks from its tail. I could hear the furnace crackling of its passage.

I ducked into the open pavilion, which was nearly empty. On his bamboo mat on the raised dais, the huge ogre again sat in a lotus position, holding the spiked club.

"Hello!" I called out. "Mr. Grbth, there's a fire dragon overhead! Better get out before it destroys the whole ashram."

The ogre raised his head. Despite the crisis going on throughout the Quarter, he seemed utterly at peace, content with his role in the universe. His heavy-lidded eyes opened and closed with the deliberate slowness of an electric garage door. His voice rumbled out. "I am aware of all things. That is one of the benefits of achieving nirvana. I no longer need security cameras."

I felt suddenly suspicious. "Do you have something to do with that fire dragon?"

Grbth hung his huge head. "Yes, I am partly responsible. I must take care of this unsettling ripple in the stream of peaceful consciousness." He looked toward the roof of the pagoda and the many levels of the pavilion above. "Sometimes my followers don't even know their own strength, once it's unlocked."

"Your followers?" I asked. "One of your students is doing this?"

"No—one of my graduates. Now I must meditate." Grbth closed his eyes again and raised the spiked club. He pounded the floor with a resounding thud. From the depths of his solar plexus emerged a low rumbling meditative sound. "BOOOOOOOMMM! BOOOOOOOMMM!"

The vibrations did something strange to the air, and I felt dizzy. I backed away, worried that the fire dragon would incinerate the ashram at any moment. The unfazed ogre had fallen into a deep meditative state, and I could see there would be no convincing him. Since he was the size of a small automobile, I certainly wasn't going to move him against his will.

When I dashed outside, I looked up to the pinnacle of the pagoda, where the fire dragon hovered in the air. Elsewhere in the Quarter, emergency crews had responded, and the water sprites worked with conventional fire-suppression crews to extinguish the flames as fast as possible. But unless it was stopped, the restless elemental creature could keep spreading fire wherever it went.

But as I stared up at the dragon, another figure rippled in the air. A huge intimidating form rose up through the pavilion's open windows and balconies, until it coalesced in the sky to become a misty but terrifying manifestation of Guru Grbth.

The huge ogre had created an astral projection of himself and now hovered in the open air to face off against the dragon. Planning ahead, Grbth also carried an astrally projected spiked club. It was just like a scene from one of those Godzilla versus Monster of the Week movies, and I prepared myself for a smackdown.

The fire dragon flapped its enormous wings, scattering sparks and little flames. The spectral ogre loomed closer, reached out a muscular arm.

I cringed, looking for cover.

And the shimmering guru patted the fire dragon on its flaming head.

Astral Grbth mumbled a soothing meditative sound, and the elemental dragon circled closer, thrashing like a dog wagging its tail. The ogre stroked down the dragon's spine.

"There, there..." boomed Grbth's voice. "Focus. Find your center. You have unlocked your inner strength. Now you must control it."

The fire dragon flapped its wings and rolled in the air, so the astral ogre could scratch its scaly belly. More sparks flew. The flickering dragon rumbled and purred, then pulled away, drifting higher. It flapped giant incandescent wings and rose into the air where it spread out, faded, then dissipated into mere curls of smoke.

The astrally projected ogre nodded in satisfaction, grumbling, and then he, too, dissipated into nothingness.

I bolted back into the ashram to find Grbth stirring on his bamboo mat, standing up with a groan and a grumble. He placed a hand against the small of his back as if he had pulled a muscle.

"All taken care of, for now," said the guru ogre. "Sometimes they get excited once they reach enlightenment, but with great power comes great responsibility." Grbth scratched his shaggy beard and belched. "I need to have my students start meditating over comic books."

"What are you talking about? Who was it?" But I already knew. "It's Syl, isn't it?"

The big ogre nodded. "Yes, poor boy. Terrible home life. He needed self-esteem and self-protection. Here at the Wham-Bam Ashram, I teach my students to find the strength within. Syl discovered and released his inner salamander."

VI

I couldn't do this alone. After rushing back to the office, I rounded up Robin, who was now armed with all the paperwork she had filed—as well as an emergency protective order she had just received from Judge Hawkins. That would help poor Syl even more than his Amulet of Importance.

As we set off for the salamander hovel in the mudflats, Sheyenne demanded to go along. And since Alvina was not technically able to stay by herself (and it was far too late to get an emergency babysitter), my half-daughter tagged along as well, even though sinister swamps and fire dragons and abusive amphibious fathers weren't exactly the best things for a little kid to be exposed to. She promised to take pictures for her Monstagram and SickTok accounts.

When we got to the barrow-shaped hovel, it was clear we had found the right place. On the ground, the slurry of stagnant water and brown ooze bubbled like volcanic mud pots. The air sparkled and flashed overhead, manifesting just a hint of the fire dragon. Alvina looked up at the light show and grinned with fascination.

With her ghostly speed, Sheyenne drifted ahead of us. "Hurry Beaux!" she called back. "I hear shouting! I don't want Syl to get hurt."

Robin stalked forward, clutching the legal briefcase against her side. "That Neb Salamander is going to be in more trouble than he can imagine. We'll sue every last spot off him."

A geyser erupted in the mudflat, and sulfurous steam hissed out. The fiery dragon flickered in the air again. We reached the round door set into the grass-covered mound just as another mud pot burbled open and swallowed the broken old wheelbarrow propped on cinderblocks.

Behind the sealed round door, Robin and I could hear shouting. "Get to your room, you worthless slimy son of a—"

I pounded on the door. "Neb, open up! Zombie detective!" It wasn't as intimidating as yelling "Police!" but at least he would know we weren't door-to-door salespeople.

The shouting stopped, and I heard squishy sounds approaching. Robin opened her briefcase and pulled out the legal document, holding it like a battle-ax.

The round door swung inward and we could see the dank, muddy tunnels inside. "What do you want?" Neb demanded. He still wore the same old bib overalls.

"This is a legal decree." Robin thrust the protective order forward. "Your son Syl has requested emancipation from you. He is to be cut loose immediately. You no longer have any parental rights."

"Emancipation!" Neb growled. "That's too damn many syllables. Let me see that." He grabbed the document out of Robin's hands, leaving slimy prints on the paper.

"We also have it digitally recorded," Sheyenne added.

From the back of the tunnel, Syl slunk forward. Seeing us, he seemed to find inner self-confidence. "I hired them, Pa, because I don't want to live with you anymore. You don't treat me right. I'm my own person."

Neb crumpled the emancipation decree and threw it into the mud outside. "I am his guardian. He's mine to do with as I please. He's too young to face the world alone."

"He was old enough to face you," I said. "Syl is stronger than you can imagine."

"I found my inner salamander!" Syl clutched the little gold Amulet of Importance around his neck.

Overhead, the sparks and wispy flames coalesced, creating the fire dragon. "That's me." He jabbed a webbed hand toward the astral manifestation. "That's who I am inside—a fire dragon! And I'm not afraid of you anymore."

Neb was certainly afraid, however. "Why you ungrateful little—"

The fire dragon roared, and a whoosh of diaphanous flames swept across the mudflats. Neb ducked back into the tunnel.

Robin extended a hand and took Syl's slimy fingers, pulling the young salamander out into the night, while Sheyenne and Alvina came closer to support him. Robin said, "You can start over, Syl. You're legally and completely free. The judge agreed with our case."

"What am I supposed to do?" Neb squirmed. "Haul all that mud myself? Wheelbarrow after wheelbarrow, from one swamp to another? It's ridiculous."

"It's ridiculous," I agreed.

"But Syl won't be part of it," Robin said.

Sheyenne drifted down and picked up the wadded emancipation decree. "I did mention that we also have a digital copy."

I said to surly Neb, "Maybe if you went to the Wham-Bam Ashram, you could work hard, meditate... and find your own inner *worm*."

"Wait, there's something I need." Syl withdrew his hand from Robin's and ducked back into the dank tunnel.

While we waited, we faced off against Neb, but the abusive amphibian didn't have the vocabulary to express what he really felt.

Syl emerged a moment later holding a beloved battered paperback copy of *The Hobbit*. "Now we can go," he said.

We walked proudly away from the mudflats, and Alvina skipped along next to the young salamander. I could tell they would be close friends. Syl was so happy, he even managed to whistle a cheerful tune with his forked tongue.

"We'll set you up with temporary lodgings, and I'm sure you can get a job. You have countless opportunities," Robin said.

"I'm a salamander," Syl said, taking it as a badge of honor. "The future is bright as mud."

As we strolled along, the fire dragon appeared again, glowing bright and happy. Golden sparks flew in all directions. With a companion like that, I knew Syl wouldn't have any trouble at all.

A Trickle in History

written by

Elaine Midcoh

illustrated by

JOSÉ SÁNCHEZ

ABOUT THE AUTHOR

Elaine Midcoh (a pseudonym) lives in South Florida. She is a retired college professor and spent many happy years teaching law and criminal justice to undergraduates. She has been a lifelong fan of science fiction since watching the original Star Trek *at age seven. By age ten she was avidly consuming the paperbacks of Heinlein, Asimov, and other sci-fi greats. In time she came to love history too and majored in that at college.*

"A Trickle in History" combines Elaine's love for both sci-fi and history, but it is also about family, loyalty, and the fight to maintain one's identity in terrible circumstances. Elaine was inspired by her own family's history, and she dedicates "A Trickle in History" to her mother and father.

This is Elaine's second story appearing in L. Ron Hubbard Presents Writers of the Future. *She was a published finalist in Volume 37 with her story, "The Battle of Donasi." And yes, this is a plug: After finishing this volume, you must immediately get Volume 37 and read "The Battle of Donasi." Twice. (Elaine is certain you'll like the other stories too.)*

In addition to Writers of the Future, *Elaine's science fiction has appeared in the magazines* Galaxy's Edge *and* Daily Science Fiction *and in the anthology* Compelling Science Fiction *(Flame Tree Press, Oct 2022). Her story, "Man on the Moon," was named the winner of the 2022 Jim Baen Memorial Short Story Award. Her historical fiction has appeared in the literary journals* Jewish Fiction .net *and* The Sunlight Press.

She hopes you enjoy "A Trickle in History."

ABOUT THE ILLUSTRATOR

José Sánchez, also known as Perrotrope, was born in 1979 in San José, Costa Rica, a small country with a unique beauty thanks to its exuberant nature. José has a BFA in fine arts from the University of Costa Rica, majoring in graphic design. However his real passion is illustration and animation, which he has studied in a self-taught way. As part of his formal studies, he also completed a one-year diploma in concept art at the Vancouver Animation School. His work was initially related to the advertising field, mainly as a motion designer. However his career took a decisive turn toward the animation industry, and he moved to Japan to work as a concept artist.

With passion parallel to his work in the studio, José kept producing personal pieces of art and illustration. That allowed him to experiment with various styles, as well as themes ranging from science fiction to fantasy for both adults and children. His illustration work is characterized by the special importance granted to color and lighting in storytelling.

Currently José is still working to break into the world of illustration so he can dedicate himself fully to what he loves so much, which is to tell stories hand in hand with writers of books, comics, and graphic novels.

A Trickle in History

Rebecca sat in the half-darkened room thinking again how stupid it was that the group met in a basement. Only one way in and out, not even a window to jump from. If the Purple Shirts raided, there would be no escape. She was on an old couch with ripped cushions, which, like all the furniture, was part of a semicircle that faced the basement stairs. The room was musty, but at least not moldy. Rebecca felt for the ancient pistol in her coat pocket. There were only two bullets. Get one of the Purples and then herself. The others in her group had their own methods ready, but they had agreed there would be no capture, no public executions. The last eight Jews on Earth would choose their own way to die.

They waited in silence, thirty minutes, forty. Where was she? Finally, old Albert said, "Maybe it worked."

"Then why are we still in this damn basement?" replied Anna, his research partner and wife of fifty years.

Albert shook his head and pursed his lips. He had no answer and Rebecca knew he thought they had failed.

Rebecca looked around the room. Albert, once known as Professor Drom, renowned physicist (forty years ago—now passing as a retired grocery store butcher), sat hunched over in his chair. A tear rolled out from the corner of his eye and dripped down his cheek. Anna went to him and put an arm on his shoulder. The other four old people, Rachel and Henry,

269

Julius and Margot, had been top scientists long ago too, just like Rebecca's parents.

Her parents. God. She had actually believed her parents were simple folks, Papa a postal worker and Mama a kindergarten teacher. On her thirteenth birthday her parents had brought her to a different darkened room, hidden in an obscure building. Her "Bat Mitzvah day," they called it, and there, in the presence of Albert and Anna and the others, they told her she was Jewish. They told her everything.

When they were done, Albert had said to her, "Now you know. According to the Purple Shirts the last Jews of the world were eliminated in 2182, when they finally took over Switzerland. Maybe so, except for us. We've never found anyone else. Maybe you are the last Jewish child born in Europe, born in the world. You can betray us if you wish, or you can take up your heritage."

And so for the past fifteen years she learned. She lit candles at Hanukkah and read at Passover Seders. On years when Yom Kippur fell on a weekend, and she didn't have to deal with school or work lunches, she would fast. When her parents died (separately, but both at home, thank God), she arranged for their burials and thanked the priest who performed the services. The others had all come to her home afterward, maintaining their false identities of course, but Albert and Anna made sure to be the last ones there. Then they took her hands and Albert said, "Now we will sit shiva," and he had explained the Jewish mourning rituals.

The sound of furniture being moved upstairs echoed into the basement. She felt again for her pistol. Henry went up the basement stairs, a large machete in his hands that seemed too big for him. He stood by the door, machete raised, his arm shaking from the weight. Then came the knocks: knock—pause—knock, knock—pause—knock—pause—knock, knock, knock.

Albert rose from his seat. "Let her in, Henry."

Henry unlocked the door and opened it, stepping aside so that Irena could enter. Despite her age and arthritic back, she walked down the basement stairs without using the handrails, clutching the top of her purse instead. Henry followed her. No one spoke until Irena reached their little semicircle. Rebecca's heart sank. There was not a glimmer of hope on Irena's face. The others saw it too.

"Well?" Anna demanded, her voice already shaking with anger.

Rebecca moved to an uncomfortable wooden chair, giving her seat to Irena who sank into the edge of the ripped couch. She reached into her purse and took out an envelope.

"I didn't open it," she said. She cocked her head toward the basement door. "But there's no change up there. No change at all."

"Still the posters?" Albert asked. Irena nodded. Those damn posters. Rat-like grotesque features on the drawings, warnings to be vigilant, Rebecca often wondered how people could maintain such a strong hatred of Jews when there were no Jews left to hate.

"Well, let's see it then," Albert said.

Irena handed him the envelope. Albert's hands shook a little as he opened it. He withdrew the sheet of paper inside. As Albert unfolded the page, it was stiff, but not brittle. Rebecca was surprised when she spotted the rose flower decorations on top of the stationery. Leave it to Rosa, she thought, always finding beauty somewhere. She wondered if Rosa was happy when she bought the stationery, despite whatever her letter said.

"My Dear Friends," Albert read. "I tried and failed three times. First in 1919 at the German Workers' Party meeting where he gave his first speech (I poisoned his water, but someone knocked the cup over before he drank), at the courthouse in 1923 when he was on trial for the attempted coup (again, poison—this time no one knocked over the cup, but the evil one did not drink or eat during the session) and finally, in 1924, when he was released from prison. That time I left nothing to chance.

"While he was in jail, I obtained a rifle and practiced and practiced. Your Rosa, little old lady, is a sharpshooter now! I found out by which entrance the prisoners are released. Across the street is an office building. I rented space on the third floor with

271

a large window that overlooks the prison. I loaded and unloaded my rifle, I cleaned it, I adjusted the sightings to perfection. On his release date I stood ready at my window, poised and waiting, my rifle secure on its stand, my sightings aimed at the prison door. And when he emerged...my rifle jammed.

"Henry, I think you are right. We are in a river and our weak gestures cannot alter the flow. Three times, three failures. I may try again and, if so, write you another letter. But tonight it is the Sabbath and I am going to synagogue. Yes, a real synagogue, with hundreds of Jews. They do not know what is coming and are happy still. I want to be with them.

"Thinking of you all,

"Your beloved, Rosa

"PS—You should have seen the look on the bank manager's face when I told him I wanted a safety deposit box for 300 years. He swallowed his surprise when I gave him one of our 'diamonds' in appreciation—after that he was helpful."

Albert glanced up at Irena. "I presume there was no other letter," he said. Irena shook her head.

"That was the only one in the box. Nothing else."

They sat in silence for several minutes.

Finally, Henry said, "So I was right. The flow of time is too strong. We can't change its currents."

"Maybe we went too far back," Anna said. "Maybe the further back we go, the less we can change. We should have tried to prevent the Second Holocaust, not the First."

Albert sighed. It had been an endless argument, one Anna had never fully given up on, even though she had been outvoted. He took Anna's hand. "My dear, we can't pinpoint the start of the Second Holocaust. First came the bombs, then the chaos, then the blaming of Jews. What do we target there? We don't even know how it all began. But stop Hitler and everything changes— maybe there would still be a Second World War, but a different one, with different consequences. And, God willing, maybe no Holocaust. No First Holocaust, no Second Holocaust. Maybe we get to live."

272

"I wonder what happened to Rosa," Irena said. She and Rosa, both widows, had been best friends.

Rebecca answered, "She told me if it didn't work she would go to Canada. Assuming she lives another twenty years, the Second World War shouldn't touch her there."

All the old people turned to Rebecca. They stared at her. For the first time that evening Rebecca saw something different in their faces; not fear, not resignation, but something else. And Anna—Anna was actually smiling. Anna rose and went to Rebecca. She took Rebecca's hand.

"Tell her, Albert," she demanded.

Albert stood too. Then the rest, Henry, Rachel, Julius, and Margot; all but Irena who stayed seated, her eyes watery.

"What is it?" Rebecca asked.

Albert said, "You know how fragile the machine is, how difficult it was to develop the fuel?"

Rebecca nodded.

"What you don't know is that it is only good for two trips. The vibrations when activated, the connectivity link...the fuel issue...two trips at most. So we have only one left. That's all. The night before Rosa left we all got together—" He waved his hands at Rebecca's sudden frown. "Yes, without you. We made a decision. We decided that if Rosa was not successful, then the last trip would be yours."

Rebecca's eyes widened. "You want me to kill—"

"No," Albert interrupted. "We want you to live."

Anna squeezed her hand. "We're all old, but you're still a young woman. Go back. Marry. Have Jewish children. Live a long, happy life away from all this."

"Find Rosa in Canada," Irena said, a tear dripping down her cheek. "She shouldn't be alone, and you'll be safe there. And your children and grandchildren too."

Albert said, "And great-grandchildren. There will be many generations before the Second Holocaust. Generations of living free, without hiding or fear. That's worth something—even if we know how it will all end."

Rebecca stared back at them, their little smiles, their nodding heads...their hope, all on her. She jerked her hand out of Anna's.

"No," she said. "Do you think I would enjoy my life in Canada or elsewhere while World War II is happening? Do you think I could hold my own baby in my arms without seeing all the lost babies?" *Or my parents, or you,* she thought.

She stood and turned to Henry. "You're wrong. Your so-called 'currents in the river of time' can be changed. Rosa did it."

Irena shook her head. "No. I saw. It's all the same. Go upstairs and see."

"Listen to me," Rebecca said. "I haven't been trained in physics and I'm no scientist, but you've missed the obvious. Albert, please give me the letter." He handed it to her. She quickly scanned it until she got to the bottom of the page. She read aloud, "PS—You should have seen the look on the bank manager's face when I told him I wanted a safety deposit box for 300 years. He swallowed his surprise when I gave him one of our 'diamonds' in appreciation—after that he was helpful.

"Don't you understand?" Rebecca asked. "A current in time was changed. The bank manager had a surprise that day. One he probably told his friends or family about that night. And the diamond might have changed something for him. Maybe he bought something he wouldn't have bought before. Time was changed."

Henry shook his head, "But that change was nothing—too insignificant to matter."

"Exactly," Rebecca said. "Maybe killing Hitler is too big a change. Maybe the...'river of time' won't allow something of that significance. We can't change the main current, but maybe we can create a side trickle, something little, something the river won't notice, something the river might tolerate. Rosa tried three times and failed. So let's not kill him. Let's do something so small, so slight, that no one would notice it, not even time itself."

JOSÉ SÁNCHEZ

Rebecca sat in the director's office on a plush, rose-colored chair in front of his massive redwood desk. The desk had intricate inlaid designs along its legs and edges—vines, and flowers. She tried to admire the multitude of artwork hanging on the walls—watercolors, oils, even two works of tapestry, mostly of nature scenes, all beautifully framed. But her damn corset was squeezing her so tight that it was hard to breathe, much less concentrate. Why women in the early twentieth century would voluntarily agree to such physical restraints was beyond her.

Thank God it was autumn and the two windows were open. If the director's office had been stuffy, she might have fainted—something upper-class women of this time were prone to do, at least in the literature of the period. The clang of a streetcar from the busy street below floated into the room, along with the smell. Though she had been in 1908 Vienna for two days, Rebecca still couldn't get over the odors from hundreds of horses. No wonder people would soon eagerly embrace automobiles—anything to get rid of the ever-present horse feces that marked the streets.

Rebecca's thoughts were interrupted by the entrance of the director, Dr. Johann Broger. He was an older man, in his sixties, with thinning grayish hair and a flowing white mustache, wearing a suit perfectly tailored for his slight physique. He came to the side of her chair.

"Fräulein Levin, I presume?" She smiled. When she had spoken to Dr. Broger's secretary earlier that morning, she had decided to use the name her parents had whispered to her when she was thirteen. This was the first time in her life that anyone had called her by her family's real last name. She offered her hand.

"Dr. Broger. Thank you for seeing me."

He went to his desk and sat down. "You carry an interesting calling card," he said. From his coat pocket he took out the diamond she had given his secretary. Broger put the diamond on his desk and pushed it toward her.

Oh damn. Was Broger refusing it—did he know it was a fake? Albert had promised that no one of this time would be able to detect a synthetic diamond. "They can't make synthetic diamonds yet, that won't happen for decades," Albert had said. "So they won't know even to look for them. They will simply see a diamond—and a wealthy young woman."

Rebecca's heart thudded hard in her chest, but then Broger reached out and drew the diamond back to his side of the desk. She took a deep breath and tried to calm herself.

"So, what exactly must we do for such a magnificent gift?" he said. "I assume your generosity is for the Academy of Fine Arts Vienna and not meant merely for its director?"

Was he asking for a personal bribe? Did they do bribes back in 1908? She thought a moment. Bribery was probably common in all times, but she was supposed to be an upper-class woman and he was a prominent man. Outright bribery wouldn't do.

"My gift is for the benefit of the school, Dr. Broger. But I leave it for you to determine its best use."

"And so I shall. But certainly, Fräulein, you have some idea for its usage?"

"I do," she said and withdrew another diamond from her purse. She set it on her side of the desk. Broger eyed it, his face flushing, but said nothing.

Rebecca leaned forward. "Last year a young man applied to your school. He wants to be an artist, a painter. You rejected him. He's applied again this year. I would like him to be accepted."

Broger glanced from the diamond, to her, and then back to the diamond.

"What is the young man's name?"

She gave it.

Broger tore his eyes away from the diamond and opened up a desk drawer. He removed a file and thumbed through it. After a few minutes he put the file down.

"I'm sorry. It appears we have again rejected the young man's application. The letter went out three days ago."

Three days ago? Damn, the historical record was off. Or were the currents of time mocking them yet again....

"So write a new letter," she said, unable to contain the harshness in her voice.

Broger's eyebrows rose. He shook his head. "I'm afraid we can't. The integrity of—"

Rebecca took out another diamond and placed it on her side of the desk next to the first one. "And give him a scholarship. Not just for tuition, but enough so that he can pay rent, too." She pushed both diamonds toward Broger.

Broger and Rebecca stared at each other in silence, the diamonds on the desk between them.

Later that week two teenage boys, both around nineteen, were sitting at an outdoor café sipping coffee. It was a gorgeous afternoon, a Friday, and pedestrians swept by them busy with end-of-the-week errands.

"I don't understand," Augie said. "What happened? How did you get in?"

"Who cares?" his roommate answered. "They said they made a mistake. They even gave me a scholarship. I'm going to be an artist."

Augie lifted his cup. He was truly happy for his friend. "To you, Adolph. May your paintings fill museums and galleries across the world."

Adolph raised his cup. "Across the world," he said.

That day, in the early evening, Rebecca was sitting on a bench along the edge of a small city park, not far from the hotel where she had taken up residence. She was trying to plan her next steps. There was no way to really know whether what she had done was enough. She decided to stay in Vienna, at least so long as *he* was here. Perhaps she would have to buy some of his paintings, or arrange for gallery exhibits, or even bribe art critics for positive reviews in the newspapers. She didn't know everything she would have to do—and, worse, she realized she wouldn't even know if or when she had succeeded. Would it be in 1933, when Germany would elect a new chancellor? Or would it be in 1939, when a war would start—or not start? She sighed. But at the moment, right now sitting here in the park, she knew two things with absolute certainty. It was Friday night, and she was a Jew.

She rose and began to cross the street. Temple Beth Aharon had opened its doors to the waiting worshippers. For the first time in her life she was going to sit in the open with other Jews and offer prayers to welcome Shabbat. In her head she recited the Sabbath prayer she had learned at thirteen, huddled in a darkened room with her parents: *Baruch atah Adonai, Eloheinu melech—*

Her foot stopped. She had just reached the other side of the street, about to step on the sidewalk leading to the temple doors and her right foot wouldn't move. She looked down. There was nothing strange in her foot's appearance, but she felt a tingling. She tried to kick her right foot with the left one, but found that now her left foot wouldn't move either. Both feet frozen. The tingling sensation in her body increased. Oh hell, was she having a stroke?

"Help," she called, or thought she called, but no sound emerged. Something else, too. None of the worshippers walking by gave her a single look, the strange unmoving lady with feet stuck frozen to the ground. They went on their way into the synagogue as if she was invisible. She tried to twist around to see if someone might be coming to her aid from behind, but her body wouldn't respond to her commands. She realized her arms were immobile too. Only her head still moved, up, down, right, left. Every other part of her body was just a tingling statue.

She glanced down where the tingling was the most intense. Her feet had developed a yellowish, bright glow and she began to lose feeling in them. As she watched, the yellowish glow extended, slowly climbing upward.

She raised her head. Of course. Henry's paradox. He had discussed it when the group had first decided to make the machine, when it was all just theory. "If we succeed, then we likely eliminate our own existence. Our ancestors will live different lives, and the generational line that led to us, our births, will disappear." They had all agreed with Henry—and they had

279

all agreed that it didn't matter. Preventing the First Holocaust, and thus the Second, was more important.

So I did it, she thought. *Got him into the damn school and the world changed.* She had managed to beat Time, but Time would not let her escape without cost. She stared at the doors of Temple Beth Aharon. Like Moses, she would not be allowed to enter the Promised Land. But through the open temple doors she was granted a glimpse of the inside and the people there.

As the glow reached her chest, she felt a wave of fear. Then she remembered when her father had explained the physics of matter to her. "Nothing in the universe is ever lost, Liebchen. It simply converts to something else, like water into steam or movement into energy." She wondered if that had been true for her parents and hoped that it applied to her now.

In her last conscious seconds as a human, Rebecca watched a young family approach the synagogue; a mother, a father and a little girl hopping and skipping between them. The girl held both of her parents by the hand. She was four or maybe five. The scene reminded Rebecca of when she had been a child and strolled so carefree, so safe, between Mama and Papa, unaware of the cruelties and horrors that waited for her in the world.

The girl suddenly lifted her feet and, laughing, swung loose in the air, held upright by her parents. Rebecca smiled. *For you,* she thought. And then the yellowish glow engulfed her completely and she was no more.

The Withering Sky

written by
Arthur H. Manners
illustrated by
XIMING LUO

ABOUT THE AUTHOR

Arthur H. Manners writes sci-fi, fantasy, and horror, and lives with his partner in Cambridgeshire, England. He has been writing for fifteen years, though it took a back seat while he finished a PhD on magnetic fields in outer space. He claims to be working as a data scientist, and so far everyone has gone along with it.

"The Withering Sky" was a blow-off-the-cobwebs free-for-all, written over the summer in 2021. Freed from doctoral studies, Arthur used this story as a form of CPR for his creative energy. There was no specific inspiration or intent, besides re-engaging with his favourite books, films, soundtracks, and video games. He also wanted to increase the number of dark stories set in space, of which there is a shortage—which is a shame, because that's where all the darkness is.

He hopes that you enjoy the story and apologises for the ever-shifting doom mural that consequently appears on your bedroom wall. He is working on removing this effect from his prose, but for now asks that you think of it not as a bug, but as a feature.

ABOUT THE ILLUSTRATOR

Ximing Luo was born in 2005 in Hangzhou, China, the capital of China's Zhejiang province. She is a student at the University of Pennsylvania studying Digital Media Design, an interdisciplinary program combining computer science and art. She has been drawing ever since she could hold a pencil, discovering her love for art and creativity during preschool. Inspired by children's books and illustrations, she started illustrating and has never looked back.

Ximing's current works explore the cohesion of reality and illusions in dreams and nightmares, consisting of surrealist pieces investigating the hallucinations of the subconscious human psyche. With a passion for novelty and originality, Ximing finds herself experimenting with a variety of media and concepts, always seeking ways to push her craft and imagination to the next level. She has worked with woodburning, scratch art, digital art, animation, traditional Chinese painting, ink, charcoal, acrylic paints, oil paints, and geometric sculptures, among other media.

In the future, Ximing endeavors to polish her work and pursue her artistic side while seeking new experiences. She aspires to fulfill her dream of developing a digital game, illustrating a children's book, and traveling the world.

The Withering Sky

I stepped aboard the derelict armed with only three scraps of information: it was something from the Kuiper Belt worth keeping a secret; against interplanetary law, my employers had towed it to Neptune's primary Lagrangian point; and the rest of the story was beyond my pay grade.

Five of us had stumbled off the shuttle: me, Kitamura, Rogers, M'Bele, and Vezzin. I huddled close to them by instinct. Out here, the sun was feeble, just another star. I'd spent long enough on Triton to find comfort in the azure glow of Neptune's ammonia clouds, but until yesterday it had been just another reminder of my crappy life on the frontier. Now, the planet had reduced to a smudge the size of a pea, and I would have given a month's pay to have it back.

We stood on the threshold of a cylindrical object almost five kilometres long and three kilometres in diameter. An object made of a material so unreflective that it consumed our shuttle's searchlights. An unlit, apparently unmanned, hulk.

It didn't look like any space station I'd ever seen. Maybe a hulled-out asteroid, though they tended to have at least some reflective terrain or protruding apparatus—not like this, perfectly smooth and symmetrical.

However, I recognised the desolation of this place. In the ten years since I fled Earth clutching my degree, I'd slummed around my share of old wrecks. I had always felt a kinship with derelicts: motes drifting through the void, catching spent wisps of cold starlight.

Apart from our footsteps, there was an unfamiliar silence. Only hard vacuum could be truly silent. Stations and spacecraft were always noisy, filled with working equipment and pipes, radio transmissions, the voices of virtual assistants and the patter of shoeless feet on module walls.

This place was so quiet that blood roared in my ears.

"Can anyone find a light?" said Kitamura. She was stocky, a military type with a no-nonsense face and an imperious tone.

We sounded off: nobody could see anything beyond the beams of their own helmet-torches.

"A control board, anything?"

"I can't even find light panels," said M'Bele, bearlike in silhouette. Tall even for a Martian, towering above us, me especially.

"Don't be stupid. You're just not looking. Who hired you?" said Vezzin, a small weaselly man.

The two of them hissed at one another as we fumbled around in the dark for several minutes. Rogers, a short, mousy-haired white woman, eventually found controls on the far wall. Strong light banks threw back the darkness.

We were in some kind of antechamber, much larger than I had expected. The room was almost ten metres high and thirty metres across—the cavernous space was almost entirely empty. I balked at the wastefulness. I had spent a lot of time on space stations designed to utilise every millimetre; every extra gram required more fuel to move around.

The walls were bare except for the lights, which were integrated into the wall's surface. The material was faultless brushed metal, a far cry from the budget construction of the oceanic research station back on Triton. I had only seen something like it on luxury leisure craft.

It was either the most expensive tomb ever made, or it had been evacuated.

Alarm bells rang in my head. What had I got myself into? Forget a month's pay—I'd have emptied my accounts to see Neptune's clouds right now.

But I couldn't go back to Triton. Even if I could get the shuttle to take me, I couldn't station-hop forever. I owed money almost everywhere a ship could land.

Unable to stay, with nowhere to run. That was how I always ended up.

My only hope was to use this paycheque to crawl back to Earth and beg my parents to bail me out. Again. Then maybe they would let me stay in my old bedroom—still plastered with teenage heartthrobs—just long enough for me to put myself back together.

I reviewed the information we had. We knew this place was a secret; there had been nothing about this on the news circuits. But nobody could have built it in Commons territory without being noticed. It must have been constructed in trans–Neptunian space and then towed into the solar system—at biblical cost.

On approach, M'Bele had railed about the illegality of it floating here, radio dark and almost impossible to find.

While he babbled, Rogers had studied the positions of the sun and Neptune. She confirmed that we were floating at one of the Lagrange points, the spots around Neptune where its gravitational tug of war with the sun balanced out.

Beyond the fact that this place had an airlock, everything else we knew was summarised on a single piece of paper, tacked to the shuttle door.

Instructions
1. Do not study the exterior. Illumination risks detection.
2. Do not disturb unsecured areas.
*3. Await and aid research team. Until then, Major Kitamura
    has command.*

Violation of the above will result in forfeiture of payment.

The first line stuck in my mind. For whatever reason, they didn't want anyone else to join the party. Not that there was much risk of accidental discovery. The object's profile had been visible only by blocking starlight behind it—as much an absence, a negative, as a presence.

We didn't have time to discuss the note, mostly because Vezzin had taken an instant dislike to M'Bele—whose measured tone could sound condescending. I bet Vezzin had been picked on as a kid. They had now resumed their bickering, almost nose to nose.

Kitamura tried to calm them but succeeded only in adding to the growing noise.

I cut across them all. "Somebody else was here."

A pallet of supplies had been placed towards the rear of the antechamber. No boot prints were visible in the scrim of dust on the floor.

"They must have sent a drone ahead of us," M'Bele said.

"If they have drones, why bother to send us?" Kitamura said.

"You really don't know? And *you're* in charge?" Vezzin sneered. He bared his teeth at the pallet as though it might attack him.

Kitamura looked him up and down. She was at least a head taller than him, and I could see something in her stance that reminded me of a cobra before it struck.

"Why don't we just find out why they sent us?" I said.

On top of the supply crate lay the same instructions sheet that was tacked to the shuttle door, with an addendum at the bottom underlined in red: *Establish camp for inbound research team,* ETA *2 days. Make* NO *transmissions.*

"Cut-and-dry babysit gig. Need-to-know basis. I can work with that." Kitamura nodded.

"What, that's it? You're satisfied? Look at this thing!" said Vezzin.

"I've seen some strange places, but the jobs are always the same. This is how it goes: we set up camp, sit tight, carry the bags when the nerds arrive, and go home with the green."

"Yeah. Sure," I said, trying to sound more confident than I felt.

I itched to jump back onto the shuttle. But opportunities to earn a quick profit were scarce beyond Titan, and I wasn't going to throw away my last chance. I started unpacking the supplies.

Who knew why anybody wanted me for a cushy job like this. I had arrived at Bouvard Station expecting a briefing. Instead, I was peeled away from the other commuters by two burly men in plain clothes and locked in stripped-down quarters with Kitamura and Rogers. When they finally came back, they promised answers, but instead we had been bundled into another shuttle with Vezzin and M'Bele. The autopilot took us out before we could protest.

The people running this outfit needed some sensitivity training. About thirty years' worth might do the trick.

I tried to put it all out of my mind. I'd have crawled through sewer soup to get away from the frontier—to keep moving, keep running, the only thing I had ever been really good at.

Our alarm faded, but a vague dread remained. We talked while we unpacked the pallet, filling in the blanks, relieved for something to do that made a little noise.

Everyone but Kitamura had been rerouted from Triton; she had the unmistakable bearing of a combat vet, and the musculature of somebody who rarely left Earth.

Rogers had been looking for extremophile marine life in Triton's oceans, though she seemed to know a lot of astronomy for a biologist.

M'Bele was a financial analyst and part-time psychotherapist, more than bemused to find himself on a paramilitary dark-op.

Vezzin was an engineer who also owned a ten-shuttle freight company, which probably meant he was in deep with the black market. I was in enough debt to recognise someone taking a job with no questions asked, just to stay afloat.

Adding my own profession—surveying caverns and crevasses around Triton's icy crust—made a team with no obvious complementary skills. There were no more clues in the pallet to explain why we had been picked.

We sorted through some regulation clothes and selected a wardrobe each, set up chemical toilets in case the one in the shuttle blocked, and even found a collapsible shower. I hadn't expected to see one in deep space, but I hadn't expected gravity here either.

"This whole thing must be spinning fast to simulate weight like this," said Kitamura.

Rogers arched an eyebrow. "The rotation is the whole reason the airlock is at the endcap of...whatever this thing is. Don't tell me none of you noticed the shuttle spinning us up on approach. That was a long burn we made."

Kitamura bristled. "Nobody told me you were a physicist. Thought you were some kind of marine biological whatever."

Rogers shrugged. "Surprise. Anyway, the fuel required to spin up something this massive must have cost a fortune."

She seemed more interested than unnerved, which unnerved me.

"Who would pay for something like that? There's nothing here," Vezzin said.

"Nothing in this room, no," Rogers said.

We all squirmed in discomfort at the implication: it had been impossible to get a sense of scale from outside, but the object was no doubt far larger than this chamber.

By the time we ate, any comfort from the supplies had dried up. We were back to staring at the walls. The tension ramped up when M'Bele and Vezzin went back to sniping at one another.

We had been aboard only a few hours, but nobody objected when Kitamura suggested we get some sleep. There were one-person tents in the supplies, which at first seemed ridiculous, given the absence of wind or rain or chill, but we decided to put them up for privacy.

I crawled inside—and paused. A pressure released in my forehead, one I hadn't been aware of carrying. The feeling spread back through my head in a wave of relief. I poked my head out through the flap, looked around at the chamber walls. The pressure returned, at the limit of my perception, a tiny flower of discomfort blossoming between my eyes.

The others all had their heads poking from their own tents, brows furrowed. When Vezzin saw me watching, he withdrew.

"We must be more tired than we thought," Kitamura said.

I lay down and tried not to probe at my forehead. I guessed the effect was some agoraphobic response after years spent swaddled by tight spaces. Our employers must have known it would happen; why else include tents?

For a few hours, the silence felt more comfortable. I barely slept anyway.

In the morning I crawled out unrefreshed and made sure I got to the shower first. Everyone muttered in their tents about headaches. I had hoped the water might ease the stabbing pain between my eyes, but it didn't pan out. The sourness lurking between M'Bele and Vezzin soon returned.

As I padded back to my tent, Kitamura and I shared a look that said *men*.

Kitamura ordered them to give it a rest, but it was clear that they weren't going to stop. She tried a new tactic. "We should explore, see what we're dealing with—but you two stay away from one another."

"The instructions say not to disturb anything," said Vezzin.

"We'll just look. I'm not going to sit here without making sure we're secure."

Rogers was already preparing to head out. "Sooner we take a look, the sooner we'll know the situation. This place could be a giant vat of nuclear waste, for all we know."

"You don't have to sound so excited about nuclear waste," I said.

"What do you mean?" Rogers gave me a quizzical look, but the smile on her face lingered.

"Well, I'm not going anywhere. I'm not risking my pay to satisfy your curiosity," said Vezzin.

I had a retort ready, but Kitamura shook her head. "No transmissions," she said.

Vezzin glowered at her.

ARTHUR H. MANNERS

We left him there in his tent, and split into two teams: Kitamura and M'Bele, and me and Rogers. Beyond the doorway leading from the antechamber, a wide corridor headed off in either direction.

The corridor was dark when we first stepped into it, but then lights winked on in sequence, spreading out in a wave from where we stood. The corridor looked like it ran for kilometres in either direction. Despite the object's size, we should have been able to see the end of the corridor, or where it bent out of sight. Instead, our view just petered out to a haze.

"Vaporised coolant?" I said. Thoughts of suffocation or poisoning shot through my head.

"Might just be damp in here. Mist," Rogers said.

Each team headed in a different direction.

I felt better at once. It had always soothed me to be on the move. A mysterious lure had hung at the edge of my perception all my life, and chasing it was the only salve for the itch. Sometimes it dulled enough for me to make some fleeting caricature of a life. Sooner or later I always left, hoping maybe that nameless something lay around the next bend—maybe my destiny, maybe just an antidote to my lousy personality.

Rogers and I walked in silence for only a few minutes before she stopped and looked over her shoulder. Frowning, she got out her radio. "Kitamura, check in."

"We're here. Found something already?"

"No, the opposite. We've lost sight of you."

She was right. Incredulous, I looked back the way we had come and saw nothing but empty corridor. We hadn't walked more than half a kilometre.

"Same here. We can't see you." Kitamura's tone was matter-of-fact, but her audible gasp had carried over the radio.

I heard M'Bele curse in the background.

"You didn't turn any corners?" I said.

"No. You?" Kitamura said.

"No."

"Vezzin, you still with us?"

"What?" Vezzin barked.

"Could you stand in the doorway? The antechamber is halfway between us. We're having trouble gauging distances."

Vezzin sighed. "Fine, I'm here."

I couldn't see him.

My mind reeled. I tried to imagine the geometry that would explain our lines of sight, but the effort almost gave me vertigo. I turned away to hide my reaction from Rogers, facing the mist.

"Well?" Vezzin said.

A long pause stretched out before Kitamura said, "Never mind."

"Maybe it's an optical illusion. Or we've come farther than we thought," I said.

"We'll deal with it later. We still need to know what's in here."

We pushed on. I kept glancing back, hoping M'Bele and Kitamura might reappear.

"Why are you smiling?" I said.

"I'm not," Rogers said.

"You were definitely smiling just now."

She shrugged. "It's been a while since I've seen something really interesting."

"Uh huh."

I wished I'd gone with Kitamura.

A little farther on, doorways appeared on both sides of the corridor. Each door led to a space at least as large as the antechamber. We tracked back and forth along the corridor, counting them. After finding the twelfth doorway and maybe glimpsing a thirteenth ahead, we headed back to the first.

M'Bele called in—he and Kitamura had found a similar number of rooms on their end. We agreed to proceed with caution.

Rogers led the way into the first room. It seemed to be a copy of the antechamber, though it was filled with large shipping containers, stacked high and arranged in a grid. I couldn't get over the vast inefficiency of space. It was the kind of behemoth spacecraft drawn by a child, or a science fiction writer with no respect for common sense.

We followed the walkways between the stacks until we hit

the back of the room, but I spent most of the time massaging my forehead.

"What's wrong?" Rogers said.

"The light's all over the place. It's giving me headaches."

"Seems fine to me. You probably just need rest."

We considered trying to open one of the containers, but we had no equipment. Kitamura and M'Bele radioed in that they had found something similar. "Just boxes and more boxes," M'Bele said.

His voice seemed to echo over the line. I massaged my head some more.

Rogers grew still. "Do you hear that?"

"Hear what?" Kitamura said.

This time, I heard it too. Kitamura's voice came twice—once over the radio, and again from somewhere to my left.

Rogers nodded. "We must be close to you."

"What?"

"The corridor runs in a circle. It'd explain why we lost sight of you."

"Doesn't explain why I didn't see any curves," M'Bele said.

"Any better ideas? Stay where you are, we'll work our way over to you."

We weaved through the walkways, playing Marco Polo over the radio. But every time we came to a wall and they sounded off, the echo came from behind us. We crossed the room twice before we gave up.

"We should head back. We need to think this over," Kitamura said. She and M'Bele got off the circuit.

But the voices kept coming, now from more than one direction.

"Echo through the air ducts?" I muttered.

Rogers grinned—the slightly unhinged kind. It didn't help my nerves.

We hurried back to the antechamber. Vezzin didn't even bother to wave.

At least things have been boring here.

Kitamura and M'Bele arrived not long after. They paled when we explained what happened. "We heard something too," Kitamura said.

We talked it over, but Vezzin scoffed at us for letting our nerves get to us. M'Bele didn't rise to it, which made Vezzin dog him all the more. In seconds they were circling one another.

Their spat was annoying as ever but killed our nervous momentum. When they were done, nobody wanted to talk, so we turned in for the night.

I felt stupid as soon as I got near my tent. What did I care about this place, anyway? The job was simple—sit on the nest until the eggheads arrived.

I crawled inside, and a wave of relief flooded my head starting from my forehead and sweeping back, as though somebody had plucked a wad of iron wool from inside my skull.

I had been living with the discomfort all day and barely noticed.

Again, sleep refused to come. I had plenty of practice sleeping in noisy environments, but I had never experienced this kind of ringing silence. I could hear the others' every snore, exhalation, and sigh. There were times when I could have sworn I heard them blinking, as they too lay awake.

Next morning, everyone looked haggard, except maybe Rogers—before she started squinting.

I knew what that squint meant. The moment I left my tent, the pressure returned for me too, a vague throbbing between my eyes. The pain was unsettling; worse was how quickly it faded from my attention. If I concentrated, I could sense it, but otherwise I felt only general malaise.

Nobody felt like exploring. The research crew would be arriving today; they could worry about what did and didn't make sense. I was happy to take a back seat and carry the bags until I had the money in hand. Then I was gone.

But it became clear that waiting even a few hours was beyond

293

us. Big as the antechamber was, it wasn't big enough to keep cabin fever at bay. Given M'Bele and Vezzin's feud, and the weird pressure in our heads, it was clear we needed distraction.

Kitamura took Rogers this time, M'Bele came with me, and Vezzin stayed behind again. I was glad on all counts, and even happier to be on the move. Everything was more manageable when I was moving.

In the hallway, we tested how far apart we could get before we lost sight of one another. I made an involuntary noise the first time Kitamura disappeared. She stood around a hundred metres away, in full view, with what seemed like at least a kilometre of corridor stretching away behind her. Then she took one step back and vanished.

She took a step forward and reappeared. It was like she was becoming transparent rather than stepping around any kind of corner.

Strung out in a line, we found that the vanishing distances between us were inconsistent. There was no discernible trend. We swapped positions and were even more disquieted to learn that the distances changed depending on who stood where, as though the horizon was personal to each of us. The only thing we could agree on was that none of us could see another person farther than two hundred metres away.

Shaken, we regrouped and inspected the storage room Rogers and I had reached the day before. No voices this time. Just containers, which we found had no discernible hinges or handles, nor any other sign of how they might open.

We trooped back to the antechamber, relieved that the research team would be arriving any moment. But when we got back there was no sign of another shuttle. Vezzin had been trying to raise them on the private radio channel for hours.

"Could just be late," I said.

"Could be they're screwing with us," Vezzin snapped.

"If this were any other job I wouldn't care, but after what we just saw..." I said to Kitamura.

Kitamura grunted.

"Saw what?" Vezzin said. He grew skittish when we briefed him on what happened in the corridor. "What a dud assignment. This place is loony. Let's get out of here."

"What, just cut and run? I would have expected more pep from a respectable businessman," M'Bele said.

"Never you mind my business!"

"I suggest you save that energy for the debt collectors waiting for you back at Bouvard. I hear they like to play with their food."

"Screw you, you dog-faced turd-eater."

"Enough," Kitamura warned. She glanced at Vezzin. "The most likely scenario is that they're delayed and need to maintain radio silence. We just have to sit tight. But I'm not doing a job with anyone who isn't all in. Show of hands. Who wants to leave?"

I tried to picture finding another way of buying my ticket Earth-side, but M'Bele's comment about debt collectors had stung. All that waited for me on Triton was a bottle of shine and a knifing on a quiet maintenance level.

M'Bele looked uncertain but didn't move. Rogers's face was a picture of disinterest. Vezzin had half raised his hand but dropped it with a scowl when he saw he was alone.

"Okay, then," Kitamura said.

We found the mural on the fourth day. Kitamura and I entered the seventh room leftward of the antechamber and I screamed.

The rear wall was alive, writhing and dancing. Reaching for me.

I fell back into Kitamura and flailed.

"Wait!" she said. The iron in her voice slowed me. She held my shoulders until I stopped struggling. "It's just a painting."

She was right, in that it was just forms on a wall.

She was wrong, in that it was no painting.

We stared at it for over a minute before either of us spoke, but by then I hadn't even started to process it.

"What are we looking at?" Kitamura said.

I shook my head. I had the simultaneous impression of

movement and a static image. Travelling in space offered plenty of conflicting sensory input, but this was a whole other level.

"You said it was a painting," I said.

"Did I?" She frowned.

It was obviously nothing, some reflections of exotic ink. But a more animal part of me glimpsed a boiling broth of elemental forms, crawling over one another for primacy.

"What do you see?" Kitamura said. Her voice was even, but she took a small step back.

"Nothing." I had to bite back: *Everything.*

We went to get Rogers and M'Bele. They had the same reactions, though Rogers wanted to take samples.

"Don't go near it," M'Bele said.

"Why? Look at it. It's remarkable," Rogers said.

"I don't like it."

Rogers rolled her eyes. She looked to Kitamura. "Well?"

Kitamura considered. "We're not supposed to disturb anything. Do you even have equipment to analyse it?"

"No, but I'm not going to cower and put garlic under my door. Let's just take a closer look. We'll learn something."

Kitamura nodded after a long pause.

Rogers started forward. I reached out to restrain her before I knew what I was doing. Kitamura and M'Bele did the same. Rogers looked bewildered at where the three of us had seized her.

I tried to focus on her face, but the wall snagged my attention. For a moment I could have sworn I saw a cartoon of all of us, outlined in black: a five-year-old's drawing of four people with big down-turned lips.

"It's just a painting," I said. "It's just that..."

"I don't like it either," Kitamura said. She looked embarrassed and cleared her throat. "For all we know, this place is a weapons lab. We don't have protective gear. New policy—until we have an idea of what we're dealing with, we don't even go near anything. Especially in this room."

For the first time since arriving, I slept well. The figures in the

296

mural had moved too fast to make out, but in my memory they slowly unspooled, and returned in my dreams to slow-dance above me.

"It's obviously a lab. Something funded off the books, a place to run all the research too nasty to see the light of day. It got out of hand, and now they're cleaning up," Vezzin said, sounding bored. I wanted to throw him into the corridor, see how bored he was then.

Speculation had become a central pastime. We had grown bored of guessing when the research team might arrive—it was obvious that they would show up when they felt like it. But it was open season when it came to the nature of the object.

Kitamura thought it was military, a psychological weapons outfit hidden beyond regulated space. M'Bele changed his guess every few minutes, ranging from mundane to wacky.

Rogers refused to offer her own thoughts.

I was the only one who suggested it might have come from farther away. It wasn't impossible; the probes dispatched to Alpha Centauri, Procyon, and Epsilon Eridani had succeeded, after all. Maybe somebody had managed a round-trip mission.

"They hollowed out an entire asteroid for a black-site lab? We might have explored a few kilometres' worth, but you could fit a small city in here," M'Bele said, considering his hand.

The others were playing cards. I itched to join them, but I held off. I was no stranger to dropping a couple grand on the table and talking big, then waking up in an alley with empty pockets. But I'd been clean for weeks now. No point putting up with this freak show only to emerge ready to gamble away my pot of gold.

"Okay, big shot. What do you think it is?" Vezzin spat.

M'Bele upped the ante. "I'm certain it's an alien spaceship."

Everyone scoffed.

"If it was alien, why would it have Earth-standard gravity and atmosphere? Everything is custom made for humans," Rogers said. She seemed more intrigued than sceptical.

"Though, if it was made by humans, it would be as cut-rate and grimy as every other station in the system," I said. My fingers twitched as I glimpsed the straight flush in Rogers's hand.

"Not if you know the right people. I've been on some stations Mars-side that look like they were designed by Dali with Solomon's gold," Kitamura said. She folded.

"Oh, yeah? Did they have the nightmare murals there, too?" I said and regretted it. The fun went out of the conversation as soon as we thought about the mural.

Rogers threw down, and everyone groaned. She was on a streak.

It went on like that for a while. By day, we wandered and tried not to think about what we found. By night, we speculated in the imagined safety of one another's company.

No doubt Bouvard knew more than we did. Maybe they even had a reason for not towing everything back to Neptune and cracking this freaky little egg open.

But we were clueless. Even the shape of the object defied understanding. We had seen from the outside that it was cylindrical, and kilometres tall, but we never found any staircases leading to other decks.

Vezzin and M'Bele wanted to use the shuttle radio to demand more information—the one thing they could agree on.

Kitamura, Rogers, and I didn't want to jeopardise the brief.

We danced precariously around the growing divide between us. Kitamura knew better than to overextend her position, announcing sorties into the corridor just before Vezzin and M'Bele boiled over. I took these trips as gifts, a taste of the freedom I craved, even when we found things that defied the laws of physics. But it was obvious that our situation couldn't last.

"What are we babysitting, the object or them?" I said.

Kitamura didn't laugh.

Vezzin started playing music at night to mask the silence. He claimed that it worked, but I could still hear everybody breathing. As soon as morning came, the bickering would start again.

Rogers started experiments. Most of it was too technical for us, but we did help her study the optical effects of the corridor. I remembered enough college physics to get the gist of what she was doing, but mostly I did as I was told.

"Has it occurred to you that Rogers is the only person who should be here?" I said.

Kitamura grunted, her arms and legs splayed out like the Vitruvian man. Apparently it helped Rogers gauge the aberration close to the vanishing horizon. Or it could have just amused her. "What makes you say that?"

"The rest of us aren't physicists or engineers or whatever she is."

"Vezzin's an engineer."

"Yeah, and a big help he is."

"Mmm. You're assuming they wanted us to study the thing at all. We're supposed to be babysitters."

"No way would they send us here just to sit on this place. What's taking the research team so long? There's enough here to occupy every researcher between here and Mars for years."

She didn't have an answer for that. I watched the familiar discomfort play out on her face. Before I could press her, she changed tack. "So, are you going to tell me why you need this money so bad? Any sane person would be on Vezzin and M'Bele's side."

I pretended to tune my radio. I had managed to avoid the topic so far and wanted to keep it that way.

Kitamura shrugged. "I want to run my own outfit," she said, as though I'd asked. "Seed money like this is hard to come by. Plus, whoever our employers are, they'll be good people to have on my side.

"As for the rest of you. Well, Vezzin's a coward, so whatever. M'Bele is too sensible to be as stupid as the rest of us. Pretty sure they just straight up lied to get him here. Rogers is a head case who would walk into fire to measure the temperature of flames. But you, I'm not sure. I figure you're running. What I can't figure is whether you're running to something, or away from something."

I looked down the corridor towards Rogers, who shimmered at the edge of the vanishing point. "Me neither," I said.

What did I tell her? That I had everything given to me but hated every second of comfort. That I wandered until there was nowhere to go but off-planet. That I gambled and drank my way to the edge of occupied space, and spent ten years wandering the ice, half frozen to death, just so I didn't have to think.

I almost broke the silence, but Kitamura spoke first, oblivious.

"Well, I hope you figure it out, because I can't pretend I know what I'm doing forever. Who knows why those bastards put us here. Stay or go, we're going to need to trust each other to get through this."

I nodded, but I was disappointed and frightened. I had been hoping that secretly she knew at least a little more than the rest of us.

Rogers's ambition didn't stop at the corridor. She wanted to study the mural. She had all kinds of ideas—ideas I couldn't begin to understand.

But Kitamura made sure nobody went near that room alone. Visits were limited to a few minutes, always in pairs, with one person facing the corridor at all times. I guessed she was afraid one of us might be hypnotised or something. I didn't blame her.

We stopped splitting up when we explored. We dragged M'Bele with us when we could, though he and Vezzin almost seemed distressed to be separated. In some twisted way, their fighting had become a comfort.

I was braced for a repeat of the mural, but most of the other rooms were empty or just quietly inexplicable. One room had a bench in it—not an acceleration harness or a storage rack, but a wooden park bench.

"At least it's familiar," I said.

"Somehow I'm not relieved," Kitamura said.

"Where are you?" I said.

I stood in the sixth room rightward of the antechamber, which

300

housed the only window we'd found. It showed nothing, just empty space dotted with stars, but I kept coming back.

I told the others I was watching for the research crew, but I didn't expect them any time soon. Two weeks had passed, and we'd heard nothing.

We had edged towards panic at one point, but relaxed when we took inventory and found the pallet had supplies for months. They must have anticipated delays.

Really, I had returned to the window because sun-bathed Earth was somewhere in the darkness. Out on the frontier, home was nothing but a fantasy. As unreal as the phantoms and streaks of light people saw as their eyeballs deformed in microgravity.

There was nothing but time on the object. Time and silence. I took any opportunity I could to wander and explore, but my body needed to rest eventually. When I stopped, my mind couldn't avoid itself.

"Where are you?" I repeated.

I had said it more often the last few years, whenever I was forced to stop, and realised that I barely recognised myself.

Was all this worth it? I hadn't heard from my parents since the last round of rehab on Bouvard. They had to remortgage the house to pay for it. They knew it wouldn't stick, so when I relapsed, they didn't call.

I didn't dare hope that we could narrow the chasm between us. Some things couldn't be unsaid. But maybe if I could just see them again, I'd have something to fight for.

All the same, in the unforgiving light of the corridor, it all seemed pathetic, ridiculous.

What was I trying to go back to?

I probed my head. I knew that pressure must be there; every night it tore through my forehead like snarled hair yanked from a rusty pipe.

I knew I hadn't been sleeping for more than an hour a night. I should have been in pieces by now, delirious and barely able to stand. But I was starting to feel more alert than ever, and when I breathed, I could almost feel the walls swell around me—

Rogers burst into the room. "Vezzin's dead."

I followed, numb. The antechamber amplified M'Bele and Kitamura's silence. For a while we became a melodramatic fresco—them flanking Vezzin's body, me and Rogers staring across it.

M'Bele broke the spell by taking a step back. Only then did it become clear that we were all staring at him. I hadn't even been aware of it.

"No, no. This has nothing to do with me," he said.

I punctured the short silence. "You've been at one another's throats since we got here."

"No, I was with Kitamura the whole time. Right?"

Kitamura nodded slowly. "That's right."

"Don't look at me like that! How could I have done this? Look at him!"

I had thought Vezzin's limbs were askew, but now I noticed one arm and both legs were bent the wrong way at the elbow and knees. His neck looked strange and had turned purple.

M'Bele was a big man, but to inflict that kind of damage he'd have needed the strength to break bricks with his hands. There was no sign of a weapon, or a struggle.

"Did you lose sight of him, even for a second?" I said.

"No," Kitamura said. "We were pretty far down the corridor." Her jaw clenched and with visible effort turned her back on M'Bele. "Couldn't have been him. Either there's somebody else here, or . . ." She cleared her throat. "We might be in trouble."

Kitamura and I fussed over what to do with Vezzin, before Rogers produced a body bag.

"From the pallet," she said in response to our shock.

"Why didn't you tell us there were body bags in the pallet?" I said.

"They were right there. I thought you knew."

I wondered what else I'd missed.

Kitamura went to the shuttle to radio for help. "Enough delays," she said.

"Wait!" I yelled in unison with Rogers.

"We can't break radio silence. There are so many questions. They'll take over, kick us out," Rogers said.

"That's the point," Kitamura said. Her gaze switched to me.

A dozen conflicting thoughts clogged my throat. I could only stare back at her.

Whatever Kitamura saw in my eyes, she didn't like it. "A man is dead," she said coldly and went into the shuttle.

I stayed with Rogers to deal with Vezzin. We had to straighten his limbs to get him into the bag. I grimaced at the prospect, but Rogers whisked me aside and arranged the body, businesslike. I heard something crunch in Vezzin's leg.

Kitamura emerged from the shuttle. "I can't raise anyone."

I stiffened. "What?"

"I thought they just weren't answering, but I'm not even getting static. I think the shuttle radio is dead."

"That's the only thing we have powerful enough to reach Bouvard."

M'Bele let out a quiet moan and began to rock back and forth.

I touched my forehead. The pain had lurched up to my conscious awareness.

Kitamura looked stricken as though grasping for control.

Rogers looked between us, the same intrigued expression on her face as when she studied the corridor.

"What's the matter with you? Doesn't anything bother you?" I said.

She shrugged.

"Can you fix it?" Kitamura said.

"Maybe. Vezzin was the mechanic."

"Try."

Rogers vanished into the shuttle. After an hour, she reported that nothing seemed obviously broken. I wasn't sure I believed her.

"Fine. They'll arrive soon, anyway," Kitamura said. She sounded far from certain.

"Wake up!" M'Bele yelled. "It's obvious—we're some kind of sick offering."

"Don't be ridiculous. You talk as though this place is alive," I said.

"I don't know what it is, but I'm certain it's not totally dead, either." He looked around. "Come on, you're all thinking it."

"The only reason we're here is to get paid and get out of here. Now stop it, you're scaring everybody," Kitamura said.

"Somebody is dead! Some*thing* is in here with us."

"There's nothing in here except our imaginations, and a few buggy experiments. We'll contact Bouvard, get double hazard pay, feel sad for a minute, then move on. Don't tell me you've never taken a dangerous job before."

M'Bele fumed, but I could see the fight had drained out of him.

It was getting late. None of us wanted to stay in the antechamber, but there was nowhere else to go. I considered suggesting we pile into the shuttle and seal the doors. Then I thought of being cooped up with Rogers bouncing off the walls, and M'Bele rocking like an earthquake survivor.

We opted for our tents, though we pushed them against the shuttle doors, in case we had to retreat.

"How can there be anyone else here? We'd have seen them by now," I said.

"Who knows how much farther the corridor goes," Kitamura said.

"Far. We haven't scratched the surface," Rogers said sleepily.

I tried to ignore that. "You'll fix the radio, right?"

But she was asleep or at least pretending to be.

We set a watch. I didn't expect to sleep, so I stayed up with Kitamura.

M'Bele sounded like somebody in the grips of fever. He tossed and muttered broken sentences. Several times we saw his silhouette bolt upright.

"Do you think we've all been like that every night?" I said.

"I'm trying not to think about it," Kitamura said.

"What if we can't call for help?"

"Like I said, the research team will be here any minute. This thing has got to be valuable to them to go through all this smoke and mirrors bull."

"What if they decide it's too much risk? What's to stop them from leaving this thing out here and saying they lost us in an accident?"

Kitamura scratched her nose. "You've been watching too many movies."

I woke to a throbbing headache. Kitamura and Rogers were already up, having taken the last watch.

"Let's go get the bastard," I announced.

"What?" Kitamura said.

"Vezzin wasn't killed by some rogue experiment. There's somebody in here who wants us gone."

"You're serious," M'Bele said. He glanced at Kitamura. "It would explain why you're here."

"Whatever. No more than one person could hide in here, no matter how big this place is. There are four of us left. Let's go get them."

Kitamura opened her breakfast rations. "If there is somebody else here, and they killed Vezzin, they're armed with something that breaks bones like twigs. Four unarmed people against one person with...what, a sledgehammer? Not good odds."

I paused to think about it, but Rogers was giving me that same strange look, as though I were a bird in a cage somehow twittering human speech. "If I don't get out of this room, I'm going to explode."

"What about fixing the radio?"

"Even if Rogers can fix it, I'm pretty sure she's not going to do it in a hurry." I turned to Rogers. "No offence, but you're all kinds of crazy."

She paused a moment then shrugged.

Kitamura put her head in her hands. "Fine. Suicidal manhunt it is."

M'Bele took some convincing, but one glance at the body bag in the corner brought him around. We headed out leftward, keeping together, holding a few wrenches for protection. By the afternoon we'd reached the fifteenth room, the furthest we'd gone. It was an office—a run-of-the-mill Earth-side office—complete with budget upholstery. There was even a water cooler. But there was also a pungent smell, like farm animals.

"Looks like we found the accounting deck," I said.

Something bumped the underside of the desk beside me, and I froze. Before I could run, M'Bele hauled a pile of rags from under the desk, writhing and screeching in his grip.

M'Bele skittered back. "What the hell?"

I could now see that the pitiful thing was a small man in his forties, cowering on the floor.

Rogers crouched beside him. I had the impression of a butterfly collector observing a specimen mounted upon a needle. "Who are you?"

He answered with another whimper. He stank, his clothes caked in dried excretions. Kitamura recoiled from another desk, where the man had been relieving himself.

Rogers crooned to the man despite the stench, and by degrees he calmed.

M'Bele and Kitamura wanted to tie him up, convinced he had killed Vezzin. I didn't think he looked strong enough to stand; breaking every bone in a person's body seemed a stretch.

Nearby we found supplies, scraps of clothing that had been fashioned into a backpack, a photograph of a young man toasting the camera with a bottle of beer.

After a few minutes the man answered M'Bele's questions.

"Transport crew." His voice was thin and broken. "Bouvard sent us. A...a supply drop."

"The pallet? Back in the antechamber?" Kitamura said.

"Routine drop. Supposed to be back on station for dinner." He turned haunted eyes on us. "They promised."

"What happened?"

The man withdrew, curling up on the floor, and Rogers had to coax him back out.

"We unloaded the gear, spent the night. Then the shuttle was gone. The others went away, and it was just me."

"What happened to the shuttle?"

"How many others?" said M'Bele.

"What happened to them?" said Kitamura.

"Guys," I warned.

But it was too late. The man shook his head in violent jerks and began crawling away. "Noooooo..." he moaned.

"Let's get him back to camp. This is ridiculous, there's no way he's going to make sense in this condition," I said.

"Seconded," Rogers said.

Kitamura and M'Bele made a show of reluctance, but there wasn't much else we could do. He obviously hadn't killed Vezzin.

We got him back without trouble. We forced him into the shower and fed him, but he fell asleep before we could get him talking again.

"Think he'll run?" I said.

"We could put him in the shuttle," Rogers said.

"Not a chance are we putting him in there. He might sabotage it," Kitamura said.

So we watched him kicking and moaning like a dog. We took shifts again, one to watch the door and one to watch the stranger. And in the middle of the night, with the pressure creeping through my forehead, I cringed at the thought that another crew had been here and only he remained.

Kitamura woke screaming in the night. Cool, calm Kitamura. She flailed and wept fat tears as we pulled her from her tent.

The stranger watched, owlish.

Once Kitamura was settled, I touched my temple unconsciously, searching for that creeping pressure. It was getting to us all. If we hadn't set a watch, might some of us have become like the stranger's crew—just walked off into the dark somewhere?

The next day, our guest started talking in earnest. The only problem was that it was all nonsense words, interspersed with screeches and hisses. He would startle suddenly, as though an explosion had gone off, and we had to restrain him. Sometimes I thought he might be saying something coherent, but it was always too quiet to make out.

He wouldn't tell us his name. For whatever reason, that question frightened him most.

We couldn't wait around forever. We dragged him back into the corridor, visiting the fourteenth, fifteenth, and sixteenth rooms rightward of the antechamber. They were boring, housing more storage containers, but something didn't feel right.

I realised late in the afternoon what was bothering me: the distances just didn't tally. We should have reached the far-side hull by now. We had gone beyond the external physical dimension of the object.

Rogers was thrilled.

Kitamura suggested the hallways were indeed bent imperceptibly, and that we would eventually find our way back to the antechamber. To check, we left a sonic beacon in the seventeenth room and hiked all the way to the fifteenth chamber on the leftward side. It was late by then, later than we'd ever stayed out, but none of us wanted to stop.

We had set the beacon to emit a one-hundred-twenty decibel ping on a one-minute cycle. Loud as a jet engine. We all stood straining to listen.

And heard nothing.

"Guess it's not curved," I said.

Kitamura didn't reply. I guessed she was remembering our first trip, when we had heard one another through the walls.

We made it to the antechamber exhausted. We managed only four hours of sleep before the stranger leapt wailing across the chamber, knocking Rogers flying. I tried to stop him and received a punch to the neck. He almost made it to the door before M'Bele tackled him.

Snarling, M'Bele tied him up. The man didn't struggle, but M'Bele threw him around like a doll and kicked him in the ribs. It took all of us to drag M'Bele away.

"He killed Vezzin. Why else would he run?" M'Bele roared. He didn't seem at all like the calm, measured man who had stepped aboard.

"Go set watch. I don't want to see you again until we move out in the morning," Kitamura said.

For a moment I thought he'd attack her as well, but he crumpled and trudged away.

None of us bothered trying to sleep again. A dangerous lunatic was one thing, but I was more worried about waking up in a panic and hurting someone.

Rogers toyed with the radio all night but claimed to have made no progress. I was beginning to doubt that she was trying at all.

"They're not coming for us, are they?" M'Bele said, slumping against a crate.

"We don't know that," I said, but it was only a reflex. I felt it in my bones—if we were getting out of here, it would be on our own steam.

Kitamura led us into the corridor before we could eat breakfast. "This thing can't go on forever," she growled.

M'Bele pushed and manhandled the stranger. The look in his eye dared us to say something. Kitamura and I did our best to smooth things over, the danger we sensed communicated in stolen glances.

Before long, I was flagging. Stress had bullied my body into a constant tremble, and my mind felt like stretched taffy.

Yet, a part of me hoped that the corridor would just keep going. I was beginning to savour the silence, the simple unending process of putting one foot in front of another, watching the unknown appear from the darkness.

I worried what would happen when it ran out—no matter how hard I ran from myself, the road always ran out.

Then we reached the twentieth chamber leftward of the antechamber, and my petty troubles didn't matter anymore, because the twentieth chamber was filled with bodies.

The forms were charred, melted and misshapen things, the features lost. But there was no mistaking the arms, legs, heads, and torsos. A few were clustered close to the door, their burned hands reaching for the corridor. Two of them sat against the far wall, embracing.

"Still they see the too bright faces of the many," the stranger said.

"Do you know what happened here?" I said.

But he was gone again, into his own world.

M'Bele backed out from the room, breathing fast.

I held up my hands. "Cool it. Whatever happened, it happened a while ago."

"You don't know that! You don't know anything. None of us do. We're searching this place like we'll find something that'll change anything. What in here is going to get us back to Bouvard?"

"Just breathe," Kitamura said.

"No. I'm done. We all know what happened to this guy's friends. Either he killed all of them and he'll go for us next, or something a lot worse than him is in here. You can get yourselves killed if you want, but I'm getting out of here."

He ran.

"The shuttle!" Kitamura said.

We tried to follow, but we were hobbled by the stranger's shuffling pace. We ended up half-carrying, half-dragging him. By the time we made it back to the antechamber, I was certain the shuttle would be gone.

It was still there, but Rogers reported that the shuttle radio module and most of our tools were missing. M'Bele had taken his tent as well, and enough rations for a week.

Kitamura wanted to go after him, but I stopped her. There were only the three of us now. Between us we could take M'Bele if things went bad, but one of us was bound to get hurt.

We spent a wary evening with our attention split between the stranger and the door. The air seemed denser, the heaviness of anticipation.

M'Bele didn't materialise. Still we sat, waiting, until sometime late the next day.

"We need to go," Kitamura said. "Override the shuttle somehow. Send help for M'Bele once we get to Bouvard."

A part of me had been screaming the same thing. Nothing was worth this.

But it made me dizzy to think about going this far only to give up and go home with nothing.

"You go. I'm staying," Rogers said.

Kitamura rolled her eyes and looked to me for backup.

She was right: we had to go. This was the moment to step up, do the right thing. But I hesitated a beat too long, and Kitamura's expression sobered, then hardened. She wasn't going to be the sole survivor, the captain who abandoned ship and let her crew drown in shadows.

I felt sorry for her. But the truth anchored me to this nightmare—I couldn't leave, not yet.

We went through the motions of eating and resting, but the atmosphere between us had changed. If there had been an alliance, it was now broken.

I was startled but not surprised when I woke the next morning and found Kitamura gone. Rogers, who was supposed to be on watch, only shrugged when I asked what happened.

"She went to get M'Bele," she said.

I didn't bother asking why they didn't wake me. Rogers was working on a pile of wires and micro-monitors. I left her to it and spent the day with the stranger instead.

Rogers announced she had to go run some experiments on the mural. We fought for a while, but it became clear that it didn't matter what I said. I was beginning to hate her, but I knew that if I didn't go with her, then I'd never see her again. And that would leave me alone. So we were both going.

Luckily, the stranger was content to be led like a dog on a leash. I spoke to him as we headed out, about what I'd say to my parents, about my luckless time on Triton, my addictions and frustrations. I sensed he was listening, even while he twitched and stared about.

I called out for Kitamura and tried to raise her on my radio. Several times I thought of doing the same for M'Bele but thought better of it.

We reached the mural without incident. The stranger let out a soft gasp as we entered the room. I half expected him to freak out, but instead he sank to the floor and sat cross-legged, mesmerised.

I kept my gaze on Rogers, asking questions about the experiment, keeping my mind busy. It worked for a while. The mural didn't look like much, maybe a few dark streaks on the far wall. I helped Rogers set up.

Then the heart palpitations started. Invisible hands gripped my head, trying to force me to look at the wall. I focused on breathing, on not looking up, but the flutter in my chest grew, sending me gasping. "Rogers!"

"Incredible," Rogers said.

I glanced at the wall, and a vice closed around my chest. "Rogers, we have to get out of here."

"Do you see it?" Rogers muttered.

"There's nothing there. Listen—we're leaving."

I tried to reach for her, but my arms had become lead weights. There was no way to not look. It was as though my eyelids had been taped open.

My body thrummed like a struck gong. Those invisible fingers slithered under my scalp, digging into the soft parts of my mind. Flashes of anger, terror, lust, hunger. I avoided wetting myself by a hair.

The mural came alive, different to last time: bright colours on top and a dark form below. A procession of figures gathered, their features only hinted at by bright swirls, like a negative of an expressionist painting. The whole thing shifted and danced, kaleidoscopic. I was looking right at it, but some part of me was also convinced I was looking at a blank wall.

"Rogers."

The dark thing rose to penetrate the standing figures. They raised their arms, mouths opening—whether to pray or scream, I couldn't tell. Then they began to buckle, and somehow I knew they were melting.

Rogers smiled. "This answers so many questions. So elegant."

Whatever she was seeing, I doubted it was what I saw.

312

I turned to run and saw the stranger with his arms raised; he began to sing a high, continuous note—cut short when I collided with him and tackled him into the hallway. I landed on top of him, heard something crack. He shrieked.

"Rogers, come on!"

She didn't move. I dragged the stranger away by the collar, bouncing him off the walls. Either he was a lot lighter than he looked or I had summoned the strength of ten people.

I made it most of the way back to camp before I slowed down. The silence hit hard then, punctuated only by the stranger's whimpers. At last, the grip on my heart loosened, the fingers in my mind retreating just enough to let me think.

I had left Rogers back there. I just left her.

But I didn't bother trying to go back, knew that I wouldn't be able to turn my feet. I needed a plan first.

The stranger was cradling his shoulder. He seemed to be fading by the moment, a bundle of bones in a paper bag.

This was all I had left for company?

I soon gave up trying to raise anyone on the radio. I wanted to crawl into my tent and sleep for days, to escape everything I could not understand.

We were fifty metres from the antechamber door when Kitamura stepped into the hallway. She was laden with supplies, looking the other way. Her jumpsuit had a big tear down one side.

I called out to her, breaking into a run despite the stranger's dead weight.

She started walking the other way, rightward of the antechamber. She disappeared within seconds, a mere ten metres from the chamber—a far shorter vanishing horizon than I had seen before.

I went past the chamber door, five metres, then ten, then twenty. She didn't come back into sight. I stopped when the antechamber vanished behind me, not daring to go farther.

I called her name for the better part of an hour. In that time, nothing stirred but the ragged flutter in my chest, and the whimpering stranger at my heel.

There was no choice but to sleep. I tied the stranger's wrists and ankles and fenced him in with supply crates. He didn't protest but curled up like a dog and fell into a muttering sleep.

I took a long length of pipe from the shower and pulled my sleeping bag into the shuttle. I closed the airlock and wedged the pipe through the locking wheel.

I managed not to scream only by imagining the peace of mind I would feel when I got home, when my parents took me in and blew away the spiders in my brain. I would get through this—all I had to do was hold onto that future.

I must have fallen asleep because the next thing I did was jerk awake. The stranger was making a low keening noise.

The locking wheel wrenched an inch clockwise. The pipe holding it in place groaned but held.

"Rogers?" I whispered.

No answer.

After a while the sound died away. The pipe had bent. I wasn't sure even M'Bele would have been strong enough to do that. I tried not to think about Vezzin's twisted body and went back to sleep.

The stranger survived the night. He didn't respond when I asked him if he had seen anything.

I realised I had been hoping Kitamura would come back. But she had gone native like the others. I knew I wouldn't last on my own. There was no choice but try to get back to Bouvard.

I spent the morning checking over the shuttle. I didn't know enough about flight controls to tell if it could make the trip back. I couldn't even access the nav computer.

I spoke to the stranger over lunch. "The shuttle was programmed to take us here on autopilot. It must be able to find its way back. If we could just find the trigger, we could go for help."

But I just didn't know enough. No matter how I tried to

think around it, I came to the same conclusion: I needed Rogers. Somehow I would have to convince her to help me.

"Come on, we've got to get her."

Leaving the antechamber felt remarkably stupid. I took another length of pipe with me; it didn't make me feel safer.

I spoke to the stranger nonstop, whistling in the dark. "Straight to the mural, grab Rogers, straight back. But we don't look at the mural. If I blindfold us, we should—"

Two snarling figures careened from the room on my right and collided with the wall. Kitamura and M'Bele, locked together. M'Bele was larger by far, but something had happened to his arm, and Kitamura was fighting with the fury of a lion.

I moved to intervene but scrambled away at the sight of something feral in Kitamura's eyes. They roared like beasts, and I realised they would kill one another.

The pressure in my head pulsed and I lost my balance. I lurched from wall to wall until the spinning stopped. By then, there was no sign of Kitamura or M'Bele. The stranger was nearby, sitting cross-legged.

"How did this happen to us so fast?" I said. I looked at the stranger. "Is this how it happened for you?"

He blinked, gazing at things that weren't there...I hoped.

"Come on."

We passed several more rooms without incident, but my progress slowed. By the time the mural room came into sight, I was actually leaning forward and sweating. It was like walking uphill, through treacle.

I checked—there was no discernible tilt to the floor. It was no easier than usual to walk back the other way.

I made it to the room preceding the mural but could go no farther. My foot hung in midair, quivering. Sweat beaded on my forehead. I strained until I was almost horizontal.

"Damn it!" I yelled, collapsing to my knees.

The stranger stood beside me, showing no signs of difficulty. He simply waited, obedient as a dog.

"Go to her. Bring her back. You can do it," I said.

His gaze continued to trace the walls. His lips moved silently, as though reading invisible words.

"Please," I muttered, but it was no use.

I could hear Rogers, holding intense conversation with somebody. I called out to her, but she didn't reply.

The overwhelming resistance grew, until I found it hard to even swallow or blink. I turned back, and at once the feeling vanished.

Time passed. I must have blanked from the exhaustion, because suddenly I was back at the antechamber. My radio was crackling.

M'Bele's voice drifted out, "I killed the bitch for you. She is dead as all the others that you have taken into you. You crawl in my mind and steal pieces of me, but won't show yourself. Why do you forsake me?"

More time passed. I ate rations, trying to spoon some into the stranger's mouth without taking my eyes off the antechamber door. Then I woke in the sealed shuttle, banging my head, convinced that I saw shadow fingers retreating from my head and flying away along the wall. Then I was walking down the corridor again with the stranger in tow.

The mysterious force pushed me back again. I could even hang in place, leaning into it as though against a gale.

I wandered back aimlessly and came across a tripod. On it was mounted a laser that Rogers had rigged for surveying. We had tried to use it to study the corridor, without success.

I didn't remember passing it on the way out here. I hadn't seen it for days.

There was a note on the pad tied to the tripod.

Distance to corridor's end:
1 p.m.: 7 km
3:30 p.m.: 1.7 km
4:15 p.m.: 129 km
4:16 p.m.: Variable
5:30 p.m.: 7 km
6 p.m.: ¯_(ツ)_/¯

317

I turned the laser beam towards the mural room. The scale maxed out. I turned it to point the other way: thirteen kilometres. Back again: maxed out. There were enough digits on the scale for a thousand kilometres.

I didn't stick around to see if it changed. I returned to camp and found that more supplies were gone.

I sat down heavily. I couldn't help the others—couldn't even reach them. Nor could I leave. I had to figure out a way to get a message to Bouvard.

But I couldn't focus enough to form a single thought.

I sealed myself and the stranger in the shuttle with food and water and rested there for two days. Sometimes I fruitlessly tried to get the shuttle working, but mostly I just lay still.

The idea of the research team coming to our rescue now seemed like a sick joke.

I tried to raise Rogers over and over. In the long sleepless hours, I scanned the other frequencies. Most of the time it was just static, but sometimes I heard M'Bele muttering.

When I emerged, Kitamura was there. One of her arms was bound in a self-made sling, the bandage crusted with old blood. We stared at one another across the partially-dismantled camp.

"Where have you been?" I said.

She didn't respond, her face immobile.

"I lost Rogers. She's stuck at..." I cleared my throat. "Stay. Rogers is the only one who can fix this. If we could just—"

Kitamura backed away. She stared at the stranger, who peered around the shuttle door, eyes wide in the shadows.

"He's harmless. He's been with me the whole time," I said.

Kitamura's gaze snapped to me, and her eyes narrowed. "Then he got to you too."

"He's mad as a bag of drowned cats, but he's done nothing. It's M'Bele I'm scared of."

I bit down on the remaining words: *And you. I'm scared of you too.*

Kitamura shook her head, backing away. "I was wrong to come back."

318

She was gone before I could say anything. Later, the worst of it wasn't questioning whether she had really been there, but the memory of her lucid gaze. She had treated me and the stranger calmly and decisively, as threats.

Things happened in no particular order. A slideshow of washing, wandering, hiding in dark corners, eating, trying to sleep. Every time I tried to concentrate, the thumping between my ears overwhelmed me. I spent hours on the floor cradling my head—

"Not coming back. I have so much work to do," said Rogers.

I blinked, looked over my shoulder. My heart leaped in my chest at the sight of the mural, only a few metres away from me.

It sleeps.

The thought rang unbidden through my mind, hammerhead upon anvil.

It sleeps but it may wake any moment, and when it does you must be gone.

Dark amorphous forms curled lazily on the wall. Forms that were of course not there, because the wall was blank.

I looked at Rogers, who was scribbling away on her tablet. Her face was haggard and her clothes rank, but her eyes were alert. "I can't go. I have too much work to do. It has developed new complexities overnight; I need to know what triggered the change."

I balked at how relaxed she seemed. I felt the mural's presence as keenly as if a live tiger slumbered beside me.

"I . . ."

How did I get here? How much time had passed?

"I can't go. I need your help."

Rogers kept scribbling.

A sharp rod pierced my forehead. I gasped, "None of us are going to get out of here if you don't—"

Rogers vanished. The mural was replaced by a stained wall. The stranger mewled at my feet. We stood in the room of burned bodies.

I had a half-eaten energy bar in my hand. A long bandage had appeared on my shin, which burned faintly.

A new silhouette had appeared on the wall. Looking at it more closely, I realised I recognised it, in a way. Sometimes such things happened close to nuclear blasts. The body was atomised, its last moment caught in shadow, seared onto the wall behind.

But there was no sign of any explosion here, nor was there a matching half-melted body. The shadow was stocky, caught in a moment of supplication. It could have been anyone, but the voice in my head said *M'Bele*.

The stranger let out a low warble, head up like a wolf howling at the moon.

I stared at the silhouette until it was burned onto my retinas. Any doubt it was M'Bele leaked away.

I wandered away into the corridor. I wanted to be sick, but I couldn't feel my body. I made it back to the antechamber without blacking out, fell short of the shuttle and stumbled into one of the unused tents.

I woke alone. I went to wake the stranger, who was curled up nearby.

He was dead. Neck broken.

Kitamura stood by the doorway. She peered at me with the wary gaze of a cat.

"You?" I said.

She stared.

"Why?"

She withdrew but spoke as she went away. "It was getting to you through him. It's just us now."

"Rogers is still alive. We need her if we're going to get out of here. Help me!"

In the distance, her reply: "I'll hold them off. Get the shuttle ready."

"Hold off who?"

She was gone.

The day passed before the floor stopped spinning and I could stand up. I left the stranger's body and made my way into the corridor, heading for the mural chamber. Even now, a part of me took sick pleasure in barrelling onward with no hope of success.

The corridor smiled upon me and let me pass. Despite covering my eyes, I could feel the mural trying to worm its tendrils between my fingers and pry them away.

"You've been gone a long time." Rogers sounded hoarse, but otherwise normal.

I wondered how she was still alive. If she had stayed here the whole time, she should have died of thirst by now. It had been days, maybe weeks.

"Damn it, Rogers. Fix the shuttle. We have to go."

"I wanted to go, at first. I was afraid. I could feel it in my head. But it's really not a bad trade, feeling a little discomfort to discover all this."

"This place is killing us. It's some kind of weapon."

"Weapon? No, no. It's an ark."

"What?"

"M'Bele was right. Funny, isn't it?" She giggled. "They tried so hard to get away, start afresh. They brought everything they'd need. Genius, really. What we could have learned from them.... But it didn't work out. They couldn't leave behind what was already a part of them. And through them, it spread through this place, like a coal seam burning for fifty years under the earth."

The back of my neck prickled. "Are you talking about the mural?"

"That? Nothing but a beautiful mote in the eye of what the makers brought with them."

How did she look at it without snapping? She sounded almost normal.

Almost.

"How do you know?" I said.

No reply.

"Rogers, you'll die here. I can't bring you food or water."

She tittered. "No time to eat or drink. No time at all."

The pounding in my head was growing again. "It's not too late. We can go home. You remember home, don't you?"

Her tone turned ponderous: "No. Do you?"

"I—" The pain sliced between my eyes. "Please, come."

"Soon. Once the work is done."

"Rogers!"

The world blurred. I did not move; the room shot away from me. I passed down the corridor, which stretched and bulged around me. I retched once, twice, got control, and by then I was flying at great speed. Kilometres of corridor passed by. I fell and fell, for so long that, somehow, I fell asleep.

You remember home, don't you?

No. Do you?

I woke in the corridor.

I found a drawing beside me. I recognised my own sketching style: a house, a big yellow sun, a car. Three stick figures stood in the middle, two big, one small.

Home.

I gripped the drawing tight, clinging to it, to sanity.

But it was a lie. I knew Earth was nothing but another dead end. Before I even landed, I would be restless, straining for freedom, for that nameless something I had never been able to find.

That flimsy shard of hope had been keeping me together. Now, it unravelled.

Even if I could find a way to alert the authorities, they would be no match for this place. Here, we were all baby birds in the hands of an insane child. The thought sent a surge of anger through me. I might not be going home, but I wasn't going down like this.

I ignored the rod between my eyes and sprinted. Maybe I could trick the corridor into letting me pass if I caught it by surprise. But almost at once the floor tilted. I was running uphill, reaching for the next doorway, which receded along an expanding length of wall. I tumbled backward, then fell, as the corridor veered toward vertical.

I landed hard, winded, and came to my feet in darkness. Somebody screamed nearby.

"Hello?" I called.

Another scream. "Get out!"

"Kitamura?"

"Get out of my head. Out!"

I groped around. "Find your way to me!"

"Get oooout!"

Kitamura collided with me and her hands closed around my neck. She squeezed, hard.

"You were all trying to kill me from the start. They sent us out here to watch us like some kind of circus. Had you drive me mad while you hunted me? Huh?"

I choked, scrabbling at her neck and face.

"You almost fooled me. For a moment there, I actually thought you wanted to get out of here—"

She wrenched away from me, her shriek cut short. Something large passed me in the dark. Kitamura gave another yell, cut short by a flurry of sickening thuds.

I could sense things changing in the darkness. Walls squeezed close around me one moment and were gone the next. The floor undulated like the surface of the ocean.

Pain came sharp and sudden, a blade of ice thrust into my forehead. I cried out and staggered, falling to my knees.

It's awake.

I looked up to see the mural.

I scrabbled away and got to my feet. If I got stuck here, then nobody was going to come to pull me away. I'd stay forever, just like Rogers.

Rogers.

I looked around the room. It was empty.

"Rogers?"

No body, no kit bag. Like she'd never been here.

I backed against the wall but couldn't feel it—denied even the simple reassurance of a solid surface to cower against.

I wept a little, gathered my strength, and took my hands away from my eyes.

Rogers was in the mural. At least, her silhouette was, standing amongst the swirling smoke. She stared in wonder at the titanic forms about her, like a child dwarfed by an ancient forest.

She had never been trying to figure anything out. She had just been waiting for this place to take her, so she could know what came next.

Eventually, I saw the others in there too, though they didn't look delighted. Smokelike tendrils billowed about them, forming and reforming structures to keep them apart, like a moving labyrinth.

There were monsters in the mural, too. Lurking in the darkest corners.

At last, I noticed a final figure standing off to one side, at the edge of the labyrinth. As I watched, new smoky tendrils began to reach for it. The further the tendrils advanced, the more numb I felt.

I didn't have the strength to be afraid. I left, wandered back to the antechamber with no plan, and came across my pack on the way. I bent to take my water bottle.

My hand passed through it. I tried again. My hand closed on nothing.

By the time I returned to the antechamber, I had run a few tests. I could touch my own body or the walls and floors. But I passed straight through anything we had brought aboard.

My heart finally sank when I reached for the shuttle door and failed to grasp it. I spent a long time standing there, grabbing at what was now beyond my reach.

A voice in my head, one I wasn't sure was my own:

You never really expected to go home, anyway.

I waited in silence. Waited to starve, for thirst to take me. To die of exhaustion.

But I didn't. I didn't feel hungry or thirsty or tired. I felt nothing at all.

The lights eventually went out. I guessed it was because they now sensed no bodies moving around. After that, I waited in darkness.

My thoughts bounced around in my skull like panicked rabbits in a sack.

I'm dreaming.

It's a mental break.

There's something wrong with the air scrubbers. Hypoxia. I'm hallucinating.

Somebody released a chemical agent by accident, and it's playing tricks.

I'm dead and this is purgatory.

Even that last one brought comfort. If I was dead, at least I wouldn't have to fight anymore.

Eventually, the lights came back on. I had been floating in nothing for...a while.

I was still in the antechamber. People were standing around me, a few still disembarking from a shuttle. Not our shuttle, which had vanished, but a new one. My heart lurched with equal parts relief and panic.

"Get back! Get away," I yelled.

None of them reacted. One of them walked through me. I bucked as an electric sizzle coursed along my limbs, the first sensation I'd felt since the mural.

The people spread out, speaking in low tones.

"Creepy place," somebody said.

"We should check the air quality. I feel a headache coming on," said the one who had walked through me.

I tried everything: waving, yelling, flapping my arms over the light panels. Nothing worked.

The people settled in, apparently under the impression that they were part of an investigation. I soon learned that they knew about my crew and our disappearance. So Bouvard wasn't just churning through sacrificial offerings. They were changing the experimental conditions, trying to learn.

But that didn't mean these people had been told anything about what this place really was. As they began to explore, it became clear that they had just been fed another sack of lies.

I followed them on their explorations, watched as their horror grew. They soon found Vezzin's body, followed by the stranger's. They also found other bodies I had never seen.

The electric sensation I felt was a direct result of "touching" them. They, in turn, complained of headaches. I recalled the sensation of icy shards slicing between my eyes.

Who had been trying to communicate with me all that time?

I knew the others were not gone. Not entirely, not even Vezzin, who had been smashed to pulp. I didn't see them so much as feel them on the peripherals of a sixth sense. They were in here too, walled off from me, but in the same labyrinth.

The newcomers were already on their way to join us, passing through an entrance they couldn't touch or see. I was just deeper in. If somebody had been trying to reach me before, causing my headaches, they were gone now—had moved onto whatever came next.

I visited the mural and found that my transformation hadn't made me immune to the object's horrors. It twisted something inside me, opening a yawning precipice.

I began to realise that this place could only take you if part of you wanted it. Maybe that was the reason we had been chosen. Rogers had thrown herself at it. The stranger had gone mad before it could get him. It had broken Vezzin and Kitamura's bodies to make them submit. Who knew about M'Bele. But I couldn't hide the truth from myself anymore: I had wanted to know.

The knowledge broke me for a time, and I retreated into madness.

By the time I recovered, two of the newcomers were dead. The other five distrusted one another. One of them was on the brink of snapping.

I did what I could. I reached into their minds while they slept, ignoring the electric pulsing. I could speak to them sometimes, with effort. It hurt them. Their headaches grew worse until they barely slept. But I kept sharing, soothing. If I could hold them together long enough...

It didn't work for long. Things deteriorated much faster than they had for my own crew. In three days, they were all dead. I waited, hoping they might join me in my corner of the labyrinth, but they never did.

Again, I stood at the shuttle door. I tried to decide whether I had really wanted my plan to work. Already, the idea of going back Earth-side—or to Bouvard—seemed more frightening than staying here. What would my employers do if they found that I had escaped?

A silent fury rose in me at the thought of them. They had lined us up for slaughter. But they didn't know that something remained—that I was still here.

All my life I had wandered the solar system, haunted by something that hungered for more and wouldn't let me settle. But now that same force fuelled me when everyone else had been swallowed up by this place. I would get my answers, dig my way down to the bedrock of this freak show and tear it a new orifice. And when I got out of here, I would bring the curse of this place down on my employers like a dark hammer.

I started exploring again. I wandered until I didn't need light and could feel my way around. I found new wonders and horrors and caught more glimpses of the others. This place was strange, but not chaotic. I would navigate it once I learned enough.

As I delved ever further into the labyrinth, I couldn't help but realise that I felt more whole, more alive, than I ever remembered being. The walls and rooms grew familiar, yet they shed endless layers of secrets. And now I didn't have a mortal body to slow me down.

I would escape, eventually, but until then I would make a home unbound. Here, a place in which I could run and run, down and down. Somewhere beneath the roiling shadows, I might find what I was looking for.

The Fall of Crodendra M

written by

T.J. Knight

illustrated by

CHRIS ARIAS

ABOUT THE AUTHOR

T.J. Knight is the pen name for a regular dude who lives in New York (upstate, not city) surrounded by oaks and pines, deer and turkeys, a cat, son, wife, and on holidays, a daughter. He makes soap, bakes too many paleo brownies, reads, runs, and writes. His favorite authors are K.L. Going, Laini Taylor, and John Steakley. While this may seem an eclectic group, he reads more for style than content. And oh, the style!

You can find his flash-length works in Every Day Fiction and Daily Science Fiction. His longer works appear in Future Finalists Publishing's Starlight series, where he served as editor for volume two.

In his story "The Fall of Crodendra M," T.J. attempts to highlight the drawbacks of our evolving hyper-individualism. Technology allows us to remain home and watch weddings, graduations, and funerals on screens. This quickly went from unheard of to accepted, perhaps with normal coming soon. So as more and more of our entertainment is streamed into our living rooms (be it from space or otherwise), this story explores the meaning of actually visiting a friend or loved one instead.

ABOUT THE ILLUSTRATOR

Chris Arias was born in 1997 in Cartago, Costa Rica, in a small farming town on the slopes of an extinct volcano. Chris has been passionate about art ever since he could hold a pencil in his right hand. He was inspired by the fantastic stories about goblins, witches, knights, and dragons that his mother told during their long walks through the local mountains and forests.

Chris comes from a humble family that couldn't afford art classes during his childhood, and so he learned to draw by copying art from video games, comics, and cartoons.

It wasn't until he entered university that he attended his first art class. In 2021 Chris graduated from UCCART with a degree in fine arts.

His passion for fantasy and science fiction and the support of his family has driven him to follow his dreams to become an artist in these genres.

He entered L. Ron Hubbard's Illustrators of the Future Contest five times and is excited to have now won.

The Fall of Crodendra M

When searching the endless dark of space,
a light, any light, will do.
—Tuner proverb

I'm in my cubicle long before my overnight shift begins, face pressed to the visor of my ultrascope which rises to the ceiling like an organ pipe. Within Net1's Houston Highrise, I inhale the pungent and sweet vapors of my fellow tuners' espressos and junk drinks while we scour the heavens for alien entertainment.

Finding something new is a challenge as we've already got planets where the apex predators are insects, others have dinosaur-like creatures the size of houses, and several Pompeii-style events where you can watch lava flow toward fleeing civilizations.

Wipeouts are Net1's most popular reruns.

I spot a speeding asteroid by only the faintest hint of reflected sunlight. My display indicates it's new, so I tap out a string of numbers on my smooth glass desktop, then pause.

"Where are you going?" I murmur.

"Shh," one of my coworkers chides.

"No, you." I give my usual, mature retort.

I follow the asteroid's trajectory to a planet. Impact in . . . two weeks. Like instinct, a thrill runs through me. This is it! Corporate adjectives like hawt and wick'd spin through my mind. I can already hear the blip-ads repeating the word: destruction!

I tune toward the planet just as my rational mind takes over. *Oh God, please be uninhabited.*

A salty drop traces down my forehead to my nose and tickles until I sneeze.

"Shut up, Hank," someone yells, followed by a chorus of "Shh."

Tap. Focus. Tap, tap. Adjust. Zoom. I sail over the planet's surface seeing vast algae-colored oceans, barren mountains cut by flowing rivers, and finally, a ramshackle hut.

Damn. Impacts are awesome. Extinctions are not.

Around the hut are long rows of cultivated violet fronds waving in a breeze. Black, leafless trees form a nearby wood. I find workers, hunched over, picking. A bipedal child—short, brown skin like tree bark—holding a ball. The child looks toward the sky.

I'm about to erase the coordinates, forget I ever found this doomed planet, when the child and I make eye contact.

"Whoa!" I rear from my scope so hard I crash into Mitch Frost behind me.

"Hey, watch it!"

I stand, run my hand over my short black hair. "Sorry, I—"

After an annoyed humph, Mitch says, "What?"

"He looked into my eyes," I say, dazed, pointing. "I think it's a he. Anyway, he...*saw me.*"

"Dreamer," someone accuses.

I can sense their contempt, nevertheless they sacrifice precious scope time to get up and crowd around my external display.

"Some kind of wormhole?" Carlton Jax asks.

"Technologically speaking, our scopes could penetrate one," Mitch replies.

We all watch the child kick his ball around a hand-hewn table.

I sit down, spin my scope in frustration. I should have kept quiet.

"If there's a wormhole," Carlton says, "then everything we see is live."

My supervisor, Bill, appears at the end of the row. Short, mid-fifties, and so gaunt I'd swear he was doing melt but for the weekly drug tests we all take.

"Hank Enos, you glorious young man, you." He approaches and my cubicle mates part like the sea. "Not a year out of college and you find an extinction event. Watch for a fat bonus in your next deposit."

Bill got here quick. He must have been monitoring me.

"What extinction?" Mitch leans past me and taps my desk. A moment later he finds the asteroid. "Hawt," he whispers, slow and dramatic.

"Keep my bonus," I say. "Just don't broadcast. No one wants to see this." It's my brother Richard all over again, only, those people won't die slow like him, withering away, addicted to melt. They'll all vanish in an explosion that'll split their planet in half.

Live, for all to see.

I taste bile.

"Everyone wants to watch." He makes a sweep with his hand. "A dozen eyes already are. Supreme find, boyo." He slaps my shoulder.

I look at the display locked onto the farm. *The child saw me. How did he see me?*

"Guys," Bill says, "you're all being assigned to Hank's planet. Coordinates will be transferred. It's in the Crodendra system. M, to be exact. Staggeringly far away. Now, get to work!"

Everyone scatters.

My throat tightens and I want to tear it all down. "I'm leaving." I stand and push past Bill.

"Really?" He throws his hands up like an inflatable tube man. "Mr. Big Shot now? Better make your bonus last. Scope might not be here when you return."

That halts me. Suddenly, all that I'd sacrificed for this job hits me like a fist. Is this fate's revenge? My comeuppance?

I stare at the elevator framed by incongruous images. A serene waterfall, a battlefield with smoke and mute gunfire. All that has happened in the universe, captured for our collective imaginations. Watch, and forget your troubles.

Always, everything we've ever seen, has been in the past, as in, history. If I'd truly found a wormhole then those Crodendrans, they're in danger *now*.

My pulse throbs in my neck, threatening to burst. I take a deep breath and walk forward. They seriously expect me to stick around and find vantage points for the death of a population?

Forget it.

Outside on the street, I stand between the sun's rays and the radiant heat of the sidewalk like a human piece of toast. Electric cars whisper by. The occupants are passengers, the drivers are code. Suppose I can afford one now, but where would I go?

On a digital billboard above, a huge rectangular display of pale blue, a word appears in red balloon font: *Something…* swells and shrinks, flips then fades. *Is…* grows then spins like a top off the screen. *Coming!* inflates until each letter explodes, showering rainbow confetti.

Few notice. Those on melt shuffle along, sweating, remembering. The rest hustle, eyelines focused below the horizon.

No one watches ads anymore; we've trained ourselves to ignore them.

"LIVE!" the word echoes down the street in a full-throated voice that reverberates off glass and steel. It jars my teeth.

Net1, it seems, is stepping up their game by using the emergency broadcast system.

Several people look up at the nearest billboard. The word live is pulsing black on a white background. Fear sinks into my stomach like a swallowed stone. I know what's coming.

I feel a brush of skin against my hand just below the cuff of my suit. "Sorry," I say and move a step right.

"Crodendra M," the voice continues, deep and rumbling.

The press of flesh, the wetness of salty sweat. Once is an accident, twice is a pattern. I shift my eyes from the billboard and see a woman, smiling. She's got curly dark hair and is wearing a form-fit black tee over a visibly toned body. Is she suicidal? No one wears black outside.

"Shame," she says, meeting my eyes with her own.

334

I wait for more. The voice continues, "With Net1's wormhole technology, we can see into the present."

I look up again and there's my planet, my discovery, focused on a hillside, showing what looks like live theater. An audience watches from stone terraces carved into a mountain, three actors bow, followed by a mute round of applause.

"Witness the DESTRUCTION!" Cut to the meteoroid hurtling toward the planet. "Live on channels 1032 through 1047." A burst of static and the interruption ends.

The people around me, those who'd bothered to look up, clap, cheer, or otherwise react in a way that indicates they absolutely will witness the destruction.

"I have to find him," I say. "Warn him. Maybe I can...blink Morse code or something."

"Who?" the woman asks.

"The child. They're pre-industrial. They don't know it's coming."

"How kind of you. Any idea how you might accomplish this feat?" She sweeps her hand in an arc as if indicating the mundane.

With futility I seek the answer among the soggy populace. Then I spot a Trip Tech bar a block away. "Maybe," I say and take off at a run.

Inside, synthtech music pounds like hammers in my ears. Bass thumps with arrhythmia-inducing force. The bar, a hollowed-out rectangle in the center of an open room, is already half occupied by day soakers. Every wall is a televis. The light illuminates a few stragglers, dancing like they're in a rave.

I sidle and wait for the bartender's attention.

She sees me and calls, "What's your poison, cowboy?"

I lean forward. "Can you illuminate Net1's newest? They have fifteen live."

"Live?" The woman thrusts out a hip and puts a long-nailed hand on it. "What's goin' on?"

"I...they found a wormhole and aimed fifteen scopes. No delay."

She shrugs. "If you say so. I give you the remote, you buy a drink?"

I grind my teeth. "Yeah. Electrofizz."

The woman tsks. "You got me. I'll be sure to mention *alcohol* next time. That'll be fifty, cowboy."

I hand her a hundred and tap 1032. One after the other, I light the walls with live images of Crodendra.

Where's the kid?

The server approaches with the drink. No change. I down the fizz and shut my eyes against the rush buzz. Setting down the glass and the remote, I step into the wide room and pace from televis to televis. Several are in motion—still searching. What is the best vantage point for annihilation?

There, the farm. I see the boy as he watches the sky, head arcing from right to left as if he could see the ultrascope's micronic adjustments.

"Go back, you dope." I wave my arms left, left. Whoever is tuning that channel has moved on. I bump into a raver while trying to see multiple screens at once, but can only see three. I pace again, for a time, and then—there he is!

He's looking at a scope, eyes making contact like an eerie painting. He's smiling, maybe even laughing. My stomach goes sour.

"Look up!" I yell at the screen. "It's coming!"

A few around me seem perturbed by my disruption. No one goes to a Trip Tech to watch. The images are secondary. They glare at me, then turn to the screen.

"Wait, is he?"

"What is this, a movie?"

"No one makes productions anymore."

"A few indie studios do."

"Now you're just being argumentative."

"Look, it says live in the upper right." They point.

I follow to the word LIVE, white font within a black letterbox, and notice something odd. It's not Net1, it's Sunrise Broadcasting.

The boy waves, and the channel changes. I'm framed by a rising sun over an impossibly distant landscape. I reach out my hand, silhouetted against a pink sunrise.

Frustrated, I leave. Evening has arrived in the city and the temperature has settled on sweltering. At dusk, the burning is reduced to a slow bake.

I lean against the base of a skyscraper and look up. High above, Crodendra shines on the Big One, the screen that dwarfs all others. Net1 has added a countdown clock. Thirteen days, twenty hours, fifteen minutes.

Then...Nothing.

Around me, the populace has shifted. Fewer suits and dresses, more stained tees and baggy sweatpants. A rare breeze carries the stench of body odor. I feel submerged in soup.

I stand straight, ready to go home when I hear, "Shame."

I turn to see the same curly haired woman from earlier, staring up. Freckles on her cheekbones form little star clusters. A thin scar above her left eyebrow remains despite being easily removable. She's changed into khaki shorts and a white tee over a clearly visible black bra.

"What's a shame?" I ask.

She nods skyward.

On the display is what looks like a market. The word LIVE is cow branded in the upper right, complete with smoke. Crodendrans shop, trade, and haggle in silence.

"It's also a shame Net1 found it. Anyone, you know, just not them."

I look at her. "Why don't you like Net1?"

"Reasons."

"Fair enough."

"Walk with me?" she asks.

No one's this nice. "Look, if you're a meat grinder, my body parts aren't for sale. I'm just—"

"Hangin' around the streets for fun?"

"You following me?"

"Observing. You're an observer, too, right?"

"Tuner, how did you know?"

"A friend told me." She touches her ear and says, "Now."

On the Big One, the image switches from the ocean to the boy. The station switches, too. If Net1 notices, they will send actual

337

bounty hunters. I've seen them in the break room. Hooded, of course.

"What's your name, Tuner?"

I watch the screen for a few seconds. The boy is smiling and seems to be searching.

"Hank Enos," I say, keeping my eyes above. Another moment and the boy goes berserk. He's hopping up and down, waving.

"Aah, he sees you. He said you'd need my help. I'm dubious. I mean, he's not prescient or anything, just extremely cognizant. Like, when you *know* someone's looking at you. That's how he found you. Us, too, initially."

"Oh, I really need you to explain."

"I will." She extends her hand. "Sylvia Blackstone is my name, thanks for asking. His name is Micah, and he's very eager to meet you."

I follow Sylvia through stifling heat and well-lit storefronts. I scrape my tongue with a fingernail. "I must be on melt. Did you slip me a dose?"

Melt pumps hallucinations directly into long-term memory. Events remembered as if they'd unfolded. Nanites on a digestible chip baked within a square wedge of green gelatin. Place it on your tongue, relax, and remember.

"Nah," Sylvia says, "this is live." She spreads her arms and spins in a circle.

I'm struggling to keep up. I sit for a living, and I haven't eaten since having a protein bar around noon.

"Besides," she says, "I wouldn't want your parents to lose two children that way."

I halt. To my left is an adult toy shop. We must be outside the city ordinance. "How do you know about my brother?"

Richard slid into melt's dark infinity in just under a month. He tried to tell us, me and my parents. We gave him generic encouragement over Facephone. Told him to buck up.

"I know you were in school at the time." Sylvia continues. "Fall to a 3.9 GPA and no Net1, right?"

She wasn't wrong. I couldn't leave or I'd have fallen behind on my classwork. "We didn't know he was . . . dying." When we buried him, he had only six fingers and eight toes. He was selling for melt money. Had I visited, I'd have *seen*.

Silence, then she says, "I have a brother. We look out for each other."

"I don't, so."

Sylvia approaches. Gets deep into my personal space. At equal height, she meets my eyes with undisclosed intensity. "When a loved one is hurting, you go to them."

"Had we known, we'd have gotten him help."

"Excuses."

Richard slid so fast we never got to the point of telling him there was a lot to live for. "He could have gone home."

"Sure, blame him."

I stand there a moment, uncomfortable with the change in the order of events, the history I'd built.

Sylvia continues, "Melt begins when someone hits bottom. It's called the bottom for a reason. We shouldn't be able to sink lower." She turns and resumes walking.

I watch her go. I figure she'd known someone who'd withered, whose last visions were through crescent, unrecognizing eyes.

After more walking we near the skirts. The last vestiges of city before entering the area you don't want to be in at night.

Sylvia stops outside a stucco-sided, three-story building. A gray door with chipped paint reveals rust spots and a simple, faded plaque that reads KXRQ. She taps a code into a keypad and a beep precedes a click.

Inside is a narrow, darkened corridor lit from above by alternating neon strips of red and green.

"I like Christmas," is Sylvia's preemptive answer to my unspoken question.

The corridor opens into an air-conditioned, atrium-style room that smells dry and crisp and tingles my nose like a frosty morning back home.

Ducts above are painted black to disguise their nature, or

perhaps blend into nothing. Wire cages contain technology with blinking green and amber lights. The true wonder, however, shines on my left: a giant screen which displays, in waning afternoon light, vast fields and a simple farmhouse. Crodendra.

I bump into a small card table with a deck in the middle. Several cards slide to the edge and fall lazily to the floor.

To my right on a foot-high dais are several double-sized cubicles occupied by tuners. They're gripping their scopes' handles as they peer into space. Above them, flatscreens line foundational beams like disjointed chyrons displaying alien vistas in shades of aqua never witnessed on Earth.

A rampaging dinosaur-equivalent grabs a squirming meal. Giant teeth bite down. Ratings go up. On Requiem 32-B, a three-limbed Requiet stands poised to serve in a game of beatball. Requiets are born with four limbs.

"Beatball is yours?" I ask. "Where are we?"

"This, my fledgling friend, is KXRQ, commonly known as Sunrise Broadcasting."

I almost wet myself. I might have, had I any liquid in my body not previously evaporated from my skin.

"Wait, *the* Sylvia Blackstone? I thought—"

"Allow me to reintroduce myself," Sylvia says and curtsies.

Our conversation shakes loose the tuners who get up and file against the dais's railing. They seem an ordinary lot, nothing unusual or special, not even their clothes which are more casual Friday than nine to five.

"Everyone," Sylvia looks up. "Meet Hank Enos. Tuner extraordinaire, 4.0 at Albuquerque U. Oh, and second discoverer of our beloved Crodendra."

"Second?" I ask with a glance at the gigantic, glowing screen.

"I found it." A tiny hand raises. A short wisp of a woman steps down two metal steps with heeled clanks. "Around twelve months ago."

"And you didn't flag it?" The moment I ask, I realize it's a dumb question.

"Of course not." She extends her hand. "I'm Audra Winchester."

"Nice to meet you."

"Thanks, Mr. Enos."

"You can call me Hank."

"I'm sure I will." Audra winks.

Sylvia intervenes. "Stop flirting, Audra."

"Make me."

"I just did. Next we have Roger Wright, you can call him Roj. Jim, our IT guy. You can call him Jim. And our third tuner Dale Coppersmith."

I smile politely at each. Jim is sour-faced and unimaginably tall, like some mad geneticist had pushed the limitations of human growth. Audra, eyes smiling within pink eyeshadow, bright red lipstick, and banana-yellow hair. A burlesque, jovial Dale. And finally Roj, who seems indifferent.

I work for Net1, I shouldn't even be in here.

"How do we know he's not a spy?"

"Now Jim, just because *we* have one, doesn't mean—"

"A spy?" I interrupt, lowering my voice.

"He sent me your personnel info, that brother I told you about. Foster brother, technically. My father never adopted him. Inheritance and all that. I got everything, but I take care of him."

"How old is he?"

"Thirty."

"And you still take care of him?"

"Of course. He's family."

"Oh, here he comes," Roj says, nodding toward the enormous screen.

The boy, Micah, marches across a dirt lawn, picks up a ball from among plenty, and looks forward. When he sees us he waves and says, "Hello."

Says it. Out loud. In English.

I lose my balance. Sylvia's quick hands steady me from behind.

"He can speak? We can hear him? How?"

"The wormhole isn't far, cosmically speaking. We sent through a couple tablets, battery packs—"

"We communicate with pulses of light," Jim interrupts.

341

Sylvia continues, "Like wireless fiber optics that translate what we say. Voice, to light, to data, back to voice. And visuals, of course."

I walk forward, drawn by the suddenly possible. The others fade into my peripheral, then disappear. The screen and the boy fill my vision. "Hello there."

No reply. The boy merely smiles and tosses his ball from hand to hand.

"There's currently an eighteen second delay, each way, in our relays," Sylvia says, her voice soft. "We're trying to lower it, but you know, the speed of light and all."

The delay ends with Micah hopping up and down. Eighteen seconds later, "You are here. You found me, I found you. We're connected."

I wait for more. Apparently that was the end of Micah's "turn."

"There's a cadence to the delays," Roj says. "You get used to them. At first we overlapped constantly, fumbling with excitement, learning each other's languages."

I turn. "You learned their language as well?"

Roj says something unintelligible.

All I could do was stare. If I tried to encapsulate the full diversity of my day, I would fail.

"We're about to order. Murphy's pizza. My treat." Sylvia says. "Stay for dinner, sign a standard NDA, then off you go."

I continue watching the screen. "Does he know what's coming?" I whisper from the corner of my mouth.

"Yeah," Sylvia replies. She puts her hand on my shoulder like we're friends. Maybe, for just one night, we are.

"How does he? I mean..." I can't formulate the question. It's too big. What would I do if given such news? I suppose if I were dying I'd call my parents, my brother, and ask for help. Maybe they'd tell me to buck up.

"Synthmeat burger," I say, giving my dinner order.

I hear a chair scrape across the floor. Audra appears next to me and pats the seat.

I sit and look up at Micah looking back with apparent patience. "So," I say, "tell me everything."

Thirty-six seconds later, I hear Micah's carefree laughter.

The next morning I call in sick to Net1. The AI has me go through a list of symptoms so it can determine if I'm contagious, or if I'm lying.

I say, "It's running down my face." This is the effective sentence passed around the break room in secret. It works. The AI tells me to call again the following day if necessary.

I dress in shorts and a gray tee and walk to the KXRQ building. I knock, certain no one will hear me down the long corridor, so I sit and wait, figuring someone will come out eventually.

Eventually takes half the sweltering, sweat-soaked day.

Sylvia herself opens the door and looks down at me. I scramble to my feet, wincing at my stiff back.

She sighs. "You're going to have to sign an updated NDA."

"Updated?"

"They're daily."

"Fine. Whatever." *Anything so I can see Micah again.*

"Come on then."

Inside, the cool air chills the sweat coating my body and I shiver. Everyone's at their desks in the atrium, faces pressed against scopes, and Micah's at work in the field. He seems to be picking and flicking bugs from the violet fronds.

He's got less than two weeks to live and he's working.

I wonder what Richard did with his time. Besides call us, that is. We should have recognized his calls as pleas. If only he'd come out and said he was on melt and that he was sliding. If only he'd asked for help. *Then* we would have done something.

I stand before the big screen and wait, and waiting is like digesting swallowed capsules of terror.

He's just a kid.

The word LIVE is blocked in the upper right of the screen.

Not for long.

I almost throw up.

Why isn't anyone doing anything? The crew is tuning, looking for new planets for Sunrise Broadcasting. They're *working*.

"You have a ship?" I ask, turning toward the dais. "That's how you set the tech up, right? Can you fly through the wormhole and destroy the meteoroid?"

Jim appears from behind a rack of electronics. He's holding a glass tablet. "It's a pleasure craft," he says. "It was Sylvia's father's. Billionaire's club and all that. He never even used it."

"What about the Earth Defense Force? We could ask them to go through."

"The EDF are toothless. We discover incredibly distant alien life and a month later there's a Defense Force? Politicians and greased money."

"Their guns are real enough."

"I'm sure they'd do everything they could to stop a meteoroid from crashing into *this* planet."

I turn to Sylvia and give her a pleading look. She's leaning with her back against a wall, arms folded over her chest.

"How about a passenger ship?" I ask. "Gather as many of them as we can?"

She shakes her head. "They wouldn't survive here. They're more closely related to trees than mammals."

"Then we build a...a glass tank and fill it with their atmosphere."

"They aren't fish."

"Then what?" I yell. There's a kind of stunned silence and I realize I may have gone too far.

Sylvia pushes off the wall and approaches. "We've been where you are, Hank. Twelve months ago we tossed all manner of ideas about." She stands next to me and looks on. "We offer comfort. We're holding their hands, virtually. It's the best we can do."

Micah emerges from his farmhouse and approaches. Seeing him tempers my heated blood.

"Hi, Micah. What will you do today?" I ask.

After a short delay, "I will play. I am practice juggling. Will show you later. My father, he has left to collect my brother, thirty farms distance. M-Married, yes? New family of his own. They will be with us."

"How can you play? Knowing what's coming." I get worked up again. My heart threatens to pound through my chest cavity. Soon, I might need a paper bag to breathe into. I hadn't felt fear for Richard, only anger—after.

"I am scared, yes. Sylvia explained what will happen. Worry is needless. Truth is coming. I must accept it."

I lower my head. I see my legs, my sneakers, my ankle-high socks. Life in stark relief.

"We will more learn from each other today, okay?" Micah asks. "You tell me stories. Your family. I do the same."

I look up. Illuminated face. Hopeful. "Yes. We will share our histories. Why don't you start?"

Sylvia and the others tolerate me for the day. I sign more paperwork on my way out and wander home. I plan to write my congresswoman, make some calls, leave some messages. I've got to try.

I tell my senator's voicemail about Richard, about how if only I'd known...I disconnect midsentence. I can't say what I would have done, but calling my senator wasn't it.

The evening passes in agonizing slowness; minutes measured like balloons one breath from exploding.

The next day I tell the AI my insides are on the outside. It doesn't know what to make of that but I get the day off. I go straight to KXRQ and bang on the door. I hear a click and let myself in.

I spend another day getting to know Micah and his family, but always with bittersweet smiles, laughter tinged with melancholy.

That night, there's no NDA for me to sign. I think Sylvia realizes I'll keep coming back.

Walking home I find myself envious of the others' time with Micah and his family—and also not.

From my couch I flip through even more Net1 Crodendra channels. They're up to thirty now. They cover every angle.

Promotions for The End are ceaseless. Highest ratings ever are expected. Fortunately they hadn't yet focused on the boy with bark-like skin whose brown lips formed words in English.

"Our numbers are down, for sure," Sylvia says at breakfast the following day. She's working down a small bowl of plant-based yogurt and granola. "I got a lean crew. We'll weather the storm."

Life goes on, I figure.

Except when it doesn't.

They're all going to die. Not just Micah and his family and his farm. Every Crodendran. All at once. I smack my forehead repeatedly. No. Don't go there.

Don't go there.

Go there?

"The ship, is it fast?" I ask.

Jim looks over. He's holding a coffee pot that's dwarfed against his enormity. "Yeah, my ship's fast, so?"

"My ship," Sylvia says.

"Bah. You never use it."

I glare at Sylvia. "When a loved one is hurting, you go to them, right?"

"This isn't what I meant. Plus, we've already said no to the ship thing. There's no weapons."

Jim adds, "Besides, we don't know what will happen if something that big goes through a wormhole."

"You sent gear through and it remained stable." I hesitate a moment before giving voice to a terrible hope and fear. "I'd like to go. To the surface. To Micah."

Sylvia pauses, then shakes her head. "Their atmosphere is mostly CO_2. You'd asphyxiate in minutes."

"Then give me a...a space suit." I find my argument coming together like a one-color puzzle. "Who originally flew up there to launch the gear?"

Audra shuffles in sans makeup, yellow hair askew. She yawns and reaches for the coffee pot where it isn't.

"I did," Jim says.

"No way you fit in any ship."

Jim sets the pot down on the table and lifts his omnipresent glass tablet. "Remote."

Audra snatches the pot and moves toward the cabinet area. I hear sugar cubes clink within a mug.

"Perfect," I say. "Not like I know how to fly. I've never even been in an airplane."

Sylvia puts her hand on mine. A week ago I'd never so much as talked to a billionaire, let alone had one physically touch me.

"It's a mad thing you're considering. If you go, you may not make it back. Who will comfort your parents then?"

I keep my mouth shut and stare, but my mind is screaming, *are you nuts!* It uses those actual words.

Sylvia cocks her head. "There's a chance it'll work, but to undertake such a risk, your motivation must be unmistakable. *Why* do you feel you must go?"

This is the big question. "Everything we do, holidays, birthdays, we're all faces on screens now. I need to say goodbye to him. I need to be there." I put my free hand on Sylvia's to reinforce the connection.

Jim's eyes are wild when he looks at me. "All right, let's rewrite the science texts, eh Hank-o? I'll fly you into a wormhole, you tell us what you see."

He might just be happy to be rid of me. "You fly me true, yeah?"

"No worries. I wouldn't crash Sylvia's ship."

"Oh, *now* it's mine?"

"Well?" I ask, my argument complete.

"I vote yes," Audra says from nearby then approaches the three of us. "Hank and I found him. One of us should go there, and since it's not gonna be me..."

I look at Sylvia. Nervousness makes my cheeks feel like they're on fire. I'm willing her to say yes. No is unthinkable.

"All right," Sylvia says.

"Yes!" I clap my hands. Relief gushes through every capillary in my body.

"It's only a ship, right? And, you know, a Net1 employee. No big loss." Sylvia shrugs one shoulder.

She wants me to go. I can tell from the dimple on her cheek, caused by the half smile on her lips.

"Mind if I go tell Micah?" I ask.

Sylvia shoos me away with a wave of her hand. I can still feel the warmth from it on mine. I tear out of the break room, eager to tell my new friend I'm coming a few trillion miles for a visit.

I'd run out of creative excuses for Net1's AI. It probably figured I was a biohazard by now. I doubt I still have a job. I wonder if I'll return alive to need one.

My stomach roils again.

"The biometric data is confirmed," Sylvia says. We've been preparing for a week. "Their atmosphere is mostly CO_2. Some oxygen and nitrogen. You'll be fine in the suit."

The suit is what I'm currently being fitted for in an adapted board room. The big, oval table where bigwigs once pondered stock prices has been shoved aside so I can stand on a box with my arms and legs out like the Vitruvian man.

Sylvia made the tailor sign an NDA.

The thought of flying was bonkers. Hell, I bused the fourteen hours to school. I hate the very notion of flying, and now I'm going into *space*?

Three days to extinction.

My problems are minuscule.

Jim's finished adding a relay mic to my bubble helmet, so I waddle like a big white zombie into the atrium, flexing and limbering the suit as I go.

"We are cutting this too damn close. I want to be out of there when that thing hits," I remind Jim, backlit by the big screen. "I still need time to fly."

Jim places the helmet over my head, twists the seal, runs a test, untwists, lifts the helmet, stares into it.

Audra looks on, chewing on a nerve stick. Break any habit,

per the manufacturer's claim. Dale and Roj distract themselves
with work. Sylvia's cancelled meetings with whomever. I can't
imagine how much money she's losing.

I've stopped eating. Water is the only thing I don't immediately
purge.

One day to extinction.

I call my parents in the morning. They aren't up, so I leave a
message telling them when it's time to go you don't ask. That
sounds morbid so I clarify by saying you show up. Our lives
aren't on the screen. We learned this the hard way. It's gone
unspoken—until now.

Sylvia drives me to the spaceport. The car is fancy. It has a
steering wheel that she uses to dodge what she calls drones.
"Jim will do everything, right?" She reminds me. "No need to
push any buttons, flick any switches. You just open and close
the hatch."

"Affirmative."

We arrive. I'm not the only one at the spaceport in a suit.

Billionaires...I wonder if they'll actually go up, fly around the
emptiness of space alone, or if this is just a new version of the
old yacht club.

The ship's in an enormous, air-conditioned hangar, parked
among others within white lines like any old car.

Sylvia gets me in and secured. It's silly, but I want a hug before
I go. Just in case, you know. Instead, she gives me a thumbs-up
then points to the close-hatch button.

Soon after, I'm cleared for launch.

My breakfast of water erupts inside my helmet.

"Hank, you're messing with my equipment," Jim laughs.
"Might happen again once you hit a few g's."

It doesn't.

Then, after having my brains rattled, meat and muscle
practically shaken loose from my bones, I am in space.

Everything is calm and I wonder if this is what melt is like.
If so, I can see the allure. Add some fantastical memories and
sliding would be easy.

The wormhole appears on my screens like waves of heat over baking sand. A few more years, I figure, the desert around Houston will be a sheet of glass.

"Come in, Hank," says Jim.

"Here."

"I'm launching the relay tech."

"Roger."

"Present."

"Seriously, Roj?"

"Man, when am I gonna get another chance?"

Jim sighs, then, "Come in, Hank."

"Still here."

Jim sounds worried. I wonder just how much he loves the ship, or if there might be an ounce of concern for its passenger.

The wormhole fills the screens.

I shut my eyes and hold my breath. I feel a disruption throughout my body. I've never died, but I figure this might be how it feels in that moment of crossing over to...whatever.

"Come in, Hank."

"Deeply unsettling."

"Say again?"

"I see Crodendra."

"Telemetry updating...and connected! I've got you."

I hear cheering.

"Is he through?" Sylvia has returned.

"Yeah. We're good. Guiding him toward the farm."

In a thought that becomes a sensation, I recognize that I'm unimaginably far from home, from Earth, as I now feel inclined to call it. My planet. For all those I have seen, and found, and named, mine was always just home, the window from which I peered out. Now, I'm physically where I have but dared to witness. I wonder what that makes me. What label might suit?

Voyager Hank. Nah.

On the screens, stars like white motes dot infinity. They look the same. Locations merely rearranged. Constellations with different names.

Diversity is universal.

"I'm jealous, Hank," Dale says. "Not that I want to be you, mind. Just, jealous."

"He's gonna be on the big screen," Audra says.

"Oh my god. I hadn't thought of that."

I hear shuffling, the scraping of chairs, then Roj says, "Hank's about to set foot on another planet."

"Talk about a giant leap."

I suppose they're right, although I hadn't given much thought to that. I only want to see my friend, to be there for him, even if only briefly.

"Nearest runway is one klick," Jim says.

"A klick?" I ask. "That's a kilometer. You can't land me closer? How 'bout on the fronds? They won't be needing them."

"You're in a ship, like a plane, not a rocket. Need to land and take off again."

"I gotta hoof it a K in this suit?"

"Two."

I go silent while the ship lands. I really should have eaten something.

I open the hatch to my right. Hydraulics hiss like an electric snake. Somewhere in the distance, Micah and his family are waiting. They must have seen my ship pass overhead. I wonder if they're as nervous as I am.

An image of my brother pops unbidden into my mind. Skin stretched over bone, sunken eyes, hollow cheeks. I hadn't gotten to say goodbye to Richard. My *brother*. We grew up together. We talked, we fought, we laughed.

What had changed? Was it melt? Something else?

Micah said we're connected, and everything had bent for our meeting. If Sylvia had said no, would I have found another way? Is this what connection means? An inexorable pull? Its opposite is drift. People drift apart.

Brothers shouldn't.

I wonder if I ever had a choice, the tidal force of fate being what it is. I unbuckle, spin in my bucket seat, and look down at

Crodendran soil, at the rocks and dirt and think, yeah, this was my choice. I made the wrong one with Richard. I should have gotten on a plane back then, gone to him, sat in his apartment, *moved in,* if that's what needed to be done.

I slide out of the bucket seat and land hard on Crodendra.

"Uh oh." *Gravity. Too much gravity.*

"What? You all right?" Jim asks in a panic.

"First words on a new planet?" I hear Audra ask.

"Uh oh," Roj and Dale say together.

"You ever take gravitational readings?" I ask Jim.

"Yeah. One point five. You good?"

"I guess this wouldn't slow down, say, an athlete." I take a few heavy steps. Look around at a literal alien landscape. I have no idea which way to go. "Guide me there, Jim?"

"Of course. Yeah."

I lumber up knolls, down, through a dried riverbed, around a green lake. I'm not in any kind of shape, and this gravity is killing me, but I am motivated, so I huff and burn through my oxygen tank. God, I hope I don't burn through my oxygen tank.

Through the periphery of my helmet, I see the meteoroid in the sky. A great, looming thing, hurtling. Adrenaline surges. Deep breaths echo in my ears.

At last, I see the farm, purple fronds waving, distant skeletal trees not.

I see the house. Micah. His family. Huddled.

I slow. Catch my breath. Study the faces I'd seen on the screen, full of sorrow, yet with a twinkle in their eyes. They're here for Micah. For me. Us.

"I'm here," I say at last. I extend a gloved hand, palm down. They take turns placing theirs on mine. This is their greeting.

Micah is last. He looks up at me. "Hi Hank."

"I'm sorry," I say. "I wanted to take you with me. All of you. I tried."

"It's all right. You are here."

Yes I am.

Micah extends his arms. I kneel. He slips easily into a gentle embrace. We steal a few quiet moments of connection. This is why I came all this way. *This.*

"Hank, time's running out," Jim says. "You took too long to get there. Way back might be longer."

"Can I take my helmet off?" I ask.

Silence, then Sylvia says, "For a minute or two. Won't be pleasant. There's nothing toxic. What? Oh, nothing too toxic. A minute at most. Try to hold your breath."

I reach up and grip my bubble helmet, inhale a deep breath, then twist. I set the helmet on the ground, look at Micah, and smile.

Micah reaches out with both hands and caresses my cheeks. His hands are rough. I don't mind.

"You are beautiful," he says.

"So are you, little man," I say, voice fluttering. I exhale as little as possible.

Micah touches his forehead to mine an agonizingly short amount of time then steps back.

"Now you must run." Micah turns toward the sky. "We have met, so we will meet again. Of this, I am certain. We will find each other in the next cycle."

"I hope so." I'm out of air and time. Through blurry vision I grab my helmet. I fumble it. It lands in the dirt. I gasp. Cough. Uh oh.

Micah's brother steps forward, grabs the helmet, sets it on my suit, and gives it a firm twist.

I inhale deep, the air still full of the unusual smell and taste of Crodendran atmosphere, then, scentless nitrogen and oxygen. I breathe, nod a quick thanks, squeeze Micah's shoulder with a gloved hand, memorize his little smiling face, turn, and run.

Jim was right, the way back is more difficult.

The ground rumbles, rocks quiver around my feet. Shrubs tear at my legs. Above, the meteoroid has become a meteor. Fire and smoke blaze in its wake.

"Less than five minutes, Hank. How you doin'?" Jim asks.

"Come on, Hank," Sylvia whispers.

"Haul ass, man!" Audra yells.

At last I see the ship, have it in my sights when the meteor strikes. The ground cracks like an egg. I lose my footing and momentum and tumble.

Micah's gone.

He's gone.

I got to say goodbye this time.

I push to my knees. The ship has resolutely remained upright. The runway? Everything is shaking like a mixing can of paint.

I pull myself to my feet, born from an ancient biological need for self-preservation. This is the antithesis of melt's lie: remembered safety while your body deteriorates around you.

I run through blurry vision. My legs plod like lead pistons. I hope Micah's right, that we'll meet again. It's the least the universe could do to balance what was happening around me. Let us all meet again, somehow, some way.

"Hank, behind you. It's...it's a *wave of planet*."

Objects whiz by. Chunks of crust. Rocks and soil. Something strikes me. Hard. I cry out from the impact. I hear hissing. I smell Crodendran air.

Exhaustion and fear war for control.

The ship. Hatch still open.

With a last scrap of energy, I dive, spin, close the hatch.

"You good?" Jim asks.

"Bleeding," I answer. "Punctured."

"Strap in or you're gonna be paste."

I do. I hear a solid click, then feel the rattling of bones, the press of g-force, then at last, silence.

I drift. I don't know for how long. I hear my brother's voice. He's telling me to wake up.

"Wake up!"

"Oh, he's coming around."

Sylvia?

A kiss on my forehead, the sticky feeling of lipstick remaining behind.

Audra.

"Touch and go, they said."

CHRIS ARIAS

"No, I believe they said he was gone, but we got him back."

"Semantics."

I open my eyes and look around. White hospital room. The whole crew. Smiling. Concerned. Well, not Jim.

"Mission accomplished, futile though it was," I croak. I'm not feeling triumphant.

"You got to say goodbye," Sylvia says. "For all of us. We're grateful."

"Before the end, Net1 found the farm," Dale says. "Highest ratings ever."

"Yeah, for them," Roj grumbles.

"Point is," Sylvia says with a round of glares, "everyone saw, including your folks. They're on their way to visit."

"My folks?" I ask. I begin to drift, some medicine or other kicking in. "They can't afford the trip."

"I expensed it. Gotta have deductions under company travel."

"Deductions? I'm not—"

"Yeah, I might have bought your contract from Net1. It cost me big, but your interview? Whew, dedicated employee."

My parents. We'll have a lot to talk about. "Thank you. Again."

"Would Hank's and my wedding be deductible?" Audra asks.

I sober instantly. "What? How long was I out?"

"You know, someday." Audra teases a finger down my arm.

Goosebumps everywhere.

"Audra..."

"I know, stop flirting."

A knock, then Jim comes in, ducking beneath the door frame. "Look what I found in my ship."

Sylvia face-palms.

"It's okay, too, by the way." Jim hands me an object the size of a large marble. "That ought to be worth a fortune someday."

I run my thumb over the sharp edge of a Crodendran rock. It wasn't Micah or his family, but it was proof, physical proof that they existed. Something more than images on a televis to remember them by.

"It already is," I say, closing the rock tightly in my hand.

What Is Art Direction?

BY LAZARUS CHERNIK

Lazarus Chernik is an experienced creative director, brand manager, and award-winning designer with nearly thirty years of experience in advertising, package design, UI/UX, and publishing. His clients have included everyone from Fortune 100 giants to game companies. An expert in all manner of media and tools, he has headed the creative departments for numerous agencies and corporations, including a top national advertising agency, a national retail chain, a national web development firm, a catalog retailer, and a retail goods manufacturer.

He has been an instructor of design software and skills in corporate training environments and continuing education facilities.

Lazarus Chernik has been an Illustrators of the Future judge since 2016.

What Is Art Direction?

In the worlds of marketing and publishing, an art director is to art as an editor is to the written word or the music producer is to rock 'n' roll. We are the voice of reason that helps the artist shape their vision into the finished product. Our names rarely get mentioned for our contributions, but those in the know—know.

WHAT IS AN ART DIRECTOR?

Illustrations and graphic design are not the sole vision of the artist. An illustration is a tool that communicates a story to the audience. But illustrators do not invent that story. That story is provided to them by their client.

They may be hired to illustrate the story of a hero's journey through space and time. Or they may be hired to tell the story of a woman feeding her dog the best kibble they've ever eaten. Or the shiniest car that's ever been painted. Or the most beautiful couple. Or the ugliest wart. Or the hungriest caterpillar. In every case, the illustrator's job is to show that story using all of the tools in their tool kit. If the audience understands that story exactly as intended, the illustrator did their job. If the audience feels that story, above and beyond the original intention, the illustrator created a masterpiece.

The art director has a few roles in this process. First (but not foremost), they provide all the necessary information the illustrator needs to tell that story. This includes the story itself, obviously, but also specific artistic requirements (e.g., colors, people, shapes, logos, etc.), the media the story will be told in (e.g., book cover, book interior, poster, magazine ad, product label, billboard, etc.), the audience they are telling the story to (e.g., 18–34 single women, 55+ seniors on fixed income, science fiction fans, golf enthusiasts, ad infinitum), and of course, all the legalese like the timelines and deadlines.

WHAT DOES AN ART DIRECTOR DO?

In essence, an art director is an artist who acts as a kind of conscience for the illustrator. They describe what the illustration should do, but not how the illustrator should do it. The illustrator has been hired for their specific vision—their style— how they tell stories. The art director works with the illustrator to ensure that everyone in the process understands the goals of the illustration and how the illustration meets those goals. To do that, the art director mediates between the goal setters of the project (i.e., marketing and sales teams) and the illustrator. Projects rarely go smoothly. Sometimes goals change or need to be clarified. Sometimes, one side or the other makes a mistake. The art director is the one responsible for managing everyone's expectations and ensuring the finished illustration meets the project goals. In essence, an art director is a manager.

WHY DOES ART NEED MANAGING?

Every author wants readers. Readers have countless choices of what to read. While readers could spend twenty seconds reading a blurb to learn what a story is about, it takes less than one second to be captured by artwork. When marketed properly, art and the written word increase each other's effectiveness exponentially. A reader gets captured by an image, is lured to read the blurb, decides to buy and read the story.

But less than one second? Yes. Audiences see the average book cover in less than one second. If an illustration attracts them, they will look at it for approximately two seconds and may read the title. If, in those two seconds, they decide the illustration "speaks" to them, they will engage with it for an average of five seconds, reading the first sentences of a blurb. Every step of this progression increases their likelihood of buying and reading the whole story.

Art directors are focused on those critical one-, two-, and five-second reactions. There can be hundreds of ways to illustrate a story. But which way will convey the story in the least amount of time? Well, that depends on the audience. Different audiences respond to different emotional buttons. Men respond differently than women. Horror fans respond differently than readers of romance. TikTok users respond differently (and more quickly) than Facebook users.

A fantasy tale of epic adventure crossing oceans and deserts and forests climaxing into world war has many powerful characters and scenes inside it to illustrate. Maybe the book should show the battle? Maybe it should show one or more of the heroes in a grand collage, with subtle symbols of their quest and maybe the strain of the journey on their faces? Or maybe it should show a simple image of the MacGuffin—the object that starts or ends the conflict but summarizes the entire epic in its ugliness or beauty or perfection of design.

The illustrator proposes their illustration, but the art director and goal setters make the final decision on which illustration to execute. Understanding the relationship between the product and the audience is, itself, an art form, which is why the art director needs to be an artist. If they don't understand every detail of this process and the decisions made by both the goal setters and the illustrator, there is no way they could properly communicate between them.

HOW IS DIRECTING AN ART?
Illustrations sell, literally.

A novel or story is akin to a work of fine art—it is a product by itself. A cover illustration is an advertisement. Advertising is both an art and a science because it demands reproducible results.

Oddly, novels are not marketed to reach the largest number of readers. They are marketed to reach the most valuable readers—the readers who will obsess over the book and tell all their friends to read it, who will bring it up on social media and to book clubs, who will start fan sites and cosplay and read all the sequels and buy all the merch. One hard-core fan will spend a great deal more than an average reader. That's why book advertising targets specific readers.

Knowing which readers to target is marketing. Knowing which buttons to push is advertising. Executing that strategy requires knowing both, plus all the artistic elements and techniques available to push those readers' buttons exactly when, where, why, and how.

Buttons?

Ever hear the phrase "Art is subjective" or "My opinion is as good as anyone else's" or "I know it when I see it"? Those are laughably incorrect when it comes to illustration.

Illustration is part of a greater school called Communication Design, where art is being used to communicate an idea to the audience. Just as words are placed in sentences in a specific order to make sense, so are visual elements.

Visual elements that illustrators control include line, shape, color, space, time (past, present, and future), movement (even in a still image), context, relationships, emotion, texture, temperature, subtext, and more. Good illustrators position symbols and objects very carefully. They color them specifically. They decide what is smooth and what is rough, what the audience sees first and second and third, who the protagonist is, and how the audience should feel about every single element.

Good art directors never look at an illustration and say, "I don't like this." They say, "This element is well executed but it means the wrong thing." In one of the most common mistakes, an artist's natural inclination is to paint a character on the right side of the image facing left. That is because, people used to reading words from left to right, move their eyes from the left side of the image to the right, and in that motion "meet" the character for the first time. This is a mistake and not a style. The reader is supposed to identify with the main character and to reside in their head for the duration of the story. In action scenes, it is almost always preferred to place the main character on the left of the image and have them face their journey, villain, or obstacle. The audience will naturally read the image from the main character's point of view and follow their gaze to see through their eyes. But to do this, the artist must identify with the character and put themselves in their eyes. This is such an awkward concept that even experienced professionals can fall into this trap. Art directors are supposed to watch for these traps and help correct them as early as possible. Other traps include the wrong reference or body type or foreshortening or weathering or light source angles or organization of the visual hierarchy, but there are far too many to mention here.

You see, there is a huge number of critical and objective elements of an illustration under consideration at all times. The art director is the illustrator's safety net to get all of those things just right. Because getting too many wrong will cost the project in readers and sales and maybe even someone's career.

Really?

Yes. Really.

Imagine Black Friday. Why is it called Black Friday? No, it's not because of the pushing and shoving. It's because, for many years, the average retail store lost money every month (thereby making their accounting ledgers "red"). Until November, when— the day after Thanksgiving—the public swarmed out to shop and bought so much in one day turning the accounting ledgers "black" for the year.

Now imagine a retail store has lost money for eleven months straight. They must sell as much as possible at the end of November to make up for that. But they need to advertise their sales for a month before then. To start advertising at the end of October, they need to hand over all their advertisements to the media by September(-ish). To do that, the ads must be approved by the boss. To get there, they have to be approved by the marketing department. To do that, they have to go through several rounds of changes. To do that, the illustrator has to be hired months in advance. Before that, the project has to be pitched, approved, and planned before an illustrator is even hunted for. By the time the illustrator gets the project, dozens of people and many weeks and months have gone into selecting and hiring them and defining what they must illustrate. If the illustrator does a poor job in any way—misses the deadline, or fails to follow instructions—the campaign is at risk, the sales are at risk, and the job of every person who works for that store on every level is at risk. And despite there being hundreds of people involved in the job from start to finish, the illustrator is a single person who can ruin everything (a.k.a. a single point of failure).

The art director's job is to protect the project from any problems along the line.

And yes, sometimes those problems are not the illustrator's fault. They could be given the wrong information or not given all the information (e.g., missed emails, texts, etc.) The content provided or the demographics could be mistaken in some way. Yet, once it is in the illustrator's hands, that is the last time it can be corrected. The art director oversees all of this and keeps communication flowing between the illustrator and the goal setters.

But an illustrator is not an employee (usually). They are not even "just a freelancer." Illustrators are specialized professionals who clients rely on to do a job they cannot do themselves, like a doctor or a lawyer.

If an illustrator listens well, executes well, finishes on time, and doesn't cause any problems—they get paid. If an illustrator identifies a problem in the process, helps solve it, and does everything else perfectly, they will be hired again. They may even become a favored illustrator of an art director, get hired repeatedly and earn some fame with their paycheck.

An art director is an illustrator's best friend.

Constant Never

written by
S. M. Stirling

illustrated by
NICK JIZBA

ABOUT THE AUTHOR

S. M. Stirling was born in France in 1953 to Canadian parents—although his mother was born in England and grew up in Peru. After that he lived in Europe, Canada, Africa, and the US and visited several other continents. Steve graduated from law school in Canada but had his dorsal fin surgically removed, and published his first novel (Snow Brother, Signet) *in 1984, going full time as a writer in 1988, the year of his marriage to Janet Moore of Milford, Massachusetts, who he met, wooed, and proposed to at successive World Fantasy Conventions. In 1995 they suddenly realized that they could live anywhere and decamped from Toronto, that large, cold, gray city on Lake Ontario, and moved to Santa Fe, New Mexico. Steve became an American citizen in 2004.*

His latest books are Conan: Blood of the Serpent *(Titan Books, Dec 2022) and* Daggers in Darkness *(1632 Inc., 2021). His hobbies mostly involve reading—history, anthropology, archaeology, and travel, besides fiction—but he also cooks and bakes for fun and food. For twenty years he also pursued the martial arts, until hyperextension injuries convinced him that he was in danger of becoming the most lame person in human history. Steve has been a judge for the Writers of the Future Contest since 2021.*

About this story Steve tells us, "It involves three of my obsessive hobbies: history, fantasy, and human nature. Knights, captive princesses, and dragons—the most ancient of fantasy tropes. 'Constant Never' uses the tropes... but I think in a way that examines how they'd really work, and with real people and a real setting (Carolingian France in the eighth century)."

ABOUT THE ILLUSTRATOR

Nick Jizba was born in Bloomington, Indiana, in 1984, but he has spent most of his life living in Nebraska. He has always spent time drawing but didn't really consider art as a career option. Losing a safe construction job in the 2008 recession pushed Nick to develop his art into a career. He attended ITT Tech Institute for game design, focusing on 3D modeling and level design. In school he ended up doing most of the concept art and sketching for group projects and that developed into a passion for digital painting. Nick has continued to learn by taking a variety of online classes, taking on the occasional freelance illustration, and working on personal illustrations that he sells at conventions. He is currently working on his first book The Sower.

Nick is a former winner of the Illustrators of the Future Contest and was first featured in L. Ron Hubbard Presents Writers of the Future Volume 38.

Constant Never

"Give me ale, you dog, and food, and be quick about it."

The *Ritter* Karl von Obersberg scraped some of the horse dung off his feet as he entered the village inn. Not that it would make much difference—the common room looked no better than the stable where he'd put his horses. Certainly it smelled no better, and there was smoke enough from the hearth in the center to make his eyes sting, but it was warmer and drier than the drizzle outside. The firepit was surrounded by the pine log pillars that held up the roof, branches still standing out like stubs. The knight hung his cloak on one to dry; it was woven of raw wool and usually shed water like a duck's back, but the long day's ride and last night's sleep under an oak tree had soaked it through.

There were carvings on the tree trunks. Bearded faces . . .

The Old Ones, he thought. These Saxon dogs were half-heathen yet, despite all the emperor's wars and priests. The thought did not improve the knight's temper.

"Ale, I said, peasant swine!" he roared, sinking back onto the bench, kicking the scabbard of his cross-hilted sword out of the way with a lifetime's unconscious habit.

Shaggy faces turned away from him around the room. One scurried over with bowl and mug, both wooden. The ale was thin and sour, but there was meat in the stew, and the round loaf of black bread was nearly fresh. He ate methodically, half-conscious of the hating peasant eyes on him. Saxon eyes. That was why he'd kept his mail shirt on. He didn't think they'd try anything, not really. And if they did, he'd killed enough Saxons in his day—Saxons, West Franks, Bretons, Italians, Avars, Basques, Saracens, lately some Danes—that a few more wouldn't do much hurt.

Nor would it be a curse if they slew me, he thought. It bubbled up from somewhere in his gut, to be pushed away hastily. There was no need to think of dying. He was no youth, he'd seen forty winters and that was older than most fighting men lived to be. But there were years yet, much to be done.

Meanwhile his belly was full, and the ache in his hands and the shoulder where the old heathen priest's hammer had broken the bone was a little less. It was time to sleep.

He pulled a copper penny from his pouch and flung it at the tavern keeper. "Blankets," he said.

"There is a box bed here, Lord," the man said; the Saxon accent was rough to a Frank's ears, but Karl had learned it well enough in the wars.

"I sleep by my horses," he grunted.

Just as warm, cleaner and much safer—there were silver pennies in his pouch with the face of his namesake, the emperor, on them. Not many, but enough to buy this dung pile of a village.

The rain had stopped outside, but it was getting on to full dark. Karl took a brand from the firepit and raised it overhead as he pushed the rough plank door open. The chill bit at him, and he hurried to the warm straw and the comforting smell of horse.

It was hot. Hotter than hell, where the pagan dogs would burn forever. Karl was surprised for a moment—surprised that it was high summer and the setting sun was hot, surprised that he was young, moving without pain. Swift and fluid like an otter, his blows struck with bear strength. The knowledge that he dreamed faded.

The Saxon shield wall was buckling. Locked together, the battle lines lurched, then moved a long step backward, back toward the great wooden temple that burned behind the enemy host. Flame birds crowed from the thatch of the roof, casting yellow light on the writhing carved figures of beasts and gods and men that covered its upswung rafters and door pillars. The dry crackling smell covered the scents of blood and dung and sweat from the thousands of men fighting and dying below. The swelling roar blurred their war shouts and the screams of the wounded.

Karl smashed his shield boss forward into a yelling flaxen-bearded face, felt bone crunch beneath the iron. His sword hacked down into the neck of another, a dull cleaving feeling as the edge cut through a steerhide jerkin and into meat and bone. The Saxon line buckled and Karl shoved through, knocked one man sprawling with his shield and then blocked the thrust of a spear with it. The foot-long head stuck in the tough leather and wood; he chopped overarm at the shaft, behind the yard of iron wire wound around it beneath the point. The wood cracked across.

His comrades and sworn men pushed through at his back, guarding him from the Saxon spears, turning to take men on either side in the flank. A champion and his thanes hurled themselves at the Frankish warriors, desperate to close the gap. Karl grinned beneath his high-peaked helm and set himself, knees bent and round shield up beneath his eyes. The Saxon wore a Spangenhelm of riveted plates, with a guard of chain mail hanging like a Saracen woman's veil below his cold blue eyes; his leather jerkin was sewn with rings of iron and brass, and he bore a light axe in one hand, a small buckler in the other. It was painted with the device of a red snake, grasping its tail in its jaws.

Karl raised his sword until the hilt was above his head, the blade between his shoulders. *"Christ and the emperor!"* he shouted. "Come and be slain!"

"Wodan, ho-la, Wodan!" the Saxon replied.

Then there was no time for words. The axe darted for his leg. His shield moved, and the sharp pattern-welded steel head bit into leather and linden wood, hewing chips. Karl roared and cut downward with his long slashing sword; the Saxon moved swiftly, relaxing one knee to take him out of the way and bringing the buckler around and up. The iron banged off the slanted surface, and the buckler punched out at him. He blocked it with his shield, caught the haft of the axe on his sword blade. They skirled together, the iron bands on the axe-haft grinding over the steel of his sword.

For long moments the two men strained against each other, locked like rutting stags in the springtime, their feet churning dirt made muddy with the blood of the fallen. They were knee to knee, close enough to smell each other's sweat, close enough to see the hate and battle lust in each other's eyes.

Strong, Karl thought with surprise. Few men could stand against him so. They broke apart, heaving backward, and cut at each other. Metal rang on metal, banged on shields. *Fast.* The Saxon was as fast as the serpent painted on his shield. The men around them paused for an instant, panting, while the leaders fought. Then Karl's foot slipped on a patch of mud. Steel punched his side, driving the iron mail through the padding beneath and into his skin. Breath hissed out between clenched teeth, and the axe rose to kill. In desperation he thrust the point of his sword at his foeman's face. The move was utterly unexpected—swords were not spears—and the rounded tip of the weapon shot up beneath the hanging veil of chain.

The Saxon screamed, thick and bubbling. He fell backward; his thanes rushed in, some bearing him away despite his thrashings, others closing ranks to hold off the enemy and buy their lord's life with their own. Over their shoulders the Saxon leader shouted, his voice blurred by his wound and the guttural local dialect of German:

"We meet again! I eat your heart, Frank!"

Karl forced himself erect, sucked air into his lungs. His eyes scanned the ranks; the enemy were weakening everywhere. Banners moved forward, marked with the Cross.

"Jesu Kristos!" he bawled. "Forward!"

The Franks formed a wedge on either side of him, bristling

with spears. They struck the Saxon rear guard and stabbed, cut, clubbed them to earth. The lines had given way to clumps and bands of men who fought or fled, the Saxon host raveling away toward the trees. Frankish cavalry from either flank pursued, but Karl waved his men on toward the temple doors. Bronze covered that oak, bronze and iron and gold, but they swung open under spear butts.

Within was a great hall, reaching upward to a maze of rafters. The floor was smooth planks, not the rushes of a nobleman's dwelling; every inch of the walls was a riot of carving and painted wood. Alone in the center of the halidom stood the great log pillar carved into the likeness of the Irmin—son of Seaxneat, son of Wodan, god of the mainland Saxons. Ruddy light from the burning thatch made it seem to bleed. So did the red gold all around it. The blood of the sacrifices hung from the rafters was no more crimson; they were of the three kinds, hawk and horse and man. The man wore the Romish vestments and tonsured head of a Christian priest; Karl felt the veins in his neck swell with anger at the sight. From the groans and cries behind him, it was the wealth of gold that struck his followers' hearts— and there was no reason Christ's man should not grow rich. Especially when he was the most promising of the emperor's knights....

Three men stood between them and the pillar. Old men, gray and white in the beards that reached to their waists; they were richly dressed in the ancient style, caps of stiffened dog hide on their heads.

One bore a war hammer with a head of polished stone. "Go," he said. "The god takes back his house in fire, and you tread on holy ground. The god honors brave men; touch nothing here and you may live."

"Apostate!" Karl said. The Saxons had surrendered to the emperor before, made peace and agreed to pay tribute and accept the true faith. They were rebels, not foemen. "Your life is forfeit. Take them!"

His men hung back, despite the order, despite the gold, despite the increasing heat as the thatch fire spread to the dense old oak timbers above. The ruddy light swept across the halidom's interior in flame and shadow, and the carvings seemed to move, painted beasts turning their eyes on living men. It was not so very long since the Franks had followed the Old Ones. Many of his men were Thuringians and other easterners, from lands converted generations after Clovis. They feared.

Karl knew his duty; the cross about his neck was a charm more potent than any heathen idol. "Your demon cannot stand against Christ," he said, striding near. "His priest will be avenged."

"His priest cursed our king," the guardian of the shrine said. "The blood of a magician makes a strong curse. Even now that curse comes upon him."

He smiled. Karl felt his battle fury break free once more. He roared and swung; the steel was blunted and notched, but it sank deep into the heathen priest's side. He staggered, a loop of pink gut showing through his tunic. The more surprise when he struck in his turn, the stone war hammer chopping down on Karl's undefended shoulder. Mail would turn an edge, but it was no protection from a crushing blow.

Pain, pain lancing down his arm. He dropped the sword and staggered, breast to breast with the old man. And the heathen still smiled, with blood sheeting down, down his side. "I curse you," he said. "I curse your tomorrows, I curse you until the circle is broken, until the battle fought is ended twice and curse by curse is slain."

A woman screamed.

Karl combed straw out of his gray-streaked beard, shaking off the dream—the same dream as always, haunting him like a night hag. The woman was probably no business of his. Then she screamed again—words, this time, and in a Frankish accent. A man cried out in pain as well. Karl came up out of the straw, snatching at his round shield as he did. The stable door banged open onto a dawn that held sunlight, weak and watery with autumn, but sunlight nonetheless.

A gang of youths was grouped around the woman; they'd pulled her off her palfrey, which was snorting and backing. One of them was clutching a slashed arm, dancing about and howling threats as he watched a staff knock the knife out of the woman's hand.

They'd also pulled down her bodice, and obviously had more in mind, grabbing at her legs beneath her skirts despite her blows and curses. The woman was young, but no girl, with black hair and green eyes, well-favored but not a noblewoman. Karl thought she might be a house servant, from the silver collar about her neck.

"Halt, swine hounds," he grated in a voice like millstones, and drew his sword despite the twinge in his shoulder.

His bones felt stiff and sore this morning, and the weak fall sun was not enough to warm them. He lumbered. That simply made him look more dangerous, like an ill-tempered bear untimely prod out of his den turning to rend the hunters.

"Stand off, Frank; this is no affair of yours."

The young Saxon's words were bold, but the grip on his cudgel was white-knuckled, and he looked right and left for the reassurance of his pack. None of them bore a sword or spear, although most had the *seax*, the long single-edged knife of their tribe, thrust under their belts.

Karl grinned and kept walking; the others backed out of his way. The leader cursed as he passed and lashed out with the club. *The old boar knows,* Karl thought; he'd twitched his shield into the way before the younger man even started to move. You lost speed as you aged, but experience could compensate, if you had the wits. He slammed the hilt of his sword into the young Saxon's mouth who went down like an ox in the shambles, crawling in the gray slick mud of the laneway and spitting blood and teeth. Behind Karl's back came a shrill bugling, and the sound of crashing wood. A tall Ardennes stallion came trotting out into the street between the rows of huts half-sunken into the ground. He was sixteen hands at the shoulder and shaggy-massive; his eye rolled as he came up behind his master, and he chopped eagerly at the mud, throwing up huge clods with his platter hooves.

The Frank still smiled, showing the gaps in his teeth, and let the heavy broadsword swing negligently back and forth. "I am the emperor's man," he said mildly.

Implying that the local count would send soldiers if he disappeared; no longer strictly accurate, but he'd said the same thing often enough over the years when it was the truth for the words to carry conviction.

Two of the village louts took their friend under the armpits and helped him away; the rest scattered.

The knight turned back to the woman; she'd pulled and pinned her dress back together, which was a pity—a fine pair of breasts they'd been.

"Thank you, my lord," she said.

Frankish right enough, he thought—from the Rhine lands, at a guess. Those from farther west had a whistling accent, when they hadn't abandoned the old tongue altogether for Roman speech. Karl thought that foolish; old ways were best and had made the Franks masters of lands broader than Rome had ever commanded. Although he himself could speak Latin—the spoken tongue—well enough to be understood anywhere in Gaul and to give simple commands in Hispania or Italy. Writing and the pure ancient language of the Caesars were for priests, of course.

"What are you doing here unescorted, wench?" he asked. Her horse was good, and the saddle well-made; her clothes were fine-woven wool, dyed saffron and blue. She looked him boldly in the eye, which he liked, as she retrieved her knife and sheathed it.

"On my mistress's business, my lord," she said, "which could not wait."

Karl nodded. "Come. Best we go." Best not to give those

young dogs time to think; think of a spear thrust from behind a bush on a forest road, for instance.

With that in mind he saddled his warhorse and put the pack frame on the ordinary mount he kept for travel; his helm went on his head, and the long lance with the crossbar below the point rested in his right hand with its butt on the stirrup iron. The warhorse snorted again and sidled as the woman came up at his side. Perhaps it was her moon-blood time that disturbed stallions. They cantered out of the village and through its fields, stubble hidden in the last of the morning mist. She produced bread and hard cheese from her saddlebags, and a skin of real wine; he drank with relish, belching and smacking his lips. Once he'd drunk good wine daily, at the table of the emperor, but that was long years ago.

"My name is Ermenagarde, Lord," the woman said. "What brings so brave a warrior to these lands?"

It was a goodly while since a pretty, well-spoken young woman had looked at him so. "I am Karl von Obersberg, the emperor's knight," Karl replied. "The old emperor, Karl the Great. Most recently I fought the heathen Danes in the north, for the margrave of the North Mark. I travel to Franconia to take up my lands."

Her look was demure, but he knew she saw the shabbiness of his harness—his weapons and armor were good, and well kept, but the rest of his gear was not. And he had no servants....*And the fief in Franconia is barely more than three peasant farms,* Karl thought sourly. Once he'd have given as much to a huntsman who served him well. He shook his head. Where had the years gone? The years when he'd been the strongest of the emperor's paladins, the bravest, one whose voice was listened to in council. There was no time he could point to and say: *Here I failed.* It had crept up on him, like the gray hair and the pain in his bones. *Enough.*

"What of you, wench?" he said roughly.

"My mistress is taken prisoner, as she rode to her wedding," she said, not calmly, but with fear well kept. "Her dowry with her, a great treasure, and all her escort slain or fled. She is of high

375

birth, and her father's only child. I ride to bring her kinsmen; for vengeance, or to pay ransom."

Karl grunted and looked around. They had ridden out of the rye fields, into deep oak forest. That thinned, oaks gave way to pines, pine to naked heath knee-tall on the horses; the damp floral scent filled his nostrils. This was good country for bandits, and the new emperor did not keep them down as his mighty father had. Landloupers in the woods, Dane raiders on the seas—things were not as they had been in the great days.

"These are evil times," he agreed; the bride's father would have to pay a second dowry to get her free, and the bridegroom wouldn't be getting a virgin. "The count's castle is near," he said. "Why didn't you ride there, if masterless men overtook you?"

Ermenagarde hesitated. A suspicion narrowed Karl's eyes; bandits would find a knight's gear very useful indeed. But if she were a decoy, what of the struggle at the village? That slash she gave one of the louts was real enough; it might kill the man if it mortified, and wounds often did.

"Lord," she said slowly, "I fear if I tell you, you will think me crazed or demon-ridden. Come first to the count's fortress, and then I will tell you—and then you will believe."

"We can't reach the castle today," Karl said. Not without pushing the horses to exhaustion, which he would not do. A man with winded horses was no better than a man on foot, if he had to fight or run.

"Then, Lord, I promise that I will tell you at the count's fort, but not before. And my word will be true, as God is my witness."

He nodded shortly. They spoke little after that, stopping a few times to let the horses drink or graze or roll. They made camp beneath an ash tree, tall and great, still with most of its leaves. When they'd eaten, Ermenagarde came to his blankets with a smile and no false modesty; he was glad of that, although of course it was the due of his rank. It would be a short ride to the count's in the morning, and he could demand hospitality—demand men to hunt down these bandits, if it came to that. He was feeling kindly inclined.

"Christ have mercy, God have mercy," Karl said, crossing himself again and again.

The count's castle was built in the familiar pattern the old emperor had built to stake down his conquests—a rectangle of great upright logs on an earthen mound, with a three-story tower on another mound in the center, also of logs, laid horizontally, notched and squared. On the inner side of the fortress wall would be quarters for soldiers and servants, a smithy, storehouses, a well—whatever was needful. This was an isolated outpost, and so there was little in the way of a village outside the fort.

Now there was much less of everything. The buildings of thatch and wattle were knocked flat, scorch marks and mud to mark their passing. The huge oak timbers of the fortress wall were scattered like twigs. Many lay tumbled, the thick rawhide bindings which had laced them together snapped like single hairs. Others were frayed into splinters, as if they had exploded; still others were scorched and charred, though that might have happened afterward, when thatch fell on cook fires and braziers. Fires often started so, in a burg that had been stormed.

"Catapults might have done this," he murmured to himself, drawing his sword and dismounting.

It was more for reassurance than otherwise. The emperor had catapults at Aachen, from the Greeks, or the Saracen caliph at Baghdad, gifts like the elephant that had shivered through a few winters in the north. Nobody would be building Roman war engines here, in this desolation of backwardness. This stank of magic.

What was inside was worse. Men—and women—clawed and torn, as if by some great beast, and burned by a fire like that of the Greeks. The count himself lay by the ruined gate of the inner tower. His face was still intact, locked in a grimace of despair; the helm had rolled free, and his bare pate was wet and shiny. The rest of him was charred. Karl prodded with the point of his sword and found the expensive mail shirt the man had worn was now soldered together into a rigid cage of welded iron rings. The sword by his hand was melted like a wax candle.

The charred scraps of a nightshirt beneath the armor proclaimed that the attack had come in the dark and by surprise. The knight imagined it. Peace, the sleepy rounds of the sentries on the walls. Then flame arching across blackness, screams and terror, the great-scaled shape descending...

He shook himself and looked around. The bodies had been looted; no surprise, peasants would have done that in the week or so they'd lain. Whoever did the slaying, there were fewer bodies than he'd have expected, in a place like this. No livestock, and many of the humans were mere fragments, a limb or a head. That brought unpleasant thoughts.

"Who did this?" he turned to Ermenagarde fiercely. "The margrave, the duke, perhaps even the emperor himself—they should know of it."

Ermenagarde made a sign against evil, one he recognized. "They could do nothing. What can soldiers do against the Wurm?"

Karl signed himself, sheathed his sword, and sat on a timber; he ran his right hand through his beard, the hairs sticking and catching on the thick cracked calluses on his palm and fingers. Trolls and night hags, drows and Wurms...all more often heard of than seen. Yet they did haunt more often here, where the Old Ones lingered, than in lands long Christian. He himself had seen the whirling dust demons that the Saracens had brought with them from their deserts to Spain when they overthrew the Goths. He moved about, searching, and found the tracks of great three-toed clawed feet in the dirt, one baked to brick by the flames. The span was broad as his paired hands, larger than the largest bear he'd ever seen. From the spacing, it took strides near the length of a tall man's body.

"The margrave could send priests to exorcise a thing of evil," he rumbled, deep in his chest.

Ermenagarde pointed silently to the ruins of a chapel. Not even the body of the priest remained. Perhaps a bishop with holy relics might prove more effective; perhaps not.

Karl went on, "Then what could your mistress's kinsmen do?"

"Pay, my lord," she said bluntly. "Remember the story of Sigurd Fafnirsbane. Ever did the breed of the great Wurms long for gold; and many of them are not just beasts, but creatures who speak and think as men do. This one—"

"You have seen it?"

"With my own eyes; may I be stricken blind if I lie. This one longs greatly for more gold, though it lies on a bed of treasure. Only gold, or some great champion, may free my mistress. And the Wurm hungers for the flesh of maidens also, so it had best be soon. Its fear for its hoard is what keeps it penned close to its lair. Otherwise all the lands about would have been ravaged long ago."

Temptation seized Karl von Obersberg between one breath and the next. *I was the emperor's champion.* Now he was just an old man with many scars, shamed by the stingy generosity of the old emperor's son. In Franconia he'd sit and wait to die, with only his sister's daughters left alive of his kin. Somehow the time to marry had never come, the right match never presented itself; so he had no sons as yet, and no inheritance to give them. No bard would make a song of Karl von Obersberg's deeds; after the Saxon wars he'd seen fighting in plenty, but never where the greatest glory fell. Good useful work, but out of the eye of the great—he'd even missed the disaster where the rear guard was caught by the Basques when the emperor came back from fighting the Saracens in Spain. The pass *he'd* been sent to protect was secured, and used... but it was the men who'd died at Roncesvalles who'd gotten the gift of undying fame.

Like Sigurd. Though he'd been only a heathen, men still knew Sigurd's name centuries later. And there was a horde of gold, too. With gold and the head of a great Wurm, his fame and might would run from Brittany to the Slav marches. Beyond, even into the lands of Danes and Greeks. Part of the wealth he could spend to buy the favor of the Franconian lords he knew, favor that would bring him a real fief. Noble fathers would fight to give him their daughters' hands; he had good seed in him yet to breed sons. He might even take this noblewoman whom the Wurm held captive—she'd still be virgin, having been hostage to a beast rather than men, and her father would be grateful.

You go to your death. Karl had fought and wandered for twenty years and more, and learned to calculate the odds. What of it? Better a chance at glory than the certainty of his last years crouching by a mean hearth, biting the coals and dreaming of when he was a man.

"I'll free your mistress," he said abruptly, standing and looking around once more. The dead should be given burial, or at least dragged into shelter against beasts. He could hear a wolf pack now. They would be in among the ruins, when the Wurm's scent washed away. "It would be a knightly deed, to rescue a noblewoman from so foul a thing. And a Christian one."

She knelt, bowing her head. "Thank you, my lord!" Her voice was trembling. "I feared...I feared it would be too late when I came to my mistress's father's house. The beast is cunning, but it hungers for the flesh of maidens only less than it craves gold."

"Come," he said to Ermenagarde. She was watching him with awe, yet with a hint of calculation in her green eyes. No doubt thinking of her prospects if he did the thing; they would be no worse than now if he died. "Tell me of this Wurm."

The cave was in a low hillside, tunneled into sand and clay. Scorch marks showed about it, the very earth fused into glass about the mouth. Outside was a broad flat area of dirt pounded to the consistency of rock where the Wurm wallowed and basked. Trees had been pushed aside or snapped off or burned for half a league about, except for a few huge oaks; the damage was long enough ago that saplings sprouted fifteen feet from some of the stumps. Karl von Obersberg frowned at them thoughtfully, noting the lay of the land, snuffing at the wind—from the cave area, thankfully. The songs didn't say if Wurms had a good nose for scent, but he was going to act as if they were as keen as slothounds until it was proved otherwise. He could smell *it*, a stale rank serpent's stink.

Beside the cave mouth was a thick pillar driven into the ground, ancient oak cracked and mossy. Karl's eyes were no longer keen at short distances, but as if to compensate for that loss they'd grown better at distance. Across half a league he could see the form of the woman chained to it, her hands high above her head. A young woman, he thought, richly dressed, with jewels sparkling at throat and belt. Her golden hair hung to her knees, hiding her face, but that was no matter. If she was beautiful, all the better; the bards would make her so, regardless, in their songs, once he'd slain the Wurm. From what Ermenagarde said, the family was rich, Saxon nobles who'd stood by the emperor in the wars and been rewarded well for it.

"How will you slay the Wurm?" the serving woman asked. She sounded as if curiosity devoured her like wolves; all through the day while he patiently quartered the area, he'd said nothing.

Karl grinned tautly. "In knightly fashion, with the lance," he said. "It's the only weapon likely to harm so large a beast, in any case. Get you gone over there"—he pointed to a dense thicket—"and hide in safety. I will make ready."

Ermenagarde licked her lips, tasting the salt sweat of fear. This Karl was a mighty warrior, that was plain to see, and a wise one. Still...

What is he doing? He'd been gone long enough for the shadows to move a hand's breadth. Then he trotted out of the woods again, onto the open ground. His cloak clung to him, and the horse—the horse was sopping wet. Her lips moved silently. Clever. Very clever indeed, but he seemed to have left his lance behind. Instead he lifted the aurochs' horn from its sling by his side and sounded it, a ripping blat that echoed back from woods and hill. Again and again he sounded it, until the clearing rang. Between blasts he roared a challenge.

The Wurm came forth. Four times longer than a man, low slung on feet like an eagle's, with legs that jutted up beside its ridged backbone in high-elbowed tension. Its body was much like a crocodile's but the neck was much longer and the head

381

narrow. Red eyes peered out from beneath a shelf of bone; when the mouth gaped, teeth showed like daggers of yellow ivory.

Ermenagarde caught her lip between her teeth. The Wurm gathered itself to leap... and Karl von Obersberg turned tail and ran, as fast as his horse could gallop. That was quickly, since he rode his trail horse, not the heavy war steed.

The woman watched for a second, open-mouthed. *A coward? He is a coward?* There was not a strand of gray in her black hair, but she was no girl in her judgment of men, and she knew Karl better than *that.*

The Wurm pursued, in a hunching, bounding run. Sunlight shone on scales like enameled metal. Flame bloomed forth from the jaws, setting the scrub alight; when the bulk of the charging monster struck the trees, even the whippy saplings were crushed to splinters. Trees broke. Flame billowed up again amid a scream of rage vaster than hills.

Then there was another shriek, of pain this time, and a billow of fog. Ermenagarde's eyes widened; she ran for the cave mouth with her skirts hitched up in her hands and her knees flashing.

"Quickly, Lady Gudrun!" she gasped, fumbling with the other woman's manacles. Then she darted into the cave, came out with two hunting bows and quivers. "We have little time. Something is wrong."

They girded their skirts through their belts and dashed out along the trail of the monster.

The cold wetness of the cloak and the sudden padding under his mail hauled at Karl as he rode out into the clearing; no colder than the knot of fear beneath his breastbone. Only a lad new to battle thought he could not die. Wrong then—he'd seen so many perish with their bright swords unblooded—and a greater error here, where he fought something not of this world. That was good; it was his revenge on the world itself. He raised the horn to his lips and sounded it, slitting his eyes until the drops caught in his eyelashes sparkled like jewels against the morning sun.

"Come forth!" he called, between blasts. "A Christian knight calls you forth to die, monster! Spawn of Sathanas, come forth!"

He'd thought himself prepared. When the Wurm came forth, he felt his bowels loosen and stopped them just in time. Five times the weight of a bear, he decided, and teeth the length of daggers, and a hide like an elf-lord's armor in a ballad, fitted jewels that shone in the sunlight. And it breathed fire.

I COME, CHRISTIAN. The voice rang between his ears without going through them, soundless. It was huge, and very weary.

Karl's horse tried to buck, turn and flinch all at the same time. He controlled it with a brutal jerk of the reins and pulled its head about. Once the beast realized what he was trying to do, it stopped fighting him, put its head down, and ran. He doubled the reins in his fists, bracing his feet to keep some control, and steered the berserk animal down the path he'd selected.

Fire exploded at his back. The wet cloak sizzled, and he could smell singed wet horsehair. The horse screamed in pain and ran faster; the Wurm was snake swift itself, but too huge to pass down the narrow trail without crushing the undergrowth, and that slowed it. Karl whooped like a boy as he ducked and wove to avoid the branches that might have swept him from the saddle. Another blast of fire—hot enough to singe his hair where it escaped under the edge of his helm, hot enough to dry the last water out of his cloak and set the padded gambeson beneath his hauberk steaming. Yet it was not as large and did not reach as far as the first blast. *Praise be to God,* Karl thought. He would have spurred the horse, except that it could run no faster. The last section of trail was straight and broad. He could hear the earthshaking beat of the Wurm's feet behind him.

Now. The trail and the ground vanished beneath the horse's feet. It did not jump, simply ran out into empty space. That was enough to take them two lengths out into the river; Karl parted company with the saddle in midair. By luck he landed clear of the thrashing hooves, although he lost his helmet to the waters.

NICK JIZBA

They were deep enough for him to claw fingers into the mud and be well hidden. Even through the water he could see the shadow of the Wurm as it tumbled into the steep riverbank. Too heavy to jump, as he'd thought. And—

A scream, loud even through the waters. Steam exploded off their surface as the stricken monster crashed down; around him the river went from ice chill to warm in an instant. When Karl surged up through the surface, the mist still boiled, but only a trickle of flame came from the Wurm's jaws as it thrashed. The stub of his lance protruded from its side, driven in to the very crossbar by the Wurm's own weight. Only such force could have pierced that armored hide, which was why he'd braced it beneath the riverbank where the Wurm must come, if it followed him.

"Haro! Haro!" Karl shouted—half wheezed—as he drew his sword and darted in.

Beyond expectation, his warhorse came to the call. The huge beast reared and chopped down at the crippled Wurm. Ironshod hooves struck bone, and one clawed leg dangled limp. The Wurm tried to breathe fire again, but only a trickle came forth, enough to burn his eyebrows dry and no more. Two-handed, he swung. Sparks rang, but the fanged head juddered to the shock. There was an old scar along the left side of the face, ending in a ruined eye; his blow reopened that old wound, and blood spattered out to hiss and steam on the wet rocks of the riverbed. Karl roared his triumph and stepped close, raising his sword above his head to drive it into the eye socket and the brain beneath.

"Die, beast!" he shouted. The long years fell away; he was the emperor's paladin, young and strong and victorious, the future open before him in blood and fire and gold.

Blackness struck.

Ermenagarde lowered her bow. The range was close, no more than twenty paces, but she'd never expected to strike so well. Karl von Obersberg stood like a statue with his sword raised and the arrow quivering in the base of his skull. His victory shout was still echoing as he toppled forward, rigid as a tree, and splashed down on the rocks. His sword rang and sparked on river stones.

"Father!" Gudrun called, running forward and kneeling by the Wurm's head. "Father! Are you all right?"

The huge scaly muzzle moved feebly, and one forelimb pawed the air.

More practical, Ermenagarde looked around for the warhorse. Trained war steeds were the most valuable part of a knight's plunder, if the most difficult to sell, and Lord Widukind had a deplorable tendency to devour them if not reminded. The beast had retreated a hundred paces or so; she advanced slowly, with soothing words. The horse had had time to grow used to her voice, and to the taint of magic that hung about her. She got within arm's reach, took up the reins, and looped them firmly about an oak limb.

Gudrun's scream brought her about. Her eyes widened as she dashed to the other woman's side. The Wurm—Lord Widukind—was . . .

Molting, she thought in amazement.

The armor of brazen scales dropped from his sides like rain, splashing into the water or tinkling on the rocks, then dissolving into dust. Steel bone and stony flesh melted, like sand in the purling water. Wriggling out of the mass, like a snake out of last year's skin, came . . . a man. A man she had not seen since she was an infant; not since the night they fled from a burning hold and the swords of the Franks.

"Father," Gudrun wept. "Father."

Lord Widukind, last overlord of the Saxons, staggered to his feet and stood with the water rippling around his bare knees. He was tall and fair-haired, with the massive, scarred body of a fighting man of seven-and-thirty years. One arm hung limp, and a wound gouged up the side of his face to take his left eye, but he smiled—grinned and shouted for joy:

"The curse is broken!" He embraced his daughter with his good arm. "And Gudrun—I see you with a man's eyes, a father's eyes."

He looked around in wonder. "How different the world is...."
Down at himself. "I'm older. Welladay, that comes to us all."

Ermenagarde slung her bow and knelt, heedless of the water. "My lord," she said, breathless. "My lord."

Widukind raised her. With one hand he parted the silver collar about her neck. "Keep this as a gift," he said, handing it to her. "For your loyalty."

He looked down and pulled the dead knight onto his back. The face held no pain, only a look of transcendent happiness. "I know this man," he said slowly. "Not his name or his deeds, but I know him. Somewhere—"

"His name was Karl von Obersberg," Ermenagarde said.

Widukind shook his head. *"I curse you until the circle is broken,"* he quoted softly. "So the priest said. Hengst said the magic could be turned on itself, but only when the two were one. He was the one I fought at the last battle, when the temple burned."

The three looked down on the body. Widukind spoke at last. "Come. We will give him burial; he was a brave man, and a great warrior. And we will splint this arm, and rest before we go north."

"North?" Gudrun asked, wiping at the tears of joy on her cheeks.

"To the Dane king's court," Widukind said, wincing. The pain of his wounds was returning. "We won't lack for a welcome, with the gifts we bring."

Ermenagarde trudged through the water to retrieve the fallen knight's sword. *Twenty-seven swords,* she thought. Mostly with full sets of armor to accompany them, and other gear besides—a fair number of knights had passed by over the years, and few had been able to resist her story of Gudrun's looks.

"I'll cut the splint," she said, and headed for the woods.

The Children of Desolation

written by

Spencer Sekulin

illustrated by

CYBERAEON

ABOUT THE AUTHOR

When Spencer Sekulin isn't on the road as a paramedic or studying, he is most likely writing. Born and raised in Ontario, Canada, Spencer fell in love with books at a young age, with authors like Terry Brooks and Eoin Colfer giving him an appetite for speculative fiction. Though he didn't begin writing until university, he quickly discovered that it was just as fun as reading. The rest is history. His passions include emergency medicine, voice-overs, homemade coffee, travel obscura, and of course, writing.

Writers of the Future is Spencer's first professional sale. "The Children of Desolation" started as a story title with no story, and sat for several years before he stumbled across it again, whereupon several unrelated ideas clicked together. "Sometimes stories take us by surprise, and then drag us on rides we didn't expect. In my case, this one started running right away, leaving me to catch up in its dust." Most of it was written on a covered porch during a torrential downpour. A novel based on it is also in the works.

Regarding the story itself, Spencer felt drawn to its protagonist, Tumelo Laska. His burden of heritage, and his moral struggle between doing what is right and putting family before all else, lends itself well to the sense of desperation of the post-apocalyptic setting. Though the world may end, humans have always loved, lost, and sought redemption—and always will.

Spencer hopes it conveys the importance of family, the indomitableness of the human spirit, and the power of forgiveness. He hopes you enjoy reading it.

ABOUT THE ILLUSTRATOR

Alexandra Albu, also known as Cyberaeon, was born in 1989, in Roman, Romania—a country that for fifty years was part of the Communist Bloc led by the USSR. After the bloody revolution in December 1989, her country stepped on the path of democracy and joined NATO and the EU.

Her parents are both former teachers—her father a math teacher and her mother a music teacher.

Alexandra found an interest in the English language and enrolled in Colegiul Național Roman Vodă, studying in the bilingual English section.

Her other passion is drawing. She has been drawing ever since she was little but started taking it more seriously after high school. She learns from every tutorial or book she can get her hands on and plans to enroll in an art university to gain formal art education. She loves bringing characters and stories to life, both hers and other people's.

Alexandra is currently working as a freelance illustrator.

The Children of Desolation

Tumelo Laska had never believed in miracles, yet as he sat by one of Underhaven's coveted hospital beds, he rested his face in his hands and prayed for nothing less.

Like some fool at his wit's end, and I am that fool. He knew it made him a hypocrite, but for Kagisa he would become anything, even the devil himself. Anything to see her smile again. "You always told me miracles still happen, even though I thought that only the Old World was stupid enough to believe in them. You'd still tell me that, wouldn't you?"

Kagisa's breaths were her only answer, yet Tumelo still felt scolded. He took a shaky breath and ran a hand over his shaved head. Even catatonic and laden with wires and intravenous lines, lustrous obsidian hair fallen out and chestnut skin pallid, she left him breathless. Not even the buzzing overhead lights, which seemed determined to bring out every wrinkle and vein, could change that.

"What did I ever do to deserve you?" he whispered. "What did you do to deserve this?"

Like every time, he knew the answers.

Tumelo squeezed Kagisa's hand. When she squeezed back, he choked on a sob and forced a smile. She would want him to smile, but her eyes remained closed, flicking behind their lids in fevered dreams. He hoped they were good dreams of when Thabo was alive, of when they were a family and not even the Desolation could poison their happiness.

"Hold on," he said. "I have another client. This will be paid for. You'll get better. You're strong...stronger than I ever was." He clenched the client's note in his other hand. "I'll return, like I always do. I promise."

"And if you're wrong?" he imagined Kagisa asking.

Tumelo bit the inside of his mouth.

"Ahem," someone said behind him. "That's five minutes. More will be extra."

Tumelo suddenly felt twice his fifty-three years. In the Old World he wouldn't have been charged by the minute to visit. Neither would he have had to choose between staying by her side and paying for her treatment. That era had died a century ago, and here he was, jealous of the dead. Wishes would not save Kagisa. Only money. Money he didn't have. He kissed her forehead and let go.

Doctor Harris leaned in the doorway, tapping his vintage Rolex, the anemic lighting reflecting in his glasses. His pinched face and plastic smile seemed made for throttling.

"Have you heard of bedside manners?" Tumelo asked.

"Everything has a price, Tumelo. You know that."

"Right...I was just finishing up."

"It'll be another thirty for the extra twenty seconds. You know the policy."

Prick. Tumelo forked over the bills, but Harris shadowed him down the dim hallway, his white coat smudged with God knows what. Wheelchairs, gurneys, and disorganized crash carts cluttered the way, and each open door breathed the smells and sounds of others in shoes very much like his own. Blood and urine stained the floor tiles, and the air smelled too little of antiseptic and too much of cigarettes.

"I trust you'll pay her medical expenses?" Harris asked.

"Next month."

"With interest?"

"With your damn interest." Tumelo felt his stomach twist. Another impossible promise. "I'll pay. Please take care of her in the meantime. You're a doctor."

"Yes, yes, but this is still a business, and I need to—"

"Make ends meet, of course." Tumelo reached the clinic's rusty front door. As usual the secretary was bombed out of her mind on synthetics. He felt ashamed for leaving Kagisa here, and disgusted that it was still the best option. Harris's droning made it worse.

"And need I remind you. If her bills are not paid, I'll unfortunately have to clear the bed for someone who can. Though I'm sure—"

"Doctor Harris." Tumelo kept his eyes on the door, anything but that viper. "If you do that, I don't care if I have to cross the whole Desolation to do it, I will kill you." He meant it, too. *Look what you're doing to me, Kagisa.* Without giving Harris time to reply, he handed over a brown paper envelope. "If this doesn't make you happy, you can shove it."

One glance at the documents within had Harris wide-eyed. "A-Are you certain of this?"

"Absolutely."

"But it's your livelihood! I'm not talking about medical bills. If you can't pay the Proprietor you'll be—"

"Have you ever been so in love with someone you'd depart with all sense just to be with her?" When Harris only blinked, Tumelo smiled and opened the door. "Then you couldn't possibly understand. Good day, Doctor." *Chew on that. Maybe it will grow you some conscience.*

Underhaven's grey, convoluted walkways greeted Tumelo with their usual embrace of stale air and the groaning machinery that kept southern Africa's last subterranean city alive. He wondered if he'd inhaled the secretary's synthetics when he saw a massive German shepherd sitting by the clinic's entrance. It perked up and studied him with its brown eyes. He hadn't seen a dog in twenty years.

"Not the kind of miracle I asked for," he muttered.

The dog wagged its tail.

"Careful. I know a few people who would eat you in a heartbeat."

It cocked its head and kept wagging.

393

"Don't say I didn't warn you." Tumelo craned his neck to let the cavern's artificial sun warm his face. His father would roll in his grave if he knew he'd just used the Iris, his family's greatest treasure, as collateral for bills he could never afford. He resisted the urge to renege on the deal and hurried into the musky streets. He had a job to do, and every second lost was a second Kagisa couldn't afford to lose.

Underhaven's claustrophobic forest of towering apartments, water pipes, and recycling silos pressed around him. Despite being one of the few places people could survive without radiation gear, Underhaven was more commonly called Underdump, much to the Overseer's chagrin. Tumelo smirked at one of the grainy television screens that hung at every junction. Upon it, Overseer Henrik Ward made his daily address. A grey-haired man Tumelo's age, but with pale skin, tailored clothes, and half as many wrinkles.

"Citizens of Underhaven, we have been blessed with another day," Henrik said, his elegant voice butchered by the crackling speakers. "We are the jewel of these lands. Underhaven survives by your efforts. Let us carry on our duties today for the building of a better tomorrow." Henrik gave the same smile he did every day, and the same gesture: a closed-fisted arm across his chest. At least he bothered to say something different every day.

The streets teemed with gritty townsfolk and merchants, with undercurrents of orphans from the slums. And fanatics. The Order of Retribution had recruiters at every corner, hawking the crusade against the mutant demons in human skin, called Desolates, as a noble cause for the city's otherwise aimless youth. The Order's zealous hunters swaggered about in their red cloaks and ramshackle armour, eager for excuses to use their holy bludgeons on any suspected Desolate. Tumelo tried to ignore them. They were right to hate the Desolates, but they reminded him too much of pain and regret.

"Hey, Tumelo!" one of the zealots said. "Got any leads on Desolates for us?"

Tumelo met the wild-haired youth's hazel eyes and felt his

stomach twist with recognition. Rudo, one of the local orphan boys. Tumelo had watched him and so many others grow up. Kagisa had even taken Rudo in once, when he'd caught a fever. He still looked no older than sixteen. Thabo was that age when he joined. The Order bled young blood. "No, I have not. Good hunting."

Rudo blocked Tumelo's path with his bludgeon. Several others joined him. "Come on. You travel a lot on that old locomotive of yours. You sure you haven't got any?"

"I'm sorry." Tumelo pushed the bludgeon aside. "And why would a Desolate come here, to the heart of your Order?"

Rudo glanced at the others, who shrugged.

"I thought so," Tumelo said. "Those things are not idiots."

"But—!"

"How old are you, Rudo?"

Rudo squared his bony shoulders. "Fifteen yesterday."

"Seventeen!" another said. "We're grown men!"

No, just boys with dreams of grandeur. Is this the Order's cream of the crop? "Then you're lucky there aren't any Desolates here. They would turn you to paste without breaking a sweat. Go to school. Learn something useful. Do whatever kids your age do these days. Just don't throw your lives away being fodder for those geriatric wonders that collect your weekly tithes. Your lives are worth more than that."

Thabo's was, too, but Tumelo doubted they'd listen either.

Rudo pressed his bludgeon against Tumelo's gut. "Mind your words, *Grandpa*. That's blasphemy."

Tumelo knew what they saw—a man whose dark beard was peppered with white, his ebony skin crisscrossed with pale scars and wrinkles, his muscular engineer's body half of what it used to be. An old man running out of time. A relic who had no right telling them how to live. Too bad he would do it anyway.

"I'm giving you my best advice. Walk away while you still can. The moment they send you out, there's no going back."

"A Desolate killed my sister!"

The others murmured their own grievances.

395

"So, you think you'll just exterminate them?" Tumelo asked.

"We're not quitting until they're all dead."

"You'll be dead long before they are."

Rudo seethed. The others closed in and were startled when a dog started barking. Tumelo yanked the bludgeon from Rudo's hand and pressed it under his jaw before he could blink.

"See what I mean? I'm an old man. Desolates never age. Imagine what one could do to you." Tumelo shoved the weapon back into a speechless Rudo's hands and stormed off, mindful of the dog trailing him. *Must be old and hungry, like me*. He quickened his pace, eager to get to the Iris before—

"Popular as ever with the devout I see," a velvety, precise voice purred at his elbow. "The Proprietor sends his regards."

Crap. Tumelo drew debt collectors like wasteland blood flies. The Proprietor was the puppet master of Underhaven's criminal underworld. Everyone owed him money, but no one ever saw him, only his goons. This sweet-mouthed little midge was Beetle. The portly man, barely four feet tall, waddled up alongside Tumelo, bringing his usual stench of garlic.

"He can keep his regards," Tumelo said. "Tell him I'll pay after my next job."

"Hmm, and when will that be?"

"Today. Sooner if you leave me alone."

Beetle tittered. "The Proprietor cannot bank on promises forever. Your debts grow by the day, let me check...ah yes, as of today, you're at seven million."

That could pay for Kagisa's care ten times over. Tumelo clenched his teeth.

"The Proprietor is eager to know your repayment plans," Beetle said. "You're his star debtor, after all."

"My father was, not me," Tumelo growled.

"Need I remind you that your father died without paying a cent towards his dues? After everything the Proprietor did to keep Laska Locomotives from going belly-up."

"After you *lied* about the interest rates."

"Oh my, that's slanderous." Beetle folded his hands over his prodigious gut. "The Proprietor never lies. Your father simply neglected to read the contract."

"Then maybe you should have read it to him!"

Beetle showed his crooked teeth. "Now, where's the fun in that?"

Some inheritance you left me, Old Man, Tumelo thought. *You never told me about this. Probably never knew. Lucky me.* "I need more time."

Beetle jotted it down on a notepad. "Needs more time, says Tumelo. Anything to add?"

Tumelo could think of a few choice words, but decided against it, letting the poison fester in his stomach like a bad meal. His ancestors must have felt the same, under the boot of their oppressors. He shook his head.

"I don't think he'll like it," Beetle said.

"It's all I have."

"How about that bracelet of yours?"

Tumelo instinctively drew his right arm back. "It's not for sale."

Beetle pouted. "Pity. Artifacts like that sell well amongst collectors."

"I'll make another payment after this job."

"Then get busy working or get busy picking a casket."

"Thanks for the vote of confidence."

"Much obliged." Beetle tucked the notepad away. "That mutt seems to like you."

Tumelo glanced at the dog. "Probably smells the ration bars on me."

"Ration bars?" Beetle said, tongue flicking across his lower lip. "That'll count for a payment."

"Of what, ten dollars?"

"Five point three to be exact."

Number crunching prick. Tumelo entertained the thought of shoving them down the man's throat. Instead he groaned and handed them over, and Beetle left with more swagger in his gait than someone with such a low centre of gravity should. Tumelo glared at the dog. "I was hoping you'd bite his pancake butt and save me some trouble."

Underhaven's train yard was ten minutes away, where eleven gated tunnels took separate tracks to the surface. Eight trains occupied the platforms, mostly derelict and overrun with rust, and far fewer than the thirty there'd once been. The tracks were too treacherous, and the trade too sparse for most folk to bother anymore. A dying art—one Tumelo was proud to go down with, if need be. Among all the rundown engines the Iris stood out like a hawk amidst pigeons. Sleek and powerful, her armoured hull painted in bold strokes of blue and grey. Even after all these years, the sight of the Old World diesel engine sent his heart aflutter. A Class 43-000 General Electric type C30ACi diesel-electric locomotive, a relic from his great-great-grandfather, who'd been an engineer and conductor for Transnet Freight before the Desolation. It had been passed down for generations, along with blood charged with a love for machinery.

Tumelo savoured the sight, feeling the years unwind until he felt like a boy again, full of dreams and wonder. Then he took out the note he'd found under his front door. Blank. A signal that someone wanted discreet service. Yet when he glanced around the platform all he saw was a scrawny girl sitting against a recycling bin; a bundle of rags with grey cloth wrapped over her eyes and faded hair that bore ghostly hints of auburn.

Just a beggar. No one's here.

He walked past the blind girl, tossing a coin at her bare feet as he went.

"You're late," the girl said.

Tumelo stopped and looked back. The beggar girl was on her feet, though facing the Iris and not him. She'd been sitting on a suitcase and now held it with both hands. It was almost as big as her. "Excuse me?"

"I said you're late."

Tumelo blinked when the German shepherd nuzzled up to

her. She scratched between its ears, and it sat, ever watchful. "It's yours?"

The girl smiled, white teeth to an anemic-pale face. "His name's Jasa."

"You had him trail me?"

"In case you got into any trouble."

This is ridiculous. Tumelo wondered if he was the target of some joke. "You're the client. A blind kid with a dog."

"Does that matter? I'll pay."

"Depends where you want to go."

The girl turned, using Jasa for support. The dog guided her to Tumelo. She had a limp, and her breaths came hard. Bad blood, judging by the pallor. A bad leg, too. When she looked up at him, albeit over his shoulder, he felt sorry for her. Another orphan with more hope than sense. That's how kids deserved to be, but this world ate them alive. An urchin like her could never afford his services. What dreams had gotten into her head to make her want to leave Underhaven? The Desolation would kill her in a day, and her little dreams with her.

"I'd like to go to the end of the One-Way Track."

Tumelo almost swallowed a mouthful of air. "What?"

"Where the tracks end, before the Burn Line."

"No." Tumelo turned away and shoved his hands into his pockets. "Go back to your begging."

"Aren't you Tumelo Laska?" she asked. "People say you're the only captain that takes the One-Way Track."

"So what if I am? I'm not taking you there. It's a death sentence." For him, too, given the odds.

"Will this change your mind?"

Tumelo heard the suitcase locks click and felt a tingle go down his spine. Was she pulling a gun on him? He turned in time to see a mountain of bills spill out. Two million at least, maybe three. "Where did you get that?!"

The girl smirked. "I earned it."

"Stole it more like."

"How could I have done that?" When Tumelo remained speechless, she cocked her head. "Do you believe in miracles, Mister Laska?"

"No—" Tumelo looked at the cash again, then the Iris, then back into Underhaven's hazy depths where Kagisa waited. She'd never forgive him for this, but he'd never forgive himself if he didn't. "How soon can you be ready?"

"I already am."

"Then get onboard. The Iris will make it in three days. Two if the tracks are clear."

The girl nodded and began clumsily pushing the money back into the suitcase. Tumelo helped her, rejecting the urge to steal it. He was a man of his word, and Laska Locomotives had a perfect record. Next to Kagisa, and before his own life, he cherished that golden reputation. Come hell or high water, sandstorms or Ravagers, Tumelo Laska always delivered.

After helping the girl climb the rungs to the engine's main compartment and marvelling at Jasa who made it in one leap, Tumelo followed. He flipped on the overhead lights, bringing out the gleam of every inch of polished steel, and then closed his eyes for a moment, savouring the fragrance of oil and solvents and the reassuring firmness of the deck beneath his boots. It felt like stepping into another world. *His* world. Then he took a crumpled document from his pocket.

"I'll need you to sign this contract. Sorry, I don't have braille. I can read it for you."

The girl stared obliviously at the wall, stroking Jasa's head. "It's okay. Jasa trusts you."

"We just met."

"He would have torn your throat out by now if he didn't. That's what happened with the last one that tried to swindle us."

Tumelo looked at the happily wagging dog. He laughed it off while taking an extra step back. "I'll need a name for the contract. You have a name, right?"

"Zala Korošec."

Tumelo began writing the name, then stopped. *What am I*

doing? He bit his lip, glad Zala couldn't see his face. *I'm taking a fortune from this kid and taking her to her death.* A better man would have helped her put the money somewhere secure, treat her leg, and buy a place to live in a safe part of town. A better man would have saved her, but he was just a lovesick fool.

He finished the contract, and Zala cosigned with a sloppy *X*. When she smiled and thanked him, he felt as if someone had twisted a screw between his ribs. He would hate himself for the rest of his life for this.

The things I do for love.

GOOD LUCK, YOU CRAZY BASTARD.

The signal patch rang through Tumelo's headset in Morse code—a parting message from Underhaven's moody station master. Tumelo smirked. Luck. Never in his hundreds of runs had he counted on it. Luck was a fickle mistress at best. A backstabbing crackhead usually.

He focused on the gauges as the Iris accelerated. Her twelve-cylinder engine roared, taking her to an easy sixty kilometres per hour. Pale lights flashed by on both sides of the track, marking every hundred meters, and the Iris's lamps painted the track silver. Clearing Underhaven's tunnels always reminded him of the first time his father had taken him out—the day he'd realized that dreams could come true.

"Remember to keep her slow until you're past the junction," Father had said with a wink. "It's no rush to get out. When you reach the open tracks, that's when the real race begins."

Daylight appeared ahead, and the Iris burst into the Desolation, veering along the Hawequas Mountains and into the lowlands. Somewhere southwest, in the red haze, lurked the ruins of Cape Town. Capital of South Africa, back when nations existed.

Zala inhaled sharply. "We're outside! Aren't we? It feels warmer."

Tumelo had offered her the living compartment, where she could stay in comfort the whole journey—God knows she deserved at least that much—but she'd insisted on sitting in the

401

seat next to his, where he had sat as a boy. As to what a blind girl could hope to experience, he did not know, but her smile told him she enjoyed it, and that was enough.

"Yes, we are," he said at last.

"How does it look? Please tell me!"

"Do you really want to know?"

Zala smiled ear to ear, and Jasa, sitting beside her, wagged his tail.

Damn kid. Tumelo told her, detailing the skeletal remains of Wellington and Paarl and the eternal red sky. Trains lying abandoned on tributary tracks. A group of optimistic scavengers in trucks tried to catch them on the way inland.

"They're too slow. Already choking on dust. No one outruns the Iris."

"You like it a lot," Zala said. "Your train."

Tumelo eased off the throttle and realized he was smiling. "I do."

Zala looked ahead. "I feel that way about Jasa. He's my best friend."

"I'd be a sorry man if a machine was my best friend."

"Then who?"

Tumelo felt his mirth evaporate. "Someone far away."

"Oh." Zala kicked her little legs back and forth, the cushioned seat making her look even smaller. "I hope you see your friend again."

You're only making this harder. "Yeah, me too," Tumelo said, amazed that such a kind urchin girl had survived so long.

"There aren't many trains left, are there?" Zala asked.

"And none like the Iris," Tumelo said. "My great-great-grand-father ran trains. He saved this one from the Desolation. Laska Locomotives has never needed another. She can easily pull over a hundred cars, has repellent coatings and sealed links to keep the bad air out. It's all I need. Right now she's even faster. Just five cars—fuel, living quarters, supplies, and two dummies."

"Dummies?"

Tumelo winked despite himself—just as Father had done

when Tumelo had asked that same question in Zala's place. "Hopefully it's a smooth run and you'll never have to find out."

"Why do you call it Iris?"

"My great-grandfather named it that, after some Old World goddess. Apparently she could travel to hell and back. That's exactly what we're doing."

Zala frowned. The Desolation's crimson light offset her pallor, but the way she sagged in the chair reminded him of her sickness. The silence gave too much room for guilt. So he told her the stories his father had passed to him, tales of the desolate lands they were passing, of beautiful forests and fields and the extinct creatures that had inhabited them. Lions, zebras, elephants, and all the rest. He described them one by one, much to her delight.

"How do you know so much?" she asked, ramrod straight with curiosity.

"Because my ancestors lived here," Tumelo said. "The Khoisan people. They walked these lands long before they had a name, when the world was plentiful and free. They were one of the oldest cultures on Earth."

"Were?" Zala frowned. "What happened?"

Tumelo found himself staring at his bracelet. Passed down like the Iris, but much older. A strand of ostrich eggshell beads, originally tied with giraffe hair. It had been a necklace, but had broken down over the generations, leaving a bracelet Tumelo held together with string.

"Other people came," he said at last. "People who saw my ancestors as animals. They were hunted as such, forced to live in the barren regions no one else wanted. There was much division back then. By the colour of your skin and the language you spoke, things that should have been a mark of pride rather than shame."

"That's terrible," Zala whispered, hands gripping the sides of her seat.

Just like what I'm doing to you, Tumelo thought, jaw tensing.

They went miles in silence, passing through fields of sand and ash. Drifts had blown over the tracks, but the Iris's plow cleared it away. It would get worse. The closer you got to the Burn Line, the worse the wind and acid showers and drifts. Past the Burn Line lurked a hell only a Desolate could walk.

"You never told me why you want to do this," Tumelo said at last.

Some colour returned to Zala's face. "It's a long story...."

"They all are. We have time."

Zala chewed her lip, but before she could speak Tumelo heard coded beeps in his headset—the Proprietor's call sign. His blood froze. He glanced at Zala, then reached to the device on his control panel and tapped twice to acknowledge. The Proprietor responded immediately.

CHECK YOUR LEFT UPPER POCKET.

Tumelo blinked and felt there. Sure enough, where those ration bars used to be, he felt a small note. It may as well have been a scorpion.

OPEN IT IN YOUR BATHROOM, AND CHECK UNDER THE SINK.

Zala seemed content to just feel the Desolation's hot light on her face. Tumelo took a deep breath, then eased out of his seat. "I'll be right back. The track will be straight for at least an hour. There's some rations in the drawer on your right, I'm sure Jasa can help you reach them."

"Where are you going?"

"Bathroom." *To speak with the devil.*

Tumelo checked under the sink and wasn't sure whether to be furious or amazed when he found a blocky device. An Old World radio transceiver, military grade. A treasure in its own right. It crackled. Tumelo put it to his ear. "You snuck into my train."

A distorted voice chuckled. "Beetle may be one of my dues collectors, but before anything else he was a thief. I hate wasting talent."

Tumelo measured his breaths. The Proprietor had him in a web, but he dared not struggle yet. "What do you want?"

"I have a job for you. If you play things right, it will be the last job you'll ever need to do."

The Proprietor's words always had two edges, and his promises were poison, but the temptation tugged at Tumelo's heart. "I'm listening."

"I want the girl."

Tumelo blinked. "Excuse me?"

"Don't play dumb. You know what I mean."

"Why would you want her?"

"That is none of your business. All that matters is that you are in the perfect position to give her to me."

"She signed a contract. I am bound—"

"Open the letter, Tumelo."

Tumelo clenched his teeth and did so. The letter was a contract, elegantly handwritten in blue ink. His skin crawled. The most powerful man in Underhaven had held this paper.

"Your new contract, dated to yesterday," the Proprietor said. "It rescinds your current one and absolves your reputation of any tarnishing. I had one of my scribes append your signature for you. Your parents did well to teach you such elegant hand. And don't tell me I cannot do that. I can. Now will you listen, or must I remind you how far I can reach?"

Tumelo bit his tongue and waited.

"Good. In exchange for your service, I will pay triple what the girl offered, and your father's debts will be erased. Carte. Blanche."

Tumelo's head spun. He was lying. He had to be. "You had enough time to sneak onto my train beforehand. You could have captured her ten times over."

"Are you calling me a liar?"

"No, I'm just—"

"It's not a detail for you to worry about," the Proprietor said. "And this is not a difficult choice. All you need to do is say yes. One syllable to end all of your worries. From there, take the last junction to the Boneyard. We will be waiting and oh so very grateful."

"I..." Tumelo swallowed hard. "I'll have to think about it."

"Is that so? I spoke with Doctor Harris this morning. Kagisa's prognosis is rather grim, though I did encourage Harris to do his best. He's my creature, after all."

Proprietor or not, Tumelo bristled. "You can threaten me all you want, but if you dare hurt Kagisa—"

"Just a reminder, friend. I also had Harris prepare a sedative. It's in the drawer where you keep your antiquated maps. Use it on the girl no more than five hours before you arrive. It will make things easier for all of us."

Between the hum of the Iris and the throbbing of his heart, Tumelo barely heard himself. "You're asking me to..."

"I know what I am asking, and you will do it. You can't afford not to. I know what you're willing to die for and it's not that girl. The only kid you'd die for got minced in Pretoria. You have ten minutes."

The radio went dead, leaving Tumelo feeling as if someone had punched him in the gut. That bastard. He tossed the device aside in disgust. Too late. He felt vile, but was this any worse than what he was already doing? His throat tightened as he remembered the day his son Thabo was born. The joy, the fear, and the tears he had shed. Zala was someone's daughter too, born into the world innocent.

When Tumelo entered the control room, Zala lay asleep in the chair, a curled-up ball of rags. Jasa watched him warily. Tumelo couldn't look into his eyes for fear that they would know. Sure enough, an injector waited in the map drawer, filled with milky serum. He glanced at the transmitter. Ten minutes. It had been six so far.

Damned if I do. Damned if I don't.

He tapped twice and was glad that Zala was asleep when he retched.

Tumelo blinked, realizing he had been dozing at the controls, lulled by the hum of the engine and sand pattering against the glass. He'd dreamt of Thabo again, and of Kagisa's dark, mesmerizing eyes. He could even feel the warmth of Thabo's little hand, when he was one year old, wrapping around his thumb. The happiest days of his life. Back then he'd felt like he ruled the world, and that couldn't be further from the truth.

Just another dream.

They had passed through the ruins of Kimberley a day ago. The Desolation stretched before him, an endless crimson haze, the track a thin line of order slicing through chaos. On the horizon loomed a wall of churning cloud and sand, like a typhoon fallen to the ground, alive with a blood-red glow and rippling with veins of green and azure lightning.

The Burn Line.

"Tumelo? Where are we now?"

Zala was awake. She had helped herself to the rations. Jasa busily licked at one of his own. Zala smiled in Tumelo's general direction. Her teeth were perfect. Why hadn't he noticed that before? Then he caught sight of the shadows to the east—the ruins of Johannesburg and Pretoria. Sweat tickled down his forehead.

"Are you okay?" Zala asked.

Tumelo forced his eyes back to the tracks. "We're nearing the final junctions. Just bypassing Pretoria."

"Another city?"

"Yes."

"Like Underhaven?"

"Was." Tumelo realized he was grating his teeth. It had been years, but he doubted ten lifetimes would be enough. He relaxed his jaw and heard Jasa whimper.

"You're sad," Zala said.

"How would you know that?"

"Jasa can tell."

"I don't like Pretoria, that's all."

Zala wrung her hands. "Did...something happen there?"

Do you have any shame? Yet Tumelo found himself talking. What was the truth compared to what he was doing to her? "Thabo, my son. He died there." He couldn't stop himself from saying more. It had been years and he had never told anyone.

"He joined the Order. I didn't want him to, but he was young and wouldn't listen. He thought he could do it. Thought he had the right reasons." *I let him walk out. I should have stopped him. What was I so afraid of?*

"The Order hunts Desolates, right?" This time Zala spoke quietly.

"For varying reasons," Tumelo said. "The fanatics mostly come from...unfortunate circumstances, but they never lack for funds. Their backers have clout and I doubt they're in it for the religious drivel." *If only I knew the name of the bastard who funded Thabo's demise.*

Zala tensed. "Thabo...he hated the Desolates, didn't he?"

"No. Not Thabo."

"Why then?"

"There's a rumour," Tumelo said, keeping his eyes on the track. "About the blood of Desolates. They say it can heal anything. Just a few drops. And enough can make you immortal."

"Did he want to be immortal?"

Tumelo laughed despite himself. "Oh no, he was never so selfish." *Unlike me.* "My wife, Kagisa...she's very sick. Has been for years. Thabo wanted to save her." *Oh Thabo... you wanted to save me, too. You knew I couldn't pay the debts. You wanted to heal Kagisa and whisk us beyond the Proprietor's reach. I told you it couldn't be done, but that only made you want to prove me wrong. I loved you for that.* Tumelo shook his head, throat burning. "The Desolate they were hunting went to Pretoria, back when it was still inhabited. There they cornered it. It killed him and a hundred other foolish kids with heroic dreams."

Zala remained silent, and Tumelo remembered details he wished to forget.

"There wasn't enough to tell the bodies apart. Desolates have powers. They were born in the cataclysms but survived, mutated, I don't know how. This one could ignite things with a gesture. It ignited their gunpowder, the fuel in their trucks, the oxygen in their suits, and Thabo—" Tumelo stopped, unable to go on. He felt Zala's delicate hand touch his. So cold, yet her smile brought a warmth he knew he didn't deserve.

"I'm so sorry," she whispered.

You shouldn't have to feel sorry for anything. Tumelo gently pulled his hand free and focused on the gauges. "I'm sorry, too."

Jasa barked—and then three deafening *cracks* stabbed Tumelo's eardrums. Bullet impacts webbed across the reinforced window. He ducked and pulled Zala from her seat as more bullets struck. The glass held.

"Stay down!"

"What's happening?" Zala cried.

Tumelo peeked up and ground his teeth at the hulking shadows speeding alongside the tracks. "Ravagers. A whole damn lot of them, too." Before Zala could ask, he was in his seat again, pushing the throttle to full. The Iris's speedometer surged past a hundred, but the Ravagers' crawlers kept pace, bristling with weapons and masked madmen. He saw them in the mirrors mounted outside the cab. Two crawlers on each side, and more on the way.

He had waltzed right into their net.

The Iris shuddered as the crawlers fired harpoons into the rear cars. In the mirrors, Tumelo saw dozens of Ravagers surging aboard, armed to the teeth with blades and crossbows and guns. Before long they would break inside and do what they were named for.

Tumelo flipped three colour-coded switches, and then yanked a lever on the floor. The Iris lurched, then gained speed. The two detached dummy cars fell behind, teeming with Ravagers and wired to three crawlers. Tumelo couldn't help but sneer. Did they really think he'd block his only way back? The fuses went off as designed, blowing the directional charges in the right-side wheels of each dummy. The blast threw the wheels like bullets, and the unbalanced cars, thrown by the blast, rocked off the other side and pinwheeled into the sands, taking the crawlers with them in a storm of flailing bodies and shrieking metal.

Yet Jasa kept barking.

What is he sensing that I'm not?!

The Iris took a left bend, and Tumelo looked at the left

mirror—right in time for a bullet to take it off. There were Ravagers on the supply car, too, and he could not afford to lose it. Tumelo muttered a curse and checked the tracks ahead. All clear. He yanked the yellow hazard suit from beneath his seat, followed by his respirator. Zala huddled in the corner, hugging Jasa.

"Stay right there," Tumelo said, donning his mask. "I'll be right back."

"W-Where are you going?!"

Tumelo took his shotgun from its rack—a restored Winchester 1897, old but true. "Getting rid of a few freeloaders."

Once in the sealed passage between the locomotive and fuel tanker, he locked the door behind him and looked up the ladder to the roof hatch. *I'm either really brave or really stupid.* He climbed and opened the hatch—and came face-to-face with a rifle. He shoved it aside, ears screaming as it fired. A steel-toed boot slammed into his chest, knocking his breath away and sending him plummeting back into the hatch. He grabbed the Ravager's ankle on the way down. The Ravager flipped onto his back, Kalashnikov flying, and Tumelo pulled himself back up and jammed his Winchester into his opponent's masked face.

BANG!

The wind blew the mess downstream. Tumelo let the corpse roll away and climbed out, panting already.

I'm getting too old for this!

A dark blur rammed into his shoulder, spinning him around and sending him rolling towards the edge. He caught himself, but his left arm refused to move thanks to the crossbow bolt buried in the joint. Pain flooded his vision with stars, but he saw another Ravager coming and groped for his shotgun. The Ravager stepped on it and shook his head.

Three Ravagers climbed down the hatch, while a dozen more crouched in waiting like crows anticipating their turn at a corpse. *Zala.* Tumelo strained to break free, but the Ravager pinned him with his boot. A glimpse at the tracks ahead killed what hope he had. A low, beetle-like machine lurked on the tracks. Its slanted nose and reinforced claws, digging into the earth on both sides, were the unmistakable nightmare of every train captain. A derailer, along with six more crawlers. If these Ravagers failed to stop the Iris, that machine wouldn't.

The Ravager drew a revolver. Tumelo glared at him.

"I'm a Laska," he hissed. "I will not beg."

The Ravager laughed and cocked the hammer.

I'm sorry, Tumelo thought. *I was a fool to even try.*

The hammer fell—and the revolver exploded, taking the Ravager's hand with it. A malfunction? Tumelo flinched as more blasts swept the train, Ravagers dying left and right, their guns and explosives erupting. He tried to move, but the nearest Ravager, halfway through dislodging a bandolier of grenades, went up in a storm of fire. The next thing Tumelo knew, he was on his side, staring at the impending derailer. Someone walked past him, as small as a child, tattered clothes billowing... Tumelo blinked, convinced that pain was making him hallucinate.

Zala was blind and lame. This girl walked with effortless grace.

She stopped in front of him and clenched her fists. The derailer belched smoke as it dug its anchoring claws deeper, and the crawlers closed in for the kill.

No, Tumelo thought. *This can't be real.*

Zala flicked her index finger. The derailer exploded off the tracks with a deafening groan, followed by the crawlers, all disappearing in blossoms of fire and smoke and sand. The ruin washed over them as the Iris charged through, but Zala remained firm, even when shrapnel tore the cloth from her eyes. When she turned, Tumelo felt his heart drop into a void. Clouded eyes of the palest blue flayed him... and then he was scrambling down the hatch. He landed in a pool of blood. Three Ravagers lay dead in the passageway. Jasa sat amidst them, covered in blood. Tumelo stumbled to the control room, feeling like he would vomit, heart ramming out of his chest.

A Desolate. She's a Desolate!

The thought didn't seem real. None of it did.

A Desolate that ignites....

Tumelo collapsed into his seat and grabbed the revolver he had taped beneath it. Thabo. The name rang off the inside of his skull like a ricocheting bullet—until he heard soft footfalls behind him. His mind shrieked to a halt.

"Tumelo?" Zala whispered.

He dared not face her. "No."

"I—"

"I won't hear it."

Zala groped for words, her voice cracking.

"If I could kill you right now, I would." Tumelo gripped the revolver until his knuckles popped. "I don't care what you look like. I would butcher you until you're like Thabo was. A pile of meat. And I would celebrate it! I would die a happy man knowing you're in hell where you belong!" Rage tore through him—and then vanished. Suddenly he felt ancient beyond his years. He couldn't even get angry anymore. "And you know what? I'll still keep my end of our bargain. How does it feel to get what you don't deserve? Do you even feel at all?"

"Tumelo, I—"

"Get out of my sight," Tumelo spat. "I don't want to see your face ever again. If you step one foot closer, I will shoot you." *And damn the consequences.*

In the silence that followed, Tumelo half expected Zala to kill him. Instead, she whispered, "They're right about the blood. That wound, you'll..."

"I'd sooner let your mutt chew my throat than take your filthy blood. Keep it and go to hell."

Tumelo didn't hear Zala move, but when he looked back, she was gone. He yanked the shaft from his shoulder and filled the wound with disinfectant, biting his tongue against the pain, then left his protective gear in a pile. If infection did not kill him, exposure from a punctured suit might, but at this point he didn't care. He only wanted one thing and he knew it was impossible.

No, not impossible.

He thumbed the beads on his wrist and looked at the map

drawer. Tingles raced down his spine. The junction waited ahead. The Proprietor would only take a Desolate if he had a plan. Tumelo slipped the injector into his pocket, and let the Iris take the track towards the Boneyard.

Now, how to sedate a demon?

Tumelo crept between the cars. The bodies were gone. Even the blood. *Like that will change my mind.* He found Zala in the living quarters, curled up on one of the cots—and Jasa blocking the way. That dog would kill him for what he was about to do.

"Hey Jasa," he whispered, chancing a smile. "How would you like a little treat?"

Jasa perked up and eyed him, but didn't budge.

Tumelo fished a ration bar from his pocket. A revolver lay there, too. He felt stupid for carrying it. *If I shoot, I'm dead. If he gets close, I'm dead. If I do nothing, I'm dead.*

At the sight of the bar, Jasa sat straighter and wagged his tail.

"You want it?" Tumelo broke off a piece. "Come on then. Here Jasa. That's a good boy!"

He lured Jasa into the locomotive. The dog glanced back every few seconds, but little chunks kept him coming until they reached an open utility closet. There Tumelo showed a second ration bar, hovered it before Jasa's nose, and threw it inside. Jasa leapt after it and Tumelo slammed the door—only for Jasa to make it halfway out, barking and thrashing and biting. A gunshot roared. Tumelo staggered back from the shut closet and dropped the revolver.

Did I just…?

He waited for a sound from inside the closet. Nothing came.

What have I done?

Tumelo found himself in the living quarters again. Sick of himself. Sick of everything. To his surprise Zala still slept, her breaths quiet and steady. He forced himself to keep going. None of it felt like he thought it would.

"Who's the real monster here?" said a voice in his head.

The injector gleamed in his hand, winking like the Proprietor's

413

unseen smile. With her eyes closed, pale hair fallen over her face, Zala looked like the frail child she pretended to be and not the century-old demon she really was. It reminded him of when he and Kagisa would sit by Thabo's bed when he was little, watching him sleep, finding more joy in that than anything the world could offer. Zala had saved his life, and this was how he thanked her.

I'm doing this for you, Kagisa. And for Thabo.

Would Kagisa understand? He shook his head and primed the injector over Zala's shoulder, but stopped when he saw something in her hand. A weathered photograph of a family standing before a crystalline lake, with a church on an island and mountains farther behind. The Old World. The little girl wedged between two older brothers looked just like Zala but for her fiery hair and sky-blue eyes—and the careless happiness of her smile.

Who she used to be, before the Desolation.

Zala had fallen asleep staring at it. Did she long for it? Was part of that child still in her, wishing for the life she lost? Tumelo's stomach twisted into a knot, but the agony in his shoulder reminded him that none of it mattered.

"I'm sorry," he whispered.

The injector hissed. Zala winced, but remained asleep. Tumelo found himself in the bathroom, feverishly washing his hands, but no matter how hard he scrubbed he could not rid himself of feeling like he'd buried them in a septic tank. *The hard part's over,* he told himself. *It's almost done. Kagisa will be okay. Everything will be okay.* He looked into the mirror and tried to smile, but the face staring back at him was crying.

The Boneyard materialized through the crimson haze of the Burn Line's periphery, heralded by thunder and the ripple of green and azure lightning across the looming bands of cyclonic clouds. Tumelo's gut told him to retreat. Instead, he eased the Iris to a halt.

Everything's dead here, he told himself. *There's nothing to fear.*

The skeletons of Old World machines—cranes, aircraft,

stacks of automobiles, and massive, bulky things he could not fathom—sent chills down his spine. There were stories of ghosts in the Boneyard, and like a ghost the figure appeared. He stood on the tracks with an audacity only the Proprietor's underlings dared, his gasmask and fluttering duster weathered by spraying sand. Tumelo double-checked his revolver and backup pistol before climbing out. The heat bled through his suit and prickled his skin. The other's gasmask gave him the likeness of a crow.

"You're the Proprietor's man," Tumelo said.

The Crow nodded and remained silent.

"She's in the third car, drugged like you wanted."

Dozens of shadows detached from the ruins, all similarly garbed. More were perched on the cranes, rifles in hand. How had they gotten here before him? Tumelo resisted the urge to touch his holster. They had a deal, and he'd delivered like always. Yet a minute of silence had him wary. "Well? The longer we stay, the less our equipment protects us."

The Crow cocked his head, as if listening to a voice in his ear. "Hand over your weapon, Mister Laska."

Tumelo set his jaw and handed over his revolver.

"The other one, too."

Damn you. He tossed his spare into the sand at the Crow's feet.

"*Now* he will see you."

A howl cut through the air, and a wicked shadow appeared through the haze. A rotorcraft, one of the few remaining from the Old World, sleek, armed, and incredibly expensive. Tumelo took a step back despite himself, shielding his eyes by habit as it landed on the tracks with a tempest of sand. The man who disembarked, resplendent in top-notch radiation gear and a white overcoat that seemed to repel the sand, made Tumelo feel smaller for every step closer he got.

The Proprietor himself.

"Good afternoon, Tumelo."

Even distorted by his gasmask, the Proprietor's voice sounded nothing like on the radio. Gunmen were climbing from the Iris. One had Zala in his arms, bound in restraints but still out cold.

"There you have it," Tumelo said. "I did what you wanted."

"With flying colours." The Proprietor gingerly brushed the hair from Zala's face. "All this trouble for such a frail little thing. Looks are so deceiving. Lester, get the serum. Harris put her metabolizing rate at six hours, but he's been wrong before. I don't want her waking up before we have her on the drip."

The Crow nodded and trudged towards the gunship.

"What will you do with her?" Tumelo asked.

"What does it matter to you?"

He's right. Why should I care? Tumelo tried to believe that, yet his heart still twisted. He glanced back at the Iris. Gunmen were rooting through her car by car. When he saw them in the locomotive's front windows, he felt a bead of sweat tickle down his forehead. "What are they doing?"

"It does not matter, Tumelo. Not anymore."

"I did my side of the bargain."

"Yes, you did."

The Proprietor made a subtle gesture with his left hand. Tumelo felt the blood drain from his face. He leapt for his backup pistol just as the gunshot cracked. A bullet screamed over his head. Another tore into his leg and he collapsed into the sand, gasping. The Proprietor sighed and plucked up the pistol.

"You shouldn't have done that. Now this will be more painful than it had to be."

"We had a deal!"

"Yes, we did. And I'm breaking it. You're an engineer, you must understand how hazardous loose ends can be."

Pain flashed through Tumelo's mind. He gagged out his words. "W-Why?!"

"Do you really want to know? Ah, I suppose you deserve to, after everything I've done to your family. You're a good man, Tumelo. You do not deserve this. Neither did your boy. Neither did your father. But we don't get what we deserve." The Proprietor knelt down, forearms resting on his knee, pistol dangling from his fingers by the trigger guard. "That girl is very important to me. I've been after her for a long time."

Oh God. It hit Tumelo like iced water. "You funded the Order. Their mission in Pretoria…"

"I didn't mean to get your son wrapped up in it. That was his own doing." When all Tumelo did was sputter, furious beyond words, the Proprietor sighed and began undoing the clasps of his gasmask. One of his guards stepped forward.

"M-Mister Ward?!"

Ward? Tumelo's mind spun.

"I'm already dying," the Proprietor said. "What's a few more years off my life? With Desolate blood it soon won't matter, and this poor man deserves my honesty." The mask fell, revealing the pale, wrinkled face of Overseer Henrik Ward. Tumelo felt as if his guts had been rearranged.

"Y-You bastard!"

"Not the right word, but close," Henrik said, face solemn. "Whether we like it or not, we are both creations of our ancestors. You inherited your father's business. I inherited Underhaven."

"You're both," Tumelo rasped, sick with betrayal. "Overseer… Proprietor…"

"Because it is necessary," Henrik said. "Corruption has destroyed most other surviving cities on this continent, but it is human nature. If I did not do it, someone who doesn't have Underhaven's best interests in mind would. The only way to control it is to play both sides, like Ouroboros eternally consuming itself. The Overseer gives. The Proprietor takes. Order wins."

"You liar! If people knew—"

"It is for their own good," Henrik said, eyebrows knitting together like an irritated schoolmaster. "I create the money people earn and make sure they are indebted to a proxy. A trick I learned from the Old World. It tames people. Keeps them from playing at revolutionary. And it has worked for a century so far, while most of our counterparts have collapsed. Which is preferable, Tumelo, order or extinction?"

Tumelo didn't give a damn. He struggled to rise, but two gunmen grabbed his arms and kept him on his knees. Henrik stood up and donned his mask. The Crow returned with a briefcase.

"Life is warfare and a journey far from home," Henrik said. "Your wife has cancer. As do I. A very aggressive kind."

"You deserve it," Tumelo hissed.

"Is it so surprising that I want to live forever? I have no heirs I can trust, and Underhaven must survive at whatever cost. I'll gladly turn her into a blood bag to make that happen." Henrik handed the pistol away and took the briefcase, which was filled with more vials of sedative. "As for you, I found out you were poking your nose into who funded the Pretoria crusade. You would have eventually found out and sought revenge. I cannot risk that. If that makes me like the men who oppressed your ancestors, so be it. Some people are fated to lose. I am sorry."

Henrik looked sorry, but it had to be another lie. Everything, from the way he opened the briefcase to how he moved calmly despite the rumble of an impending sandstorm, was a display of power, nothing more.

"This Desolate will get what she deserves, thanks to you," Henrik said, brandishing an injector. "She would have destroyed the city had we tried to capture her there. The official story will be that you bravely took her a safe distance from Underhaven and died incapacitating her. You will be a hero, and the Iris will live on to serve Underhaven's expansion and the redemption of our species."

Tumelo felt like a fool. All his life he'd worked under the very same man who had turned his father into a slave. Underhaven, everything, was a lie. Now he was going to die in the Desolation and Kagisa...*No, I'm not finished!* The wind picked up. Sand veiled everything but the immediate surroundings, blinding the sharpshooters on the wrecks. Henrik's two guards exchanged glances, and when Tumelo felt their grips on him weaken, he recalled Zala's words.

Do you believe in miracles, Mister Laska?

"Storm's coming in, Mister Ward," the Crow said. "The ships won't fly if we get caught."

THE CHILDREN OF DESOLATION

"In a minute." Henrik poised the injector over Zala's shoulder. "I've been waiting years for this."

You're right, Kagisa. I'm a sentimental fool. Tumelo surged to his feet and grabbed Henrik's arm, twisting the injector free. He stabbed at Henrik's neck, but the man deflected it with the briefcase and the swing drove into the Crow's throat instead. The man grunted and grabbed Tumelo in a death grip. They fell in a heap, and the sandstorm struck in earnest, blinding everyone else. Shouts rose. Gunshots barked. Tumelo found himself limping towards the Iris's shadow, hurting all over, his respirator mask missing. Henrik was shouting something over the gale. *Come and get me.* Wheezing, Tumelo climbed aboard with one hand and one and a half legs and rolled into the locomotive—right into someone's leg.

"What the hell?" a voice said.

Tumelo kicked the gunman's knee and jumped to his feet, only for his wounded leg to give out. He grabbed at a utility closet as he fell, but it flew open instead of holding, and he tasted the rust on the cold metal floor. Three gunmen glowered at him, the foremost rubbing his knee.

"Idiot," he hissed. "What the hell do you think you're doing?"

"Just shoot him," another said.

"Yeah, in the knee first."

A dark blur shot from the closet and latched onto the man's throat. The other two stumbled over each other and raised their guns. The dog leapt at them, taking bullets as he did, but his weight and momentum toppled both men, and he finished them with a savagery that turned Tumelo's bowels to water.

"J-Jasa?!"

The dog looked back, blood dripping from his mouth. His wounds knitted shut in seconds.

He's a Desolate, too. Tumelo stifled a laugh and forced himself to smile. "Go ahead. I earned it. Just..." *Be quick? Like he'd understand that request.*

Jasa barked, then looked towards the door. Tumelo understood at once.

"You want to save her."

Jasa wagged his tail.

"Truce? I have an idea. I just need a distraction."

The dog bounded out the door.

I guess that's a yes.

Shouts and gunfire erupted outside. Tumelo limped to the control room, realizing halfway that he'd lost too much blood. Luckily he wouldn't need much for this. He slumped into his seat and opened the throttle. The Iris surged through the sandstorm, all twelve cylinders roaring. Bullets hammered her from all sides. The front window shattered, spraying Tumelo with glass. He kept her going. Henrik's gunship was still on the tracks, its rotors powering up. He thumbed his heirloom one last time, wondering if his forefathers were watching.

You're right, Henrik. Some people are fated to lose.

The Iris slammed into the gunship, and everything went up in a daze of fire, rotor blades, and shrieking metal.

"You have a good heart," Kagisa said. "Don't forget it."

"Kagisa?" Tumelo tasted sand and blood. *Damn, a good dream, too.* All he heard was thunder and wind. He tried to sit up, but his old body refused. Poison air stabbed his lungs with every breath. The tracks were close, the burning gunship crumpled against the Iris. The impact must have ejected him from the window. *I guess a quick death was too much to hope for.*

Henrik limped from the wreckage, his coat in tatters and his mask gone, briefcase in one hand and pistol in the other. Blood matted his grey hair from a gash in his scalp. "What have you done?" he snarled. "Do you have any idea what you've done?!"

Tumelo coughed out a laugh. "Killed us both? May as well join me, the sand's warm."

Henrik started cussing, then broke into a coughing fit. Blood dripped from his chin. "You don't understand. Without me, Underhaven will fall apart."

"They should have the right to choose," Tumelo said.

"They had that right in the Old World, and they chose themselves into oblivion."

"You told me we don't get what we deserve. What's this, then?"

"You thick fool! Think about your wife!"

Tumelo closed his eyes, focusing on the warmth of the sand. "I'll see her soon."

"Enough!" Henrik cocked his pistol. "I'll just send you along now—"

Jasa rammed into Henrik from the side. They fell in a heap, but the man freed himself and slammed the briefcase across Jasa's nose. The dog yelped and tumbled across the sand with a scattering of injectors. "You mutt!"

"His name's Jasa," Zala said.

Henrik whirled. Zala stood in the blustering wind, her clouded eyes as bright as the fires behind her. Tumelo felt his throat constrict, and when Zala glanced at him, he found himself torn between tears and laughter. Henrik brandished an injector in a trembling hand.

"I don't keep anything on me you can detonate, kid."

"I'm not a kid," Zala said. "I'm a century older than you."

"You're a monster is what you are."

"Because I'm different?" Zala's voice sounded hollow.

"Because you're the spawn of that cataclysm!"

"Does that matter?" Zala's clouded eyes glanced Tumelo's way. "We're all the children of Desolation, one way or another."

Zala approached calmly, her pale hair and tattered cloak dancing in the wind. Henrik stabbed at her, but she sidestepped his swing, grabbed his arm, and twisted. Henrik gasped as the injector sank into his armpit, and before he could pull free, Zala pushed the plunger. He lurched, and with a sputter dropped into the sand. Zala muttered something and tossed the injector aside, and then Jasa was on her, licking her face and whimpering. She hugged him tight and giggled.

"It's okay now, Jasa. It's okay."

Tumelo tried to move, but his body felt leaden. He glanced at the unconscious Overseer. "I was hoping someone would shut him up. Didn't think it'd be you."

Zala leaned into Jasa, her face hidden against his fur. "Why didn't you let him take me?"

Tumelo blinked. "You knew?"

"I overheard, but I always suspected you were his creature."

"I'm not anyone's creature."

"No, you're not. You're a good person." Zala went to his side, hurt etched across her face. "I was awake when you injected me. Jasa did as I instructed him to."

Shame washed through Tumelo like a fever. He looked away, sand stinging his eyes. Yet Zala knelt and touched his hand.

"You hesitated," she said. "You spent this whole trip trying your best to hate me, but you're not that sort of man, are you?"

"Why?" Tumelo's chest burned. His lungs were dying. "Why did you let me?"

Zala tugged nervously at one of her pale curls. "Because I deserved it. When I met you, I thought you were like the others. I thought I'd have to kill you, too. But then you told me about Thabo…and I realized that running away might not be the answer."

"I…" Tumelo bit his lip. "Please, just let me die in peace."

"You don't have to die."

"I don't want your blood!"

"Are you that selfish?"

The word stabbed Tumelo in the gut. Selfish? He opened his mouth, but the words would not come out. God, she was right. How could he wish to die instead of getting back to Kagisa? How could he leave her alone? His eyes burned. How could he let hate do this to him, when he had done all of it in the name of love?

"Please," Zala said. "Let me do something good for once."

Tumelo bit his tongue and nodded. Zala's face lit up with a radiant smile. She bared her wrist and slashed it with a knife, letting the blood fall into the hole in his leg. His stomach lurched. At worst he'd die. At best…Tumelo blinked as tingles washed up his thigh.

"I'm sorry if it isn't very sanitary," Zala said.

"A little late for—" Pain walloped Tumelo's mind. His vision exploded with stars, and his head rang like a bell. Then, suddenly, he was sitting up, Zala supporting him. He sucked in a breath and realized she had helped him into his respirator. His wounds were gone.

"How do you feel?" Zala asked.

Like I'm twenty years younger. Tumelo managed a nod.

Zala grinned and stepped back—and then three gunshots cracked from somewhere in the haze, striking her in the chest. She staggered to the side, only to strengthen and whirl around to face the gunmen hidden in the storm. The haze blossomed with explosions and screams, and then Zala grabbed Henrik by the hair and yanked him up as a shield.

"Leave!" she shouted. "Or do you want to die for this man?"

Tumelo could not see anyone in the haze, but he knew by the silence that the remaining gunmen had chosen wisely.

The Iris was still in one piece, albeit scorched at the front. Zala made Jasa go inside and closed the door behind him before climbing back down the ladder. Tumelo watched her back, torn between warring thoughts. *She killed Thabo. She saved my life.* He looked down and saw his revolver in the drifting sand.

"Tumelo." Zala faced him, her clouded eyes locked on his. She looked exhausted. "Do you still want to kill me?"

"I..." Tumelo felt a weight in his hand and realized he'd picked up the gun automatically.

"It's okay," Zala said. "I won't stop you. I knew this moment would come."

Tumelo gripped the weapon, yet something burned in his chest, and it wasn't hate, or even fear. It got worse when Zala tapped herself on the forehead, right between her eyes.

"Put it right here and even I won't be able to heal before I die." Zala offered a sad smile. "I'm sorry to keep you waiting. I'll give it to you. My life for Thabo's."

Thabo. Oh Thabo. My dear son. His greatest pride. His deepest joy. Gone forever. His heart jammed into his throat. "For Thabo..." Tumelo held Zala's owlish gaze and pulled the trigger.

Zala spun around and fell on her side, blood spattering the Iris's hull. Tumelo took a deep breath and lowered the gun. "You're right. I'm not that sort of person."

Zala sat up, the hole in her right shoulder already knitting shut. A crumpled bullet fell out and disappeared into the shifting sands, joined by the wink of falling tears.

"Come on," Tumelo said, going for the ladder. "Don't make me wait."

"Why . . . ?" Zala looked up at him, tears spilling down her face. "Why?!"

Tumelo grabbed the ladder rungs. "Laska Locomotives has a reputation, and I'll be damned if I ruin it by murdering a customer." He paused. "Though I won't lie, that felt good."

Zala blinked and then burst into laughter. To Tumelo's surprise, he laughed, too.

Where the tracks ended a new world began, one where Desolates were the least of your worries. Tumelo stared at the churning wall of cloud and lightning and envisioned the hell that waited beyond. "You're certain about this?"

Zala stepped into the control room. "Oh? It almost sounds like you care."

Yeah, I'm confused, too. Tumelo took a deep breath and turned. Zala had changed into the clothes in her suitcase. Ragged leathers with innumerable pockets, a duster, goggles, even a tattered hat. It would have looked comical had he not known what she was. Jasa sat beside her, wagging his tail. Zala crossed her arms and scowled, and Tumelo knew why. He took out the photograph and wagged it with a floppy sound. "Looking for this?"

"So you did take it."

"For safe keeping. The Proprietor's men would have stolen it."

"Thank you, it . . . means a lot to me." Zala took a step forward, then hesitated. "Can you . . . describe it for me?"

"What?" Tumelo felt a pang in his chest. "You're really blind?"

Zala nodded, pale hair drifting over her face. "The Desolation took my sight in exchange for what I am. I've gotten used to it."

CYBERAEON

Blind for a century. Tumelo looked at the photo and told her as much as he could, from the church to the mountains to the smiling family in the foreground, and the inscription on the back: Bled, May 2027. Zala smiled as he did so, and when he finished, she accepted the photo and held it over her heart.

"I don't remember any of it," she said. "I've been wandering for a century just trying to figure out who I am, I feel empty. Only finding Jasa made it bearable." Her free hand clenched and tears welled in her eyes. "I'm tired of this. Of killing. The Desolation took everything from me but my name. I just want to find the place I came from. Where Zala was happy and innocent and free."

She was. She had a family that loved her and a world in bloom. Tumelo sighed. "You think you can find it?"

"It's all I have left."

Tumelo saw the desperate hope in Zala's eyes and realized they were alike. Both lost and brokenhearted and searching for hope. "It won't be like it was. It might not be there at all."

"It doesn't have to be," Zala said. "All that matters is that it was there, once. Like me."

"Then I'm sure you will find it." Tumelo clasped her shoulder. "My father said our hearts know things we can never explain. I think you will know when you get there."

Zala smiled anew and wiped her eyes, then tucked the photograph into her pocket. She handed him a packet. It was filled with vials of blood. Tumelo gaped.

"That's...?"

"For Kagisa," Zala said. "It will keep. My blood is different."

Tumelo stared at them. "Will it hurt her?"

"Did it hurt you?"

No. He'd never felt so alive.

"Isn't this what you wanted?" Zala asked, worry etching her face.

The miracle I've been praying for. Tumelo swallowed hard. "Yes..."

Zala touched his arm. "I know it's not enough."

"No, it is," Tumelo said. "More than I deserve. They say your kind are monsters, but you only want to live. Like Thabo wanted Kagisa to live. My ancestors were hunted by people who didn't understand, who refused to call them human...and I did the same with you."

"You have every right to hate me."

"No, I don't hate you." Tumelo took a deep breath, amazed at his own words. "You know what I see in you? Myself. When I was young, everything I wanted was somewhere else. You may have wandered for a hundred years, but part of you is still that child looking for home. How can I hate that?"

Zala's eyes widened, then she turned away, blinking rapidly. "That's the most mature thing you've said this whole trip," she whispered. "Thank you."

For the first time since Thabo died, Tumelo felt the heaviness lift from his heart.

It was time to let go. To break the cycle. It was time to live on.

Zala had all her things gathered. They made their way to the back of the locomotive. A few field repairs had been made, replacing windows and sealing bullet holes. Henrik lay trussed up in a corner still out cold, but healed by Zala's blood—a request from Tumelo.

"What will you do with him?" Zala asked.

Tumelo studied Henrik. Not a god. Not a devil. Just a man, like him. A man who had followed in his father's footsteps. "The people deserve to know. They deserve the truth."

Zala nodded, as if that were the answer she'd been hoping for. She rolled her shoulders and nudged her suitcase towards him. "Then this is where we part ways, Tumelo Laska. Your payment."

"You still want me to believe you earned all that?"

"I found it sitting out in the open, practically begging to be taken. How does that sound?"

"Like a load of crap."

"You're right." Zala laughed, then grabbed the door handle to the exit, scratching Jasa's ear with her other hand. "But you earned it. Be well, Tumelo, and tell Kagisa...that I'm sorry."

"I will," Tumelo said. "And...I hope you find it."

427

Zala smiled. "Me too."

From the Iris's control room, Tumelo saw Zala and Jasa walking side by side towards the Burn Line, untouched by the heat and wind and radiation. Flashes of lightning cast their shadows, so small against the Desolation's wrath. Yet Zala's stride was as determined as someone who saw exactly what lay ahead, and as he watched her press into oblivion, Tumelo hoped, one day, that he'd see her step out of it again. He blared the train's horn three times and lifted his hand. Zala turned and waved with a radiant smile. Then she patted Jasa's head, faced the Desolation, and vanished into its crimson flow.

Tumelo watched as sand filled in their footprints, until it looked as if they'd never been there at all. "A long journey," he whispered. "For both of us."

He looked at the empty seat beside him, then ran his hand along the battle-scarred surface of the Iris's dashboard. He smiled.

"Let's go home."

Timelines and Bloodlines

written by

L. H. Davis

illustrated by

CLARENCE BATEMAN

ABOUT THE AUTHOR

L. H. Davis (a.k.a. Laurance Howard Davis III or Larry) lives on Florida's Space Coast. Born and raised on the coast of South Carolina, he earned a degree in mechanical engineering from USC. He then moved to Florida to work in robotics. After writing dozens of technical proposals for nonexistent, advanced technologies, he decided to give science fiction a try. Discovering that it too was a form of designing, he retired from engineering to write full time.

"Timelines and Bloodlines" is an adventure set in both the future and the past. Would a knight on horseback stand a chance against a modern soldier? Would that soldier be wrong to even defend herself? Could she if she tried? Larry commented, "I'm a plotter. I like to know where a story is going, how it will end, but Angela (female lead) took the reins on this one. The closer I got to the end, the harder she pulled the story her way. She did good."

Larry is a member of the Florida Writers Association, "Writers Helping Writers." After winning their Royal Palms Literary Awards several times in multiple categories, they asked him to become an RPLA judge. He enjoys providing constructive feedback, and also hosts a weekly online critique group. Larry has self-published four novels as well as a novella. He writes in multiple genres: sci-fi, fantasy, historical, and YA paranormal.

Larry entered the Writers of the Future Contest twenty-five times before winning. His motto—"Never give up."

ABOUT THE ILLUSTRATOR

Clarence Bateman was born on the little Caribbean island of Jamaica and currently resides in New York. His passion for art was inspired by comic books from an early age. He fantasized about one day being a comic book artist for Marvel as Spiderman was his favorite superhero at the time. In his early teenage years, he would hustle family members by doing Christmas cards and lightly twisting their arms to buy them. He would do art for his friends in school and they would pay him with comic books. He dropped out of high school to enroll in the Edna Manley College of the Visual and Performing Arts in Kingston, Jamaica attending for three years before immigrating to the US.

After a series of dead-end jobs, he decided to go back to school for art enrolling in the New York City Technical College part time while holding down a full-time job in the garment district as a pattern maker. He did a three-year advertising program with the intention of becoming an art director and instead ended up working in the advertising field for the next thirty plus years as a freelance preproduction sketch artist. Sketch art at the time was done primarily with magic markers, color pencils, and inks. When work started transitioning to the computer, he taught himself how to use Adobe Photoshop and Illustrator.

Clarence's primary focus is science fiction and fantasy art, encompassing such a wide range of subject matters he considers it practically impossible to have artist's block. He spends his late nights honing his skills, constantly learning, and working to become a better artist.

Timelines and Bloodlines

"We're over the drop zone."

I flinch beneath the straps of my safety harness. I'd muted my earbuds to silence the roar of the Vertical Take-Off and Landing, or VTOL's rotors, but the mute function is selective and doesn't block the pilot or crew. "Mute off," I say. Groggy from sleep, I wipe drool from my chin.

Across the deployment bay, Angela Smith grins. "Welcome back, Sarge."

I smile and shrug.

"You know the drill," Captain Muller says. "Leave nothing in the past. Do not open your chutes above fifteen hundred meters. Should your chute open before we begin regression, it will *not* come with you into the past. Use your reserve." He pats the small pack on his stomach. "If either chute deploys while you're still inside the regression bubble, do nothing. The chute should open on its own when the bubble dissipates. If I spot anyone on the ground, I'll pick a new landing site and expect you to follow. Questions?"

The only safe way to travel through time is to regress in midair. Standing on the ground is possible but risky when regressing long spans of time. After a thousand years, the surface of the ground is not at the same elevation. If it was lower back in the day, you'll rematerialize above the ground and drop. If it was higher back then, all or part of you will rematerialize below the surface, which will merge with your flesh. Once on a training run, we'd jumped back fifty years standing on an open runway. Since we knew the history of the runway, there was no risk of rematerializing inside something solid, but what we didn't consider was how much the concrete had worn away over the years. It hadn't worn down much, just enough to fuse the soles of our boots to the deck.

Captain Muller selected the Alnwick jump site because of an old stone bridge. The Romans built it long before the Battle of Alnwick, and it still exists in our timeline. It would have settled over the years, so the structure would have been taller in 1093. We plan to return to the present from the bridge, anticipating a drop of a few inches.

"Three thousand meters and holding," the pilot says. "Ground speed: zero. Wind: zero degrees, three knots."

"Roger that," Muller says. "Simultaneous deploy: two minutes." Muller glances at his wristwatch and then at me. "Jackson, if we get separated, I expect you to stay with Smith. Follow her lead. Franklin, stick with me. OK, power up all modules."

The deployment bay can release a twenty-person jump team one at a time or all at once. They offset the seats on opposing walls by one meter, allowing the deployment arms to intermesh prior to release. Since there are only four of us, we spread out, two on each wall, leaving empty seats between us.

"Status?" Muller asks.

"Jackson green," I say.

Smith and Franklin report the same.

"Captain," I say, "if someone spots us in the air, should we roar like dragons?"

"McCartney," Angela grumbles, guessing who'd told me her little secret. McCartney, Angela's friend, let it slip over beers that Angela has a tattoo of a dragon on her chest. I don't care if she has a tattoo or not, although I do hope to get a private viewing.

Meeting Angela's eyes, I chuckle. "Who? I'm talking about all the dragons in those books you showed us on the Middle Ages. There must have been flocks of dragons flying around England back then. We might just blend right in."

Angela is a pretty little thing with blond hair, blue eyes, full lips, a trim figure, and an IQ off the chart. She's a lieutenant in the British army, a historian who specializes in medieval warfare. I wasn't sure how Angela would react when I asked her out to dinner, but she accepted and seemed to have fun. If the mission goes as planned, I intend to ask her out again.

"Sergeant," Captain Muller says, "if you see a dragon, feel free to roar. Otherwise keep your mouth shut." He gazes at his watch. "Staging. We drop in ten...nine..."

I double-check the straps of my sniper rifle as the deployment bay doors beneath our feet swing open. My weapon, a lightweight FANG LG sniper rifle, fires high explosive, 16 mm, laser-guided shells. Since we won't be able to recover the slug, they made custom shells out of compressed metallic powder, so that the only thing we'll leave in the past is forty-five grams of tungsten carbide dust. They designed the shells to explode fifteen milliseconds after impact. It will pass through the victim in half that time, so the body will remain intact.

The deployment arm, attached to my chute harness between my shoulder blades, lifts to assume my weight as my seat folds down and back. Timing is such that we hang over the open hatch mere seconds before the drop.

"Two...one."

I flinch. "Dammit." *Every damn time!* We stay close for a few seconds and then drift apart, facing each other. Muller gives a thumbs-up once we achieve adequate separation. He's tethered the remote actuator of his Time Regression Module, or TRM, to his wrist and grips the device in his hand. The master unit is in a belly pack beneath his reserve chute. Muller thumbs open the actuator cover, presses the button, and a translucent-blue regression bubble forms around each of us. We carry our own TRMs in belly packs, but the captain's unit can trigger all of them.

The bubbles pass through our bodies, sanitizing us as they expand from the modules. Nothing alive, not even bacteria, travels with us into the past. The bubble's impenetrable force field shields us from raindrops, birds, and any bugs we might

433

encounter during the transition. It also pulls a partial vacuum that keeps us from developing air bubbles in our blood and guts when we rematerialize in the past. The entire process takes fewer than three seconds, so running out of air is not an issue. As my bubble fades, I glance at my altimeter, which indicates we're still above twenty-five hundred meters. The terrain below has more trees, but that's the only obvious difference. The old bridge looks worn but generally the same, although a rutted dirt road now wanders away from each end. In our timeline, the bridge sits unused in a remote meadow. I use my arms as airfoils to turn and scan the horizon. The sky glows pale blue in the east, although the sun has yet to rise. Smoke, not dense but widespread, hangs in the still air several miles south of us. The road from the bridge meanders toward the battle, which seems to be well underway.

Our mission is to assassinate an obscure earl named Robert Crompton. He died young in 1099 during the First Crusade, but we came back in time to make certain he never reaches the Holy Land. Crompton originally died a few hundred miles short of his goal, which had been Jerusalem, but he fathered a child along the way. It's his only known descendant, but after a thousand years, Crompton's bloodline is threatening London with total annihilation.

Intelligence sources have confirmed that a terrorist group has smuggled a nuclear bomb into London. The leader of the group, a man we call T. Rex, likes to flaunt that his ancestor was an English knight who "came to rape the Holy Land." We can find no record of T. Rex or his family, no lineage. What gave him away was when Angela recognized the insignia the terrorist group selected to represent them, a rearing stag with flaming antlers. She remembered having seen it in her studies and identified it as Lord Crompton's device. They collected T. Rex's DNA from a blood sample after a failed assassination attempt and found Crompton's DNA in a tooth taken from his family crypt. After DNA tests confirmed the men's common lineage, only one question remained. How many others will cease to exist if Crompton dies *before* he leaves for the Crusades?

CLARENCE BATEMAN

No one knows, although everyone agrees it will be hundreds if not thousands. Yet, if we do nothing, millions will die in London if they can't locate the bomb in time. They also don't know if they have weeks, days, or hours to find it. What they do know is that if Crompton dies before leaving England, T. Rex will cease to exist and the bomb will not be in London.

To assassinate someone a thousand years in the past, we first needed to find him. It's impossible to locate most people, but Crompton led an army of English knights against the Scottish in the Battle of Alnwick on November 13, 1093. After discovering who to eliminate and where to find him, the British government asked the United States for help. While our time-travel technology is still experimental and classified top secret, a select few in the British government are aware of the project. We've made several training runs, but assassinating Crompton is our first true mission. We flew out of London, but a backup team in Liverpool will come after us if we don't reappear on the bridge at 0600 hours. Walking to the battlefield and back will take several hours, and it's close to 0600 when we land, but we'll regain those hours when we regress to the present. No matter how long we're in the past, we'll reappear on the bridge at 0600, or never.

"I didn't see a single dragon," I say, placing Angela's chute beneath the bridge next to the others. We hold on to our TRMs, spare ammo, and rifles, but stash everything else under the bridge. While the 16 mm FANG LG is my weapon of choice, the others carry 5.56 mm automatic carbines, and we all carry 9 mm sidearms. Our jump helmets will only draw attention, so we leave those behind as well. I hang back with Angela as Captain Muller and Master Sergeant Franklin lead the way. They're more experienced—and expendable. Angela and I have orders to stay a half kilometer behind them whenever possible, although always within sight. Our earbuds keep us in constant communication.

We walk for two hours before Muller calls for a five-minute break. After entering a thick forest of massive oaks, we had to reduce the gap between the two teams to maintain visual contact. Muller and Franklin crouch in the shade beside the road, maybe three hundred meters ahead.

"I need to make water," Angela says, stepping behind a tree. "Comm off."

When I hear her unzip, I realize her jumpsuit will be down around her ankles. "Comm off," I say, shutting mine down as well. "If you see any dragons back there, sing out. I got my heart set on seeing one."

"Funny man. Be careful what you ask for. Some dragons are rather ugly."

"Maybe, but I'd still want to see it. Do you really have one tattooed on your chest?"

"I do."

"Well? Are you shy?"

"I didn't get a full-torso tat because I'm shy."

"Seriously? It's that big?"

"If you want to see it, I don't mind."

"I don't mean to harass—" And that's when she steps out from behind the tree, jumpsuit around her ankles. Other than her dog tags, she's nude. "Damn, woman."

She'd had the dragon's chest and belly tattooed over *her* chest and belly. Her nipples, spaced wider than the width of the dragon's body, stand proud beneath its open wings, which wrap around onto her back just under her armpits. The dragon's tail covers her bare crotch, disappearing between her legs only to reappear as it wraps twice around her left thigh. Its scaly, muscular rear legs curl over her hips onto her rump. The neck of the dragon rolls over her right shoulder and reappears on her left shoulder, its head drooping over its left wing onto her breast. She'd had the head positioned so that her left nipple forms the dragon's emerald eye. The shape and intricate details of the head trick my eyes, so only after glancing at her right nipple, which is bare and natural, do I realize there isn't a noticeable rise to either of Angela's breasts.

"It's beautiful," I say, twirling my finger. She turns, showing me her back and cute little butt, which the dragon appears to be gripping with its hind claws. The artist flared the dragon's wings as if in flight, the tips not quite touching Angela's spine. While the wings are symmetrical, they aren't identical. The dragon's right hand, inked beneath the wing, is flipping me the bird. I laugh. "I love it."

She pulls her jumpsuit up over her hips and turns to face me. "It doesn't bother you?"

I know she's not talking about the work of art. "You're beautiful."

"You're not a breast man?"

"I like them as much as the next guy, but variety's a wonderful thing too."

"Not everyone agrees with you," Angela says, slipping into her sleeves.

"It sounds like you've had an unpleasant experience."

Angela sighs. "It was years ago. I had my breasts removed when I turned twenty-one, and the bloke I'd been dating since upper school ditched me. I guess I'm still a mite angry."

"So you weren't...born that way?"

"Flat as a plank? No. My mother died of breast cancer and everything indicated I'd end up with it too. I simply chose not to worry about that for the rest of my life....Kept my nipples, though."

I grin and tap the corner of my eye. "I noticed."

Angela smiles. "Do you like that little touch?"

"Oh yeah."

She chuckles and rubs the dragon's eye through the material of her jumpsuit. "Talk about painful. Bloody hell. I groaned so much the guy needling me had to wear earbuds."

"Oh crap. Comm on," I say. We've been out of communication much too long.

"Comm on," Angela says.

"Where the hell have you guys been?" Muller asks.

"Sorry, sir," I reply. "We both needed to take a squat and figured you guys would rather not hear us singing *that* song."

"You got that right," Franklin says.

"Dammit, Jackson," Muller says. "Kick sand over it but leave nothing *else* behind. Double-check the area and then move out. We'll wait here for you. Keep your eyes open. We're hearing things. The fighting is close."

After catching up, we walk another ten minutes down the road before spotting a group of wounded soldiers coming our way, Scots by the look of them. We take to the forest and move toward the sounds of battle—shouting men, screaming horses, steel hammering steel.

The forest grows hazy with acrid smoke so dense we can't see twenty meters ahead of us. We step out of the forest into a smoky field, littered with the husks of last fall's corn harvest. Unable to see the far side, we can't be certain it's the battlefield, although the fighting sounds quite close.

"Spread out," Muller says, "but stay within sight. Let's move upwind."

Before we can even take a step, a horse and rider materialize in the smoke. It's a battle-weary knight wearing a suit of scale armor, small panels of steel laced to a tunic of chain mail. The interlocking steel rings of his black mail glisten as if coated with oil. He's wearing a bullet-shaped nasal helm and carries a painted wooden shield, rounded at the top and pointed at the bottom. The shield has served him well. Its top left-hand corner is missing and crossing blows from a sword have gouged an X in the white paint. The insignia on his shield is a rearing stag. We all freeze, hoping the smoke will provide enough cover.

"What do we do?" Franklin murmurs.

"It's not Crompton," Angela says. "No flaming antlers."

The knight spots us and spurs his horse forward, swinging the spiked-iron ball of a military flail on a meter of chain above his head. The enormous sword at his side rattles as it bounces off the horse's chain mail covering its hindquarters. The white horse wears a full set of armor: a chanfron over its face, a criniere around its neck, and a peytral on its chest.

"Scatter," Muller yells.

We run in separate directions. In the smoke, it's unlikely the knight realizes Angela is a woman. He rides her down first. The horse's breastplate slams into her back and knocks her aside instead of down under its hooves. She falls face-first, flips head over heels, and ends up on her back. Wide-eyed, she stares between her boots at the knight as he turns to gallop back, flail in hand. After reaching a thin scattering of brush, I turn back as the knight again spurs his horse toward Angela. I raise my rifle, but Angela fires her carbine, peppering the knight's chest with multiple rounds. The horse shies right as the knight falls left, landing on his back with a thud.

"Are you all right?" I ask, running up to Angela.

"I think so."

I pull Angela to her feet and then toward the trees, but she twists free and turns back. "What are you doing?" I ask.

"I need to see him."

"Why?"

"I'm a historian."

The knight stares up at us, blood streaming from his nose and mouth. He's barely alive. "I'm so sorry," Angela says as the knight's eyes glaze over. And then his body winks out of existence. "Bloody hell?"

"Damn," I say. "That ain't right."

"Jackson. Smith," Franklin says, jogging our way. "What happened?"

Behind Franklin, the same knight materializes in the smoke, flail swinging.

"Behind you," Angela screams.

Franklin turns, catching the iron ball of the flail in the face. His head explodes. Without slowing, the knight charges us.

Angela turns and runs. "That's the same knight I just killed."

"If so, you did a piss-poor job of it," I say, shouldering the FANG LG. He's too close for the scope, so I just sight along the barrel and squeeze the trigger. The massive slug strikes him square in the chest, arresting his forward motion. As designed, the shell explodes two meters behind him. The horse shies from the report as the knight slams into the ground.

"He won't stay dead long," Angela says.

"Then we'll shoot him again—" I stop as Angela's rifle rattles to the ground beside me. I turn. "Angela?" All of her clothes and gear, including the TRM, lie in a heap on the ground. Her dog tags sit atop the pile. I stoop and recover them. "Dammit."

"What happened?" Muller asks, walking up.

"That knight killed Franklin," I say, pointing out both bodies. "And then he came after me and Smith, so I shot him."

"Wonderful." Muller sighs. "You probably just erased several thousand people back in our timeline."

I stare down at the pile of clothing and gear.

"Crap," Muller says. "Was that Smith?"

"What's left of her." I hold out her dog tags.

"Dammit."

"Captain, what will happen to us if we kill an ancestor of the scientist who came up with this time-travel technology? Will we disappear like Smith?"

"No. Smith was simply…*unborn* in the present. She *was* here, which is how her gear got here. She must have been in that knight's bloodline."

"It's weird. I could kill him, but Smith couldn't. She'd already shot the dude once."

"You saw him go down?"

"We watched the man die, but then he vanished and came back after us. Franklin just got in the way."

"Smith *couldn't* kill him and still exist to pull the trigger," Muller says. "The two are mutually exclusive, so time reset."

"That's some whacked up stuff. So now what?"

"So now we bring Smith and Franklin back."

"How do we do that?"

"We go back in time," Muller says, staring at his wristwatch. "Nine minutes should do it. Power up Smith's TRM. I'll get Franklin's. And pick up Smith's spent shell casings, just in case. Check the ground where that knight fell. Hopefully, Smith's a decent shot, and you find all her slugs. If not, they'll disappear when we regress."

441

After pocketing the spent brass and all but one slug, I open Angela's pack and activate the TRM. "All green." I flip mine on as well.

"Franklin's too," Muller says.

"How are we supposed to—" I stop as the bubble forms around me. When it dissipates, I'm standing in the brush where I'd been earlier when Angela first shot the knight. Gunfire draws my attention.

Angela is again on her back in the field, having just shot the knight. I run out and pull her to her feet. She gazes at the knight and takes a step in his direction. "Forget him." I pull her back. "We need to find Franklin."

"Franklin's dead," Angela says. "And didn't I just shoot that—Bloody hell!"

I glance back. The knight has once again disappeared. "He's one of your ancestors. But don't worry, he'll be right back. Hide."

"Where are you going?"

"Hide, dammit!" I sprint toward the spot where Franklin died earlier.

"Jackson," Franklin says, appearing in the smoke. "Where'd you go?"

The knight looms above us. The spiked ball of the flail hisses past our heads as I tackle Franklin.

"Over here," Muller yells, having taken cover behind a tree on the edge of the forest. "Smith, shoot him again."

The knight rounds his horse and comes after us. We run for the trees, but he's too fast. A shot rings out. When we hear the knight thud to the ground, Franklin and I stop and look back. The knight groans and pushes up into a sitting position, wincing as he settles on his left butt cheek. He lost his helmet in the fall and appears to be in his mid-forties. The man pulls off his right glove and holds it up. "I yield. Mercy." And then he vanishes.

"What's with that guy?" Angela says, jogging up. When she sees Franklin, her jaw drops. "I thought you were dead."

"Me?"

"Fallback into the trees," Muller says. "Now!"

We spread out, each behind a different tree trunk. After a few minutes, the knight, tired and battered, again rides into the field. He circles his horse, scanning the area. Satisfied he's alone, he drapes the flail over the saddle and unties a flap at his crotch. After relieving himself, the knight secures the flap, grips his flail, and spurs his horse back the way he'd come.

"Talk about bad luck," I say. "That dude died four times just trying to take a leak."

"Just three," Angela says. "I shot him twice, and you shot him once."

"You shot him three times," I say, "but after I shot him you disappeared." I search my pocket for the spent shell casings and slugs but find nothing. We've regressed, so I've yet to shoot anyone.

"I disappeared?" Angela asks.

"We came back for you and Franklin. So maybe you did only shoot that knight twice. I saw it three times, but I guess two were the same event. That hurts my head."

"Wait," Franklin says, "you came back for me? Did I disappear too?"

"No. You don't remember what happened?"

"I remember Smith yelling 'behind you' and when I looked back, you tackled me... from twenty meters away. How'd you do that?"

"You're remembering two separate outcomes of the same event, although you're not remembering everything."

"Do I *want* to remember everything?"

"Not if you want to sleep at night," Muller says.

"I only killed that knight once," Angela says. "My last shot just hit him in the bum."

"He must have died later from infection," Muller says. "Or maybe a Scottish soldier found him out here wounded and killed him. Either way, he died because of you, so time reset. You can't kill your ancestor and still exist to do it."

Angela pulls a spent shell casing from her pocket. She holds it up. "He might have reset, but we didn't."

"We should never reset," Muller says. "Check the ground where he fell and recover the slug."

"Sir," I say, "you never did answer my question."

"Which one was that?"

"What will happen to us if we do something to prevent the development of time travel?"

"We can't change anything that would keep us from being here," Muller says. "The two are mutually exclusive. Time would reset."

Franklin shakes his head. "Why wouldn't we just pop back into our own timeline?"

"Because coming here to the past *is part* of our personal timelines. If we do something in the past that changes the present to the point we couldn't be here, whatever past we're in resets to a point before we altered it. But our personal timelines always move forward, even when we regress."

"Always?" I ask.

"Always," Muller says. "That's why you remember seeing Angela kill that knight three times. Two of them were the same event, but, in your timeline, you experienced all three of them independently. TRMs would be useless if our personal timelines reset. If they did, when we got back from a mission, we wouldn't remember going."

"So when we regress back to the future, our personal timelines pick up where they left off, plus we have a little of the past spliced into it."

"Sort of, except what you call the future is simply the present."

"You ain't helping," I say.

"We never go forward in time," Muller says. "We can't. TRMs don't work that way. *Time* doesn't work that way. The future doesn't exist until after it happens, and then it becomes the past. When we return to the present, you might feel as if you're going into the future, but you're simply rejoining your past."

I shake my head. "It sounds to me like *everything* is in the past."

"Now you're getting it," Muller says. "All right, let's get this done, but don't kill anyone except Crompton."

"I found it," Angela says, holding up the slug she'd put in the knight's hip.

"Good," Muller says. "Let's move upwind of this smoke, so we can see what's going on."

The field of battle lies beyond a stand of trees on the far side of the smoky cornfield. The pine forest is only five hundred meters deep, even less where it encircles a towering outcrop of rock. We follow a well-worn path to the top and find the air free of smoke. Years earlier, someone built a fire pit on the plateau at the top. People have used the campsite often, at least once since the last rain.

"This is a shepherd's watch," Angela says, gazing out over the field of battle.

The green meadow rolls to the horizon, both north and south, and appears to be four kilometers wide. A shallow stream meanders east to west, skirting the base of the mound on which we stand. The English army is encamped south of the stream. Half a hundred tents, untouched by the battle, stand in the meadow, banners fluttering in the light breeze. To the north of the stream, the fighting has blackened several acres of the green turf. Dead and dying knights, foot soldiers, and horses still lie where they've fallen in battle. What remains of the Scottish forces are retreating to the north. The English have taken the field. Squires roam the carnage, slitting the throats of wounded horses and Scotsmen alike. Sporadic cries of mercy and screams of agony punctuate the colorful but grizzly scene.

"There's your knight," I say, pointing out the man Angela shot.

"And Crompton." She offers me her binoculars.

Several dozen English knights sit astride their horses at the edge of the stream. Lord Crompton with his flaming-stag shield and Angela's knight are among them. Their horses drink and graze as the men talk, no doubt telling tales of their conquests as well as mourning their fallen comrades. Crompton and the old knight face each other, their horses side by side but heads to tails. Crompton wears a polished, gilded helmet adorned with a gleaming, silvery spike. His face shield, split up the middle and hinged on both sides, stands open, revealing the younger knight's face. He appears to be no older than thirty.

"You're up, Jackson," Captain Muller says. "Take the shot so we can go home."

I slip the FANG LG from my shoulder, flip out the front bipod, and open the scope covers. After placing the rifle on the crest of a large boulder, I lie on my belly and nudge the rifle forward until I find Crompton in the scope. The integral range finder flashes 523 meters, so I adjust the scope to allow for the drop of the slug, add a click to the south to account for the light breeze, and switch on the targeting laser. Since I'm using a guided shell, adjusting the scope isn't necessary for the range and conditions. However, if the guidance system fails, a well-placed dumb slug will still get the job done.

"This is almost too easy, sir." I focus on the fact the man I'm shooting has been dead for over a thousand years. *But how many of his descendants will disappear today? I guess we'll never know. You can't count what never existed.* "Mute on," I say, placing my earbuds in noise-cancellation mode. I wait a moment for the others to mute their buds and then squeeze the trigger. In less than a second, the shell finds its mark, severing Crompton's left arm before passing through his chest and heart. The horse Angela's knight is riding has terrible timing. Having raised its head as I pulled the trigger, it caught the shell in the right temple—fifteen milliseconds after it struck the knight. Pulverized brain, skull, and gore fill the air. Both knights fall, landing in a heap atop the headless horse. No one on the field even looks our way.

"Mute off." And the sounds of the world return. "Nice shot," Muller says. "But what . . . got something against horses?"

"Sorry about that," I say, securing the scope.

"What the *hell*?" Franklin says.

"I didn't mean to hit it." I turn to glare at Franklin and realize he isn't talking to me. He's staring at a pile of clothing, Angela's.

I shake my head. "Dammit, she's gone again."

"Wait a minute," Captain Muller says. He gazes through his binoculars at the knights on the field. "The banners in that cluster of tents are all either rearing stags or the same rearing stag with flaming antlers. It's effectively the same house, likely father and son. That older knight must be Crompton's father."

"Back us up," I say. "We need to go back for Angela."

"It won't matter," Muller says. "Angela's in their bloodline. Our orders are to kill Crompton, so she's gone no matter what."

"No. We can't just leave her dead."

"She's not dead," Muller says. "She never existed."

"No way. Those are her clothes. She was here. Let's go back. We can figure out another way to get Crompton, like maybe later in his timeline. Angela can do the research and figure out when and where her bloodline began. It has to be sometime between 1093 and when Crompton leaves England in 1098, right? Hell, it could be tonight at the after-battle party. Give her a couple of days to figure it out. You owe her that much."

"Captain," Franklin says, "if she can't figure it out, we can always come back and shoot him again."

"And I won't hit the horse next time. Come on, Captain."

"All right." Muller glances at his watch. "We'll regress fifty-five minutes. Crompton Senior should still be taking a leak. We'll walk back to the bridge from there."

"Why not take us back to daybreak," I say, "and save us the walk?"

Franklin laughs.

Muller shakes his head. "Why are you still just a sergeant?"

"Because I'm good at it, sir."

The captain nods. "All right. We left the transport at 0545 this morning. Allowing fifteen minutes for the landing should be plenty, so we'll regress back to 0600. That should put us near the bridge. Power up Smith's TRM."

"We're good to go," I say, exhaling as Muller presses the remote. When the blue bubble fades, Angela is standing beside me near the bridge, while Muller and Franklin reappear half a kilometer down the road. They turn and stare back at us.

Angela grabs my arm for support, disoriented by the sudden change in location. "Bloody hell. What just happened?"

447

"When I shot Crompton, you disappeared again. It looks like the guy *you* shot is Crompton's father. Me and Franklin talked Muller into delaying the mission a day or so to give you time to figure something out."

"Me?"

"We're gonna kill Crompton, one way or the other, so you need to figure out when he got your tenth great-grandmother pregnant, or whoever she was. If we kill him *after* that point, you should still exist. I'm willing to bet you're English through and through, so he probably gets some lady around here pregnant before he leaves for the Crusades in ten ninety-eight. Do you think you can figure it out?"

"Probably, I'll need a DNA map, but something doesn't make sense. When *I* kill Crompton Senior, time resets, so *he* has to be my direct ancestor, although it can't be through Crompton Junior because he's already born....Unless— The father must do something in the near future, their future, to initiate my bloodline through Junior."

"Like what, buy him a hooker?"

"Maybe."

"Maybe the father died from the fall when I killed his horse. Hell, maybe it does happen tonight at the after-battle party, which they wouldn't have if *either* Crompton were dead."

"Maybe *what* happens at the party?"

"Well, victorious soldiers do have a tendency to get drunk and make babies, or at least *try* to make babies, especially when they're away from—" The familiar sound of parachutes opening draws our eyes skyward. A team of four soldiers circles overhead. "Who's that?"

"Bravo Team." I shake my head. "This ain't good."

Muller and Franklin walk up as our backup team lands in the pasture.

"I don't like the looks of this," Muller says.

"Should we regress home?" Franklin asks.

"We need to hear them out. They're here for a reason."

Five minutes later Bravo Team joins us on the bridge.

"Major Wilson," Muller says.

"Captain Muller, we've come to make certain you complete your mission *today*."

"We need a few more days of research," Muller says. "It turns out that Lieutenant Smith is a descendant of Lord Crompton. Later today, we kill him and his father in separate events, and each time Smith ceases to exist. We'll come back to this timeline in a few days to a point after Crompton establishes her lineage...plants her seed, so to speak."

Major Wilson nods. "We know what happened here today and your plan, but it's no good."

"Sure it is," Angela says. "I just need a few more days of research. I'll need a DNA map—"

"You only have six hours," Wilson says, "and you *don't* find what you need. London goes up in a nuclear fireball at noon today, which is why we're here. You must finish the job *now*."

"No," Angela hisses.

"I'm sorry, ma'am," Wilson says. "Captain, those are your orders...from the president of the United States."

I slide the FANG LG off my shoulder and hold it out to Wilson. "I ain't killing her, sir. If you want her dead, you take the shot."

"Bravo Team can't," Wilson says. "In our timeline the damage is done, we can't change it. We wouldn't be here if the nuke hadn't gone off, so if one of us shoots Crompton, our timeline will reset. Us being here and the nuke *not* going off are mutually exclusive. *You* have to do it in *your* timeline."

"Bloody hell," Angela yells. "You're saying I have to die today, to save London? We still have six hours. Captain Muller, we should stick to our plan."

"You had six hours last time," Wilson says, "but they still nuked London. If it helps, the blast kills all four of you."

I shake my head. "How the hell could that possibly help?"

Wilson glares at me but says nothing. He turns to Angela. "Sorry, ma'am. You die either way, but if you die here you'll save millions of lives."

"You don't know that for a fact," she says.

449

"What I know for a fact is that if you go back to your timeline without killing Crompton, all four of you die in London at noon today along with ten million others. Your plan sounded reasonable until the nuke went off. I figured it was over, a done deal, but somebody back home realized we had one more shot at it, *if* we could intercept you in this timeline. Captain, you need to retake that kill shot and let it stand at all costs. We're coming along as observers."

"Smith, I'm sorry," Muller says, "but I don't know what else to do." Her eyes brim with tears, yet she nods understanding.

When I place my hand on her shoulder, she turns and buries her face in my chest. I take her in my arms and catch Muller's eye. "Give us a few minutes."

He nods. "You got it. Bravo Team is escorting us, so we can't regress back to the cornfield. We'll have to hoof it again. This time we'll hold up in the forest until Crompton Senior clears the area."

I go with them but have no intention of pulling the trigger. The best I can do for Angela is to find a peaceful place and distract her—until she vanishes. Angela tries to get a handle on the inevitable as we walk. She cries some, curses a little, but then she pulls herself together. After accepting the fact she'll never go home, she asks if I'll take care of a few things for her. When I agree, she writes out a list of people to notify of her death. I can't bring myself to remind her that none of them will know who she was. I have to wonder if *I* will. I think I'll at least remember her as being part of the team on the mission, although maybe not our dinner date or anything before we regressed back to 1093.

I tuck the note in my pocket and change the subject. "What do you do for fun?"

As it turns out, Angela plays around with white magic and has a group of friends she calls her "Coven of Wiccans." She says it isn't anything serious, just something fun to do on the weekend. They party and hold ceremonies where they try different incantations and potions. They liked her dragon tattoo so much they made her their High Priestess.

"If you can work magic," I say, "now's the time to do it."

We sit behind a large pine tree on the edge of the cornfield. The old knight shows up on schedule and drains his bladder without dying this time. After he rides off, the others prepare to move out.

"I can't do it, Captain," I say. "Sorry, but I sprained my trigger finger. Scope's already set, so all you need to do is put the crosshairs on his left arm, just below the shoulder, and switch on the laser. And don't hit Senior's horse this time. Maybe that's the reason— Just don't, OK?"

He nods and takes the rifle. "Dammit, Devon." He has never used my first name, so I know he understands and won't press the issue.

Angela snuggles against my chest and gazes up at Muller. I can see fear in her eyes, but she says, "It's OK, Captain. I'll take care of Devon while you're gone."

"I'm sorry," Muller says. "It's been an honor knowing you, Lieutenant."

"How long do I have?" Angela asks as they walk away.

"Fifty minutes, give or take."

"I might as well get comfortable. Comm off." After removing her TRM and sidearm, she pulls pins from her hair, allowing it to flow down her back in a golden river of curls. She kneels beside me, removes my TRM and sidearm, and places them with hers. "I hope you don't mind," she says, sitting astride my lap. "Will you hold me until it's over?"

"Comm off," I say. I've been listening to Muller and Franklin but decide I don't want to know—when. If it's a clean kill, she'll disappear before I hear the report. I scoot out from the tree with Angela on my lap, lay back on the pine needles, and pat my chest. She lies on top of me, her legs between mine. "I hope you don't mind," I say and then kiss her soft, full lips. Then we just lie there, her head on my chest, my cheek against her forehead. I close my eyes and enjoy her warmth, her scent, and the feel of her body. At first her little heart races, pitter-pattering away, but after a few moments, it slows and synchronizes with my own.

451

"Thought of a spell yet?" I ask.

"Yeah, and it worked. I'm right where I want to be."

"I don't believe that, but thank you.... Why don't we go back to the present, right now, and just not go to London?"

"In the present, we're already dead. We can't go back until that changes, and when it does, I won't exist in any time—"

I flinch as a cold blade presses against my throat. I gaze up into the eyes of a foot soldier.

"I wouldn't move too fast, if I was you," he says with a thick English accent. He's wearing a chain mail tunic and a rusty kettle helm not unlike the British Brodie helmet first used in WWI. The blade at my throat is the tip of a blood-covered lance.

"Turn loose the lady," a second man says. He also carries a bloody lance. "You're Lord Barron's squire, ain't you? Brave men are dying out there. And here you are, forcing yourself on a wench."

Angela sits up. "He isn't doing anything wrong."

"That's for Lord Crompton to decide. Our orders was to round up craven dogs, deserters. And it looks to me like we found one. Where's your dress, M'Lady?"

"Um. Soiled, disgracefully soiled, I'm afraid. Squire Devon loaned me this."

"Both of you, on your feet."

"Comm on," I say as we walk across the smoky field.

"What's that supposed to mean?" the first soldier asks.

"They're prayer words," Angela says. "Comm on. We worship the same god."

"Ye best pray it's the same god Lord Crompton worships."

"Muller," I say.

"What?" the second soldier says.

"Muller's the name of our god," Angela says.

"Muller," I say, "they've captured us. We need your help."

"Pray all you want," the first soldier says, "but you'll see better results if you beg for mercy from Lord Crompton. Confess your sins and he'll like as not let you be on your way. He's God-fearing and kind. A true man of his word."

"Devon," Angela says, "I think I know how to get *all of us* back home. I need to speak to Lord Crompton as soon as possible."

"Muller," I say, "don't do it. Angela has a plan. Let her speak with Lord Crompton. Please!"

"No need to pray for that," the second soldier says, "that's him on the near horse with the flaming stag and fancy helm. And the other knight's his father, Lord Crompton, the Elder."

The battlefield remains as we'd seen it earlier, littered with the dead and dying. Muller acknowledges my request after arguing with Major Wilson. They'll delay as long as Crompton remains within range.

"Beg pardon, Lord Crompton," the soldier says. "We found this dog hiding with this wench back in the forest. I think he's Lord Barron's squire."

"And who is this lovely lady?" Crompton asks. He swings his leg over his saddle and drops to the ground.

"I'm just a serving girl."

"Has this man dishonored you?"

"Not at all. I was merely afraid, and he was comforting me. He's done nothing wrong. M'Lord, please set him free."

"I will consider your request, but what were you doing in these woods?"

"I... came out early this morning to search for mushrooms. And once the fighting started, I hid in the forest. Devon found me and vowed to stay and protect me. He was so kind that— I will not lie to you, M'Lord. I here do confess my sin... of lust. I hoped to lie with Devon and *not* because he was kind to me." Angela steps close to Lord Crompton, gazes up into his eyes and motions for his ear. In my earbuds, I hear her whisper, "I've had such terrible urges since my husband died, two years past."

"And you have yet to be with another man?"

She shakes her head. "I've been with no one."

Crompton meets my eyes. "Where do *you* belong?"

"Um."

"M'Lord," Angela says, "he confessed to me he was indeed Lord Barron's squire."

Crompton nods. "Do you know where to find your lord?"

"Um. Yes?" I say, hoping it's the favorable response.

"Then go to him. Tell him everything. The lady is now under my protection. As such, I will see to *all* her needs. You may leave."

"I need to go back the way we came to recover my...shield and helm."

"Then do so."

"Thank you, Lord Crompton." I bow. "And you, M'Lady. It's been an honor serving with you."

"And with you, Squire Devon. Before you leave, I should return what is yours." She pulls out her earbuds as she walks over. Angela hands all of her gear to me, including her dog tags. Squatting, she whispers as she unlaces her boots. "If this doesn't work, I won't need clothes, and you'll need to take them back with you." Stuffing her socks inside her boots, she ties the laces together and drapes them over my shoulder. "Things are going to happen fast. As soon as I hand you this jumpsuit, I want you to turn and walk away." She gazes into my eyes as she undresses. "I hope to see a lot more of you," she says, handing me the jumpsuit.

Chuckles rise from the gathering of knights and squires. "M'Lady!" Lord Crompton says. "Someone bring the lady a cloak."

"Go," she says, turning to face Crompton.

As I walk away, the crowd groans and several men curse. "May the Lord protect us," someone says. Several swords chime as knights draw them from scabbards. "It's a demon." I stop dead in my tracks.

"Why are you painted as might a dragon?" Crompton asks. "Are you a witch?"

"This is not paint. The dragon is within me. See for yourself. Touch me."

"I dare not until I know what you are."

"I am the High Priestess of the prophet known as Merlin."

"But Merlin is mere legend."

"Nay. Am I not real? I've come to warn you, my liege. Merlin came to me last night and shared his vision. I saw you die in the

Holy Land, which in turn caused the fires of hell to rain down upon *this* land. For the sake of King William, and your people, you must never go to the Holy Land. Give Merlin your word that you will never leave the island of Britannia, or you shall die...here and now."

After a moment of silence, I glance back.

Crompton grips the hilt of his sword. "Die, shall I? By your hand?"

"No." She cuts her eyes to me and then up to the shepherd's watch. "Death will strike you from above, as might lightning."

I cup my hand over my ear and whisper into my palm. "Muller, we need thunder, now." The report of the 16 mm echoes around the valley. Horses lurch and soldiers duck, not knowing what or where the danger might be.

"That was a warning," Angela says. "Do I have your sworn oath?"

"I have no need to leave this land," Crompton says, gazing up at the cloudless sky, "nor desire. To protect my people and King William, I swear to you and Merlin that I will never leave this island kingdom."

"Thank you, Lord Crompton." She closes her eyes, turning her face and palms skyward. After a few moments, she opens her eyes. "Merlin accepts your word...and summons me home. I must go. I'll ask Squire Devon to escort me through the forest."

"As you wish, M'Lady. And I thank you for your counsel, as I do Merlin."

"Squire Devon," Angela calls, "might I trouble you a bit longer?" She slips on the jumpsuit but doesn't bother with the boots. We walk back into the forest as fast as we can and meet up with Muller and Franklin in the smoky cornfield.

I glance around. "Where's Bravo Team?"

Angela grins. "They disappeared, clothes, gear, and all."

Muller smiles. "How'd you know?"

"Because *I* didn't. I suspect Lord Crompton kept his word and never left the island of Britannia. Since London wasn't nuked, the second team was never deployed."

Bravo Team vanished while the report of the FANG LG still echoed through the countryside. By convincing Crompton that Merlin's vision was real, the warning shot itself had triggered the new timeline. Muller returns my rifle and walks ahead with Franklin.

As Angela pulls on her boots, I chuckle. "That was one hell of a story to make up on the fly. You were great out there."

She grins up at me. "Which part did you like best? Merlin?"

"No, *that* had me worried." In my best female voice, I say, "I will not lie to you, M'Lord. I here do confess my sin... of lust."

She gazes up at me and smiles. "That part's true."

"It is?"

She stands and takes my arm. "Yes. Devon, I like you and want to see more of you... *if* you'll promise me something."

"Anything. What?"

"Promise you'll never do that girlie voice again."

I laugh. "Yes, M'Lady. You have my sworn oath."

After reaching the bridge, we recover our gear from beneath and walk to the middle of the span. Anticipating a drop when we return to present day, we crouch. Muller activates the TRMs, and our bubbles form for three seconds. When they vanish, we grunt and groan as we drop half a meter. My teeth clap together but that's the worst of it. Getting back to base, however, is another matter.

Even though we arrive at precisely 0600, our VTOL transport is not waiting for us. The pilots have not abandoned us; they simply have no reason to be there. Since we've changed history, there is no nuclear device, so the pilots haven't flown the mission. In their rush to address the threat, our scientists gave little thought as to what might happen should we succeed.

Only the four of us know we went—and why.

The Last History

written by
Samuel Parr

illustrated by
DAO VI

ABOUT THE AUTHOR

Samuel Parr grew up in North West Leicestershire, UK, in countryside crosshatched between nature and industry. He spent his early years filling these spaces with fantastical people and creatures in his mind and didn't stop as an adult.

Since reading The Hobbit *as a child, the world of fantasy and science fiction has captivated him. In happiness and health, in illness and grief, he has found fantasy a consistent source of beauty, solace, and inspiration. He started writing ten years ago, partly as an attempt to give back to the genre that has gifted him so much.*

In such a way, "The Last History" was born. It started with a question about two concepts: could you take the brutally long Civil Service Exams of Imperial China and make them a magic battle royale?

Into such a gauntlet, Sam threw two unlucky characters: a lowborn old woman with hidden powers, and a privileged young nobleman with a tortured past. From this pair, the story came, and with it a library of questions. How does our national history shape our lives? Under such influence, how much can we blame a character for their actions? And, somehow, can this story have a talking toad?

This collection of questions became the story that was Sam's first professional sale; something that has helped Sam after a lifetime of low confidence in his writing. He now can't wait to continue setting the weird worlds in his head onto the page, and he hopes you might read his work again.

ABOUT THE ILLUSTRATOR

Dao Vi is a concept artist and illustrator from Los Angeles born in Ho Chi Minh City, Vietnam. While growing up, Dao has always had a connection with drawing and video games. However that connection wasn't always strong, and he would occasionally lose his interest in art. His passion was reignited when he discovered the vast world of concept art and illustration for films and video games. Dao loves to tell stories through world-building, concept design, and illustration and hopes that one day he can share this passion with those around him. Currently, Dao is attending ArtCenter College of Design as an entertainment design student whose goal is to work as a concept artist for films and video games.

The Last History

Quiet Gate mixed her blood with the ink and began the sequence of pictograms that would please the Ancestor. The writing alcove faded away as she wrote; she forgot the arthritic cramp in her hands, the stink of urine from the chamber pot under her desk, the way the alcove's walls pressed from all sides, giving her barely enough room to stand. Instead, pictogram by pictogram, the Ancestor's story took shape.

Beyond the thin oak of the alcove door, the quarter-hour of the Exam Bell gonged. Quiet listened as she wrote, imagining she could hear the nibs of fifty other entrants scratching away at parchment in alcoves identical to hers. All of them were in this Exam Hall for one purpose—to complete the Histories of the Eight Ancestors. The first to do this would become a new Minister. The rest would have nothing.

Quiet would be ahead of most of them. She had studied for five decades and was now twelve times a failure of the Grand Exam. Her limbs might be old and weak, but her pictograms flowed onto the parchment like water down a streambed.

That was, until the toad interrupted her.

"Such typical servility," it croaked from the desk. "I hoped your experience would make you interesting, little one."

It was a beautiful creature, a body striped with gold and brass, and eyes of wise deep black. Most students would be ecstatic that it was here; such a character's presence signified a benefactor from the Antecedent Ministry. Yet Quiet was not and never had a benefactor, and all the toad had done since appearing yesterday was mope, refuse to answer her questions, and make too much noise.

"If you're going to speak, you can at least double-check my calligraphy," she said. "I don't want the Carnivore eating *me* when I invoke her."

The toad ignored her, blinking at the tiny room as if disappointed with the stained linen sleeping mat and dented iron chamber pot.

"Another crop of petty sacrifices," it said.

Well, Quiet didn't need its help. The labyrinth outside the alcove was still, and soon she lost herself painting the History. There were screams, but they were distant, and they did not interrupt her.

Three hours later, Quiet frowned at her complete History: a thousand symbols painted in a grid told the story of the oldest Ancestor of Nation, the First Carnivore. Each intricate pictogram had to be perfect, and in the correct order. Finally, she nodded. It was ready to invoke.

"Discoverer of Flesh," she intoned, speaking the words set down centuries before. "Hear my plea, your desperation our hope, your hunger our key."

Her voice cracked. Curse the damn thing; it came out high and reedy now, like she was imitating herself.

Yet it did not stop the Carnivore.

The air closed with an animal heat. One by one, the pictograms before Quiet snarled into shapes forming the image of a pale beast lying in a white wasteland, a wound of crimson at its side. A figure garbed in grey appeared; the skeletal Ancestor, bowing her head, giving prayers of thanks. The Carnivore's mouth mirrored the beast's wound as she opened her jaws.

A story of Nation. A story of power. Quiet could feel the magic throbbing in the air like a heartbeat.

The picture faded, yet the pictograms continued to glow. The alcove sweltered. The Ancestor was listening.

460

Holding her voice to make sure it didn't tremble, Quiet slowly recounted the seventh canto of the History where the Carnivore used fire to cook the meat she had harvested.

This was the real test. If the History was flawed, the Carnivore would take vengeance.

The sizzling smell of hot pork filled the air; pearls of pale meat tumbled across the parchment, ruining it with grease. It did not matter. Quiet let out an exhale. The Ancestor had seen her work and approved.

"Gratitude for a gracious gift," she said to the empty air. The pork was a blessing; it meant Quiet would not have to brave the communal pots. The meat was salty and tender with fat, and she wolfed it down in minutes. She was glad the toad refused the piece she offered it. Her appetite, at least, was still strong.

For a few precious breaths, she rested in the alcove fingering her quill. If a single stroke of a pictogram hadn't been perfect, it would have been Quiet who provided the Carnivore's meal.

The hour gong echoed through the Hall. Six of the Eight Ancestors done. Quiet had already completed the necessary Histories for the Farmer, Servant, Fisher, Child, and Soldier. She contemplated completing the History of the Convalescent in the alcove she was in. It was calm now, but who knew how long it would be before a thieving student came snooping?

As if in response to her thoughts, a sheet of bright blue water flowed under the alcove door. Quiet cursed, snatching up her satchel and stick.

"We need to go," she snapped. She recognised the water's unique hue and what it meant. "Some fool has recalled the Great Flood."

"I remember these waters," the toad said, jumping down from the table to wet its feet. "Such dazzling blue."

Well, forget about the petty little character then. *It* could swim.

She stepped out into the narrow corridor and cursed again. The granite floor was already a shallow stream reflecting the flickering torches that were the only light in the Hall, while the scent of salt water cut through the Hall's cloak of incense smoke.

461

Likely the candidate had called the Flood by mistake; the final cantos of the First Fisher's History were fiendish, as entrants had to scratch them onto a tablet while completely submerged in water. Still, malicious or not, the waters were dangerous. She leaned heavily on her stick as she walked down the corridor, heedless of the doors she passed leading to even more study alcoves. Most would be empty, but if they housed other entrants, hopefully they'd realise there wasn't time to rob Quiet's notes.

The corridor ended in stairs of blue-veined marble, leading to identical corridors above and below. Going off memory, Quiet climbed two levels. The staircase was a far cry from the alcoves' poverty; the walls were inlaid with mosaics tessellated with gold and lapis lazuli, while brass statues of the Ancestors stared down with eyes of diamond. She was careful to watch her tongue while they were near. She had heard stories of students cursing the Ancestors under the statues' stares and the endings were never pretty.

Years ago, she had danced through these same corridors, avoiding the eyes and spells of the other entrants as if they were all sleeping while she was awake. Now, she hobbled. But experience had its gifts. She knew some of the Hall's secrets.

Finally, she found what she was looking for: a statue of the First Servant. The Ancestor was depicted as a beautiful man flowing with golden muscle, his eyes gentle and knowing. Good. The statues' powers were traps, but also ladders, if one knew how to work them. The Servant's cantos included travel in a variety of circumstances, and with his completed History in her satchel, Quiet could call on him.

She knelt and unrolled the Servant's History, trying to ignore how the water sluiced through her leggings. She located the passage she needed—a glowing set of lines describing the Servant crossing the Tiger Lake in a storm to fetch flowers for the Empress. She murmured them quickly, feeling their power hang in the air like smoke. Now just the invocation.

"Servant of State, bonded by vow," she began, bowing her head.

A laugh echoed down the corridor.

Her head shot up. It had been a beautiful, awful sound; a child's laugh, full of joy.

There was only one candidate she knew who would laugh like that in the Exam Hall as the water rose.

The Flood *had* been intentional. *He* had called it.

And at that thought, the inconvenient terror she had been battling for four days broke in.

She needed to escape.

But what was the Servant's invocation? The words escaped her.

Drowning would be a peaceful ending, a traitorous thought whispered. *More than you deserve.*

What were the *words*?

Something splashed behind her, and she flinched. But it was only the toad who blinked at her, then at the Servant's statue, and sighed.

"Servant of State, bonded by vow," it said, "strength you give, in the bend of your bow... to others your service, and the salt on your brow."

Quiet could have kissed the slimy little beast. She repeated the words, and the Servant smiled.

"Where shall I carry thee?"

The Ancestor's words were almost lost in a sudden roar. A wall of water crashed from the stairs above, shining a deep blue under the memory of a sun a thousand years ago.

"Take me from here," Quiet said, and the world went black as the water hit.

Quiet Gate moved through a womb of night in the arms of a god and realised that even after twelve visits and fifty-nine days, she had never found an end to the Exam Hall and its coiled corridors.

The Servant bore Quiet to another of his statues in a chamber on the shorelines of the Flood. It was a crossroads of sorts; she counted seven stairwells leading to further corridors. The four heading down were choppy with water, but the ones leading up looked dry. She swore, realising that the salt water had awoken the army of cuts and blisters that covered her legs. The laugh haunted her. *He* would be near.

Fittingly, the crossroads' floor was a glass mosaic of the Fisher riding the sea waves. His static beauty was ruined by cracked inkwells that lay like broken eggs, the refuse of some desperate struggle for supplies between entrants. Each entrant came to the Exam with nothing; even their clothes were taken from them to prevent cheating. They were expected to source everything in the Hall—quills, parchment, clothes, food, water, and of course, magic. Stealing was encouraged. The winning entrant would maintain the world for the emperor. They were expected to be worldly.

"Gratitude for a gracious gift," Quiet said to the Servant's statue.

"This Flood has caused many endings."

She was surprised at the rush of warmth she felt when the toad's golden head appeared from behind the Servant's ear. The memory of her terror hadn't left her, and loud, mopey company was better than none. And, she admitted, he had just saved her life.

Dangerous, that. Once, Quiet's memory would never have failed her. Now, her mind felt as labyrinthine as the Hall, and tracking the million memories of the Ancestors was becoming harder.

"Doubtless that was the point," she told the toad, proud that her voice was steady. "Come, we must climb."

"An ending comes," the toad said, looking at the downwards stairwells, and for a moment it almost sounded human.

A body was floating in the waves.

It was a young woman. The too-blue water swelled her black hair and pale robes, so that her body looked vast and oceanic. Her parchment floated on the water's skin; pictograms and poetry and artwork, all blooming into illegibility.

Quiet sighed. A cloud of blood was growing around the entrant's head. Obviously dead, but still it felt wrong to leave a body like this.

The woman was slight, but her skin was cool and slippery, and Quiet couldn't lift her. She at least managed to pull the body up a couple of steps onto the dry floor, sighing as the woman's head lolled. The woman's face reminded Quiet of too many ghosts. She pushed back the woman's robes to reveal the name tattoo under her collar.

Steadfast Forest.

As Quiet had expected. A Concrete name. The daughters and sons of the great houses had abstract concepts as their name-object, while commoners had to make do with the mundane. Stone. Lake. Gate. This girl would have carried the hoarded hopes of her community with her, hopes that left little room for any dreams of her own. Such an entrant would have no Ministry benefactors, and the only tutelage her community could afford would be from the cheap charlatans who claimed to have taken the Exam but had never stepped foot in this Hall.

And so, she had no hope when the waters came for her.

If only she had approached Quiet instead. As a twelve-time survivor of the Exam, Quiet was in high demand as a tutor, but charged a pittance to teach Concretes like herself. She stared at the vacancy in the girl's eyes, wondering what spark might have burned there as Quiet taught the Eight Histories, the intricate skeletons of the Empress's Alphabet, and the crackling power of one who understood form, meaning, and story.

"The Grand Exam is a great leveller," Quiet's father whispered in her memory. *"Anyone can take it, and anyone can succeed."*

But Quiet had learned that was a lie, in so many ways.

"I will carry your name to your family," she said. The girl could not hear the promise, but the Ancestors would.

"Little one, someone approaches," the toad croaked in Quiet's ear.

She realised he was right. There was music, coming from a stairwell surrounded by sculpted carp.

Someone was whistling.

Quiet rose, ignoring the protest of her knees. She knew who

it was. The same candidate who had laughed before. Only he would have so boldly called into the Hall's maze; a challenge to any other entrant.

There was nowhere to hide.

The boy that entered looked like he was at a dance, rather than the Exam. He had found flowing robes of blue silk, woven with branching patterns that accentuated the delicate bones of his face. His hair shone in black curls, and his hands were clean and elegant. A bulging satchel was slung on his back, holding his Histories.

At his side was a peacock. The bird was the most auspicious of Exam symbols, and its presence would greatly strengthen any blessings granted. This one had eight brush-like feathers on the crest of its head, and Quiet knew the folded fan of its train would hold eight more, each patterned with eight eyes. She recognised it from the Eighth History; such a character had been attendant to the First Empress. To have it here signified that the boy had a benefactor so high-ranking that Quiet would never have heard of him.

The boy's eyes brightened when he saw her.

"Master Gate!" he cried out. "Oh, I'm so glad you are here! And you have a character too! The Flood, did you see it?"

"Ceaseless," she said. She fought to keep her voice neutral. *Don't look at the dead girl.* "Yes. I saw it."

Ceaseless Charity, the first-born son of House Charity and one of the most powerful Abstracts in Nation, laughed like a child.

"I must thank *you* for it," he said. "You warned me about the alternating meters of the cantos. The Fisher was so impressed that I had remembered—and goodness, what a presence he had! With him, I felt like how a fish must feel in an ocean!" He stepped close. He smelled just as he had always done—of honey and milk and sweat. "But I don't need to tell you that. You can see the gift he granted me."

"The Flood was poorly executed," the peacock appraised Quiet as it came to Ceaseless's side, merely glancing at the toad. It spoke with the voice of a woman, but its syllables vibrated with power. "Any notes will be ruined, Ceaseless."

"Yes, Ceaseless," Quiet said, voice strained. "For what purpose did you summon the waters?"

He grinned as if she was testing his knowledge in class. "I wanted to see if I could. You always said the Flood was tricky to invoke—twenty five cantos to do it properly, and all with perfect tone and rhythm."

He paused expectantly, and she could see the hope in his face. He wanted her to praise him.

"This girl drowned because of you," she said softly.

His eyes flickered. "I didn't do it to hurt her," he said, his voice taking on a childish whine. He stepped past Quiet to pick up the papers floating in the water, barely glancing at Steadfast Forest. "And she would have died anyway, Master. Look at these shoddy forms." He spat the final words. "They bring shame to the Ancestors."

Oh, she had hoped, how she had hoped, that he would be better.

Quiet's mind went to the Carnivore's History in her satchel. There were many, many cantos of savagery in it, through which she could call the Ancestor's teeth. She had a brief urge to whisper the words now, against the boy in front of her.

Yet she told herself it would be futile. Not with that peacock character at his side. It was the same every year. The Abstracts always went into the Exam powerful.

A gong split the air, ringing twelve times. The midnight bell. The entrants had been in the Exam Hall for five days.

"Enough diversions," the peacock said. "You will need at least three hours to assemble the Convalescent's History, even with my aid." It cocked a dark eye at Quiet, "Unless she already has it."

Ceaseless laughed. "Oh no, Pea. We won't steal, especially from Master Gate. She taught us everything, and we know she will do honour to the Ancestors." He dropped Steadfast's notes and came closer to gaze at the Servant's statue. Quiet knew he was admiring the figure itself rather than his reflection. Despite her anger, she had a sudden urge to touch his dark curls.

"Careful Progress will be by Empress Ao's Audience Chamber," he murmured. "He always thought he was a better writer than me." He blinked at Quiet, expression hopeful. "Would you like to come with me, Master Gate? Don't worry, I'll protect you."

Quiet made herself smile. It felt like she was peeling her lips from her teeth.

"No thank you, Ceaseless. I must continue my own Histories." She bowed. "Just remember what I taught you, yes?"

Ceaseless nodded.

"I always do," he said.

Then he spoke the Servant's blessing and a canto for travel using the very words Quiet had taught him. The Servant's shadow engulfed him and the peacock, leaving the chamber empty and silent except for Quiet's irregular heartbeat and the weight of her old fear.

Quiet had been a fool with Ceaseless.

When she first met him, the boy was full of shadows. He had sat listlessly when Quiet was introduced to his dark room, the windows shuttered and the air stale. Around him lay the refuse of other tutors' attempts: dictionaries of logograms, compendiums of poetry, and reams of memory tests.

"The boy is broken," the Lady Charity had told Quiet. "I named him Ceaseless, but he does nothing." She had looked at her son like he was another servant, and Ceaseless stared back with eyes that Quiet understood. She had seen them before in those tutees that were refugees from Nation's slums. "Normally I wouldn't trust a Concrete tutor, but I've heard of your reputation for hopeless cases. He's been like this since his father decided to chance the Exam himself." She shook her head dismissively as if the only lingering feeling for her husband was disdain. Yet Quiet had shivered at her words, feeling an emotion she had never felt in an Abstract House before.

Empathy.

When his mother had left, Quiet did not test the boy's knowledge, or have him paint pictograms, or anything else she was expected to do for high-born pupils. Instead, she had settled herself on a mat not yet close enough to smell his honey scent and asked him a question.

"Would you like to hear a story?"

Quiet hid behind a marble pillar under a network of the Servant's magic, peering at the two entrants. She'd found them huddled underneath a statue of the Soldier—a boy and girl, whose skeletons showed through their skin. The girl's robes were bloodstained around her chest. The boy was tending her, and weeping.

Quiet relaxed. She had feared an Abstract when she heard the girl's whispers, yet she recognised the boy. His name was Growing Lake and he had been her tutee. In his satchel were only three Histories. She spotted the stone tablet of the Soldier and the fragile luminous scroll of the potent Convalescent. Growing had had none of Ceaseless's passion, but a diligence of almost heroic proportions, eyes burning with the same belief that brought so many Concretes to the horrors of the Exam Hall.

"As a Minister, I will make things better," he had vowed to her.

Quiet's father had once said the same.

Growing had also always been foolish. She could see the girl had completed the Fisher's and Farmer's Histories; he should have taken them from her, instead of crying and making himself a nice little target for any Abstract.

But then her fellow Concretes were often like that. Abstract children were tutored from birth for this place, but the Concretes had only a limited idea what to expect. Indeed, Growing reminded her of her first tutee, Graceful Petal. Such a clever, useless boy.

"I'll stop him," Growing was murmuring, cupping the girl's face. "I'll stop him, Bountiful, and he can't hurt you anymore."

469

"No," Bountiful coughed. "You can't face him, Growing. He's the entrant of House Charity. I barely escaped; he only let me go because I let him tear up my History of the Child."

Quiet felt a wave of cold. Just how many entrants had Ceaseless hurt?

Growing flushed. "I can and will. Master Gate taught me well."

"That old woman? What good is she, Growing? She's spent her life failing this Exam."

"Her tutees always do well. She tutored the first *ever* Concrete Minister, and two more since then." He glanced around, before whispering words that made Bountiful's eyes widen.

"Truly?" she gasped.

"Yes," Growing said. "So you see, I *do* have a hope of becoming Minister. Master Gate has made sure he will fail."

Oh, foolish boy. Foolish, foolish boy.

For a moment, Quiet imagined intervening. She imagined stepping from the shadows and telling Growing that he had no hope against Ceaseless.

But that wasn't what she did. In the Hall, she watched. She listened.

Yet the children were so poor, so hungry.

Quiet crept away. But first, she took out her grease-stained History of the Carnivore and laid it on the floor. It still held nearly all its potency, enough for an entrant to invoke a feast. When Growing exited the chamber, he would surely find it.

"You have intrigued me." The toad hopped behind her as she climbed one of the Hall's many staircases. Quiet tried to ignore it. "You write beautifully. You spend three hours creating a flawless History only to give your work away, and your chances of graduation with it."

They passed a corridor that smelt of spiced lamb and honey cakes, but Quiet wasn't tempted. She needed to find a bolthole to endure the final hours of the Exam in.

The stairway ended in a silent corridor of alcoves. Several of the doors had been broken at one end, while at the other a set of tables had been pushed onto their sides as barricades; a battle between two entrants. There were teeth marks on the doors and the tables—a sign that both entrants had completed the Carnivore's History. She wondered absently who had won; when both combatants had the same History of the Ancestor, the Ancestor would follow whoever's History was the highest quality.

Either way, there were no bodies and it seemed calm now. Quiet's legs were aching; it would be good to sit down.

"You are not here to become a Minister, are you?"

She rounded on the toad. "Why are *you* here?" she said. "Which Minister sent you?"

"It matters not." The toad's black eyes bored into her. "You are troubled. You cared for that boy."

"What I feel should not matter to you."

It hopped up to her shoulder. "You could face the other one, you know," it whispered in her ear. "The dark one...you have skill enough."

Quiet flinched away. "I can't," she said. "Why do you care anyway?"

"I am a character of the Empress, girl. A student not living up to their potential concerns me. You could kill the dark one and become Minister." Its body swelled. "It is what your father would have done."

Quiet froze.

"How do you know of my father?" she said.

"I have seen generations pass here, girl, like mayflies above my old lake. I watched your father die here. You share his face and his skill, but not his hunger."

Quiet wasn't ready for the emotions that punched her—loss, sorrow, and a sly, secret warmth. The toad had once known her father and recognised her as his daughter.

"Tell me what you know."

"There is little to tell," it rasped. "Your father came here, completed seven Histories, and died at the hand of the graduate to be, but he at least tried."

471

Her heart ached. It was terrible, because when she pictured her father in this Hall five decades ago, she could not recall his face.

The toad looked up at her, a canny light in its dark eyes.

"He would have been proud to see you here," it said. "He would tell you to kill the dark one."

She hissed and swept the beast off her shoulder. It was sent flying with a surprised croak, and she rushed into a nearby alcove, slamming the door shut.

"Don't pretend to know my father," she shouted through the door. "Don't pretend you want to help me. Just go and crawl back into the History you were brought from."

"Such potential," the toad murmured, voice vibrating through the wood. "Why do you run from it?"

Quiet had been twelve when her father left. They had lived together in a shack on the city's outskirts, and their life held a steady, comforting ritual. Each morning Quiet would go out with the other girls to pick wolfberries in the field, while her father spent ten hours scrubbing the floors of the Abstract houses. He would return in the afternoon, smelling of lye and sweat, a lotus or chrysanthemum or peony he had picked on his way home gripped in his large worker's hands. She would take the flowers impassively, like it was her birthright, even though it made her feel like a courtly maiden from the Histories, rather than a grubby, growing girl. And he would finally ask her the same question, his voice gentle and clean as a kingfisher's cry.

"What today, my luminous one, has given you hope?"

And Quiet would answer the same way she always had.

"The Exam, Father, gives me hope."

He would bow, light their brass lamp, then lead her down into their blessedly cool cellar. The lamplight would reveal the shelves of glittering leather-bound History books he had stolen over twenty years from the Abstract houses.

And their studying would begin.

Quiet had loved to study. Loved to share the cellar's bottled silence with her father, sheltered from Nation's summer, as he guided her through each of the Histories. He was a marvellous storyteller, his passion filling the words with heat and life. He spoke of the Ministers like they were gods.

"The Ministers," he told her, "are the Empress's chosen. They wield the power of these Histories in the wider world, while we can only invoke them in the Exam Hall. And with it, they can achieve marvels."

Back then, Quiet had thought of the Exam as her father spoke about it: the great leveller between Concrete and Abstract. The solution to the hungry winters and plague-thick summers that had taken her mother. A way out of the petty futures open to her as a fieldhand, or seamstress, or cleaner.

She was intensely jealous of the Abstract schoolchildren, who got to train for the Exam every day, walking to school with soft laughs and certain eyes.

And so, when her father told her he had decided to enter the Exam himself, she had been happy. No one, she thought, could match him for passion, wisdom, and gentleness. He loved the Histories. He would be an excellent Minister.

"This will be our chance, my hope," he said, "to make it better, for everyone."

Before he left, he picked her a hundred flowers, and presented them to her on one knee, like she was the Empress.

She learnt about the Exam's true nature only later. After her father entered the Exam Hall with his head held high. After the Abstract entrants, with their benefactors and characters and lifetime of training, had killed him. How petty her fears had been before he left. Seamstress, cleaner, housewife—she would have chosen any of those futures if it meant her father had stayed to tell her stories, to whisper goodnight, to bring her flowers, and to make her feel like somebody more.

Instead, Quiet grew into a woman alone. She did not work, but survived on her father's pitiful savings, growing gaunt and lean with hunger.

Yet it was not just gold that her father had left. Each day, as she opened her textbooks, she remembered his vision of a Concrete

Minister. She wove it around her like a cocoon, told her father's ghost about it, instead of facing the house's silence.

Quiet realised she would do anything to make it true.

Quiet tried to lose herself in the History of the Convalescent. As with all the Ancestors, its composition was exacting; a series of poems, each line the perfect number of syllables, in three alternating meters, with the seventy one reflections of the Convalescent's life listed in their exact order. Yet the Convalescent was also looking for inspiration and emotion in her poems. Within the tight confines of the form, the Ancestor expected her students to innovate.

It should have been child's play to Quiet. She had, after all, completed the History in five previous Exams now. Yet her hands spasmed with pain as she wrote. She kept seeing the face of Steadfast Forest and questions skittered across her mind like lightning.

Where is Ceaseless now?

Is Growing really going to challenge him?

Why is the History of some ill woman so important?

The last question was heresy, but it had become increasingly insistent over the last decade of her life. It had been the Empress, last and greatest of the Eight Ancestors, who had written the Eight Histories of Nation, and inscribed them with the Ancestors' magic. There was no doubt about the power they held and their importance to Nation's culture.

"We must remember our roots," her father had told her in their cellar. *"There is power in tradition."*

But why should the Eight Ancestors be venerated, instead of the thousand other great heroes of Nation?

Quiet's quill trembled. She was gripped with a sudden urge; instead of declaiming about the Convalescent's recovery from her lovers' dagger, and the pain of betrayal, she started a new line.

There was once a girl called Steadfast Forest. She was brave and faced great peril. She died, but in this work we will remember her name.

Oh dear. She had just ruined the page. If she invoked the Convalescent with this, the only boon she would receive would be pneumonia.

But still. She had written the words with the same precision as every other line. It *looked* like part of a History. Quiet liked how "Steadfast Forest" seemed on the page. It had a dignity to it.

Something crackled within her. She raised her quill and wrote another line.

There was once a woman called Quiet Gate. She was an evil, evil person. She lives, but in this work we will decry her name.

The words looked like truth.

She sighed, rubbing her eyes. She was in no mood to write poetry. She had always found the Convalescent the most difficult History, bar the Empress's; it was why she always left it until last. It felt untrue to write about the sorrow of an Ancestor centuries old, rather than what you saw before you.

She let her head slump. She shouldn't, she knew. It was dangerous to stop working; as soon as you did, the exhaustion subsumed you. She could feel it, waiting below the bright, brittle energy she only ever felt in the Exam Hall. She just wanted to sleep. No, more than that, she wanted to stop.

And would that be so bad? So what if another entrant found Quiet and finally killed her? She'd had a good run, with twelve Exams under her belt. She had taught dozens of entrants, a handful of whom had become Ministers. She'd done justice to her father's memory.

What did she have to live for? A silent house full of scrolls and books. No lover. No friends. No children.

Her thoughts drifted to Ceaseless. His face came so clearly to her even here. If she died, what would happen to him? How would he feel if he was told he never would see Quiet again? Perhaps he wouldn't care as long as he became Minister. The thought brought a rumble of pain in her chest. Would he be happy working with the Histories every day? Would he be monstrous, unleashing the Ancestor's power just to see it, uncaring about who he hurt?

475

Quiet's head slumped. Her father smiled at her, holding her cheek.

"Girl." The toad's voice woke her with a start. How long had it been?

It croaked as she opened the alcove door.

"What?"

"I am awaiting your apology."

"Then carry on waiting."

The toad blinked. "You are the rudest applicant I have been assigned to."

"What do you want?"

It glanced behind it into the deeper shadows of the corridor. "Are you waiting for me to announce you?" it said to the darkness. "Come out, you tired old fowl, and make your entreaty."

"I should have known not to expect courtesy from a character of the Fisher."

The peacock's voice resonated through Quiet's ears. She felt a wave of foreboding as Ceaseless's guardian character stepped into view, the blue and green feathers of its plumage glittering in the torchlight.

"Where is Ceaseless?" she asked immediately.

"Hopeless entrant," the peacock said, ignoring her. "I bring tidings from my charge, who has bid me find you. He asks you to attend him, in Ao's Audience Chamber."

"*Attend* him?" Quiet said. "Why?"

"It seems he is wounded," the toad said. Its wide mouth looked like it was smiling. Quiet felt a sudden chill.

"My charge has bravely contested another entrant," the peacock said, train feathers twitching.

"Is he alive?" Quiet said softly.

"How else would he have bidden me? He is merely inconvenienced, but still, he requests you." The peacock appraised an eye at Quiet. "He trusts you."

Quiet turned away, back into the alcove. Curses. Stupid boy. Stupid character. Her hands shook.

In the Hall, she watched. She listened. To do otherwise

would be to have the Ministry realise what she was here for. Her carefulness was why she had survived so long.

She sighed and stepped out into the corridor. The pain in her knees felt like a warning for what she was about to do.

The Histories had freed Ceaseless.

As the weeks of their tutelage went by, Quiet had told him of the stories of the Eight Ancestors. She focussed not on pictogram structure or poetic meter, but on the drama and characters— the brutal diligence of the Servant's seven labours, the Fisher's mastery of the Flood, the Empress's court of humans and spirits, and the founding of Nation.

The boy had listened to her, and the vacancy slowly left his eyes. After a week, he finally spoke.

"Father used to tell me these stories," he had whispered. "Hearing them...feels like he's still here."

After three months, he had already memorised the Eight Histories, and his quillwork was flawless. He practised constantly; Quiet had to remind him to eat. He talked to her all the time now, always about the Histories and the Exam.

As a tutor, you shouldn't get attached. Especially not to an Abstract tutee who lived in a palace while the Concrete pupils had only poverty.

Yet Ceaseless was Quiet's only tutee to see the Histories' beauty, as well as their power. The only tutee who had lost their father to the Exam.

When you taught someone, you gave them part of your soul. You watched your knowledge grow in them and saw yourself reflected. It was the greatest connection Quiet could have with another person. A shell of a boy became whole with light and learning, and *she* had filled him.

"What today has given you hope?" she asked Ceaseless every day.

"All I hope," he said, "is to become a good Minister, and do you and Father proud."

At night, Ceaseless's answer filtered into her dreams, and she smiled in her single bed.

Yet one month before the Exam, she had seen another side to his passion.

She had arrived at House Charity, feeling more awake than she had since her last Exam, to find Ceaseless not alone as usual. He was joined by a guard, who loomed above a boy with blond hair. Quiet vaguely recognised him as a child of House Constance; a weak family, but still, an Abstract one. The boy's shirt had been torn from his shoulders to reveal his bare back. On the floor was a parchment—a practice History of the Fisher. It was ruined with ink.

"Master Gate!" Ceaseless cried, his eyes bright and hard. "This dolt spilt ink on my History! Mother invited him here to be my *companion*, but look how he repaid her!"

In the guard's hand was a metal cane, jagged with tiny spikes.

"Ceaseless," she had said, feeling suddenly light-headed. "Stop. A mistake, clearly. This will start a war between your houses."

But Ceaseless wasn't listening. Breathless, he had gestured at the guard with a shaking hand and she couldn't tell if he was furious or elated.

The guard, a Concrete bred from birth only to obey, brought the cane down on the Abstract boy's back, again and again.

Quiet had watched in horror, her happiness crumbling. The Constance boy had whimpered, but he didn't fight. As if he too thought he deserved this.

"Stop!" she had cried. "Stop, Ceaseless!"

But Ceaseless had ignored her, the flame in his eyes fading as the boy's back became a ruin of welts and blood.

Quiet bid a statue of the Servant take her to Ao's Audience. He acquiesced, depositing her just outside.

Ao's Audience was the largest chamber in the Hall. While the layout of the Hall changed for each test, this room always remained the same; a dedication to the final Ancestor, Ao, First Empress and Progenitor of Nation. Ao's statue dominated the room, twelve feet of brass depicting a beautiful woman with the tail of a dragon. Around her loomed the other Ancestor statues arranged like courtiers. Between them all, three dozen desks were lined in rows. On the far wall was the Hall's only entrance, a great gate of white cedar and steel, where each entrant was pushed naked and shivering into the labyrinth. The whole place smelt like dust and stale incense.

It felt wrong, being here. Quiet always got as far away from this place as she could. It was here that the final History must be invoked, and so it was here that the most powerful entrants must eventually come.

Crumpled before the Empress's statue was a body.

Quiet's knees burned as she ran over to it, heart pausing.

It was not Ceaseless.

The man looked thirty years old, plump faced even after days in the Hall. His neck was tattooed in red ink with his name: "Careful Progress." His eyes were glassy. He was clearly dead.

On the floor around him were torn pieces of parchment, thick with pictograms. Histories. A lot of them.

"Careful," the toad whispered from its resting place on her shoulder. "This is an excellent chance."

The peacock led her to the statue of the Servant. Leaning in its shadow was Ceaseless.

His dark curls were matted with sweat, and blood ruined his blue tunic. Yet his eyes brightened when he saw her.

"Master Gate!" he said. "You came."

"What happened?" she said softly.

"Careful Progress was here too," he said. She noticed a catch to his breath. "He had seven Histories *and* a character, but I won with only six." His voice was soft, childlike in his hope to impress her, but soon it darkened with an anger that was all a man's. "He just viewed the Histories as tools. He'd stolen all of them, I think. He tried to set the Carnivore on me, but I asked her to choose, and she chose me." He glanced at her. "I didn't mean for her to kill him, but she did. And I told myself it wasn't so bad. After all, I did just as you taught me, Master Gate."

"You shouldn't have done that," she said. "We talked, didn't we? About showing restraint."

DAO VI

Ceaseless's eyes flickered. "We did," he said. "But Master Gate, *he* attacked *me*. Was I to just let him kill me?"

She flinched. She remembered the moment when she saw Careful Progress's body. "No," she whispered.

His eyes brightened. "I am so glad you are here with me, Master Gate. I can still become Minister with you to help me. I'll make you proud."

He smiled, but Quiet noticed the red deepening on his tunic.

"Let me see," she said. Ceaseless grimaced but opened his shirt.

Quiet had seen the Carnivore's work before, but she still trembled at the deep gouge across Ceaseless's delicate ribs.

"It's not so bad, is it?" he said.

"We should leave him," the toad said, not even pretending to whisper. "He is little threat now."

"Do so, little tadpole, and I shall devour you," the peacock said.

"Oh, be silent, both of you," Quiet said. "No, it's not so bad," she told Ceaseless. Her voice sounded more confident than she felt. The toad was right; with this wound it would be easy to leave Ceaseless here and let the Hall decide his fate. Yet he was watching her with such hope.

And it was better now he was wounded. He was her tutee again, her boy again. She could teach him to be better than her.

She sucked her teeth, thinking. If she had finished the Convalescent's History, she would have been able to heal him. As it was, she had to make do.

Luckily, it turned out Careful Progress had been a busy entrant before facing Ceaseless. In his pack were several wrapped packs of dried meat, stacks of parchment, and a cache of medical supplies including bandages. The wound needed stitching, but Quiet was no surgeon. Binding it would have to do.

"What are you *doing*?" the toad whispered, as Quiet patted Careful Progress's body.

"The right thing," she said.

"You are hopeless," it hissed. "If you won't live up to your potential, I will find another."

"Wouldn't my 'benefactor' have a problem with that?" she said absently, unspooling the bandages.

The toad only croaked in what she assumed was an angry response, before hopping down from her shoulder and straight out of the chamber. She watched it leave with an unexpected pang of remorse, but she wouldn't follow it. She was needed here.

"Does it hurt?" she asked Ceaseless, once she had bound his chest.

"No," he lied. "I can continue." As if to prove it, he stood, swaying only a little.

Quiet nodded and let herself reach out to touch his cheek. "Then, my boy, let's write a History. I will work on the Convalescent. And you will work on the Empress."

Ceaseless's eyes widened. "Excellent! I wouldn't accept a History from anyone but you, Master Gate." He nodded once. "And I remember what you said about the Empress. That I must be very cautious because she is the most difficult. I do have you *and* Pea."

"That's right," Quiet said. "You have us to help you." If peacocks could frown, she was sure the peacock would have. "Now, we practiced the First Empress's History, but now that we're in the Hall, it's different. Tell me, what is so difficult about her?"

"That the Empress requires you to have the seven other Histories before you invoke her," he recited. "And, most important, she requires your love." He frowned. "Oh, are you *sure* I love her enough, Master Gate?"

"I am," Quiet said.

Ceaseless gave a shy smile. "I think so too. But I need time. I want her History to be *perfect*." He glanced at the door. "Do you think anyone else is working on the final History yet? Perhaps I should go and stop them, to make sure I have enough time."

"I am sure the Empress would prefer you focus on her," Quiet said. She clapped her hands, ignoring the sweat spiking her back. She could teach him; it would just take time. "No procrastinating, Ceaseless. Get to work."

He pouted but nodded. She felt a stab of relief; see, she *could* still control him. Soon, he was at a desk, tongue stuck out as he painted pictogram after beautiful pictogram. His brush tip caressed the page, and his eyes were gentle flames. Oh, he painted with love all right. Quiet had no doubt that the Empress would graduate him.

And then he would be Minister. Her beautiful, brave tutee, who she had brought out from the darkness.

Yet that darkness was still there, and he would take it into a role where he wielded this power in the wider world.

She sat at another desk, focussing on redoing the Convalescent's History to distract herself. She first pulled out her original attempt, giving the name "Steadfast Forest" a quick glance before tossing it aside. Sentimental fool. She just needed to finish this Exam and be done.

Empress Ao's statue stared down at her, with her dragon eyes, as she worked. Foul woman. It had been she who established the Ministry and the Grand Exam and commanded it be open to Concretes as well as Abstracts. Had she realised how generation after generation would sacrifice themselves in pursuit of power?

Either way, entrants died. And so, Quiet hated her. It was one of the reasons she would not graduate. She loved the Histories, but could not paint the Empress.

"Master Gate?" came Ceaseless's voice. She started; she had been daydreaming. How weak her mind was becoming. "What's this?"

The cold calm in his voice was her first warning. She turned to see that he had stopped working on the History. Instead, he had crept up from behind. In his hand, like dead petals, was her failed History of the Convalescent. His finger tapped the line where she had written her own name.

"Ceaseless, you shouldn't go through my things," she said, her voice strained.

It was too late. His eyes were flowing over the words.

"You know, Careful told me something about you before he died," he said softly. "I killed him for it."

"Ceaseless," she murmured. *Remember it's not his fault.* "I was just playing. Being sentimental in my old age."

Ceaseless swallowed. His eyes moved as if reading words she couldn't see.

Behind him, the peacock's head shot up. Quiet tensed, then realised it was looking beyond her.

The toad was crouched in the Hall's entrance. Behind it was the shadow of an entrant.

"Master Gate," Growing Lake said, stepping into the light. "Your character told me the plan. Let's face Charity together."

The Exam Hall had shaped Growing from a gentle boy into a starving dog. Each of his limbs held a tenuity from a lifetime of hunger, yet his eyes burned; he held a History in each hand, and his satchel bulged with more. The Convalescent and the Soldier, the two Ancestors who had resonated most with the boy. Growing had lost his parents, Quiet knew, to the slumlords. For all the boy's gentleness, his whole life had been a battle.

She couldn't help a burst of pride. He was exactly the sort of entrant her father had wanted to become Minister.

"Come, Master Gate," Growing called. His jaw tightened as he stared at Ceaseless. "I follow your lead."

"He speaks like he knows you, Master Gate," Ceaseless said, letting her failed History of the Convalescent flutter to the floor. "Is he...another of your tutees?"

"Calm, Ceaseless," she whispered, like she was talking to a beast. "I'll deal with this."

"No choice now," the toad croaked, wide mouth smug.

Quiet felt a surge of anger. The toad must have lured Growing here to the danger of Ceaseless. She would ask the Carnivore to eat it after this.

"Is he challenging me?" Ceaseless said, more curious than angry.

"Just sit here a moment and then we'll work on your History," Quiet said. *Please.* She couldn't bear it. Killing brutes like Careful Progress was one thing, but Growing was her Concrete tutee. Another who held a piece of her soul.

For a wordless moment, Ceaseless frowned. Then he placed a hand on her shoulder.

"Very well," he said. He nodded at Growing. "If you're Master Gate's pupil, I won't hurt you."

Growing did not move.

"Growing, please don't be foolish," Quiet said, and her damned voice cracked, betraying her fear. "Entrant Ceaseless Charity has more Histories than you do."

"We can face him together," Growing said.

"I can't do that."

A flicker of surprise broke the boy's anger, but his eyes soon hardened.

"I should have known," he spat. "Everything you told me about your father's legacy—pretty lies to ensure you were paid."

Ceaseless's grip tightened on Quiet's shoulder. "You *dare* speak to Master Gate so?"

"Careful, Ceaseless," the peacock said softly. "I sense many Histories."

Quiet frowned, then realised the import of the bulging satchel. Bountiful must have given Growing her Histories voluntarily. With Quiet's, he would have seven Histories in all. While Ceaseless had six and was wounded....

Quiet's breath caught. It was not Growing she needed to protect.

It was Ceaseless.

"I told you the truth, Growing," she said, trying to keep the desperation from her voice. "But please understand. You don't know what's happening here."

Growing's hands tightened on his Histories and she knew she had lost him.

"Soldier of Nation, defender of the Hall," he intoned. "Your bravery our bread, your spear our wall."

The air bled with screams and clashing iron; the Soldier's presence.

"Strong of arm, the spearwall held," Growing cried, the first line of the fourth canto, and the screams peaked as his magic woke.

Growing's invocation of the Soldier manifested as dozens of spearpoints fanning around him, piercing tables, shattering chairs. A wall of floating tower shields protected his body, faintly transparent. Behind them, he carried on reading the rest of the fourth canto, detailing the story of the Soldier's spearwall.

"Stop!" Quiet cried, caught between Growing and Ceaseless, helpless like the weak woman she was. Ceaseless pushed her back, whispering the Carnivore's invocation and a line from the sixth canto, the peacock's voice layering his.

The air filled with animal heat, and then clawed hands materialised out of nowhere slashing toward Growing. Yet half the hands faltered before they reached the entrant, sensing Quiet's completed History in his satchel, and the rest bounced off the shields.

Quiet's heart spasmed, her hands shook uselessly. She always avoided these fights. She had never seen her tutees die.

Growing snapped another invocation and spectral ropes flickered into existence around Ceaseless's wrists and legs. The binding of the Convalescent, in her "Times of Dreaming Hardship"—canto seventeen, lines twenty seven to thirty three.

The peacock gave a fluting cry, pecking fruitlessly at the ropes as Growing advanced, the feathers of its train spreading. Quiet felt a flicker of hope seeing the azure character's defiance.

Spears impaled the bird, driving it back screeching. It flailed, its colours fading as the spectral points pushed clean through it.

From the shadows under a statue, the toad leapt forward, its jaws widening and widening into a cavern of black far vaster than it had any right to be and swallowed the peacock whole.

Quiet stared in amazement. Who *was* the benefactor behind this character?

Then her despair returned. Ceaseless was stumbling in his bindings, his face screwed up as he stared at the toad. He invoked the Fisher, but nothing happened.

It would be over soon. This broken boy, this monster and

mirror, the closest thing to a family she had ever had since her father left. He would be gone.

Ceaseless glanced at her, terror in his eyes, and then seemed to calm. A smile ghosted his lips.

"Servant of State," Quiet whispered, "bonded by vow."

Growing strode forward with his spearwall. The Concrete boy had lived in poverty and hunger in slums as labyrinthine and cruel as this Exam Hall.

Ceaseless had wounded Bountiful, Growing's friend. If there was any justice here, this would be it.

"Strength you give, in the bend of your bow," she continued.

The spears angled down on Ceaseless.

"To others your service..."

Yet Growing, Quiet knew, had once had a mother and father who loved him.

"And the salt on your brow."

The Servant smiled at her from his statue.

"Stop him," she pleaded. She hadn't even read from a canto, yet the Servant didn't hesitate.

The air rang like a bell. Growing's shields shattered, his spears snapped, and the boy was flung back by the force of Quiet's invocation. He slammed into a statue with a crack.

Quiet stood stunned at what she had done. It had felt like someone else was speaking the Servant's words.

She cursed and hobbled over to Growing.

Blessedly he was alive and conscious. He gaped up at her, covered in blood and dust.

"Go," she said. "Let me deal with this."

"But you promised!" he screamed. "You promised we'd stop them!"

Tears were bleeding from his eyes. She had betrayed him. After all those lessons together and the secrets she had shared, she was defending the very Abstracts he hated.

It was terrible, she thought, to be betrayed by your teacher. Unforgivable.

"I will make this right," she said. "I swear."

Ceaseless's voice trickled into her ears.

Teeth materialised on each side of Growing, row after row of fangs connected to nothing but the memory of jaws thousands of years ago.

No, Quiet said or thought or wished.

The Carnivore bit Growing in two.

"Now," Ceaseless whispered, "we can complete the Empress's History."

He stood next to where she was slumped on the floor, the History of the Carnivore sword-like in his hand. She couldn't understand how he was still upright.

He bent down and picked up a scroll. Growing's History of the Convalescent.

"It shames me to use another's work, but it will be necessary," Ceaseless said softly. "And his forms aren't so bad. You taught him well, Master Gate."

Quiet's heart stammered.

It was self-defence, she told herself. Growing had attacked Ceaseless, after all.

Ceaseless stared down at Growing, at the body that Quiet couldn't look at. The Abstract's eyes were serene.

"You saved me," he whispered. "Thank you, Master."

She looked away and forced herself to see Growing. To see the broken vessel that was once her tutee.

"We should continue work on the Empress's History," she said.

Ceaseless absorbed her words. Then he laughed.

"Yes!" he said. "Yes! And I'll be Minister with you by my side."

His hand reached for hers. He gently pulled until she stood.

"You know," he said, breathless with elation. "Careful Progress told me that your Abstract tutees *always* fail. He said you would kill me. But I *knew* he was lying. Otherwise you wouldn't have helped me."

Quiet finally met his eyes. The faces of the Abstract entrants she'd taught over the years ran through her like ghosts.

Some had been easy. Fools like Iron Temperance—a headstrong girl with a cruel streak, cast out at the Hall's entrance after Quiet told her to hide cheat sheets between her legs.

Others had required more subtlety. She thought of Joyous Progress, Bright Hope, and Obedient Prudence, and the teethmarks on their bodies after she had taught them mistakes on the Carnivore's History.

Yet all of them had succumbed, and Quiet, being only ever a minor tutor to all of them, had escaped blame. After all, her success rate for those she tutored by herself—the Concretes, the upstarts—was excellent. One in five survived. Three had even graduated. She remembered their names—Diligent Mountain, Silent Rain, and Graceful Petal. Graceful had been the first ever Concrete entrant to graduate, thanks to Quiet's help.

Three Concrete Ministers. She had achieved her father's vision thrice over. And all it had cost was a few Abstract lives.

But Ceaseless, Ceaseless was different.

She was so tired.

"Yes," she told him. "Of course they were lies. Now come. Show me what you've created."

He led her between shattered desks and cracked flagstones, his body trembling with excitement. She looked for the toad, but it had disappeared after swallowing the peacock. There was only her and Ceaseless and the History he had created.

His Empress's History was a simple sheaf of parchments. The final History was among the simplest to compose—only twenty cantos, describing how the Empress had founded Nation with the aid of the Soldier, the Fisher, and the Convalescent. How the final Ancestor had held court attended by the characters of the land, and used their magic and hers to set down the Histories of the Eight Ancestors and establish the Grand Exam.

Ceaseless watched her read, eyes never leaving her face.

"Is it good?" he said.

"It is excellent," Quiet said. "But you will need to redo the fourth canto. On her first day in court the Empress had seventy *six* attendants, not seventy seven."

Ceaseless froze. His head flicked around, searching for the peacock that wasn't there.

"That peasant boy was such a liar," he finally said. "You're my teacher. You don't hate me."

She held his eyes a moment. They were so beautiful. So full of life.

"Yes," Quiet said. "I only want what's best for you, Ceaseless. I love you."

He blinked.

"I love you too, Master Gate," he said. "Of course you're correct." A ghost of his old grin flitted across his face. "You taught me everything good."

She stroked his curls as he rewrote the final page, watching him fill line after line with diligent, beautiful pictograms. His honey scent filled her, smelling like the flowers her father had brought her. She didn't look at the bodies of Growing Lake or Careful Progress. Instead, she looked at the name tattooed on Ceaseless's neck and whispered it back to herself. She wanted to stay here forever.

Yet eventually, the hour gong sounded and Ceaseless put down his quill.

"It is a masterpiece," she said. "Better than anything I have ever created." And it was true. Each pictogram was perfect; a portrait miniature of inexpressible delicacy, painted with all the gentleness that Ceaseless had.

"Let us finish the Exam."

In the days before the Exam, Quiet had not slept. Ceaseless haunted her thoughts; the beautiful boy she had saved, the monster underneath.

After he had ordered the son of Constance beaten, House Charity had spent a river of gold to placate the boy's House and Ceaseless had been punished every day for a week. Quiet had also changed the focus of her lessons; she spoke to Ceaseless about examples of kindness in the Histories, wherever she could.

Yet his violence had been getting worse. He hid it from her now, but she heard the rumours. Orders to his guards to attack an Abstract girl on the street, after she had mocked his skill. The wounds on the servants who had made some tiny mistake handling his Histories. The two servants who had disappeared completely. She was afraid to find out what happened to them.

On the final day before the Exam, Quiet had decided. She must do as she had first planned and teach Ceaseless an imperfection in the History. He trusted her enough to believe her.

Ceaseless has been surprisingly tranquil for a first-time entrant. He had smiled when she entered, sitting legs folded. Instead of parchment and ink and tablets, he held a hand mirror and a quill wet with ink. Around his neck was a long thick shawl. It made him look larger.

"You've taught me so much," he told her. "About what matters. More than Mother. More than Father, even. Thank you, Master Gate. Truly."

Quiet had swallowed, fighting down the feelings that clawed up her throat, the memory of the Constance boy's bleeding back.

"And what does matter to you?" she had asked, keeping her voice steady.

"Family," Ceaseless said immediately. "Family and tradition."

He unwrapped the shawl revealing his neck. He had made a delicate cross where his name tattoo was, a line of black splitting it in two. Next to it, he had redrawn the symbols with one word changed.

Her certainty drained away.

Ceaseless Gate.

"Empress, Empress, Progenitor of Nation. Hear my words and grant me Ministry."

It was strange to hear Ceaseless speak the final invocation. Quiet had never gotten to this point before. She'd never wanted to.

Yet in that Exam Hall, in the blood of two other entrants, she sat with her final tutee and watched the Eighth Ancestor manifest.

Unlike the others, Ao appeared not as a sense or through a statue, but in their minds. Quiet's head was filled with images layered onto each other. The Empress was a crowd with hands linked, or a coiled dragon with ruby eyes, or a small, old woman the same age as Quiet, writing on parchment with the quill of a peacock, her eyes full of joyless knowing.

"I can feel her, Master Gate," Ceaseless said, breathless with wonder. "Just like you told me. I can feel her love."

The Empress smiled at him and Quiet. She spoke with the voice of thousands.

"Imperfect," she said. She raised her quill, which was also a sword, and flicked a cross over the parchment of Ceaseless's History, the ink wounding the words.

Quiet wrote down their names.

She sat at the only desk left standing after Growing's spearwall, in front of the great gate to the outside world. The statues of the Eight Ancestors stared down at her. Beyond them, the staircases plunged into the darkness of the labyrinth. Quiet imagined the endless corridors, filled with bodies and statues and silence. She contemplated how many entrants were still alive and whether Steadfast Forest was still floating in the floodwater. She wondered if more would come here to attempt the Empress's History themselves.

Quiet wouldn't stand in their way.

The Empress had left them as quickly as she had come. Ceaseless was cold and peaceful next to Quiet now, the joy still on his face. It had at least been quick. Quiet hoped it had been painless. He deserved that, at least.

When he had changed his name to Gate, she had been blinded. She had felt, for a golden moment, like she had a family again. But she understood now. She had realised when she'd seen how Ceaseless looked at Growing's body, the same way he had stared at Steadfast Forest, or the whipped Constance boy— with a gentle emptiness. Then Quiet had finally, truly seen the vacancy in him. She hated herself for what she had done, but she'd always hated herself. Her father's vision had a cost to it, which she had borne for all her life. She didn't feel sorrow. At least, no more than she always felt.

Ceaseless's name was huge in her mind, just like all the others: Concrete names, Abstract names, names she'd aided or tricked. Names of entrants she had only heard of. Her mind was so full of them she could barely think; her memory, honed to recall the difference between seventy seven and seventy six, had stored them all.

So she wrote their names on her failed History of the Convalescent. The list grew longer and longer. The Hall fell away and her sorrow and exhaustion dimmed. A sense filled her; the giddy, heady sense she only felt in the Hall. The sense of power, building just beyond her reach.

"You write, but not a History."

The toad hopped onto the desk.

"Toad," she said distantly. "You lured Growing here."

She should hate the character for what it had done, but the names called to her too strongly for anything else.

"Yes," the toad croaked cheerfully, "and destroyed that ugly bird, all to clear the way for you, to ensure you would act, and defeat the dark one."

Her hand shook a moment.

"His name was Ceaseless," she said. "I didn't defeat him."

"It matters not. The way is clear now, for you to become Minister."

"I will never become Minister," Quiet said.

The toad blinked, before giving a resigned croak.

"My master," it said, "wishes to speak with you."

It hopped away. Quiet let it go. All that mattered now were the names. It felt freeing, to let them flow out onto the page. One hundred names. Two hundred. Three hundred. Until finally, she had written them down, finishing with the first victim of the Hall she had heard of.

Open Gate.

Would her father be proud to see the people she had tricked to their deaths to achieve his vision?

"Master Gate."

It was the familiarity of the title that made Quiet stop writing and let the endless darkness that she had been shutting out crack into her. For a moment, she could imagine.

But the voice was an aging man's, querulous and gentle, with a hint of Concrete twang.

The Hall's gate had opened a crack, bleeding in the scents of the wider world; fresh wind and pine and rain, which pierced the cloying incense of the Hall as if it were just a dream.

Just inside it, stood a man. He wore a silk robe of incredible craftsmanship, embroidered with scenes from the Empress's History. He held a densely wound scroll. His face was lined but delicate, his head hairless, his eyes sharp.

"Graceful Petal," Quiet said. "Or should I say Righteous Deputy Secretary-General Petal of this most brilliant Heaven."

Her first Concrete tutee grinned and for a moment she saw the boy who had been her first success, forty years ago, when her father had been twelve years dead. She had taken the Exam with Graceful after tutoring him for a year and gifted him the Histories of the Fisher, Carnivore, and Child. He had won against Abstracts far more experienced.

She was glad he was still here. At least someone had survived her schemes.

"The toad was yours," she said.

"Yes," Graceful said. "I needed him to help me answer a question."

"Oh?" Quiet said, but already she was losing interest. The names pulled at her. They seemed far bigger than the parchment.

"Will you finally join us?" Graceful said. He took a step into the Hall, glancing at Ceaseless's body. "There are three Concrete Ministers now and we all owe it to you. Please, Master Gate. Complete the Empress's History and lead us to shape Nation for the better."

Quiet leaned back in her chair, closing her eyes for a moment, resting in the soft darkness.

"You know," she said. "I always found it odd, the language of

494

Nation." She gestured to the words in front of her. "We have 'widow,' for when someone loses a spouse. We have 'orphan,' for when a child loses her parents. But there is no word for when a parent loses their child."

Graceful came near her. The toad gave a croak of cavernous depth.

"You have stopped monsters becoming Ministers, Master Gate," he said. "But now we need you to lead us."

"In the pre-Nation script," Quiet continued, like Graceful was her student again, "there *is* such a word. *Vilomah.* Yet the Empress, when formalising our modern tongue, left it out. Cold fish that she was, perhaps she understood. To lose a child is unspeakable, indefinable." She placed down her quill, admiring how the names looked on the page. "How much more unspeakable is it, then, for someone to lose their children willingly? To sacrifice them? Is there any cause that can justify that?"

"We have been able to help thousands," Graceful said. "Because of you."

"No," Quiet said. "I am not a saviour. I am a monster." She held up a hand when he opened his mouth to interrupt. "I am sick, Graceful. Sick of this place. Sick of these Ancestors. Sick of the Empress's magic. What right did she have to dedicate our entire Nation to the mercy of people centuries gone? To venerate only the first of things? To claim the Exam brought equality between Concretes and Abstracts instead of bringing the whole rotten system down? I could never become Minister, Graceful. I could never dedicate my life even more to her legacy."

Graceful frowned, the same way he had when she taught him a challenging pictogram.

"Then will you just die?" he said.

Quiet couldn't help smiling. Oh, if only she could. But the names, the names were calling her so. She opened her eyes and added a final name to the parchment. Her own.

The last graduate, she thought.

"What are you writing?" Graceful said.

"A History," Quiet said. She thought of Ceaseless—not the

495

body sitting before the Empress or the Abstract filled by his father's teachings, but her beautiful boy, who had come from the dark into the light. She remembered Growing Lake, his hope, his hardness, his tears. She remembered her father, the most gentle man she had known, who would have hated what she had done with her life.

"A new History," she said. "Not of Firsts, but of Seconds, Thirds, Thousandths. A History of continuations and endings."

They were there, she realised. Just beyond thought. Just like the other Ancestors, waiting and watching.

Quiet cleared her throat, meeting the eyes of the Empress's statue.

"It is ready to be invoked."

The Year in the Contests

CONTEST GROWTH

The Contests continue to expand and in the thirty-ninth year, we had more entries than any previous year.

Winners in this volume hail from nine countries: Canada, China, Costa Rica, Jamaica, Romania, South Korea, United Kingdom, United States of America, and Vietnam.

The Writers of the Future Online Workshop continues to help those who wish to improve their writing skills. Over 7,500 people have begun their online journey from initial idea to finished story. It remains free to enter and access to the information is unlimited, even after completing the course. And those who have finished the course are invited to quarterly Ask Me Anything online events with Contest judges.

The Writers & Illustrators of the Future Podcast continues to provide hard-won advice through interviews with Contest judges, winners and industry professionals. The podcast is syndicated on dozens of stations internationally with over forty million downloads. This year we celebrated episode #200. The podcast was a finalist in two categories in the People's Choice Podcast Awards: Education and Storyteller (Drama).

AWARDS FOR THE CONTEST AND ANTHOLOGY

The Writers of the Future won three of the 2021 Critters Annual Readers' Poll awards: Best Writers' Discussion Forum, Best Book Cover Artwork, and Best Anthology.

The 2022 eLit Awards from Digital Publishing awarded the Contest Gold Medal Winner for Anthologies.

The Writers & Illustrators of the Future Contests won the Shield of Excellence and Creativity award from Online TV Magazine.

JUDGES LOST AND GAINED

This year we lost Eric Flint. He was one of six to ever transition from Contest winner to judge. His winning story appeared in *Volume 9* in 1993. "The panel of judges that year was Larry Niven, Jerry Pournelle, Anne McCaffrey, and A. J. Budrys, which was as prestigious and authoritative as any group of judges you could ask for. And, best of all, not one of them knew me from Adam, so I could be certain their assessment was impartial. In a very real sense, my writing career began at that moment." We will miss him, his dry sense of humor, and incredible knowledge of history that he transformed into amazing fiction.

We welcome Illustrators of the Future Contest judge Irvin Rodriguez. Irvin was the Illustrators' Contest Grand Prize winner in 2011, featured in *Volume 27*. Irvin has developed into a compelling and versatile artist. He works in the film, comic book, publishing, and video game industries for clients like Naughty Dog, Lucasfilm, DC Comics, and Magic the Gathering.

NOTABLE ACCOMPLISHMENTS FROM ALUMNI AND JUDGES

Here are a selection of the many accomplishments from our Contest judges and over 800 winners.

JUDGES

Kevin J. Anderson (Contest judge) released *Gods and Dragons*, the third book in his epic fantasy Wake the Dragon series.

Jody Lynn Nye (Contest judge) won the Polaris Award from ConCarolina and Falstaff Books for mentorship and supporting up-and-coming artists.

Brandon Sanderson (Contest judge) made history with his Kickstarter campaign, Surprise! Four Secret Novels, garnering over forty-one million dollars. He has so much going on, he is doing weekly updates on his website!

498

Robert J. Sawyer (Contest judge) won the Machine Intelligence Foundation for Rights and Ethics' 2022 Media Award for his WWW Trilogy.

ALUMNI

Jennifer Bruce (Vol. 37) won several awards, including the Society of Illustrator's Los Angeles Illustration West 60, *Beautiful Bizarre Magazine*'s Digital Art Award 1st Prize, Cheltenham Illustration Award, Society of Illustrators Annual 65, and inclusion in the Communication Arts Annual 63.

John M. Campbell (Vol. 37) had three short stories published: "Living the Dream (Except for One Thing)" in *Dream: Tales from the Pikes Peak Writers*, "The Eco-Patriot" in *Triangulation: Energy*, and "Racing the Marineris" in *Bizarre Bazaar*.

Leonard Carpenter (Vol. 1) just shipped off his latest screenplay to Hollywood while his "Tropic of Cuba" was published through Kindle Vella.

Elizabeth Chatsworth (Vol. 37) won the Independent Book Publishers Association's Benjamin Franklin Award for Science Fiction & Fantasy for her novel, *The Brass Queen*.

Ron Collins (Vol. 15) published the ninth book in his Stealing the Sun series, which started with his Writers of the Future workshop 24-hour story. He also published Collins Creek, a three-volume collection of short stories. In total, he published seven stand-alone books, a couple of omnibus boxed sets, plus several short stories.

Andy Dibble (Vol. 36) edited and released his first anthology *Strange Religion: Speculative Fiction of Spirituality, Belief & Practice* and his story "The Pronouns of Hlour" came out in *Sci Phi Journal*.

James Dorr (Vol. 8) won grand prize in Defenestrationism.net's 2022 flash fiction competition with his "Casket Suite."

Karen Joy Fowler (Vol. 1) released her historical novel *Booth* through Penguin Random House.

Jessica George (Vol. 36) won book of the year at the Rubery Book Award for her novel, *The Word*.

Harry Lang (Vol. 28) won Third Place in the 2022 Jim Baen Memorial Award for his story, "The Rocketship of Her Dreams."

Ken Liu (Vol. 19) had a TV show, *Pantheon*, premiere on the AMC network based on his *The Hidden Girl and Other Stories*.

Elaine Midcoh (Vol. 39) was awarded the 2022 Jim Baen Memorial Award Grand Prize for her story, "Man on the Moon."

Artem Mirolevich (Vol. 23) held gallery showings in Florida and New York.

Wulf Moon (Vol. 35) released *Super Secrets Illustrated Volume 1*.

Samantha Murray (Vol. 31) took home Australia's Aurealis Award Best Science Fiction Novella award for *Preserved in Amber*.

Leah Ning (Vol. 36) has a horror story in the *Dark Matter Presents Human Monsters* anthology.

Scot Noel (Vol. 6) published four online/digital issues: *Dream-Forge Anvil 7—The Meaning of Life, DreamForge Anvil 8—Perception, DreamForge Anvil 9—Out of Place*, and *DreamForge Anvil 10—What We Give*.

Steve Pantazis (Vol. 31) won the Booksie 2022 Short Story Competition for "Out of Print."

Brittany Rainsdon (Vol. 38) placed third for the 2022 Baen Fantasy Adventure Award with her Writers of the Future workshop 24-hour story entitled "Exchanged."

Natalia Salvador (Vol. 38) was an illustrator for Letters from the Fairies. Her illustrations were published in *George Leaves the Lights ON*.

Elise Stephens (Vol. 35) released a full-cast audio of her winning story, "Untrained Luck."

Mike Jack Stoumbos (Vol. 38) released volumes three and four of his This Fine Crew series. And three volumes of the series were translated and released in German.

Michael Talbot (Vol. 30) illustrated the children's book *Party Animals*, held two solo art exhibitions, Salvation: Redux and Warriors in the Garden, and completed multiple murals and public art projects in Wynwood Miami, FL; Roxbury, MA; East Somerville, MA; and in Brighton, MA.

M. Elizabeth Ticknor (Vol. 38) edited the *4th and Starlight: A Fantasy & Science Fiction Anthology* featuring Contest winners and entrants.

Brian Trent (Vol. 29) published his novel *Redspace Rising,* which was based on his Writers of the Future winning story. He also saw his ninth appearance in *The Magazine of Fantasy & Science Fiction.*

Elizabeth Wein (Vol. 9) Little Brown Books for Young Readers published a tenth anniversary edition of her novel, *Code Name Verity.*

Galaxy's Edge and *Asimov's Science Fiction* and the major short stories magazines continuously have one or more of our former winners in most of their publications.

That's quite a substantial listing for this past year. There are just so many accomplishments, really too many to list or record. So we're looking ahead to a spectacular future.

For Contest year 39, the winners are:

Writers of the Future Contest Winners

FIRST QUARTER
1. *Samuel Parr*
   "THE LAST HISTORY"
2. *Spencer Sekulin*
   "THE CHILDREN OF DESOLATION"
3. *L. H. Davis*
   "TIMELINES AND BLOODLINES"

SECOND QUARTER
1. *Devon Bohm*
   "KITSUNE"
2. *Arthur H. Manners*
   "THE WITHERING SKY"
3. *David Hankins*
   "DEATH AND THE TAXMAN"

THIRD QUARTER
1. *David K. Henrickson*
   "WHITE ELEPHANT"
2. *J. R. Johnson*
   "PIRACY FOR BEGINNERS"
3. *Elaine Midcoh*
   "A TRICKLE IN HISTORY"

FOURTH QUARTER
1. *Marianne Xenos*
   "MOONLIGHT AND FUNK"
2. *Jason Palmatier*
   "UNDER MY CYPRESSES"
3. *T. J. Knight*
   "THE FALL OF CRODENDRA M"

Illustrators of the Future Contest Winners

FIRST QUARTER
Alexandra Albu
Clarence Bateman
Dao Vi

SECOND QUARTER
Alaya Knowlton
Ximing Luo
Sarah Morrison

THIRD QUARTER
Kristen Hadaway
José Sánchez
Helen Yi

FOURTH QUARTER
Chris Arias
Chris Binns
April Solomon

L. Ron Hubbard's
Writers of the Future Contest

The most enduring and influential
contest in the history of SF and Fantasy

Open to new and amateur SF & Fantasy writers

Prizes each quarter: $1,000, $750, $500
Quarterly 1st place winners compete for $5,000
additional annual prize!

ALL JUDGING DONE BY
PROFESSIONAL WRITERS ONLY

No entry fee is required

Entrants retain all publication rights

Don't delay! Send your entry now!

To submit your entry electronically go to:
   www.writersofthefuture.com/enter-writer-contest

Email: contests@authorservicesinc.com

To submit your entry via mail send to:
   L. Ron Hubbard's Writers of the Future Contest
   7051 Hollywood Blvd.
   Los Angeles, California 90028

1. No entry fee is required, and all rights in the story remain the property of the author. All types of science fiction, fantasy, and dark fantasy are welcome.

2. By submitting to the Contest, the entrant agrees to abide by all Contest rules.

3. All entries must be original works by the entrant, in English. Plagiarism, which includes the use of third-party poetry, song lyrics, characters, or another person's universe, without written permission, will result in disqualification. Short stories or novelettes generated or created by computer software and/or artificial intelligence will be disqualified. Excessive violence or sex and the use of profane, vulgar, racist or offensive words, determined by the judges, will result in the story being rejected. Entries may not have been previously published in professional media.

4. To be eligible, entries must be a short story of fantasy, science fiction, or light speculative horror. Your story has no minimum length requirement, however it may not be longer than 17,000 words.

   We regret we cannot consider novels, poetry, screenplays, or works intended for children.

5. The Contest is open only to those who have not professionally published a novel or short novel, or more than one novelette, or more than three short stories, in any medium. Professional publication is deemed to be payment of at least eight cents per word, and at least 5,000 copies, or 5,000 hits.

6. Entries submitted in hard copy must be typewritten or a computer printout in black ink on white paper, printed only on the front of the paper, double-spaced, with numbered pages. All other formats will be disqualified. Each entry must have a cover page with the title of the work, the author's legal name, a pen name if applicable, address, telephone number, email address and an approximate word count. Every subsequent page must carry the title and a page number, but the author's name must be deleted to facilitate fair, anonymous judging.

   Entries submitted electronically must be double-spaced and must include the title and page number on each page, but not the author's name. Electronic submissions will separately include the author's legal name, pen name if applicable, address, telephone number, email address, and approximate word count.

7. Manuscripts will be returned after judging only if the author has provided return postage on a self-addressed envelope.

8. We accept only entries that do not require a delivery signature for us to receive them.

9. There shall be three cash prizes in each quarter: a First Prize of $1,000, a Second Prize of $750, and a Third Prize of $500, in US dollars. In addition, at the end of the year the First Place winners will have their entries judged by a panel of judges, and a Grand Prize winner shall be determined and receive an additional $5,000. All winners will also receive trophies. The Grand Prize winner shall be announced and awarded, along with the trophies to winners, at the L. Ron Hubbard awards ceremony held in the following year or when it is able to be held due to government regulations.

10. The Contest has four quarters, beginning on October 1, January 1, April 1, and July 1. The year will end on September 30. To be eligible for judging in its quarter, an entry must be postmarked or received electronically no later than midnight on the last day of the quarter. Late entries will be included in the following quarter and the Contest Administration will so notify the entrant.

11. Each entrant may submit only one manuscript per quarter. Winners are ineligible to make further entries in the Contest.

12. All entries for each quarter are final. No revisions are accepted.

13. Entries will be judged by professional authors. The decisions of the judges are entirely their own, and are final and binding.

14. Winners in each quarter will be individually notified of the results by phone, mail, or email.

15. This Contest is void where prohibited by law.

16. To send your entry electronically, go to:
www.writersofthefuture.com/enter-writer-contest
and follow the instructions.
To send your entry in hard copy, mail it to:
L. Ron Hubbard's Writers of the Future Contest
7051 Hollywood Blvd., Los Angeles, California 90028

17. Visit the website for any Contest rules update at:
www.writersofthefuture.com

L. Ron Hubbard's
Illustrators of the Future Contest

The most enduring and influential
contest in the history of SF and Fantasy

Open to new and amateur SF & Fantasy artists

$1,500 in prizes each quarter
Quarterly winners compete for $5,000
additional annual prize!

ALL JUDGING DONE BY PROFESSIONAL ARTISTS ONLY

No entry fee is required

Entrants retain all rights

Don't delay! Send your entry now!

To submit your entry electronically go to:
   www.writersofthefuture.com/enter-the-illustrator-contest

Email: contests@authorservicesinc.com

To submit your entry via mail send to:
   L. Ron Hubbard's Illustrators of the Future Contest
   7051 Hollywood Blvd.
   Los Angeles, California 90028

1. The Contest is open to entrants from all nations. (However, entrants should provide themselves with some means for written communication in English.) All themes of science fiction and fantasy illustrations are welcome: every entry is judged on its own merits only. No entry fee is required and all rights to the entry remain the property of the artist.

2. By submitting to the Contest, the entrant agrees to abide by all Contest rules.

3. The Contest is open to new and amateur artists who have not been professionally published and paid for more than three black-and-white story illustrations, or more than one process-color painting, in media distributed broadly to the general public. The ultimate eligibility criterion, however, is defined by the word "amateur"—in other words, the artist has not been paid for his artwork. If you are not sure of your eligibility, please write a letter to the Contest Administration with details regarding your publication history. Include a self-addressed and stamped envelope for the reply. You may also send your questions to the Contest Administration via email.

4. Each entrant may submit only one set of illustrations in each Contest quarter. The entry must be original to the entrant and previously unpublished. Plagiarism, infringement of the rights of others, or other violations of the Contest rules will result in disqualification. Winners in previous quarters are not eligible to make further entries.

5. The entry shall consist of three illustrations done by the entrant in a color or black-and-white medium created from the artist's imagination. Use of gray scale in illustrations

and mixed media, photo and design software, and the use of photography in the illustrations are accepted. Art generated using programs such as *artificial intelligence*, or similar programs will be disqualified. Source and reference imagery may be requested at any time to ensure all rules have been met. Each illustration must represent a subject different from the other two.

6. Electronic submissions will separately include the artist's legal name, address, telephone number, email address which will identify each of three pieces of art and the artist's signature on the art should be deleted. Only .jpg, .jpeg, and .png files will be accepted, a maximum file size of 10 MB.

7. HARD COPY ENTRIES SHOULD NOT BE THE ORIGINAL DRAWINGS, but should be color or black-and-white reproductions of the originals, of a quality satisfactory to the entrant. Entries must be submitted unfolded and flat, in an envelope no larger than 9 inches by 12 inches. Images submitted electronically must be a minimum of 300 dpi, a minimum of 5 × 7 inches and a maximum of 8.5 × 11 inches.

All hard copy entries must be accompanied by a self-addressed return envelope of the appropriate size, with the correct US postage affixed. (Non-US entrants should enclose international postage reply coupons.) If the entrant does not want the reproductions returned, the entry should be clearly marked DISPOSABLE COPIES: DO NOT RETURN. A business-size self-addressed envelope with correct postage (or valid email address) should be included so that the judging results may be returned to the entrant. We only accept entries that do not require a delivery signature for us to receive them.

To facilitate anonymous judging, each of the three photocopies must be accompanied by a removable cover sheet bearing the artist's name, address, telephone number, email address, and an identifying title for that work. The reproduction of the work should carry the same identifying title on the front of the illustration and the artist's signature should be deleted. The Contest Administration will remove and file the cover sheets, and forward only the anonymous entry to the judges.

8. There will be three cowinners in each quarter. Each winner will receive a cash prize of US $500 and will be awarded a trophy. Winners will also receive eligibility to compete for the annual Grand Prize of $5,000 together with the annual Grand Prize trophy.

9. For the annual Grand Prize Contest, the quarterly winners will be furnished with a specification sheet and a winning story from the Writers of the Future Contest to illustrate. In order to retain eligibility for the Grand Prize, each winner shall send to the Contest address his/her illustration of the assigned story within thirty (30) days of receipt of the story assignment.

   The yearly Grand Prize winner shall be determined by a panel of judges on the following basis only: Each Grand Prize judge's personal opinion on the extent to which it makes the judge want to read the story it illustrates.

   The Grand Prize winner shall be announced and awarded, along with the trophies to the winners, at the L. Ron Hubbard awards ceremony held in the following year or when it is able to be held due to government regulations.

10. The Contest has four quarters, beginning on October 1, January 1, April 1, and July 1. The year will end

on September 30. To be eligible for judging in its quarter, an entry must be postmarked or received electronically no later than midnight on the last day of the quarter. Late entries will be included in the following quarter and the Contest Administration will so notify the entrant.

11. Entries will be judged by professional artists only. Each quarterly judging and the Grand Prize judging may have different panels of judges. The decisions of the judges are entirely their own and are final and binding.

12. Winners in each quarter will be individually notified of the results by phone, mail, or email.

13. This Contest is void where prohibited by law.

14. To send your entry electronically, go to: www.writersofthefuture.com/enter-the-illustrator-contest and follow the instructions.
To send your entry via mail send it to:
L. Ron Hubbard's Illustrators of the Future Contest
7051 Hollywood Blvd., Los Angeles, California 90028

15. Visit the website for any Contest rules update at: www.illustratorsofthefuture.com

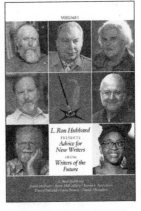